JOHN JASPER'S SECRET.

A SEQUEL TO

CHARLES DICKENS'

UNFINISHED NOVEL

"THE MYSTERY OF EDWIN DROOD."

WILDSIDE PRESS

CHARLES DICKENS' WORKS.

PEOPLE'S DUODECIMO EDITION.

Reduced in Price from $2.50 to $1.50 a volume.

This edition is printed on fine paper, from large clear type, leaded, and contains Two Hundred Illustrations on the finest tinted plate paper. Each book is complete in one large duodecimo volume.

OUR MUTUAL FRIEND	1 50	LITTLE DORRIT	1 50
PICKWICK PAPERS	1 50	DOMBEY AND SON	1 50
NICHOLAS NICKELBY	1 50	CHRISTMAS STORIES	1 50
GREAT EXPECTATIONS	1 50	SKETCHES BY "BOZ"	1 50
DAVID COPPERFIELD	1 50	BARNABY RUDGE	1 50
OLIVER TWIST	1 50	MARTIN CHUZZLEWIT	1 50
BLEAK HOUSE	1 50	OLD CURIOSITY SHOP	1 50
A TALE OF TWO CITIES	1 50	DICKENS' NEW STORIES	1 50

AMERICAN NOTES; AND UNCOMMERCIAL TRAVELLER......1 50
HUNTED DOWN; AND OTHER REPRINTED PIECES...... ...1 50
THE HOLLY-TREE INN; AND OTHER STORIES....................1 50
MYSTERY OF EDWIN DROOD; AND MASTER HUMPHREY'S
    CLOCK 1 50
DR. MACKENZIE'S LIFE AND WRITINGS OF CHARLES
    DICKENS...1 50

Price of a set, in Black Cloth, in Twenty-one volumes.......................$32 00
Price of a set, in Full Sheep, Library style...42 50
Price of a set, in Half Calf, sprinkled edges.......................................53 00
Price of a set, in Half Calf, marbled edges...58 00
Price of a set, in Half Calf, antique..63 00
Price of a set, in Half Calf, full gilt backs, etc.................................63 00

GREEN CLOTH DUODECIMO EDITION.

This is the "People's Duodecimo Edition," in a new style of Binding, in Green Morocco Cloth, Bevelled Boards, Full Gilt descriptive back, and Medallion Portrait on sides in gilt, in Twenty-one handy volumes, 12mo., fine paper, large clear type, and Two Hundred Illustrations on tinted paper. Price $40 a set: being the handsomest and best edition ever published for the price.

Above books are for sale by all Booksellers and **News Agents.**
Copies of any or all of the above books will be sent to any one, to any place, post-paid, on receipt of their price by the Publishers,

T. B. PETERSON & BROTHERS,

306 CHESTNUT STREET, PHILADELPHIA, PA.

PREFACE

A FEW words of explanation are obviously necessary, in connection with the publication of this work, presumably unexpected by the reading world. These few words, however, will not take the shape of an apology, although a certain proportion of readers may suppose such a disarmament of judgment to be politic, and while a certain segment of the critical circle may be disposed to quote the effective axiom : "Fools rush in where angels fear to tread."

When the lamented death of MR. CHARLES DICKENS occurred, in June, 1870, it is well known that a special pang was added to the general sorrow felt for his loss, in the knowledge that he left unfinished a work which had commanded the widest attention for its opening numbers, and which promised to be one of his most effective and popular books. Very soon thereafter the inquiry came to be made whether the work would not be completed, from materials understood to be in existence, by some capable hand; but that question was almost as quickly answered, by the statement that no such continuation could be made, because there existed no remaining materials whatever.

The truth, meanwhile, as usual, lay between the two suggestions. "Materials" there were few, reckoning only written records or data as coming under that name. But the author, doing what he believed to be his life-work, had not been entirely reticent as to the scope of that work; and hints had been supplied by him, unwittingly, for a much closer estimate of the bearings of those portions remaining unwritten than he could probably have believed while in life.

All these, with many more particulars, laboriously but lovingly procured, have fallen into the hands of the writers of this concluding story, who believe that they are conveying a benefit as well as a pleasure to the world in setting partially at rest the thousands of speculations to which the non-explanation of the "Mystery" has given rise. They have written in the fullest love and admiration of the unfinished original work, as well as of the great novelist who so suddenly laid down his

wonderful pen, to the grief of all lands and all
time; they have carried out, however feebly, what
they have fully traced and identified as the intention of the writer, every intrinsic and extrinsic fact
and hint being carefully considered. Thus they
make no apology, because they believe themselves
to have been really offering homage to a great
name in faithfully gathering up materials, and
completing, it may be unskilfully, what its bearer
left merely a brilliant fragment. That they have
failed to sustain the delicate shades of character
of the actors in the original story, only to be imparted by the *one*, or to gem the conversation of
those characters with that irresistible oddity of
blended wit and pathos for which that *one* was unequalled in the age or the language—these defects
no one can know more profoundly than the writers
themselves; and for these they make the only
apology connected with the affair : they have *done
their best.*

No close imitation of the style of MR. DICKENS
has been attempted, as it would have been, had
there been any intention of foisting a pretence
upon the public. If something distantly approaching his manner has been frequently assumed, a
sufficient explanation will be found in the atmos-

phere which necessarily surrounded those who have devoted months to the studies indispensable to their task, and in the anxiety naturally felt to make the contrast between the two works as little as possible apparent to the non-critical reader.

Since a large portion of this story was written, a new motive for its completion has been supplied (had one been wanting) in two or three dramatic "continuations" and "conclusions" of the original story, made or commenced by writers in America, where MR. DICKENS is well known to have had a host of readers and admirers. In these, so far as knowledge of them has reached the writers of this concluding story, it is not too much to say that the American *entrepreneurs* have principally shown the absence of their alleged national characteristic of keenness, by falling into the delicate traps of pretence in plot and action, so skilfully set, in the earlier portions of "Edwin Drood," by the writer who mystified the whole body of readers through a long portion of the career of the Golden Dustman, in "Our Mutual Friend."

LONDON. *March* 1871.

CONTENTS.

CONTENTS.

JOHN JASPER'S SECRET.

A SEQUEL TO

"THE MYSTERY OF EDWIN DROOD."

CHAPTER I.

MAYOR SAPSEA GIVES AUDIENCE.

THE Worshipful the Mayor of Cloisterham sits in high state in his Mansion House. Perhaps not in these very words, but certainly in the same spirit would *he* put it, to the ear of confidence, in describing the state really held by the head of the ancient and honorable borough, at any period during the present term of official incumbency, when men have returned once more to the allegiance so often departed from, and when, in at least one of the high places of England, talent and originality hold power.

His Mansion House, and he the Lord Mayor, instead of being merely the Worshipful. Why not? His stereotype imitation of the Dean, once his ideal, has faded and changed more than a little, thinking of this—into a shadowy copy of some magnate of the bench, once seen, or some puissant states-man temporarily flashing across the line of vision. We grow —do we not?—in stature; then it is only fitting that we should grow in self-estimation, in aspiration, and in all those other things which make up the surroundings of " getting on."

Why not the Lord Mayor instead of merely the Worshipful ?
—the indignant question may be asked once more. The
blending of private residence and auctioneer's premises, on the
High Street, over the door of which the newly-incarnated
figure of Time, taking the place of the old, and substituting
the hammer for the scythe, daily and hourly cries, "Going !
going ! gone !" to the hours, and knocks down any lagging minutes straggling along after the main body—that might possibly need certain ameliorations, within and without, before venturing to claim place beside the civic palace of the world's metropolis ; but beyond this, what more ? That imposing room,
but one pair from the street, and overlooking it, alternately devoted to valuatory conferences and vendatory conflicts innumerable, between the professional talent for inducing belief in
the high value of faded carpets and decayed furniture, and the
proverbially-stubborn tendency of the British mind to hold all
articles once touched by the hand of use as worthless, unless
rank has hallowed or celebrity sanctified—this might well be
the recognized seat of power, police-guarded and urchin-
dreaded, if Cloisterham really had its rights and privileges, instead of continuing the victim of cruel precedents. Why not
a Mansion House, indeed, with the desk of the civic dignitary,
at certain hours of the morning, holding behind it a stately
person, fur-mantled and gold-chained, and at least announced
on entrance as " The Worshipful the Mayor !" even if that
higher flight should not be reached, and the proclamation fail
to be " The Right Honorable the Lord Mayor !" Why not
here, instead of in that less-impressive place, the Town Hall,
with its bench of magistrates dividing honor and labor—why
not here, and into this awful presence, offenders be haled by
the alert and vigilant constabulary, to expiate the offence of
illegally conveying from barrel to pocket, one red herring, value
three farthings, or to bide the punishment so certain to fall on
the unlawful violators of heads and illegal debruisers of countenances ? Yes, why not all this ? ruminates Sir Thomas
Sapsea, Knt., so created—

But of this latter, anon. Merit does not always receive complete recognition in the first instance, even when there is some approach towards justice ; and, the course of amelioration begun, its completion can always be more patiently waited for than can be endured the first tedium of absolute neglect—just as two hours of time following the dawn, and yet preceding the sunrise, seem far less tedious to the watcher than appears one half hour of that thick darkness before the first grey in the east. It may or may not be that the trumpet of fame shall become filled gradually with the complimentary words successively bestowed upon a certain Epitaph, in which centre the best energies of a not inactive brain, and the fullest results of an experience far from narrow, from the lips of pilgrims from distant lands as well as distant sections. And it may or may not be that some other historical event will chance, like that connected with the return of a banished sovereign and the gathering around him of the chief notables of the honored city, such as the brown old gabled Nuns' House opposite, once saw, in those days when the right divine was less questioned than now, if not better defined—titles and honors flowing from the momentary contact with royalty in a specially generous mood, and the chief magistrate of the city necessarily first remembered. And, failing this, who can say at what day it may be necessary for Cloisterham, loyal as well as tenacious of privilege, to send up that Address before briefly referred to, of which the before-mentioned chief-magistrate, active or retired, must be the appropriate bearer, being on that occasion "put to the sword " in that pleasant manner so well known in local history, and so grateful to the sufferer ? And then, if at no other time, and in no other way—then Sir Thomas—

The reverie of Mayor Sapsea, in which that type-donkey has been indulging to quite the length of the lady with the basket of eggs, at this stage changes its character, and the rude present resumes the place of the possibly golden future. The dignitary has been indulging in it, seated alone in his chair of imaginary state and chamber of fancied power; and his chair and desk stand in such a position that, looking directly before him, he sees the quaint overhanging gables and latticed windows of the Nuns' House. From the house his active thought—that active thought which travels around the world by atmospheres, so to speak, sees China in a tea-caddy, and the Arctic regions in a fur tippet—naturally recurs to the young ladies who, during the school season, make the old house and gardens musical, and thence to that one of the late member who was said to have borne a close personal connection with the great event of his administration.

An unfortunate event, so far, he cannot but think. He does not ignore the fact that in the history of Cloisterham yet to be written, more than a little of importance will be imparted by the knowledge that during the Sapsea Mayoralty occurred the mysterious disappearance and alleged murder of one Edwin Drood; but is it not just possible that the surpassing lustre of that period may be dimmed by the additional record of the mystery remaining unravelled, in spite of the (naturally supposed) bending of the chief magistrate's gigantic mind to its elucidation? More than once, of late weeks, this has occurred to him, until there is danger of this new mortification taking rank beside the one already sapping his vitals—that the late Mrs. Sapsea, albeit possibly a victim to the effort of looking up too high, had not been spared to look up yet higher, to Mind incorporated with Mayor, before crawling, in her abasement, into her chaste monument, and giving occasion for that brow-contracting Epitaph.

He has said to Mr. Datchery, some weeks before—a most meritorious person, this Datchery, showing creditable deference to both Intellect and Position—that his friend, Mr. John Jasper, man of iron will, swaying the long and strong arm of the law, will undoubtedly succeed in tracing home the guilt to the suspected perpetrator. But additional time has elapsed; Mr. Jasper seems to have made slow progress, if any; what if——

At this juncture there is a knock at the door, and a ser-

vant conveys the request of the respectful and approved Mr.
Datchery, that he may be allowed to intrude for a few moments on the valuable time of the Worshipful the Mayor.
He is permitted to enter, more truly from the grand wave of
the magisterial hand than the word of permission ; and the
man of the white hair and the dark eye-brows is immediately
in the presence. He has worn his hat to the door; Mr. Sapsea observes how quickly he removes it as he crosses the
threshold, and the incident strengthens the toleration with
which this highly-respectful visitor to Cloisterham, temporarily become a resident, is regarded by its first magistrate.

"Thanks for the permission. I may hope that the Worshipful the Mayor is in good health," courteously suggests the
new comer; adding, however, in a moment, "Now that I
look a second time, may I take the liberty of remarking that
His Honor the Mayor is scarcely looking at his best ? shows
signs of—what may I be allowed to call it ?—possibly mental
fatigue ? "

Mr. Sapsea passes his hand over his brow, then runs it
upward across the front hair, and ends by sweeping away a
little of the hirsute encumbrance from the temples, after the
manner of one suddenly made aware of the weariness of long
mental effort. He is evidently gratified—as this man seems
to have the faculty of gratifying him on all occasions, simply
by feeding more adulatory oats to the pompous donkey nature,
than the average of those thrown in contact with him. It
almost seems that he might be covertly a relative of the
defunct and much-respected, from the facility with which he
subjects his mental vertebræ to the straining curve of the
glance directed above its level.

The Mayor, as already said, experiences intense gratification at finding that mental efforts are beginning to tell upon
his face, and is thereupon amiable to a degree which might
have gone far towards conciliating even the impracticable
Durdles.

"Highly pleased to see Mr. Datchery," he says. "I trust

that you find your residence in Cloisterham as agreeable as
you expected on first taking lodgings. As to mental efforts
and fatigue," another stroke of the fat hand over face and
hair, and another pretence of sweeping away some annoying
anxiety, " as to that, you will recognize, Mr. Datchery, that
we who are charged with the public interests, in responsible
positions, do not sleep upon beds of roses—that is how *I* put
it—not upon beds of roses; and if sometimes the eye and
manner evince fatigue, those cares which none understand
except such as bear them, must plead the excuse; as connected
with the legal profession by occupancy of the bench, I say
again that these must plead the excuse."

"Good heavens!" says Mr. Datchery, as if struck to the
heart by the manner of the great man's last remark, "Do I
hear aright? Do I hear the Worshipful the Mayor speaking
of 'excuses' for that which really covers him with respect?
May I beg that His Honor will give me his hand, in evidence
that I have not been so painfully misunderstood?"

Mr. Datchery, without taking his eyes off the Mayor's face,
commences fumbling for the coveted hand, upon which demonstration the official, his broad meaningless face informed with
all the gratified vanity of Justice Shallow, superadded to the
asinine profundity of Dogberry, holds out the member with
impressment, and warmly returns the shake instantly given it.

"No, Mr. Datchery," he says, with profound appreciation
of that duty of putting his visitor at ease, devolving on him
as both host and superior. "No,—I am pleased to say that I
do not misunderstand your remark, which I take to be intended as complimentary, however liable to possible misconstruction
if not analyzed by Mind. We *are* at times fatigued; such a
possibility *does* exist; and the strongest back—I used that
phrase on the bench, only a day or two since—the strongest
back, as *I* put it, can only bear one load at a time."

"So pleased that His Honor the Mayor does *not* misunderstand me," Mr. Datchery replies, with effusion. "And I am
the more anxious that such a misunderstanding . should not

arise, at the present moment, as I am about to take what may be held an unwarrantable liberty."

It is not too strong a term to say that Mr. Sapsea is alarmed, and that he shows the alarm, unconsciously to himself, and yet as plainly as he has lately shown his swelling self-complacency. About to take a liberty; the phrase is seldom or never a welcome one. What may it not mean? Possibly borrowing of money? Ah, then, how likely the mental hands are to go down to the pockets and button them, even if the physical are restrained by very shame! Tendering of unpalatable advice? What hardening of the heart and sharpening of the will, in advance, to meet that most violent of all assaults upon the liberty of the individual! Revealing of unpleasant facts and letting out of skeletons from dark closets? Then what homicidal wishes, half covered with hollow thanks, and what regrets that in the days of Job some process had not been discovered and put in operation by the patriarch, for the benefit of all his descendants, having the office of exterminating all "comforters" and bearers of untoward news, at the instant when they break silence!

It is not to be supposed that Mr. Sapsea feels or philosophises all this, in the brief space following the threatening words of Datchery; he would be less a pompous fool, and so less fitted for the straw mayoralty of Cloisterham, had he that capacity. But he recognizes an uncomfortable feeling creeping through the numb skull and the thick cuticle; and the lips are pursed a little and the full cheeks puffed additionally, immediately thereafter.

"A liberty?—Mr. Datchery—I do not quite understand,"—— He flounders and pauses. Datchery comes in at once with great vigor and readiness.

"The liberty I was about to take with the Worshipful the Mayor," he explains, "is merely to venture upon consulting with him, if he will permit such a term of apparent equality, with reference to one of those very cares of his office, of which mention has just been made."

2

"Ah!"

This interjectory reply of Mr. Sapsea may mean anything or nothing, like the Italian "altro," which sounds all the gamut from satisfaction to despair. It may be relief from a worse fear; it may be surprise at the audacity, not yet declared enough for violent repression; it may be a mild form of tacit permission to the other to go on. Judging from the self-satisfied smirk accompanying, the latter may be presumed, and the man of liberties presumes accordingly.

"His Honor the Mayor did me the great courtesy, at my first coming to Cloisterham, to speak of a case of great local interest, not long before occurred."

"Referring," says Mr. Sapsea, with a wave of the hand at once explanatory and magisterial, "to the disappearance and understood murder of the young man Drood. Yes, I remember speaking of the affair to you, in the presence, as I think, of Mr. Jasper. Humph! you are about to ask, I have no doubt, whether anything additional has been discovered; and I am obliged to reply that—as I may have before remarked —mills turn slowly that grind exceedingly fine. That is how *I* put it—slowly, sir, for fine work. Nothing as yet, because the time has not yet arrived; though there is reason to believe that the investigation has not been conducted without Intellect and a certain amount of Energy."

"Ha! the Worshipful the Mayor puts it with his usual force and felicity," suggests the visitor. "Only personal presence prevents my pointing out that place in the combination in which Intellect reigns; may I be pardoned for adding that I presume at least a part of the Energy incarnated in Mr. Jasper, of whom the Worshipful the Mayor also spoke— the man who, if it is possible for a single buffer of careless habits to remember correctly, was mentioned as a man of strong will, and as having the reason of relationship for seeking out the murderer?"

Mr. Sapsea bows. The sentence is a slightly long one, and necessarily a little confusing; but it has the requisite flavor

of adulation, and the waves of anxiety on the erewhile
thought-ruffled forehead are placidly smoothed as the dignatary replies :

"Not only very well guessed, Mr. Datchery, but I may say
very well turned.   Mr. Jasper has Energy : it is not for me
to deny, any more than to accept, your remark suggesting the
presence of Intellect."

Mr. Sapsea has bowed, Mr. Datchery followed him in that
genuflexion, and the *entente cordiale* may be said to have
arrived at that position which it often holds in the intercourse
of nations—being very warm in spite of being blind and
meaningless : possibly *because* of those characteristics.

But something definite approaches, likely to be as disturbing as definite understandings between the powers so calmly at
peace in their ignorance.

Mr. Datchery, with the air of a single buffer, who is not
only idle and careless, as he has before proclaimed himself, but
also exceedingly indolent, thrusts his hand into his pocket
empty, and withdraws it holding a dark brown object of some
four inches by two and a half, and possibly an inch in thickness, leathery and damp-looking, with suspicion of spots, and
suggestions of dirt.

It is a pocket-wallet of which he loosens the straps and
throws back the folds, holding it out to the Mayor.

"The Worshipful the Mayor supposed, very naturally, that I
was about to ask some question as to the progress of the
Drood mystery.   On the contrary, it is my high privilege, as
I hold it my duty, to assist His Honor, even in the humblest
way, and the most unimportant of particulars, with a single
link that may be of eventual use in—may I borrow from His
Honor's epigrammatic habit ? in forming the fetters of the
criminal."

The fat magisterial hand is extended to take the object
offered ; while the magisterial face assumes an aspect of innate
stupidity and want of comprehension, struggling with a pretence of that wisdom understanding all things and impossible

to nonplus by the announcement of any new discovery in thought or physics—which would be irresistibly ludicrous if a certain element of the pitiful did not enter into it.

The magisterial eyes, glass-assisted, take in the object handed by Datchery; and at last they take in one peculiarity, at first ignored. Then the lips of wisdom speak again sententiously.

"Pocket-wallet, dark brown leather, wet, name of E. Drood under the flap. Likely to have been on the body of the unfortunate young man, when murdered by—by one whom we will not name. I see in this, Mr. Datchery, if you can fortunately prove before the court that you came into possession of it without taking part in the crime—I see in this, sir, possible means of tracking out the criminal, and of convicting him; that is how *I* put it, nothing less than tracking out the criminal, and convicting him."

So much in words, Mayor Sapsea. But what mode of expression, appreciable by the mere reader, shall convey the additional and unspoken words involved in air and gesture? As thus, in corrugation of the laboring brow, wave of the fat hand, and throwing back of the shoulders to a distance delightful to His Honor's tailor:—"You have brought to Mind and to Power something; but you have no more idea what, than the slave in one of the Brazilian mines, who picks up an ounce diamond in the rough, and carries it in his pouch as a mere pebble, while he seeks for something of a thousandth part the worth that happens to glitter. Here is the crucible in which the true worth of objects must be determined; here Intellect will deal with that which has thus far been only the sport of Accident."

But far is it from the idle, careless, and indolent buffer, who possibly sees all this in the demeanor of his interlocutor, to show any knowledge beyond that conveyed in words. He merely responds, with a wondrous sustaining of his old air of humility, not to say subserviency.

"So pleased that the Worshipful the Mayor recognizes at

least some worth in the slight link that I have been enabled
to supply. Possibly, however, His Honor will be more gratified as well as instructed, when I inform him how this wallet,
which undoubtedly was the property of the missing Edwin
Drood, and probably on his person at the time when he met
with his sad end, came into my possession."

"Humph," responds the Mayor. "It is very well, Mr.
Datchery, that you see the necessity. How, sir—that is how
I put it, as I must do—when—if called upon to act upon the
case, on the Bench—how does it happen that I discover in
your hands this article, which I believe—yes, which I may
say I am confident, from my past experience, to have been in
the possession of the murdered man at the time of the commission of the crime ? "

Mr. Datchery is not staggered, as well he might be, at this
somewhat forcible adoption of his own words against himself.
Possibly he has been quite prepared for this, as for nearly anything else that could occur in that peculiar presence. At all
events he is quite as bland and good-humored as ever, as he
accepts the permission, and in his own rambling way gives the
story of the wallet.

"I have already had the privilege of telling His Honor the
Mayor the fact of my being a single buffer, and an idle one ;
but I may also tell him that I am an odd one as well, and that
I habitually do what others are not much in the habit of
doing. Suspicious, in the eyes of the Worshipful ? Let me
hope not, or at least let me try to remove the impression.
My arrangements are simply a little odd, nothing more. For
instance, I often employ the fishermen's boats and go fishing
up the river, though I am free to say that I do not remember
having caught a single fish as yet, since I came to this pleasant town. I do not deny that I have had nibbles, though I
may be encroaching on the valuable time of the Worshipful
the Mayor, by presuming to mention such a trifle. However,
it is to be supposed that the supreme authority desires *all* the
information at my command—not simply a part of it ?"

"All, Mr. Datchery—all : that is how *I* put it in examinations from the Bench—all or nothing. Be good enough to go on, sir!" replies the Mayor, with one of those commanding and benevolent waves of the hand which show him entirely unsuspicious of the narrator's good faith.

"Thanks for the permission"—continuing. "I was about to say, then, that there is an old fisherman, occupying a cabin not far from the Weir, named Crawshe, whom I have several times employed to row me up the river, and help me in indulging my odd humor. He has a poor boy, his son, whom they call Little Crawshe—helpless from some accident—the falling of a stick of timber, I think, which has broken away some of the cords of the back of the neck, compelling him always to hold one hand under the chin, to keep the head from falling forward on the breast. May I hope that His Honor the Mayor knows anything of Crawshe and his boy? No—of course not : they are not likely to approach such Position. Well, the poor fisherman often asks the privilege of his employers of taking the crippled boy with him in the boat, as a means of amusing him in his inability to share in the rough play of the other boys. Yesterday I went up the river, rowed by Crawshe, and Little Crawshe accompanying. I gave the boy some pence when about to leave the boat, and he took this wallet from his pocket to put them into it. Watching him a little closely, to see how he managed with one hand, I caught the name under the flap, and at once pretended a certain interest in the looks of the article, and bought it from him for a shilling. Inquiring on that point, though I had no doubt on the subject, I learned that neither Little Crawshe nor his father could read a word, so that neither could have had any knowledge of the name on the inside. Inquiring further, in my idle way, I learned that the boy had picked up the wallet on the river bank, very near the Weir, only a day or two before, in such a spot that it would seem impossible that it could long have lain there without attracting attention. I need not ask if His Honor follows me, and if he arrives at the obvious conclusion to be drawn from the latter fact ?"

Datchery pauses, as he may well do after so long a story without interruption. At once the Mayor brings to the subject the force of Intellect.

"Conclusion obvious," he observes, sententiously. "Wallet not long found, criminal been lately along river bank, and dropped it accidentally, after having robbed it of contents. You are quite excusable, Mr. Datchery, as a man without legal training, for not having arrived at such a conclusion, which demands Mind and Experience. But that is how *I* put it, sir—late dropping of stolen article, late presence of criminal, possible remaining even now in the neighborhood."

"Reasoned with the well-known acuteness of the Worshipful the Mayor!" exclaims the other, with glee. "May I take the liberty of shaking hands again, in felicitation? Thanks, many. And now may I beg to offer one more suggestion?"

His Honor the Mayor nods loftily but suavely.

"More than once, as the Worshipful the Mayor will remember, the name of Mr. John Jasper has been alluded to, as the person most interested in tracing out the crime. Might I suggest that this wallet should be placed at once in his hands, for his information and encouragement?"

The Mayor seeing no objection, and briefly expressing himself to that effect, Mr. Datchery adds:

"And should I be contravening the wishes of His Honor the Mayor, in requesting the privilege of being present at the exhibition or delivery to Mr. Jasper (whichever His Honor may think proper under the circumstances) of this—this article, as His Honor has well called it, which suddenly assumes a certain interest and value in this case?"

Mr. Sapsea at once retires within himself again to a certain extent; and the pomposity is much more marked as he enquires:

"Humph! I do not understand, Mr. Datchery. Desire to be present at Mr. Jasper's receiving this—this article? I am not to presume that any connection exists, in this affair, between Mr. Jasper and yourself?"

"Certainly not, as the Worshipful the Mayor should be assured at once," replies the man who has again fallen under tacit suspicion; and replies somewhat hurriedly. "Let me implore His Honor not to place me under impressions which I should deprecate, in spite of my high respect for the energetic Mr. Jasper. No; my motive is easily told, and, I may hope, not a discreditable one, as appealing to the cultivated Intellect which I address. I have the honor to be a student of humanity, though an idle buffer; and I find a singular pleasure, sometimes, in observing the first moments of sensations in minds bent to special objects."

"Ah!"

This interjectory comment of the Mayor again conveys relief, if not satisfaction, and the other proceeds:

"Now, venturing to make use of the information kindly imparted by the Worshipful the Mayor, in this permitted interview and others, and assuming all Mr. Jasper's great energies to be worthily bent upon pursuing this concealed though suspected murderer, may I not name, as some slight compensation for the benefit which I have been accidentally enabled to bestow upon the search, the privilege of watching Mr. Jasper's triumphal sensations when this new link of evidence is put into his hands? I take the liberty of asking His Honor the Mayor if this may not be allowed, without derogation to the dignity of his position, and without compromising my own, so much more humble."

Mayor Sapsea is finally conquered, as it would seem. What mere mortal would not be, under corresponding circumstances? however the gods of old might require the rising of additional incense to the divine nostrils. Certainly the idle buffer has smoked the very-wooden god sufficiently, and it is time that some answering blessing should be reached. It comes, in one of Mr. Sapsea's most benevolent and condescending waves of the hand, and in the full accordance of the required permission, which the donor no doubt considers compensation enough for a life-time of service.

"You may be present at the delivery to Mr. Jasper of the— the article, Mr. Datchery. It may be contrary to legal precedent, sir—and that, when on the Bench and off it, I consider the palladium of English liberty—that is how *I* put it, in occasional consultation with my learned brothers — the palladium of English liberty. But this shall be waived, Mr. Datchery—this shall be waived," waving the fat hand, meanwhile, as if unconsciously punning on the word. "We will call upon Mr. Jasper, and I will show him the article, and possibly deliver it to him, you being present."

The conference is ended with these words, as conferences must end between the highest of earthly dignitaries and those who are temporarily permitted to approach them on terms of conversational equality. Mr. Sapsea rises from that chair which has for the preceding half-hour been more or less a throne; assumes that hat so marvellously French in the bell of the crown and the curl of the brim, and with which Cloisterham is now quite as well acquainted and almost as loftily, as with the Cathedral tower itself; and the two make their way, the Mayor the least trifle in advance, and Mr. Datchery only putting on his hat at the latest possible moment,—to that interview with Mr. Jasper which is to fortify him with a new prospect of revenge on the murderer of his dear boy.

CHAPTER II.

DURDLES, SCULPTOR; AND HONEYTHUNDER, AVENGER.

DURDLES at work. Impossibilities become possibilities, and falsehoods absolute facts — just as while all the Old philosophers were demonstrating, with a laborious persistency and an equally laborious folly, that no vessel propelled by the steam of a kettle could ever cross the great ocean, and that no needle could ever be induced to carry a thread regu-

larly through any fabric, by blind mechanical power — the
New philosophers were quietly perfecting the ocean-steamer
and inventing the sewing-machine.

An anomaly, certainly, and yet no less a truth. Durdles,
known never to be at work, actually at work—and at work
with a will, whatever there might have been, or failed to be,
of that judgment which should control the will, and without
which it is somewhat more dangerous than indecision.

And Durdles sober. At least so nearly freed from the habitual sottishness of his ordinary life, that if it hung around him
like a murky atmosphere it did not envelop him in its close
embrace like an impenetrable fog. Grim, stolid, heavy-looking and stone-dusty as ever, there was yet something about
the man, just then, elevating him above the wholly-debased
and sordid, if it could not lift him into the realm where dwells
romantic interest. Perhaps it lifted him even there, in spite
of dirt, squalor, ignorance, ill-temper, drunkenness. We are
not very expert at measuring personal positions or calculating
moral distances—most of us ; and Stony Durdles may at some
moment be found quite as severe a strain upon the mathemati-
cal faculties, as the new planet discovered last month, or the
comet that is to flaunt its luminous tail in our view next year.

It has already been said of the Stony One, that fame called
him a wonderful workman, while actual observation only saw
him doing nothing, with much accompaniment of two-foot
rule, dinner-bundle, accepted outlawry, and self - satisfied
comments upon himself in the third person. Who knows,
meanwhile, but Fame—who must possess wonderful (if never
mentioned) ears, to gather up all the intelligence spread
abroad in the world through the medium of her trumpeting
mouth—may have been wiser than the speakers who saw and
heard at a lower level, may even have caught the occasional
clink of a hammer and chisel, the use of which brought the
dusty old stone-mason within the scope of her duties ?

Then, too, Fame may have had an assistant or two, the
post of observation being the ordinary level. Who knows

but Mr. Tope, the verger, so likely to be acquainted with all the minor details of the lives of those with whom he was much thrown in contact—and Mr. Crisparkle, so careful of the grammatical accuracy of Durdles' language when addressing his Reverence the Dean—may have been the means through whom there crept to the outer world of Cloisterham certain indefinite rumors of an ability belied by every appearance and surrounding?

Durdles' den or cave in the city wall was deeper than most people knew—even as possibly so was the solitary tenant, if a modern and not-too-classical secondary use of the word may be permitted. Few persons stumbled over the broken stone and chips of the yard, to enter the precincts at all; still fewer knew that the miserable apartment, which only they saw, had any other outlet than the broken door; and yet fewer dreamed that within that inner apartment was carefully hidden one of the most notable oddities of the century—the "studio" of Durdles the Sculptor!

"Stony Durdles," indeed, and in how different a sense from that in which the ordinary little world of Cloisterham understood it! Durdles the Sculptor. If laboring for immortality, doing so with scarcely more than a clientelle of two or three; if for some other end, it may not be easy to number the invisible beings coming into the calculation.

That Mr. Tope knew of the "studio," and yet carefully concealed its existence, who could better tell than himself, remembering the thousand gruff importunities first and last addressed him by the odd human compound, to assist in procuring privately some bit of stone that promised to serve the one great purpose? And that Mr. Crisparkle, the bright, fresh, clear-headed but excessively-human Minor Canon, possessed equal intelligence—what better proof was necessary than his presence at the very moment when the clink of mallet and chisel was being heard in the unsuspected recess?

Durdles the Sculptor—once more. Think twice, careful student of the calculus of probabilities, before adding to the mistakes of human arrogance by declaring such a thing impossible, except in some sense involving the broadly ridiculous. For if we live a dual life in sleeping and in waking hours, so different each from each that scarcely one can recognize the other of those twin components when meeting on the border of the shadow-land—so surely, too, our powers and our capacities are dual, making the rule of life more strong by forming the exception, and balancing the blemish showing to the eye upon a surface otherwise so brilliant, by some small spark at least to light what otherwise would seem too base and common for the Forming Hand.

There is an old German story, having to do with the life of Albert Dürer, which has been told once and again by those who love the great art of which he was declared the "evangelist," but which may be briefly told once more, with the title indicated, if not expressed—"The Unexpected."

Samuel Duhobert was color-grinder to the great painter—a poor little humpbacked fellow, who seemed especially made for the drudgery of the studio, and for the Xantippe words, and often blows of Madame Dürer. To escape the last, he built him a little hovel of retreat under the bank of the Pegnitz; and there he ground the colors which, under the master's hand, were to form hues of immortality. But the poor fellow was not without leisure, and not beneath *ennui*. In a mere spirit of imitation of what he saw every day, he used a few scraps of the colors, and *daubed*. Pictures he had none to copy, even had he possessed the capacity; so he did the only thing possible—he tried in his own feeble way to reproduce the scene spread before him at the door of his hovel—a reach of the silver-winding river, a few trees, an old castle crowning a distant height, and the blue Franconian mountains bounding the prospect. This was what he—*daubed;* what else than daubing could be the work of the poor color-grinder?

But there came a day when he was expelled from his master's service, during that master's absence, by his proud and violent mistress. He was penniless and without resources.

Stay—there was *his picture ;* that might buy him enough of bread for at least a day or two, if he could but sell it. As fortune ordered, there was to be a sale of pictures the very next day, at a seat about to be dismantled in the neighborhood. The auctioneer knew him, and might favor him, in his distress, by offering the picture as the humblest portion of the refuse of the collection. The auctioneer took pity on him, as he had hoped, after a certain amount of objection. The unpretending effort was brought to view, fortunately before the representatives of rank and wealth, as well as cultivated tastes; and the poor hunchback, shivering in his corner, saw it sold—admittedly the equal of the best effort of Claude Lorraine—to an agent of the Emperor, at the price of *the original for the picture ;* eventually to confer on the color-grinder the Barony of Duhobart, and to become one of the leading attractions of the Imperial Gallery at Vienna.

But what of this ? Was it not simply an instance of the bringing to light of genius before unknown ? Not so, the bow was never drawn again; there were no more arrows in the quiver. If Duhobart ever painted again, to meet the demands of his own awakened self-love, and the expectations of the world of art, he only *daubed.* He had done his life-work at a single stroke. His story has place here, because there was a similar life-work flashing out a single spark from amid the dust, squalor and stupidity of Durdles.

" How are you getting on, Durdles ? The morning was so bright and cheery, that I said to myself, Durdles will be at work, to take advantage of the excellent light; and I will drop around and flog my own indolence and self-indulgence by observing his industry."

It was the voice of Mr. Crisparkle, cheery as he had described the morning; and the whole man indefinably informed and irradiated by the atmosphere of sunrise, bird-songs, and the flash of falling water.

He stood just within the low inner door, to pass under the stony lintel of which he had been obliged to bend himself at

least two feet from the perpendicular, without reckoning the
height of his hat; and he saw the miserable walls of broken
stones, rather thrown together than built, with a bed of little
else than rags in one corner; and in the other—beneath a
broad ray of morning light, which came in from what would
have been called a loophole in the days of mediæval attack
and defence, a short bench of heavy wooden planks, bearing a
block of stone, drab-colored and slightly friable, like that of
Caen, with which the French have managed so to brighten up
the architectural tone of their cities.

This block, some three feet in height, and a foot square,
stood on end, the bottom portion as yet all unworked, but the
upper beginning to assume some rough resemblance to the
head and face of a woman. A rough resemblance, only bearing the same comparison to any possible completed bust that
the first crude idea of a project bears to its succeeding self
when elaborated into a full plan of action. There was the
recognizable shape of a head, life-sized and really well mould-
ed; there was a hint of hair, evidently designed to be flying
loose and wavy; there was a suspicion of nose and chin, of
which the shape could not yet be determined; and at that
point the thick cloud of uncertainty settled down, and obliged
conjecture to supply all the remainder.

Before this Stony Durdles was standing, mallet and chisel
in hand, alternately chipping away at the figure, with that
caressing carefulness known only to the master sculptor, and
never achieved by his students or helpers until they themselves become masters, engaged on works of their own,—and
falling back a pace to note the effect produced by a touch or
two of the chisel, as no doubt did Phidias two thousand years
ago, and as certainly did Thorwaldsen yesterday.

This, before the shadow of the Minor Canon darkened the
dim cross-light of the entrance, and even after he had spoken.
The sculptor must not be broken in upon too rudely, whether
his material be stone or marble, or the intruder must take the
risk of a certain *brusquerie* in reception; for what if a pre-

mature turn of the head, leaving the hands to complete a stroke thus far only designed, should be the means of causing a slip of the chisel, the chipping off of the whole end of a nose, or the ploughing of such a furrow in a cheek intended to be plump and fair, that even the plough of Time (which he uses quite as often as his scythe, though all attention seems to be concentrated upon the other agricultural implement) could scarcely be held capable of such a devastation ?

Clink, clink ! and chip, chip ! Then, before the gruff and stony one desisted for a moment, he said a good morning so unamiable that it would have driven away any one knowing him less thoroughly than his visitor. Then he turned back to the bust, improved his variety of view by throwing his head to one side, as if the object, when finished, was to be principally inspected by persons in bed; then laid down hammer and chisel, thrust both hands and wrists to their full depth into the pockets of his horn-buttoned jacket; then drew out from the right one a villanously soiled handkerchief, which might have done previous duty for at least a year as an envelope for the dinner-bundle (indeed Mr. Crisparkle thought that he remembered having seen it fulfilling such an engagement), wiped with it the dusty brow on which some drops of perspiration may have stood from other reasons than those affecting the corresponding portion of Mr. Sapsea's physiognomy ; then opened his mouth, and spoke, in his own peculiar growl.

" Ye ask Durdles, Mr. Crisparkle, how is he getting on ? Durdles puts it back to *you*, and asks *you* how he's getting on ? 'Cause,—— " and here Durdles, no doubt gnawed by a half-hour's hunger, which he had up to that moment managed to control if not to suppress, made a sudden clumsy lunge towards the other end of the bench, where the dinner-bundle doing present duty had lain unperceived by the clergyman, extracted therefrom half a square foot of bread, and an only smaller modicum of cold bacon, and commenced improving the time to be otherwise wasted in conversation, by munching with at least the effect of toning-down his gruff voice, if not making all his words more intelligible—" 'Cause, though Durdles knows his work, specially when dealing with the monuments and the Old 'Uns, he may like to know how things like this, that may be called his *fine work*, looks to eyes that has more larnin' than his own."

Thus appealed to, the Minor Canon took a little closer survey of the work of art, Durdles for the moment withdrawing all attention from the work to look upon him and stolidly read the verdict in his face. The survey seemed to be satisfactory, for the bright face expressed something like pleasure, as he said,—

" Getting on very well, very well indeed, Durdles. This, I think, is better than either of the others. More of life and vigor about it, though of course very far from being finished. By the way, perhaps you will allow me to look at *them* again for a moment, as a means of comparison."

" The Old 'Uns that *I* have stuck away, 'cause they were dead, never comin' to have any life in 'em, is all up there, Mr. Crisparkle," replied the mason-sculptor, the words seemingly forming part of a sandwich of bread and bacon. " You can look at 'em, if ye like to see vaults above ground ; Durdles don't mind, with *you*."

Mr. Crisparkle took the permission, and acted upon certain knowledge which he had no doubt before possessed.

He moved a little to the left, over the bed, and there, drawing aside a curtain of faded and dingy chintz, so nearly the color of the stone of the wall as easily to have escaped observation, revealed yet one more of the surprises of the " studio."

There was a niche coarsely built into the wall, by a hand showing at once the skill and the roughness of the stone-mason, with a certainty that the constructor had been in the habit of observing the niched altar-tombs of the old cathedrals. For, though rough in materials, and careless as to shape, this recess was almost ludicrously like some of those in which, during the last century, the remains and effigies of sainted old abbots have been found built into the walls of religious-houses, their entombing seeming to have been made under the dim prophetic knowledge of some coming transition period, during which they would need to be temporarily covered altogether from view, to avoid the hammer of the iconoclast, shattering noses and dismembering toes and fingers, if even avoiding the extreme violence of utter destruction.

And the resemblance did not quite cease with the receptacle. There is another detail of many of the altar-tombs, within and without those niches, familiar to all who have paid even the most hasty of visits to those cathedrals where Power lies entombed as well as Piety. This is a row of figures, from two or three to half-a-dozen in number, generally kneeling and invariably ruffed, arranged woodenly one in front of the other, often minus those very tender noses (which seem to be the weak point of persecuted statuary), and supposed to represent certain members of the family of the recumbent principal occupant. In this, too, the receptacle of Durdles' domestic Old 'Uns was of the cathedral, cathedrally. For there stood no less than six shadowy busts, ranging from eighteen inches to three feet in height, all in various stages of incompleteness and abandonment, and of materials as diverse as their appearance in other regards. One was of marble not far progressed with, and creating a suspicion that it had been abandoned in sheer despair of making due impression upon it with any tools at command; another seemed of granite or basalt, thrown aside from motives apparently similar, after labor progressing a little further in grim and profitless determination. A third, the largest of all, was of soft red sandstone, and this would seem to have been a success up to a certain point, for the hair had begun to be more than indicated, and the features of the face had assumed a certain prominence. But ah! the remark just previously made had been illustrated in advance; the material so easy to manage had been equally easy to mar—the nose was gone, to the very root, through either accident, sudden dissatisfaction, or malice. There were others, minor and possibly

3

older—the dynasty of the stone-mason having extended over some years, and those successive filings-away in the niche having been resorted to by the bereaved head of the dynasty, who neither knew nor cared for enough of scripture precedent to "bury his dead out of his sight," though he paid some attention to the proprieties by curtaining them.

Attempted representations, all these, of one object. The bust of a woman always attempted, with the same peculiarity of wildly flowing hair, though beyond that point the successive failures had left no opportunity for judgment. The bust of a woman. Of what? of whom? of one who had been? of one who was? of one expected? of one who was not, had not been and could not be?—such as float through the visions of the imagination, or are born in the atmosphere of those twin rosy clouds, love and wine? Little likely, at least, one of the latter, in the case of Stony Durdles: it seemed necessary for Mr. Crisparkle, who held a portion of this curiosity, to fall back upon the hypothesis that some woman of the past was thus being blindly aimed at and never hit.

"Looking at the 'Old 'Uns,' " said the clergyman, after making a careful survey of the rejected, and then dropping back the curtain, " I am inclined to think that you are getting on very well—very well indeed, and that you will make something out of this."

The compliment, albeit a qualified one, should have been pleasant to the sculptor—should have produced at least a slight effect in the way of adding to the amiability of a face not notable in that direction. But evidently the proper chord was not touched—as it is not in the case of a vain-glorious author, who, warily fishing for complimentary mention of his works, is rendered rabid by finding all approbation bestowed upon some trifle of earlier years, long consigned to oblivion, if not to shame, by himself.

"What's them to judge by?" he growled, laying down his partially-emptied bundle, and wiping his mouth on the back of his hand, the soiled handkerchief being no doubt held too

sacred for such a mere menial use. "There's only one of 'em
as could have 'mounted to much at the best; for Durdles, even
if he knows his work, hasn't the tools and other things of the
high-flyers. That one had the nose knocked off, along of them
young imps a frightenin,' of me at an unfortnit moment.
And 'something,'—what do you mean by something, Mr.
Crisparkle? What's 'something,' if I can't make it look like
Her?"

He had commenced with a growl; he ended in a tone of
voice not far removed from a melancholy plaint, and in which
the Minor Canon again found some approach to that answer
which had never yet come from the lips of Durdles. 'Her,'
in that tone: who could doubt, even if no one knew, that the
romance of a life, perhaps its tragedy, lay in those feeble and
stupid attempts at art, by one who had no such vocation,
unless the heart supplied the call? Some unknown impulse
moved the clergyman then to make that reply which had
more than once before trembled on his lips, but been withheld.

"How can I tell you, Durdles, whether there is any probability of your being able to make it look like Her, when I do
not know what she is to you, or what she has been? Some
day, when you tell me so much, if you ever do——"

"Stop!" and the voice of the stone-mason now blended the
growl with the broken pathos—the latter not entirely taken
away, even if marred, by his extracting from his pocket a
stumpy and dirty black pipe, likewise extracting a roll of shag
and a match, and clumsily proceeding to light it. "Stop, Mr.
Crisparkle, you are right, and Durdles is wrong. Ye won't
mind the pipe, I'm thinking, for ye're not one of them new
lights as begrudge the poor man his pipe and his beer. Who
is 'Her?" The gal Durdles loved and expected to make his
wife, many a year ago, when he was younger than he is now,
and when the imps didn't worrit the life out of him!"

Commonplace and unattractive-looking as was the object
speaking, there was almost a romantic interest in him as he
spoke, revealing that "one touch of nature" that "makes the

whole world kin." The Minor Canon felt the influence,
blended with a corroboration of what had before been his suspicion; and there was true feeling in his voice, as he said,—

"Ay, I understand, as I thought before that I did. The
girl you loved and were about to marry, many years ago, and
whom you lost."

"Lost—yes, that is the word; you men of larnin always
knows the right word, whenever you gets 'em. Yes—lost—
that's the word for *her*."

"Died?" Mr. Crisparkle asked the momentous question in
that single syllable, and yet with some influence weighing
upon him, which made that single word difficult. He did not
see, nor did he need to see, the face of the other, its natural
homeliness and habitual neglect contorted by a strange blending of rage and grief, as he replied,—

"There some of you larned folks isn't much wiser than the
poor fools—Durdles and the rest of 'em. No, she didn't die—
not as I knows on. She'd better, no doubt, you parsons 'ud
say. Died! No, she ran away, jest a month afore we wus to
to been married, with a big, wordy, psalm-singin' chap, who
swore he would marry her (so they said), and then didn't,
so that she and her babby was kicked out into the world.
Maybe she died, then—Durdles don't know. Never seed her
since, whether alive or dead—never expect to. Seed her
child, though, too many times; wish I hadn't never! You
would make me tell it, which I've not done it afore to no one.
And what of it? Durdles has some secrets as he can keep,
and *will* keep, because they belong to others; but he has a
right to do what he likes with his own, hasn't he?"

"Poor old fellow!" said Mr. Crisparkle, sympathetically.
"You did indeed 'lose' her. But why do you wish to remember her, in a likeness, if she treated you so ill?"

"There you larned folks *is* fools—nothing less. What do I
want of her likeness as she was after she went away and
broke my heart?" It was notable that he had almost entirely
dropped the habitual third person now, and spoke in the ordinary

first. "I want her as she was afore that psalm singin' scoundrel come to her—when she was *mine*. I tried to get a picter made of her, but how could I, with no one as had seen her, and me not good at describin', as she wasn't a yard of stone wall. And I've been a-tryin', for this ever so many years, afore you ever knowed anything about Durdles, to make her out of stone. That's all; and I ax pardin for there bein' so much of it. But maybe as you can tell me, now, if I keep soberish, whether I can ever cut her all out of here?"

He touched his dusty forehead as he spoke, as indicating that *there* must be the origin of the possible likeness; and there was that in the story and its circumstances, so pitiful, that the Minor Canon may be excused for possibly having raised hopes that had small chance of fulfilment, in the reply which followed :—

"Make a likeness of her? Certainly you can, with your use of tools, and such a recollection of her as you seem to retain— that is, if you keep, not ' soberish,' but sober. You will not be the first who has done it, Durdles, even under circumstances less favorable than your own. Listen, and light your pipe again if you wish, while I tell you what a woman did, within my own knowledge—a poor ignorant woman, living down at Deal. She was the wife of a sailor, who went away before their child was born. It was born, and then only a few months afterwards it died, while he was still away—on the other side of the world. She had no means to procure a picture of the poor dead child, and yet how could she allow it to be buried without some recollection being preserved—not only that she might avoid forgetting its appearance, but that the father, who had never seen his child, might be able, when he came back, to form some idea how it had looked? What did she do—this poor woman, who had neither friends, money, nor education? She laid out her poor baby stiffening on the boards, went down to the pits, and brought home some clay; and then in the clay she modelled its little face, head, and neck, so correctly, that no one who had seen the child failed to recognize the likeness. So the father, when he came back, saw the image of his child, if not the child itself; and what the poor sailor's wife could do, without instruction, Durdles can do after all these years' practice with tools, and in stone-work, if I am not mistaken in him."

Durdles had a second time extracted the soiled handker-chief, and seemed to be wiping his eyes, when the Minor Canon concluded. Possibly the grief of the sailor's wife, like his own, but so much more painful, had done what his own duller sorrows had failed to do—brought sufficient moisture to the eyes to lay the habitual dust on the uncomely and stupid face. At all events Stony Durdles was belying his name by being more or less melted, when a sound caught his ear, changing the expression of that face much more rapidly than any observer of its ordinary stolidity could have believed pos-sible.

What he heard, the Minor Canon had reason to suppose that *he* heard also—two voices of very different key and vol-ume, though both loud and angry, coming in from the direction of the front of the hut. Durdles, who had made a mechani-cal lunge for his dinner-bundle, concluded temporarily to fore-go it, and rolled through the small door, towards the outer one with more agility in his movements, and an expression of more intense hatred on his face, than the other had ever observed under any provocation. A little surprised, and inter-ested, in spite of himself, the clergyman followed, coming upon Durdles just as he reached the door looking out upon the yard, and sharing with him in the instructive spectacle then and there presented.

The Reverend Luke Honeythunder, even more bulky in person, more overwhelming in tone, and more aggressively philanthrophic in manner, than the Minor Canon had before known him, his large eyes and his fat cheeks alike distended with anger, which seemed even to permeate his breadth of ultra-clerical garb and his wisp of white neck-cloth—not to mention his hat, escaped from his head, and cooling from late perspiration in the midst of a heap of stone-chips.

Drawn in a bent position across the left knee of the Philanthropist, with his head and shoulders held under the left arm
of that person, a peculiarly sensitive part of his anatomy
defenceless against attack, and his otherwise useless legs flying
up in the air, bannered with rags and shoe-strings, in vigorous
efforts to get himself loose or severely kick his enemy, hung
the before uncaught and unconquered Deputy, at last come to
great grief.

Great grief, indeed ; for few hands were broader or heavier
than that right member which usually managed to handle the
funds at the Head Haven of the United British and Foreign
Universal Philanthropists, and of which it was sometimes
said that a hand so large would naturally cover those funds,
and keep them for a certain time out of the public sight—not
to mention the probability that the very long digits appertaining must reach farther down into the common purse and touch
cash lying nearer the bottom, than any of less extended proportions. A very large hand and a very heavy hand, set in
motion by a temper not strictly apostolic, even if highly philanthropic ; and Deputy—long escaped but caught at last, as
the irreverent sometimes say of other fugitives, especially those
from matrimony—Deputy was becoming fully aware of the
weight of that large hand, and the strength of the muscular
system controlling it.

Whack! whack! whack! "There, you infernal little scoundrel!——" [Whack! whack!] "Man of God cannot pass
along the street, cannot he, without being assaulted by——"
[Whack! whack!] "such wretched little vermin and misere-
ants as you, who——" [Whack! whack! whack!] "ought
to be sent to prison, or to the asylum for young reprobates, at
once, and——" [Whack! whack! whack!] "would be if I
had time to attend to you!——" [Whack! whack! whack!]
"You will be a better boy after this, you infernal young ras-
cal; or if not, I will come down——" [Whack! whack!]
"to this miserable hole again, and flog the balance of the life
out of you!"

This has been given as a solo, for the sake of preserving the unity—not the unities. It was really nothing of the sort, meanwhile; those mild expostulations being continually blended with equally mild promises of reform and expressions of personal good will, on the part of Deputy, of which a few of the plums must be thrown in together at this late moment, affording a pleasant amusement to the philosophical reader, to pick them out from the mass and stick them in where they belong.

"Strike me again, if you dare—big thief!"—"Boo! hoo! hoo!—goin' and a-ketchin' of a little feller like me, and a-slappin' of him!"—"I'll kill you, you big lubber, when I get away, bellows me if I won't!"—"Boo! hoo! hoo!—let a feller go, I say!"—"Give you the next stone down yer throat—hope I may die if I don't!"—"Boo! hoo! hoo!—I hain't been a-doin' nothin'—let me go, I tell yer!"—"Smash yer eye, next time I ketch yer—see if I don't!" etc. etc. etc., with the appropriate oaths (horribly appropriate, for England's children at that age!) duly understood and likewise properly distributed.

Causes have, unfortunately, not been given for half the great conflicts of the world, even when known. The facts would seem to have been, in the case at present under notice, that the Philanthropist, once more seeking the Reverend Septimus Crisparkle for reasons which may hereafter develop themselves, and directed towards him as having been observed going that way about half an hour before—had walked, in his striding and appropriate way, which required some rods of width for safety, literally over and upon the top of Deputy aforementioned, the latter being at that moment absorbed in the use of a peculiarly well-sized heap of stone-chips, and engaged in stoning the whole world of Cloisterham, human, animal, and architectural, in one grand *feu d'enfer*, in honor of the discovery; that Deputy, aggrieved and resenting, met that affront by running head-foremost into the Philanthropist, after the legendary manner of the battering-ram, being thereupon overthrown by a vigorous thrust of the heavier combatant; that Deputy thereupon skirmished more distantly, with war-cries compounded from the various savage nations of history, in the meantime discharging continuous missiles against the bulk of his antagonist, with the end of eventually knocking off the philanthropic hat, at the same time rendering it less waterproof in certain portions; and that, finally, the Philan-thropist, chafed beyond endurance, not to say bruised corres-pondingly, opposed length of stride to agility of motion, pur-sued, with his heavier squadrons, the light cavalry of Deputy, over stone-heaps and around unfinished monuments, with the result of capture and signal punishment heretofore so feebly portrayed.

Facts ascertained; immediate results given; after-conse-quences of the encounter unknown.

And still not all even of the immediate results as yet indicated.

Mr. Crisparkle as before shown, followed Durdles to the door, and gazed with him upon the instructive spectacle. Had he failed to do so, or had the conversation of the past half-hour not taken place in the "studio," possibly the Minor Canon might have missed the words which followed his first glance, from the lips of the sculptor with one idea.

"It is very long since Durdles has seen him, but he knows him all the same. D——n him! Durdles don't forget!"

"Whom do you mean, Durdles? The large man, who is only giving your pupil what he ought to have had long ago?"

"Yes, that is him. What's his name nowadays? Durdles never seed him in Cloisterham afore. Do you know him?"

"Know him? Yes, and do not admire him much more warmly than yourself, though I should scarcely like to use the same words in expressing my opinion of him. That is Mr. Honeythunder, the great philanthropist, of the Head Haven, London."

"Head which? Philanthe — what ever is it? Durdles' head is a little thick to-day, along of the dust, and that story he has been a-telling; but he knows enough to know that yonder's the big, wordy, psalm-singing chap who ran away with my poor gal, and broke her heart and mine—if he *has* shaved his face since, and got more'n a trifle older. D——n him !—Durdles says once more."

Mr. Crisparkle, astonished beyond measure, looked around, more interested now in the man at his side than the scene before him.   But Durdles had gone back into the hut without another word.   And the next moment Mr. Honeythunder, possibly recognizing the presence of the Minor Canon at the door, had released his well-flogged victim, and stridden forward, picking up his damaged hat, and wiping the perspiration of philanthropic justice from his brow, to say,—

" Mr. Crisparkle, as a matter of choice, perhaps I am not more anxious for your company than you are for mine ; but there are reasons, affecting both and others, why I must see you at once.   Be good enough to say where I can do so."

He did not extend that large hand, now red with the increased circulation of violent use, as he spoke.   Neither did Mr. Crisparkle, as he answered, viewing the other with a new interest which the latter little suspected,—

" At my house, of course, if Mr. Honeythunder will honor me so far."

CHAPTER III.

KNOCK AND RING.

HELENA LANDLESS, the bright fresh air of the morning tinting her dusky cheek with a healthy bloom, and making her the very incarnation of that " beautiful girl of the tropics," of whom we hear so much, and see so little — is enjoying that morning in the aërial garden of which Staple, and P. J. T., have unconsciously become proprietors, with

Lieut. Tartar, lessee, and Neville Landless, Esq., possibly one day to be a bencher of the Inner Temple, sub-lessee.

In other words, the young girl is enjoying the morning air in that portion of the garden which has been arranged by Mr. Tartar in front of her brother's window. The poor young fellow, with some indefinite idea of being less lonely in less confined space, is reading in Helena's room adjoining; and the sister finds a double pleasure in catching the perfume of flowers, breathing that clear air from which the smoke of five hundred thousand chimneys has unaccountably absented itself on that special morning, and listening to the twittering of those sparrows which even outdo Mr. Tartar in their disregard of the heights at which they perch—all this without disturbing the studies of her other self, who must at the same time be pleasantly conscious of her near companionship.

To her, or into her immediate neighborhood, Mr. Tartar himself, his curling head, brown face and blue eyes just showing above the leaves, crowning that portion of the party wall dividing the two tenements, and the remaining portion of him presumptively hidden behind that wall, and immediately against it.

"Good morning, Miss Landless. Will you kindly give me a few words here, by coming up closer to the wall? or may I step over?"

The young girl gives a momentary start, as the apparition comes to her eye, and the voice to her ear, almost at the same instant. What is there in the voice, that seems unlike the usual frank, careless tone of the sailor — always with something breezy about it, as if unused to be uttered in confined spaces, and as if bearing some resemblance of broad oceans over which it has been echoed? It has a trembling earnestness now, or at least she fancies that it has; the mind is not quite at ease, from the action of which the voice emanates— of so much she is sure in a moment. And the blue eyes— why are they a shade less clear, bright and jolly? more as if a sudden earnest should have come into and shadowed them.

Almost incredible that she should see and hear so much in
that single instant—especially as there lies between the two
persons from so far away, nothing of that mysterious sympathy
informing lover and sweetheart, and giving reason as well as
convenience for the closest observation. But more than one
allusion has already been made to that keenest-eyed and most
fatally observing of all the animals of the East; and something of one of their characteristics comes into play, here, as
others may be shown at no distant period. At all events,
this she sees, hears, and marks, with so slight a shiver of
wonder and apprehension (the hunted as well as the huntress,
again), that it almost passes away before she answers his
salutation.

"Good morning. Perhaps you startled me a little, from
my seeing you so suddenly. May you step over? Certainly,
if you will be very, very careful. Something to say to me?
is it of consequence? Has anything happened?"

Mr. Tartar may not hear all the words, for the permission is
no sooner given than accepted; and with a great deal more of
exposure of himself than is at all necessary, in the way of
standing for a moment on tiptoe at the apex of the wall, with
some apparent impression that the point is a main truck open
to the view of a whole admiring fleet, he springs, swings, drops
and slides over to the side of Helena, wonderfully relieved of
any previous embarrassment by the normal manner of his
coming, and no doubt as much happier than he could have been
if forced to use the land-lubber abominations of door and
stairway, as he had been in the old days when permitted to
descend from the tops head-foremost by one of the stays, instead of clumsily coming down the ratlines.

"Ugh! I thought you were going to fall."

"I? No, thanks. There has been no danger whatever, or
I should not have tempted it in a lady's presence. Your
brother: he is within hearing?"

"No, he is reading in my room. If you wish to speak to
him, I can call him for a moment."

"Please do not, then. I asked if I might come over, and
you kindly said yes. Now I have something more to ask.
Would you mind fancying that you had seen enough of the
friend in me—or say of the good fellow, if the other expression
is too strong—to allow me to say a word in confidence, away
from your brother, and not for his ear ? "

"Neville and myself are twins, Mr. Tartar, as I believe tnat
you know ; and we have not been in the habit of having confidences apart from each other."

There is just a shade of fright in the tone of the young
girl, and her manner may convey a distrust of the sailor which
she certainly does not feel. What she does feel, for the instant, however, she would die before putting into words : she
has half a suspicion, for that instant, that she has been deceived
in certain previous impressions, and that the skilful climber is
about attempting to scale a precipice where he must certainly
fall—in other words, she is momentarily afraid that he is about
to spoil a valuable friendship by blending with it an impossible
element of *love!* This thought, not for long, fortunately ; for
the very next words of the other dispel it, to make room for a
widely different fear.

"Pray, do not think me capable, Miss Landless, of asking
you to hold back from your brother anything that could give
him pleasure ; but could you not, under some circumstances,
conceal from him, for a time, what could only give him pain,
without forwarding his interests ? "

"Could I not, Mr. Tartar ? I should be unworthy the name
of sister, if I could not. Pray pardon any seeming distrust,
which I assure you that I have not felt ; and if it is anything
affecting poor persecuted Neville——"

"You have hit upon what I mean, at once, Miss Landless,"
he interrupts. "It is of your brother's affairs, and yet of
things which I do not think prudent to mention to *him*, that I
wish to speak. Now, may I continue, with the hope that you
will not repeat to him what I say, unless permitted to do so
by Mr. Grewgious or myself ? "

"You wish me to make that promise before trusting me? Well, I trust *you*, Mr. Tartar, and I promise."

"Thanks for the confidence. Do not be alarmed, then, at what I am about to say. What seems threatening may only be, and I trust will be, the commencement of better things. Your brother is hunted, however, even more closely than any of us knew, and more wickedly and dangerously."

"Ah!" It is a cry, coming from the heart of Helena Landless—such a cry as the brave girl rarely utters; but such a cry as comes very naturally to the lips of even the most heroic, at the first moment of sudden fright or agony.

"Last night," the sailor proceeds, "both your brother and yourself left the house for half an hour or more, as you will remember."

"Yes, it was about ten o'clock, and I had persuaded Neville, who still shrinks, as you know, from venturing much abroad in the daylight, to accompany me on the briefest of walks through one or two of the side streets. Well—we were gone about half an hour. What could have happened within that time?"

"Much, Miss Landless, could have happened in half an hour. I once saw a noble ship cut literally to pieces within that space of time, and two thirds of her company left dead or dying. However, whatever occurred in this instance was not of that character, though possibly quite as *murderous*. But I must not waste words, as your brother may come to look for you, and make the conclusion of my story less easy.

"I happened to be coming through the quadrangle, though I suppose that neither of you saw me, as you left the door. By the way, did you lock that leading from your apartments into the hall?"

"No—for so short a stay, and with—what is it that they call her? oh, 'the scout,'—with the scout around, we did not consider it necessary."

"Let me advise you, then, Miss Landless, always hereafter to lock your door when you go out, so that if any crime is to be committed, burglary may be added as a neat thing to take hold of."

"Thanks, we will look after that in future. But pray tell me——"

"What was lost by leaving the door unlocked *this* time? Probably nothing: indeed, as I said before, much may have been gained. To continue what would be my 'yarn,' if I was telling it on a different deck. I went up to my room, after you went away, found the air a little hot and sultry there, and retreated to the garden, that part of it just beyond the wall. Then I seemed to have an idea, for which roving fellows, like myself, do not try to account quite so closely as the philosophers, that I should not find so much breeze anywhere else, as sitting astride the wall, and fancying that I had climbed on the bulwarks in a late watch in the horse-latitudes. I imagine, now, that I may have been *sent* there, who knows?

"At all events, I found some reason for being there, before I had occupied the bulwarks for many minutes. I sat where I could see the window of your brother's room, and I noticed that the light had been turned down when you went away.

"Suddenly I saw the light brighten; and if I committed a breach of propriety in looking *into* the window, that, too, may have been ordered by what we sailors sometimes call 'the sweet little cherub that sits up aloft, keeping watch for the life of poor Jack.'

"The light went up, as I have said; and I expected to see that your brother had given up his walk and returned. It was a very different face that I saw—that of *the man who is hunting your brother.*"

"Heavens! John Jasper! Are you sure that you were not mistaken, Mr. Tartar?" Helena cannot avoid exclaiming, in the first moment of surprise.

"No, I am not mistaken," answers the sailor. "It was that man; and when I knew so much, you may be sure that I watched more closely, and nearer. His face had a devilish expression of triumph (I am afraid that I saw *that* with my

face very near the window!) as if something long waited for
had come at last; and yet no less than twice during the five
minutes that I saw him there, that same face was crossed by
spasms of pain, one of which seemed as if it might kill him
on the spot."

"That was he—yes, that was John Jasper!" the young
girl rather murmurs to herself, than reassures the other.

"Of course it was he! We who float about around the
wide world are sometimes obliged to recognize a light or a
headland very quickly, and after not many views of it; so
that we recognize people once seen, with nearly the same
instinct. I have told you that I saw the pain on his face,
more than once. I did not know what produced the effect,
then : I know now."

Helena Landless, her brave heart nearly standing still with
a terrible interest, can only say so much in a word, and Mr.
Tartar goes on :—

"Here I am at fault, or rather I was at fault last night.
What he was doing I did not know, nor do I know at this
moment. I saw him stooping over the table, and fumbling with
things lying upon it—then pulling out one or two of the
drawers. What I *believed* that he was doing, at the instant,
I will tell you. Something against your brother's liberty, and
perhaps his life, in one or two directions. Looking for something of your brother's, that he could place where it would
seem to have been dropped during the commission of the murder; or arranging to place something apparently in the possession of your brother, that may once have been known to be
in that of the poor young fellow. But what ails you, pray,
Miss Landless? You have lost color—you seem faint. I am
sorry if I have pained you."

"No, it is nothing—pray proceed," answers Helena, with
a strong effort. She *is* pale and faint-looking; and something in the story has affected her. Ah, can it be? Was
that sudden fancy mutual, producing on the one side, months
ago, that boyish boast of how *he* would paint the sister of

Neville, on the part of Edwin Drood,—and on the other, so far, neither mark nor sign ?   Is this bright, fresh young girl, who has no excuse or privilege to wear mourning for the frank-hearted boy gone so suddenly and mysteriously to his death, really concealing, for his sake, the heart of a widow in her bosom ?   And have the words so suggestive of his " taking off," come too closely and roughly home to her consciousness, overcoming that womanly calmness ordinarily so marked, and leaving her weak as the most untried ?   Questions asked as are so many in this world of catechisms, without any expectation of their being immediately answered, and propounded as may be a larger proportion of the same class than we ordinarily admit, more for the sake of awakening thought on a certain subject than of shaping that thought into assured convictions.

But Mr. Tartar proceeds, as requested, though after a little longer pause than seems to be demanded by the circumstances of the case.

" I am glad to see that you are better, Miss Landless, though perhaps that does not assist *me*.   For I have a most painful confession to make, involving at least two crimes and possibly three or four.   Two that I am certain of: burglary, and assault and battery ; and larceny, as seems probable."

" Whatever can you mean, Mr. Tartar ? " enquires the young girl, for a moment doubtful whether the height of the aërial garden, or some other uncalculated influence, has not, after all, caused the narrator to " lose his head."

" Pray pardon my wild way of putting it," he rejoins. " What I mean is simply that at that moment I must have lost control of myself.   For I certainly sprang into the room, through the window, oblivious of all rights of property ; and I am afraid I assaulted the other intruder (though what right I had to do so, *you* must say) to the extent of knocking him down.   I think that I tried to arrest him, with the idea of giving him in charge as a burglar.   But the attempt was by no means an easy one ; and in the struggle, when we were

4

both on the floor, he managed to twist away from me and escape through the open door. I followed him down one flight, then returned to the room, to ascertain if any damage had been done to the furniture, and at first with a view to await your return. · But a second thought made me determined not to tell your brother at once, if you would consent to keep the affair temporarily from him; so I quitted the apartment, in the same way that I had entered it, only carrying away this, which I found on the floor, from its glitter, and which I feared might be overlooked if I did not take personal care of it. May I ask whether it belongs to you or your brother, or whether, as I half suspect, it may have dropped off the hand of our pleasant friend in my little struggle with him?"

Miss Landless receives, without any other emotion than must necessarily be associated with anything obtained in so romantic a manner, the object which the other hands her, and of which she knows nothing — as how should she, it never having been placed before her eyes, or mentioned in her hearing? It is a ring of blended diamonds and rubies, the conceit a rose, and the workmanship exquisite as the stones are pure and delicate. She takes it from the hand of Mr. Tartar, her eyes flashing a little with that admiration which the diamond seems to have the faculty of exciting in those human orbs of the softer sex, from which its flash is legendarily said to have been originally borrowed by the genii. She slips it upon one of her fingers, as many of those fair beings have a habit of doing with gems of price whenever a moment in their hands in that convenient form. Then she draws it off again, hands it back to Mr. Tartar, and says:—

"No; you must be correct in your surmise. It does not belong either to my brother or myself, and must have been dropped, I think, by the — by your antagonist. But it is sweetly pretty, is it not?"

She says nothing more on that point—knows nothing more. Bright as are the eyes of the young girl, trained in that far-east of the beast of prey and the deadly serpent, they have no power to follow the diamond and ruby flash of that ring for a single hour of its past history: how much less to read its future, which may be the whole future of two lives!

"Yes, it is very pretty: but what am I to do with it?" is the very natural suggestion of the man who has thus suddenly become possessed of property for which he has neither use nor title.

Helena Landless is thinking of something else now, and she says :—

"What a strange story you tell me, Mr. Tartar! and what a singular mystery it all is! My poor brother! Yes, thanks to your goodness and courage, I believe that we *do* see new danger to *him*, before it strikes; and you will help us—I know that you will—to save him from it, without even allowing him to know what is threatened."

Mr. Tartar's brown face is all aglow with the pleasant excitement of the compliment thus bestowed and the help thus sweetly requested; and his blue eyes have all their old expression of frank daring in the prospect of adventure, as he utters the first words of the promise demanded. But there is an interruption, and when the promise eventually comes, it comes in quite another shape.

Mr. Grewgious is standing in the open window—so Angular, in the clear morning air, that his face and figure seem to have assumed all the gables of the old houses thrusting themselves out on the narrow street behind doomed Holborn Bars. He has come up to see Neville Landless. He does not find him in his room. He observes Tartar and Helena standing and in conversation, in the aerial garden. And he calls as pleasantly to them as a much better rounded man could be expected to do.

"Strictly between ourselves, young people," he says, "the hour is slightly early for a flirtation, and still earlier for one that involves extensive promenades in covered walks. May I

hope that you are both well, and inquire whether Mr. Tartar
has come down from the mast-head or up from the cabin ? "

"Come from aloft, Mr. Grewgious," laughs the young man.
"May I pick a geranium for your button-hole ? or perhaps
Miss Landless will make it doubly valuable by doing so."

"A geranium ? Certainly, if you will be so good. Why
should not an Angular old fool enjoy all the privileges of his
position ?   And where is your brother, Miss Landless ? "

Helena obeys the hint by stooping to pick a flowering sprig
of the favorite named ; and Neville Landless, at last attracted
by hearing voices in his room, and the calling of his name in
that of Mr. Grewgious, comes out from the other apartment
and behind Mr. Grewgious at the window, at the moment
when Mr. Tartar, puzzled with his superfluous ring, and just
remembering that there is now some one else to consult in reference to its disposal, steps to the window, holds it up on the
end of his finger to the old lawyer, and says :—

"See what a treasure-trove—isn't that what you men of the
law call it ?—came into my hands last night. There is a
flower, now, worth wearing, on the hand if not in the button
hole."

He sees Mr. Grewgious start back, then dart suddenly forward, as his eye catches sight of the bauble ; he feels that the
Angular man, anything but angular now, grasps it away from
him with a cry which eventually shapes itself into twenty
startling words ; he hears Neville Landless, behind the lawyer,
echo that cry with variations of an equally surprising character ;
he becomes dimly aware that Helena, near the verge, is also
startled by the cry, and in danger of making one last plunge
from the roof—his quick eye and hand saving her ; and it is
only then that his sense takes in what his outward ear has
heard at once—those pregnant words of Mr. Grewgious :

"Good God ! Mr. Tartar ! have you any idea what it is that
you are handing me ? This is Edwin Drood's ring, which I
put into his possession not two days before—before he disappeared, and which was undoubtedly on him when that event

took place ! I have known it for nearly twenty years. Whence
did it come ? How did *you* come by it, young man ?   Quick—
no trifling—who can tell me anything of *this?"*

CHAPTER IV.

TARTARS OF TWO SEXES.

THERE is an impression current in the world—so current
that it has shaped itself into an axiom—that " when things
reach their worst, they must mend ; " for if, when it had
reached its culminating point of fury, a certain storm had not
abated, the world would undoubtedly have been blown to atoms,
and nothing would now be remaining, if anything whatever
did remain, except a few fragments of what was once the globe,
and its wonders of nature and art, floating about through
space, each particle blindly seeking to find and rejoin the
others, as the members of a separated family might do, de-
prived of all those senses which guide search or indicate proximity.   And if there had not been a point at which the edge
of the appetite for violence began to be dulled, when two or
more great nations were hottest in their work of devastating
and destroying each other—then, long before this time, the last
tendril of vegetable life would have accompanied the last man
to extinction, and the earth returned to be once more chaos.

The great difficulty in receiving this comforting assurance
of affairs growing better from the worst, lies in the impossibility of knowing when the worst has been reached, so that the
amelioration may be expected,—as also in the question, of some
little consequence, whether the sufferer may not perish under
the infliction, before the " coming " of the promised " good
time."   And it is just possible that Rosa and Miss Twinkleton may have considered that point with some apprehension,
suffering, the one in person, and the other vicariously, under

the wrath of the Billickin. The occupation of the premises
in Bloomsbury would end, necessarily, at no distant day,
through the necessity of Miss Twinkleton resuming her chaste
and most proper duties at the Nuns' House, at the close of the
vacation ; but until then ? For the fact cannot be disguised
(Mrs. Billickin's extreme candor being duly adopted), that a
state of affairs which had seemed to be at its worst within a
few days after the occupation of the lodgings, had continued
to increase in unpleasantness with a rapidity shaming the
boasted results of geometrical progression, until calling the
premises untenable would have been a very mild way of putting it, and only the mingled hope of early deliverance, and
desire not to pain the unconscious Mr. Grewgious by opening
his eyes to the existing status, induced an attempted continu-
ance on the part of the two ladies.

Not that the Billickin had contracted, during those succeeding weeks, any personal objection to dear little Rosebud, who
belonged to that peculiar class of little people, much more
popular with the grim and staid (from an unrecognized lacking
of those very qualities, making collision unlikely) than better
regulated persons of a more pronounced individuality ; but
that the hostilities existing between the two combatants continued to grow in fierceness if they declined in frequency ; and
that no so-called non-combatant can hope to escape all the
blows aimed at the fighting force which he or she accompanies
in an amicable relation.

Needless to say that of the two combatants Miss Twinkleton suffered most, as the less vulgar and consequently the
more sensitive. Also as, all other things being equal, the
aggressor will generally receive less damage than the party at-
tacked : the hammer will show fewer dints than the anvil
against which it is pitted in a succession of violent strokes.
Did the eggs, ordered soft-boiled, but intended to be cooked in
some mild sense of that word, come up, in the morning, so
guiltless of near approach to the fire that they might be believed to have just been laid, and only affected by the animal

warmth of the pullet ?   Then certainly the junior participant,
even if less declared than the other in her observations as to
the cuisine, might be held quite equally a sufferer.   Did the
chop, ordered well-done, emerge from the lower regions in such
a condition of blackness and cinder, that it might be supposed
to have been hung up in the chimney for at least the previous
week ? then might the same revulsion be expected in the
younger stomach, which moved the elder to digestive hysteria.
And so of the blacks in the pudding : the deal-board consis-
tence of the tart, from which the fruit seemed to have been
omitted *without* particular request ; the unsettled condition
of the occasional morning coffee (a weakness of Rosa's
indulged by Miss Twinkleton in lodgings, as it would not have
been at the Nuns' House), in which the pulverized berry
seemed always to be floating about in a state of unrest, and
violent self-assertion as to its genuineness ; and the tea, which
sometimes exhibited symptoms of feebleness, possibly consequent on its long and weary journey from China or Japan,
leading to a feeling of cruelty in taking advantage of and
swallowing it.   In all these, and an hundred other pleasant
details, for which there did not seem to be quite the proper
excuse—we may be sure that the little lady in that unseasona-
ble black, which sat upon her like a dark winter day shutting
down over a soft spring landscape, suffered quite her proportion of discomfort, without thereby affording any relief to her
elder sister in affliction.

   Whether any of the other lodgers at Billickin's, or all of
them, meanwhile, experienced corresponding sensations, it was
of course impossible for the Cloisterham twain to form an
idea.   It seemed highly improbable that any proportion of
them could have remained long under that roof of the integrity of which in rainy weather the Billickin candor expressed such doubts, without in some mode trampling upon
the weakness of that lady, and thus arousing a certain amount
of residuary antagonism ; and yet, as the changes were not
constant, it was impossible to say that the disturbance affect-

ing the two was other than local—that Mrs. Billickin was doing anything more than saving the young lady from serious consequences by keeping her at the proper alimentary moderation, while she returned to the lips of the elder that chalice from which she had herself drank so deeply, by reducing her blood to the understood boarding-school-pupil thinness and poorness.

But there were other and darker clouds in the horizon. Indefinable unkindnesses may for a long period take place, without ultra results, between the two unfriendly powers before brought into the comparison; but there comes a time when definable acts are done, and when accurately-worded complaints are the first consequence, with protocols and ultimatums following, and behind them—open war.

It was one of those hot and sweltering mornings on which P. J. T., had he experienced the like in seventeen hundred and forty-seven, would have wiped from his brow the Perspiration Juicily Trickling, and announced a Positively July Temperature, when Miss Twinkleton and Rosa, sitting at their after-breakfast sewing, and conversing over the feasibility of an afternoon stroll through the parks, became aware of the presence of the Perpetually Jostling Tartaress. She was not of those who " folded their tents, like the Arabs, and silently stole away;" on the contrary, her disappearances were apt to be more or less noisy; and it was in her entering a room that the occupants became aware of her belief that the door was Pushed Just To, and that every room of a lodging-house was Permitted Joint Territory, to be entered upon and enjoyed, at any moment, by those who Pleased Just Themselves.

The Billickin seemed pale and attenuated enough to have hurried in during one of the intervals of a succession of swoons which would be fatal at the next recurrence; and her indispensable shawl, thin in texture, as became the temperature, suggested, as it fell away from her shoulders, that it uncovered something which might otherwise have been concealed, and completed the living statue of Candor. She was

perhaps a shade more rigid than on former visits, owing to
the lingering of some portion of one of the late spasms ; but
the least observant mind could not doubt her capability of
stating, then, as at any moment, the whole of a demanded
proposition.

"Miss," she said, with the visible effort of so late suffering,
"business is business, and one doesn't always have the privilege of pickin' hout the time when it is to be done—leastwise
I don't, as I should probably pick both my time and my company if permitted."

Pausing to take breath, she left an opening for Rosa, who
said,—

"I beg pardon, I am sure : was it anything about dinner?
—and is it not a little early ? "

"No, Miss," returned the Billickin, for one moment sweeping around her eye and fixing it upon Miss Twinkleton with
the air of one who saw at a great distance some dim and
doubtful object of no special significance—then bringing it
back to her interlocutor. "No, Miss, it isn't dinner—it's
servants."

"Servants? has anything happened ? "

"That much, Miss, as things can't go on at this rate—no,
and you cannot make them, try however you will."

"Rosa, dear," said Miss Twinkleton, showing the little
consequence which she conceived the whole matter to hold, by
threading a needle with the utmost skill and nonchalance,
"the person of the house is what I should call ambiguous, if
I had reason to suppose her capable of understanding such a
word. Will you be kind enough to ask her, in any words
suited to her habits, what she may happen to mean ?—so that
this unannounced call may be made as short as possible."

This shot might have been a serious one, had it reached its
mark ; for Miss Twinkleton, for certain reasons which may
presently appear, was more than ever before disposed to make
an end of her tormentor, and made less than the usual pretence at masking her artillery. The Billickin was equal to

the occasion, however : she did not hear one of the offensive
words—at least it is to be presumed that she did not, as she
made no allusion to them in the remarks immediately following.

"No, Miss, it's not dinners," she said, severely, yet with
calm superiority to all trials of her equability; "it's not dinners, it's servants, Miss; you can't keep the respect of servants, Miss, and I defy you to try, if parties who are old
enough to know better, not to mention that they have been
all their lives in positions as ought to have taught them what
servants are and what they want, seeing that they've not been
that much above 'em—if such parties, whom we won't name,
Miss, because it would be a wasting of time and a trying of
tempers that has enough to bear—if such parties will break
all rules belonging to respectable 'ouses, which they may
know or may not, by talking to the servants of things that
they have no more to do with—no, Miss, I will not keep the
truth from you, not for one minute, though you kill me for
speaking it—no more than the child unborn."

Rosa, who found herself thus once more in the current
shuttlecock condition, and who had enjoyed quite enough of
it, though she had no idea of killing Mrs. Billickin as a relief
—Rosa looked up, a little in surprise, unable to fancy what
serious wrong had been done to the servants by her unfortunate preceptress; and while she was endeavoring to frame a
few words of reply, Miss Twinkleton, who was by no means
extinguished, though temporarily overpowered, cut in, so to
speak, and saved her the trouble.

"Rosa, my dear," said that dignified lady, "I shall really
be very much obliged if you will ask the person of the house
—I may say the remarkable person of this house, who seems to
be the victim of most objectionable manners, as well as that
very poor blood for which we give her full credit—to state
what she wants, and why she intrudes where her company is
not desired, in the most offensive manner."

This, spoken a little more loudly than her wont, and very

direct, was something that the Billickin did not find it quite
convenient to ignore. The pale face grew not a little flushed,
consequently, and there seemed some promise of another
spasm in the immediate presence of the ladies. Great is the
discipline of self-control, however, in minds possessing a certain combative power; and the lodging-house keeper of
Southampton-street, Bloomsbury, proved as yet quite equal to
the emergency.

"Yes, the servants is meddled with, Miss," she continued,
after only a moment to rally. "There has been remarks made
to 'em about water spilt at the tap, in front of one of your
doors, Miss, which some parties who have little enough if the
things they take from others comes to be picked out, thinks
that they own. Not that the water is not sometimes spilled,
Miss, along of its spirting, and the tap not bein' entirely
tight,—I will not deceive you on that point, Miss; but what
would you expect? Does those parties think as they have
taken the 'ole 'ouse, that no one else than themselves is to
have water? And whose is the servants, Miss, 'ired with
hexcellent characters, and paid good wages that regular that
there is never a word of complaint—no, they wouldn't dare to
make it!—who orders *them*, I ask, Miss? Not to mention,
on no account, Miss, that them as makes the complaint is
always a drawin' and a splashin' of the water, makin' the slop
themselves, raising the rates and using so much water that one
would think who did not know any better that they must be
uncommon dirty to need so much scrubbin' to make 'em
clean."

Miss Twinkleton's eyes flashed (she was again threading
her needle, and looking up at the light, her expression of
countenance could be easily discerned), but she answered
suavely, and with no apparent disturbance, in that tone so
well known at the Nuns' House:

"If you should ever have occasion, Rosa, dear, be good
enough to say to this extraordinary person, that you have
known some people who used so little water as to create the

suspicion that they never washed themselves at all, and that such people generally have a horror of the free use of water by others—a kind of hydrophobia, as I believe, though the fits sometimes have another name."

The eyes of the Billickin were lurid in her pale face at this juncture. Evidently she was one of those demanding to be fought with plain words, and quite as capable of taking a mortal hurt as giving one, the bolt being well directed. But she did not yet find another opportunity for a counter-thrust: for Miss Twinkleton, her blade freshly-blooded, and feeling the excitement more than ordinarily, made another lunge with very creditable effect.

"And while you are speaking with that person, Rosa, dear," she said, "it will be quite as well to intimate that the practice of coming into private rooms without knocking, is one never tolerated in respectable society; and that, if the practice should be continued, during the short time that we remain in this house, we shall suppose that our rooms are intended to be entered surreptitiously, in the hope of finding us absent, and for purposes which I need not name—so that we shall be under the necessity of keeping the doors always locked."

The eyes of the Billickin, lurid before, were aflame now. Still she fought to the last, not manfully, as naturally comes the temptation to say, but *womanfully.*

"Which I have always observed, Miss," she remarked, "that parties as was very averse to having rooms entered without knocking, was in the habit of carrying on practices that didn't bear looking into very closely. Not that I suspect any one whose name we will not mention, Miss, of having any gentleman coming to visit her. No, Miss, I will not disguise it from you that there is too much of age, and too little of that as is called good looks; and something else is to be suspected."

"You will say to the person of the house, Rosa, dear," Miss Twinkleton rejoined, calmly as ever, "that it is not the

mere fact of any one coming in without knocking, to which
we object, though that may be offensive enough ; but that in
her case, and that of her servants, we shall be obliged to
make the rule positive for *personal reasons.*   And then
you may add, Rosa, dear, a request that the person will leave
the room immediately, and not return to it in future, sending
any requests or enquiries by some one whose blood is not so
poor, and who is less offensive in manner."

This was the final blow—the death-wound.   Miss Billickin
felt the dismal fact, though she might momentarily conceal it,
as truly as ever knight of old felt the gliding in of the insidious steel between the joints of his armor, drinking his life-
blood, and making it only a question of the moments that
must elapse before he should topple headlong.   She drew the
shawl close around her shoulders, as if that might be some
protection from the verbal weapon of scorn that was lacerat-
ing her ; and the face was as pale as if there had been no
blood at all behind it, instead of that self-proclaimed so thin
and poor.

In point of fact, the discomfited fled the field at once,
thereafter, merely throwing out this Parthian shot as she
went,—a weak one, under all circumstances.

" I understand the 'int, Miss, and I shall take it for the last
time, havin' been enough insulted.   It is out of your power,
Miss, to make silk purses out of any number of sows'-ears,
and wherefore try ?   And you may tell Mr. Grewgious, Miss,
that the rooms is wanted immediately, when the time is up,
as, thank goodness, it is before long, and no renewal at any
price—not if you should offer me guineas for shillings ; and
your order for dinner, if you do not wish to go hungry, Miss,
you can bring to my room, where I can receive it decent."

Miss Twinkleton, victress without quite knowing why she
should be so, sat silent after the departure of the enemy—
more defeated than victorious, after all, because she could not
but remember what a pattern she had been setting for one of
the pupils of the Young Ladies' College, in that encounter
which had been more one of tempers than wits.

And Rosa? We have all heard of "bullets from rose-
buds;" and perhaps there may be something of the kind, in
some state of existence not yet fully understood.   But there
was no bullet in this dear little rosebud: there had never been
any missile more powerful or more dangerous, in her compo-
sition, than the little pellets of charming girlish pettishness
which she had fired off so readily, in those days already
grown so very, very old, at him whom she now tenderly
called "poor Eddy!"   And she was unquestionably a little
frightened at the repulse of Mrs. Billickin, slightly as she
had shared in the conflict preceding it.

"You heard what Mrs. Billickin said, dear Miss Twinkleton?" she asked, when the discomfited lady had departed, with
much more noise in closing the door than she habitually made
in opening one.   "She will not come here any more, I suppose;
and—we shall be obliged to remove."

"Are you sorry, Rosa?   Do you think that I could say
any less than I did say, in the face of such impertinence and
bad manners, including us both?   If so, I am sure that *I* am
sorry for anything of the kind having occurred.   But I cannot
apologize to this person, Rosa, dear, whatever may be the cost
of my refusal."

So Miss Twinkleton, with a momentary idea that she had in
some indefinable way seriously marred the fortunes of her companion by the severity of her speech.   To whom Rosebud,
transcending any ordinary relations of friendship between the
two, kind as they were (teacher and pupil understood), throwing her arm around the neck of the careful spinster, and kiss-
ing her:

"Apologize, dear Miss Twinkleton? 'consequences of your
refusal?'   What can you be thinking of?   Why, you only
did what you had a perfect right to do, and what she deserved
to have done, long ago.   Yet it was all very odd and very droll,
was it not?" and the wee thing laughed almost too merry a
peal for an accompaniment to the black dress, which seemed to
sadden without touching her to the depth of melancholy.   But

that peal blent with another, almost as silvery, in the ringing
of the bell; and that was followed, the moment after, by the
entrance of Helena Landless, the very quick disappearance,
thereafter, of Miss Twinkleton, and the two young girls, so
different in nearly every marked peculiarity, finding themselves
once more alone together, sitting on the sofa drawn to the window, and with arms about each other's waists.

Sitting as they had sat months before at the Nuns' House,
when Rosa seemed first undefinably to put herself under the
protection of her stronger and more experienced companion,
and when Helena seemed to make the same surrender to one
who should teach her something as yet unknown of the graces
of life and literature.   Sitting as they had done at that time,
and with nothing gone out from their tender regard for each
other, and yet with such a change lately wrought in each that
the half-instructed eyes of the other could not fail to see and
remark it.

What was that change, as it affected each ?   It would have
been very difficult for either to put in words what she saw, or,
more strictly speaking, what she *felt ;* and it may be equally
difficult here, to convey an impression sufficiently forcible and
not erroneous.

Helena's dusky cheek and tawny eye seemed brighter than
they had ever before appeared since the day of her first coming to Cloisterham.   They were not filled, informed, and softened, as often become those indexes of the human countenance
immediately on the awaking of a love which shall change the
whole order of being.   To tell the whole truth, they were less
amiable and possibly less lovely than in those earlier days ; and
it was almost certain that she would not have been as likely,
then as before, to awake the loving regards of some heart-whole
new-comer into her atmosphere.

There was more of power in the face—more of will, less (at
least temporarily) of that sweetly poised maidenhood to which
Mr. Crisparkle had bowed with such unmingled respect on
that windy evening, beside the river at Cloisterham—more of

what possibly might have existed in those still earlier days of
which Neville told, when wrong commanded hatred and the
wild will took refuge in the subtlety of escape. In a word,
she seemed (temporarily again) less to be loved and more to
be feared; the claw of the tiger was sensibly more protruded
from within the velvet sheath of the beautiful paw.

And Rosa, again? Nearly all that which had *not* occurred
to Helena, seemed to have fallen upon *her*. Gentle she had
always been, in her school-girlish and half-childish way; but
she seemed gentler, now, than ever; and the gentleness did
not appear to be entirely that of grief. There shone a softer
and warmer light in the eyes; the sweet lips, though they
retained their bewitching pout, curved into new lines of more
natural beauty; there was more of feeling and more of
womanhood in the whole face. Without quite being able to
explain where lay the difference, the close observer would have
said that she was three years older than she had been six
months before; and the chances are at least even that he
would have added the suggestion that she was much more
lovely in that sense which constitutes the inviting and involves
covetousness.

So much of what was in each, and a part of what each saw
in the other. It possibly remained for a few words of conversation to reveal to each the truth of what might have been
suspected, as well as to suggest other ideas by no means taken
into the calculation of either.

Rosebud had been laying her head on Helena's breast, for
the moment, and looking up into the eyes bent above her in
what seemed their old habit of protection; and then and in
that way it was that she saw what caused her to start up with
something like fear blended with her wonder.

"Why, dear," she said, holding off the other at arm's
length, as if to examine her to better advantage, "what is it
that ails you? What makes you in some way different from
what you were two days ago? Has anything happened to
you? Have you something to tell me?"

"Indeed, I have much to tell you, darling," answered Helena, after the pause of a moment. "Does my face show that something affects me? I am glad that you see it, for that makes my task the easier; and yet I am sorry, because it proves that I am not a very good actress, just at the moment when I need to be the best in the world."

"Something *has* happened, and it is not pleasant! Is it to you, or Neville, or—Mr. Tartar?"

Why did the eyes of the other scan the young girl so closely as she uttered the last word? And was there indeed, as Helena thought, a little momentary flush on the sweet face, and the least in the world of tremor in the voice, as she spoke it? At all events, the impression was acted upon before any reply was vouchsafed.

"To me or to Neville,—that is all very well, darling; but what has the name of Mr. Tartar—whom you began to know so very lately—to do with your anxieties, eh? Let us understand about *that!*"

If there had been the moment before any doubt about the color or the tone of voice, that doubt was immediately removed. The sweet pink cheek grew crimson, the fair young brow mantled with an answering flush, and the whole manner was that of the school-girl (as indeed she was, in the truest sense) detected in some peccadillo which must cause shame, while yet the very farthest removed from wrong.

"What do you mean, Helena dear?"

This was a subterfuge—at least a means of gaining leisure for thought, as nine times out of ten the same innocent question eventually proves to be. Helena Landless accepted it at its true worth. Her question had been answered, unexpectedly soon and well; and she held up her finger in playful warning, as she replied : —

"What do I mean, darling? Oh, you understand! Look at that tell-tale face. This sailor-man is becoming dangerous to my pet. He must be sent away to sea, on a very long voyage—say for five years or so."

5

"What *do* you mean, Helena dear?"

The same words used before, but with a change in the intonation, showing that an explanation, however unnecessary, was
positively desired.

"'What do I mean,' again? Why, simply that we have
found our heart—found it only to lose it to a mere stranger.
That is all."

"Oh, Helena dear!" Without another word, for that
moment, Rosebud flung herself into the arms of her friend,
hiding the blushing face on her bosom, and when she did
speak, uttering words which proved her to be the veriest child
who ever suddenly found the heart of a woman beating in her
own.

"Don't laugh at me very much, dear, if you can help it,
and don't scold me at all, please! Oh, it is so wrong—I know
that it is; and yet how can I help it? Only think of my
making such a little fool of myself, when *he* has not said a
word and I do not know whether he cares for me any more
than he does for a kitten!"

Helena Landless' handsome brown hand, with its long,
nervous fingers, went caressingly over the brow of her friend
as she uttered the best reassurance that could possibly have
fallen from human lips.

"Cares for you? yes, you baby-beauty! no fear but he
cares for you, quite enough. Every body cares for you, l
think, and well they may, such a dear little bird as you are.
Poor Neville! only think how happy I should be, if you but
loved *him* as you do this stranger."

"Poor Neville!—yes, and poor Eddy! see what a torment
I am, dear, to myself and everybody. But what ails *you*,
now? Have I said anything to pain or offend you?"

For Helena had sprung up, when the speech was little more
than begun, with a gesture like that of shaking away the arms
clinging to her. She had walked to the opposite window,
turning her back to Rosa; and there, as the latter followed
her, she found her with those long nervous fingers over her
face, weeping in what seemed a fit of uncontrollable emotion.

"Dear Helena, what have I said or done, to make you, who are so strong, cry like my own childish self? Tell me what my careless tongue has said—that is a dear."

"Nothing, Rosa, pet, nothing!" replied the other, making a violent effort to master her convulsion of feeling. "But I must tell you, or I think that my heart will break." She put her arm again around Rosa's waist, though they remained standing, and so went on, with broken words that told so much of the violence of that emotion producing such an effect upon her usually well-governed nature.

"See, I have forced away your secret, darling, and at the same moment cannot protect my own! *Don't* you understand what is eating out my heart? It is not anxiety for my brother, though that is keen enough to make me sometimes almost forget my sex: it is something so much sadder and worse. Don't be frightened at me, or think that I have been mean or treacherous, for indeed—indeed, I have not; and I would not tell you the truth, now, if they trampled me to death with elephants for refusing — only that now it is too late for the confession to do any harm."

She paused for an instant, and Rosebud looked up in her face with an unshapen pity blending with her alarm and wonder. But she said nothing—only drew closer her arm in sympathy around the slight waist it spanned, as Helena went on,—

"*Don't* you know yet what is coming, darling? How can I tell you?—and yet I wish to do so, and *must!* My heart is buried somewhere, though I do not know where; and yet it lives and aches. *I loved Edwin Drood.*"

"Oh, Helena—dear Helena!"

"Yes—you must not think that I have willingly done you wrong. Had he lived, and had there been no break between you, this would have gone with me to my grave. But I loved him, I think, from the first moment that I saw him: I could no more help doing so than I could avoid breathing."

"Poor Eddy! Yes, and he loved *you:* I have no doubt of

it, now! He could not love *me*, as I could not love *him*, with
an affection beyond that of brother and sister; we were too
much like two children together, I suppose, with no experience
in either to guide the other. But *you*—I have no doubt now
that he loved *you*, and that was why he gave me up so easily,
when—when I asked him to do so."

"Do you think so, darling? Oh, if I could only believe
that—only know that, I think I should be happy, even knowing that I had lost my dear boy from this world for ever."

Her hands were clasped at the moment; and in her dusky
eyes there shone that expression of hungry and unsatisfied
affection, only less difficult to look upon than to ray out from
a heart experience. Then she commanded herself, by a powerful effort, as one who felt that she had been temporarily
indulging a weakness unworthy or out of time; and she
seemed scarcely the same person, but a few moments after,
when, still standing at the window, and her face almost terribly earnest and determined, she herself changed the subject
with nervous suddenness, and related what had occurred at
Staple Inn on the previous night and that very morning.

Rosa listened, with an interest rapidly culminating in a
still-lingering fright at the knowledge that John Jasper was
continually coming so near her and with so deadly a purpose.
Was it possible that she could be quite safe from him even
now, with all the protection afforded by Mr. Grewgious and
(her heart whispered this, as if a little ashamed and doubtful
of the propriety of such an element in the calculation) Mr.
Tartar?

But the face of Helena Landless had grown calmly stern
and self-reliant, now; and there seemed, as Rosa gazed into
it, protection in that, if in nothing else. And though her
words of promise were few, bearing upon some hurried
expression of the young girl's fears for herself and for Neville,
those words should have been quite sufficient for more than
one who knew her blood, and the reason she might be likely
to recognize for fighting, life for life, against the suspected

murder of the man she had loved, the persecutor of the friend
she valued so dearly, and the unscrupulous pursuer of the
brother who formed her other self!

" No, darling—do not fear that man, terrible as he is !"
she said. " He has never seen an East-Indian jungle, I
think: I have, young as I am. And he may learn, by-and-
bye, that the hunter is not always safer than the game he
thinks his own, when once he ventures into that wilderness
which has no path and no end."

CHAPTER V.

JOHN JASPER'S UNEXPECTED PLEASURE.

MR. SAPSEA leaves his Mansion House on the High Street
in company with the complaisant Mr. Datchery — on that
errand which is to confer so much revengeful pleasure on Mr.
Jasper—in one of those complacent and wholly self-satisfied
moods which may bear the same relation to the ordinary mental frames of humanity, that is borne by a day of unclouded
spring sunshine, with Nature at her best in every detail of
light, verdure, flowers, and bird-music, to the average day in
which cold fogs, bleak winds, and dismal happenings combine
to prevent any mistake as to the terrestial character of our
footstool.

Complacent Mr. Sapsea is always, and under all circumstances. He wooed Miss Brobity complacently, complacently received that awe-struck up-looking which eventually produced
so serious an effect on the liver, buried her complacently, and
complacently so epitaphed her that it seems doubtful whether
any pain in the marital loss is not quite compensated by the
pleasure of the monumental opportunity. He has been complacent in all his valuations and knockings-down ; he is the
most complacent of mayors, because no man so little feels the

cares and obligations of office as the thorough donkey who can understand nothing whatever of them; and if there is a special point of his pompous and shallow existence, in which the sense of complacent self-satisfaction reaches its acme, that point is to be found at the moment when he is duly soothed by such senseless subserviency (to call it by no worse name) as that of Mr. Datchery, and when he is permitted, so to speak, to diffuse himself over the whole sphere of his honors and duties, in a gush of pompous patronage.

Mr. Sapsea is not only gushing with patronage in this particular instance, but he is literally overflowing the civic community with that benefit. He is about, unasked, to confer the most important of benefits upon Mr. John Jasper—his friend, Mr. John Jasper—entitling him to the life-long gratitude (to be duly shown in added subserviency) of that person; he is conferring an obligation upon Mr. Datchery, with the natural result of keeping *that* person at his present humble and appreciative status, and possibly bringing him a shade lower in comparison with himself; he is exercising the highest functions of the chief magistrate of Cloisterham, in outdoing all predecessors in the extent and graciousness of his condescension; and he is adding another to the multitudinous influences which shall ensure him a proud niche in the local temple of fame, by arranging for the effective employment of that link in the chain of evidence against the suspected murderer, which—that is how *he* puts it, and will some day put it on the bench—which he has discovered by patient research and constant exercise of Mind.

To say that Mr. Sapsea, thus at peace with himself and the world, assumes the outward demeanor proper to such inner beatification, would be to do that eminent person gross injustice. He "assumes" nothing; from the inner consciousness, always candid, radiates that which makes him the most noteworthy of men. Were not matter lamentably dull and stupid, with no capacity to adapt itself to changes of circumstance, then possibly we might see an additional fraction of

roll in the brim of the hat, and there might be a nearer
approach to perfection in the proud sweep with which the
trouser, tapering away from the graceful protrusion of the
abdomen, finishes the Hogarthian line of beauty at the shoe.
As things go, so much cannot be expected, and there will
always be some slight outer imperfection in the belongings of
the great, unwarranted by the completeness inwardly attained.

The Mayor is half a yard in advance, as they emerge from
the door of his house, and take their way towards their near
destination. Whether he, of himself, assumes that slight
precedence, just enough to indicate position, and yet too little
to be offensive to the humble companion, or whether that humble companion, Datchery to wit, falls back the trifle necessary
to throw the other into that prominence, as the only available
expression of that unbounded respect which would keep the
head uncovered, if the spectacle might not create too much
remark in the street of Cloisterham—this important question
cannot be easily settled : only the fact can be given. Dignity,
combined with Intellect, has its place ; Idle Inconsequence
walks half a step behind ; what more could be desired ?

They have measured, perhaps, a hundred yards from their
point of departure, and are not far from the Lumps-of-delight
shop, on the left as they walk, once momentarily holding so
prominent a place in the history of Rosa and Edwin—when
Mr. Datchery is thrown still more to the rear, by encountering
a person coming out from the near tobacco-shop, a cigar between his lips, and the amount of smoke thrown out from that
fragrant and most filthy combustible quite enough to prevent
any immediate view of his features. Mr. Datchery would
seem to recognize him in spite of the enshrouding veil ; for
the Mayor—not a little chafed at seeing any person walking
with himself hindered by any other person or persons unknown—observes, as he half turns his head, that they accost
each other, and that (this is a salve to the wounded dignity)
Mr. Datchery does not seem over well pleased with the encounter.

He hears the man with the cigar say, ignorant of the impossibility, under the circumstances :—

" Ha, Dick ! have a weed ? "

And he hears the other answer :—

" Why, Philpits, is it possible that you are *here?* No, no cigar for me : I am going to an appointment with His Honor the Mayor."

Then he, making a temporary pause, and in point of fact waving the rights of position, waiting for Mr. Datchery in recognition of the propriety of the latter's demeanor, loses the next words that pass between the two, and only knows that they are coming towards him.

This man, addressed as Philpits, is slight, and not too well dressed—his hat, particularly, being of that class designated, not euphoniously, the billicock—and his clothes, with an air about them that may be salty, and may be that of constant use, carrying another air less ambiguous—that of having been made for a larger man, or stretched in wearing if the owner has not shrunken. His complexion is dark, almost very dark, though this detail is somewhat confused by the slouching brim of the billicock ; and his age must be set down as uncertain, there being somewhat too much of dark beard, well matching the dark-brown hair, for that number of years conveyed by the complexion. He shows, as he moves, a bit of roll that (again) may be of the sea, salty, and that may be merely a slight species of swagger.

Other men than Mayor Sapsea, looking at this person, might set him down as an anomaly ; and a man from Scotland Yard, suddenly meeting him, might be tempted to look after him at greater length than the turning of the next corner. The Mayor merely sees one of whom he makes the mental note :—

" Disreputable—that is how *I* put it—disreputable, and no advantage to that well-behaved person, Mr. Datchery, to be known by him.

But by the time this observation is made, the two have measured the few feet intervening, and they approach the

Mayor, who is not flattered by what seems to be a pending
introduction.

That introduction follows, but in so unobjectionable a shape
that the great man is partially disarmed.

" Will the Worshipful the Mayor," says Mr. Datchery, adding to the intermediary bow accompanying by taking off his
hat, and the other catching the spirit of the presence and
doing the same—" will the Worshipful the Mayor pardon this
momentary hindrance, which I beg him to believe was quite
unexpected, and allow me to introduce an old college-mate,
Mr. Robert Philpits ? Mr. Philpits, Mr. Mayor Sapsea, of
Cloisterham."

" Honored," says Mr. Philpits, notably saying nothing
more, as possibly from confusion, but bowing with an
empressement which throws his face almost entirely out of
view of the Mayor, and which shows, by the profundity of the
action, that he fully recognizes the privilege conferred upon
him.

" As Mr. Datchery's friend," remarks the Mayor, with an
air of adding that only as Mr. Datchery's friend this person
can be tolerated at all by the official, and with a patronizing
wave of the hand which puts any thought of shaking that
member out of the question—" as Mr. Datchery's friend, I am
glad to know Mr.—Mr.——"

" Mr. Philpits " suggests the introducer.

" Ah, Mr. Philpits."

" Old chum, as I have just had the honor of informing the
Worshipful the Mayor," Mr. Datchery goes on to explain, the
two hats being by this time recovered, in a military sense.
" We have not met in a long time, as His Honor should also
be made aware."

Mr. Sapsea, glancing again at the sartorial adornments of
Mr. Philpits, has no difficulty in understanding why this apology is made, as illustrating the self-evident fact, that had Mr.
Datchery been in the habit of meeting Mr. Philpits frequently,
he [Mr. Datchery] would have instructed him [Mr. Philpits]

to array himself in more becoming costume before present-
ing himself in his [Mr. Sapsea's] irreproachably-costumed
presence.

"My chum, his Honor the Mayor should also be advised,"
Mr. Datchery goes on, "has been for a long time so far away
as the Danube, doing a little of engineering, something in
which an idle and unemployed buffer like myself almost envies
him, though the employment really has not improved his personal appearance.   Eh, Philpits, my boy ? "

"Precisely," answers the stranger, with no more waste of
words than he has before displayed.

"Humph ! my Time, Mr. Datchery !" somewhat severely
comments Mayor Sapsea, at this juncture.   "Procrastination,
sir, is the thief of time—that is how *I* am in the habit of
stating the fact; and we are loitering, if I am not very much
mistaken."

"A thousand pardons !" replies Mr. Datchery, much affected by the mild reproof as well as by the felicitous original illustration.   "His Honor the Mayor will be kind enough not to
suppose the hindrance intentional, and therefore disrepectful—
only an accident, which Mr. Philpits, at any risk to his own
self-love, must permit me to call a misfortune.   I accompany
the Worshipful the Mayor at once, and with real regret for the
delay."

Then moving on a step or two :—

"By the way, Philpits, old fellow, what will you do with
yourself during the little time necessary to fulfil my appointment with His Honor?   You have never been in Cloisterham
before, I think ? "

"Never."   Thus sententiously again the new comer, who is
moving on with the others, permittedly, but rather aimlessly,
and altogether uselessly in the matter of convoy, as a mean
little tug may sometimes be seen keeping company with a
magnificent departing steamer for a certain distance down
harbor.

"Never, no, of course not; only a forgetful buffer like my-

self would make the blunder of asking. Then, of course, you
know nothing of the town—a most respectable old place, and
quite an odd one, as you will see when you take a glance at it.
You can know nothing whatever without *me*, and may be lost."

"Likely," says the sententious Philpits.

"Humph!" comments the Mayor, without further explanation, but possibly meaning to imply, in his concise way,
that the world—that is how *he* would put it—the world would
have little difficulty in surviving the loss of so insignificant
and ill-clothed a person as the man Philpits.

"Now that I think of it, perhaps you had better keep with
us, if His Honor the Mayor will allow me the liberty of
extending the invitation. Only a few minutes at the rooms
of a friend here, and then I shall be at your service. May I
hope that the Worshipful the Mayor approves the suggestion,
thus giving my friend the additional privilege of being introduced, if opportunity should allow, to a man who has been
characterized by His Honor, with his usual felicitous use of
words, as energetic, and therefore a Man of Mark?"

It is doubtful whether Mayor Sapsea would consent to the
company of this unknown, ill-dressed, and supposedly disreputable person, for any longer time than necessary to traverse
the little remaining distance to the Gate House, but for the
employment of this last skilfully devised bit of extra fumiga-
tion. But, *with* that new inhalation of pleasant incense, he
yields once more to the insidious machinations of the unscrupulous Datchery, waves that fat official hand with a dignity as
impossible to convey in words as it would have been to trans-
mit to a second generation through the medium of Mrs.
Brobity-Sapsea, and says :—

"The request is a somewhat unusual one, Mr. Datchery ;
still, as I do not suppose that my friend, Mr. Jasper, could
have any unwillingness to form the acquaintance of this—
this person whom you know, there will be no objection to his
accompanying."

"Thanks for the courtesy of His Honor the Mayor—which

is, however, nothing more than his habit led me to expect,"
says Mr. Datchery, again bowing his acknowledgments, with
a side glance at Philpits, which adds : " Why do you not
humiliate yourself to the dust, miserable mortal, in view of
such condescension ? "

" Thanks — many to this and the other ! " responds the
obliged Philpits, of whom, from his extreme reticence of
words, the impression might be not unnaturally formed that
he has been for a long time in such a branch of employment,
connected with his engineering, as to induce serious daily
expenditure of voice, thus coming home with very little
remaining in his chest, and being obliged to economise, as
another man might do with a small remaining amount of
money, after long reckless expenditure of capital.

So it is that they go on to the Gate House, meeting no
adventure of additional consequence by the way ; though Mr.
Datchery once catches a glimpse of Durdles emerging from a
low door-way, and there passes between them a quick motion
of understanding that might be suspicious, if some other eye
could observe and comment upon it—as that other eye does
not. And so it is that they go up the postern stair at the
Gate House, Mr. Sapsea, again becomingly in advance, as
chief of the Embassy ; Mr. Datchery next, a subordinate,
but possessing a certain importance ; and Mr. Philpits bringing up the rear—slouching a little in his gait, and with his
billicock accidentally falling so low over his eyes as to make
observation of those features impossible—no doubt in the due
abasement of a position rather permitted than acknowledged.

They pause at the door of Mr. Jasper's room, at the head
of the stairway, however, simultaneously with a motion of
Mr. Sapsea's authoritative hand, which says, quite as plainly
as words could convey the same injunction :

" Pause. Listen. Piano and voice. An exquisitely beautiful combination and harmony of sounds—that is how *I* put
it—exquisitely beautiful combination and harmony. I know,
without seeing him, thanks to the exercise of Mind, that Mr.

Jasper is playing and singing. More than that—that he is
playing and singing a fine old religious song. Italian or German — that is what *I* say — Italian or German; Bologna,
Naples, Weimar, Prague. Pause and listen."

They pause and listen, perhaps not altogether from the
motion of Mr. Sapsea: possibly because other ears than his
(however shorter, and so at disadvantage) can catch the subtle
harmonic blendings of the grand old Gregorian chant with
which the choir-master is filling a leisure hour, and educating
his aspirations after the Infinite and the All-Glorious. They
hear and appreciate the delicate manipulations of the keys of
the instrument, by a hand evidently the worthy master of the
rich brown ivory keys it touches at once caressingly and com-
pellingly—evoking, in succession, light and fairy tinkles of
sound, that might be the musical pattering of rain in a foun-
tain, in the midst of a delicious summer-shower; bursts of
rich harmony that fill the very sense of satisfaction with their
fulness and perfection ; and deep-rolling thunders that seem to
have the faculty of becoming waves of hoarse melody, and
sweeping away the soul to some imagined empyrean where
they have at once origin and end. This with the instrument;
and combined with this a rich manly voice, forming the cross
between tenor and baritone, and perfect in every musical
phrase and modulation, while bounding with a sense of exult-
ant power which seems to make it something more than a
voice and elevate it to the height of a faculty.

They stand, as they may well do, spell-bound. When the
good man sings hymns of praise, he is exercising a very high
privilege ; when he sings and plays them divinely, he is doing
something which distantly (though not always pleasantly)
suggests the employment of celestial beings through all ages.
And even lowlier men than Mr. Sapsea may hold a weakness
for considering themselves likely, at some unguessed period
in those ages, to become celestial beings, more or less fully developed in the details of robe and pinion.

They do not interrupt the effective player and singer, for

many minutes, during which the only perceptible motion among the three is one of a certain patronizing impatience on the part of the Mayor—the employer and owner of that invaluable Time of which he makes no infrequent mention as filled to repletion with important deeds and events. Then there is a pause, which does not come, as such pauses may be usually expected to come, at the close of a movement and with sounding and measured chords, but arrives with couriers in the shape of trembling in the voice, uncertain touches upon the keys, and all the symptoms of suddenly-diminished physical capacity. Then the last broken and unsteady note is struck, the voice already fallen silent; and the three as they stand unnoticed at the open door, see the musician rather stagger than rise from his seat, and confront them as he turns to leave the recess.

They mark—some of them, perhaps all—that the face is contorted as that of one might be under an agony not yet unendurable ; and they see that the eyes have something glassy and unnatural about them, as might be those of a child suddenly awakened from sleep, at an unusually early hour—or as might be those of a man of full age, who had really been wandering away in mind, into those far-off regions suggested by the dead music, and who found some difficulty in making instant return to the lower world.

But this expression changes—compelled back, as it might be, by the exercise of a strong will, as he recognizes the presence of visitors. And there is a certain amount of graceful dignity in his reception of them, when the eyes kindle to natural life and at last take them in. He has a word of respectful welcome to the Mayor, as to one who honors his room by coming into it; one of corresponding character to Mr. Datchery, though less respectful, as to one who is only an equal; and a distant recognition — quite warm enough under all the circumstances, for the entirely supernumerary and slightly *de trop* Mr. Philpits, whose presence is at once explained and apologized for in the brief word of introduction, and who proves that he has no intention whatever of being in the way, by subsiding into the corner of the room, merely saying, " Delighted Mr. Clasper, mum — mum — mum—" in such a tone of mumble that his previous paucity of voice seems to have culminated in one last expiring breath, and who retires into the most absolute and ineffective no-thingness by engaging in close distant study of the backs of a row of opposite music-books, which he cannot understand, and a ridiculous daub of a picture of a young girl, side-long to his view, over the mantel, of which he can know even less than of the sealed books.

Mr. Sapsea, Plenipotentiary in the very mixed Embassy of which Datchery may be rated as Secretary, and Philpits as the most useless of *attachés*—Mr. Sapsea has no idea of wasting any more of that valuable Time to which time-wasting ref-erence has already been so often made by himself and others, and interrupts Mr. Datchery's attempted compliment to Mr. Jasper upon his looking well (for which there is the worst possible ground), by entering at once upon the Important Business.

" Mr. Jasper," he says, with his best wave of the fat mag-isterial hand, and with his shoulders thrown back to the full capacity allowed by the straight, high-backed, uncomfortable chair of the time of the royal heroine of Tilbury Fort—" Mr. Jasper, my call of this morning—I may say *our* call of this morning, as Mr. Datchery is more or less concerned in it— may be considered one of business ; but if I am not mis-taken, sir, it will be found, as I say—that is how *I* put it, and the expression may or may not be capable of improvement— it will be found to combine business and pleasure."

" Ah," remarks Mr. Jasper, who learns nothing whatever from the rigmarole, and who may be accordingly excused for replying thus briefly and non-committally. But Mr. Datch-ery, who has not enjoyed any opportunity for venting his boundless subserviency for at least five minutes, interjects, to the relief of Mr. Jasper and the delight of the Mayor,—

"Ah, yes, His Honor the Mayor certainly uses a most felicitous expression : 'combining business with pleasure'— what could be better ? A thousand pardons, for the interruption."

Mr. Philpits is craning forward his neck, in the stupid effort to read the unreadable title to the back of a music-book, by reducing the distance to six inches less than it would be if he sat upright in his chair.

"Mr. Datchery," continues the Mayor, "was not a resident of My Mayoralty at the time of certain occurrences, of which we are only too well aware—that is how I put it, Mr. Jasper— only too well aware. I allude, of course, to the circumstances connected with the lamented disappearance, and almost certain murder, of your nephew."

For the instant, a spasm passes across the face of the choir-master, even more declared than that which was suppressed and strangled as he rose from the piano.

For that instant, too, his hands grip the sides of his chair with a tenacity threatening to the integrity of that article of furniture. But these demonstrations are wondrously brief, and they must be unnoticed, for who has motive to observe them ?

Mr. Sapsea is absorbed in the importance of his Embassy and the contemplation of the influence of Mind on Mediocrity ; Mr. Datchery is gratifying his pet subserviency by staring at the Mayor, under his white hair and dark eyebrows, with a fond intensity suggestive of early worship, in the event of the laws of Britain being so remodelled as to allow that exercise ; and Mr. Philpits, having made the discovery, through the six inches gained by craning, that the mysterious appearance of the words on the back of the music-book is caused by the book having been accidentally placed upside down in the stand, is endeavoring to ascertain, at some peril to the already elongated neck, how it would read in the event of his being able (and permitted) to stand on his head.

"The Worshipful the Mayor is quite correct, as usual,"

says Mr. Datchery, immediately following Mr. Sapsea's introduction. "My only acquaintance with what I may be permitted to call the unfortunate and melancholy case, was
derived from information kindly furnished by His Honor, in
this very room, on my first coming to Cloisterham, as Mr.
Jasper may remember."

"I do remember, Mr. Datchery," answers Mr. Jasper,
speaking for the first time on the theme; "though pardon
me if I fail to see the importance of your knowledge. And
as for the remark just made by you, Mayor Sapsea—allow me
to inquire why you use the expression 'almost certainly murdered?' To *me* he is *certainly* murdered: what reason have
you, allow me to ask, for qualifying the suspicion? Has anything been discovered, and am I to connect your visit at this
time with the fact, throwing doubt upon the crime?"

"Nothing whatever, Mr. Jasper; on the contrary——"

"Ah!" This expression comes a second time from Mr.
Jasper, but much more pronouncedly and much more mean-
ingly than before. It betokens satisfaction now: presumptively the satisfaction of a man who discovers that his pet
theory is not to be assaulted; and that satisfaction is so great
that he does what Mr. Datchery could not be induced to do
under any provocation—interrupts His Honor the Mayor.

"No, Mr. Jasper," the official resumes; "on the contrary,
there have been certain discoveries made giving renewed force
and color—that is how *I* put it—renewed force and color to
your opinion, and leading to the hope that, as I say, the murderer may be unearthed, and brought to justice."

Mayor Sapsea has come to the Gate House with the errand
(if an Embassy can perform so low a thing as an errand) of
giving his friend Mr. Jasper a great pleasure. At this moment
it seems that his purpose will be fully accomplished; for it *is*
pleasure that glows darkly on the choir-master's face at the
announcement of "certain discoveries." Has that transitory
flush of pleasure anything to do with the action of a late night
at Staple Inn?—with the action witnessed by Tartar through

6

a high window ?—with a " treasure-trove " picked up by that
forcible person on the floor of Neville Landless's room ? Was
there something *to be* discovered and EXPECTED TO BE *discovered ?*

The pleasant flush dies out, and who shall know of its momentary existence ? For (the others as before) Mr. Philpits
has unobtrusively gone over to the music-stand, taken out the
misused book, opened it, and is attentively scanning the bars
of one of Mendelssohn's most intricate compositions, with that
air of stupid delight and half-intelligence which a Fejee
Islander might be expected to display in examining the involved figures of a work on geometry.

" Mayor Sapsea," says Mr. Jasper at this juncture, " I am
glad to hear you say that you have *not* changed your opinion ;
for be sure that I have not changed *mine.* On the contrary,
so additionally impressed have I been, within the last twenty-
four hours, not only with the fact of my dear boy's murder,
but the certainty of the near detection of his murderer, that
I have resumed a habit for awhile laid down, at the suggestion
of Mr. Crisparkle, as mentally unhealthy, and written out my
impressions—briefly this time, and not in the leaves of the
diary that I now regret. Permit me, before you proceed, to
read you those few words which have as yet gone no further
than my pocket."

Permitted by the wave of the magisterial hand, and the evident interest of Mr. Datchery, he draws from his vest pocket
a folded paper, opens it, and reads :—

" I am now so firmly impressed with the fact that the time
" for the final arrest and punishment of my dear boy's murderer
" has nearly or quite come, that I cannot resist going back to
" an old habit, which I am sorry that I relinquished, and set-
" ting down my impressions for my own satisfaction, if not for
" future reference. How this detection is to come—whether
" from the finding of some recognizable portion of the body,
" once and always so dear to me, in the waters of that river,
" where he was so certainly and ruthlessly thrown by the man

" whom he trusted—or whether the murderer himself, becom-
" ing careless in his security, is to work out his· destruction by
" imprudent words, or the bringing to public knowledge of
" some article hitherto concealed—this I cannot pretend to
" fathom in advance. But of the fact I am sure. The quest
" to which I devoted my life seven months ago is not to con-
" tinue for any long period now. The end is near. I feel this
" and know it, with a certainty defying reason as it defies con-
" tradiction.· My dear boy is to be avenged, and then my life-
" work will be done."

Mr. Datchery listens to the reading with that interest which
a single buffer of uncertain habits may be expected to exhibit
in the presence of any event or communication unexpectedly
sensational ; Mayor Sapsea listens with that complacency natural to one who hears his own opinions echoed, and his own
labors—that is how *he* puts it—his own labors in some great
cause humbly assisted ; and there is every reason to suppose
that the nonentity, Philpits, does not hear it at all, that
objectionable person having returned to his chair, with the
music-book, and being at the moment engaged in beating time
with his hand, and bobbing his head over it, as if it conveyed
a certain dumb suggestion of some audible music once heard
by his untutored ears, possibly half-barbarian and ear-splitting,
during his engineering on the Danube.

" And now that you have, in this paper, Mr. Jasper, quite
echoed the opinions — echoed is what *I* say — the opinions
already formed by myself, from the researches which the invisible hand of justice—that is how *I* put it, the invisible hand
of justice, as well as the long and the strong hand—has been
steadily making from the night when the crime was committed," says Mayor Sapsea, elevating his head still more,
and throwing back his shoulders additionally, in extracting
from his pocket an object thus far deposited there — " now,
Mr. Jasper, you will be gratified, I know, by my exhibiting
to you an—an article, discovered by—by one of the persons
engaged with myself in the investigation of the details of

this crime, only yesterday, and so near to—to My Mayoralty, that the late presence of the murderer cannot be doubted."

His hand has by this time extricated the wallet from his pocket, but the hand is by no means small, and the object is quite concealed in it, until the other hand has thrown back the flap, and the first hand holds wallet and name full before the eyes of John Jasper at the same instant.

Then follows what Mayor Sapsea, who has come to confer a delight upon his friend Jasper, could scarcely have expected at the moment of leaving his Mansion House; what Mr. Datchery, though a buffer of very easy antecedents, must be equally pained and surprised to see, the benevolence of his intentions in coming to Mr. Jasper being likewise kept in view; what Mr. Philpits cannot be supposed to see, much less to understand, he being at the moment engaged in intently surveying the picture of Pussy, from a sidelong point of view, through a tube formed of a loose roll of music, under some apparent impression that the obliquities of character may be thus looked into, as they cannot under the deception of the full face.

What is it that the two see, the third thus ignored?

They see John Jasper stiffen from his chair, into an erect position—not rise, or spring, but stiffen, as if the truth of the old fable of the Gorgon's head had outlived the belief in it, and the commencement of a transformation to stone may yet be seen by the curious, at intervals and under favorable circumstances. They see one hand go up to his head, as if the hidden pain came there at first; they see the eyes sink away into the sockets, with such suddenness that they seem extinguished, until a look of fixed horror, raying out from them, belies the fear; they see the face contort again into shapes of agony before undreamed of, and thick drops start on the forehead, dampening the hair that falls over it; they see the hand, momentarily uplifted to the head, fall away from that to the throat, and seem to clutch at the neck-cloth; they hear a gurgling attempt at utterance, with no words reaching the outer air; and then they see the stone change to boneless and nerveless flesh with the same suddenness as that of its first transformation, and the figure collapse back into its chair, its whole upper length not more than two feet from the seat, and the suspicion, a strong one, that a dead man has flopped down there, with the stony eyes wide open.

To say that Mayor Sapsea is surprised at the reception of his benefaction by his friend, Mr. Jasper, would be sheer waste of words. He rises, but stands in such an attitude of helpless horror and bewilderment, that some of the stories traditionally told about the great always exhibiting extraordinary presence of mind, may well come under fresh examination in the light of this circumstance.

Mr. Datchery mutters something about " great joy affecting persons nearly as much as great sorrow, and that the Worshipful the Mayor, no doubt, sees Mr. Jasper thus affected, under the influence of this memorial of his dear boy, and this new hope of avenging him ; " but how much of this the Mayor hears or understands must remain problematical. For the very moment after the catastrophe, the disreputable-looking Philpits, who should never have been in the place at all, discovers the fact, drops his music-roll telescope, and literally rushes from the room and down the stairs, without farewell, and in such undignified haste, that he may well be suspected of rank cowardice in the presence of death and suffering; and the next moment Mr. Datchery, unable to recall him by the shout of " Philpits ! Bob! come back, I say ! " springs out of the door and down the stairs after him, leaving only the Mayor and his friend together.

Mr. Jasper may be breathing again now—probably he is so, for the eyes, that were fixed, seem to roll. And when Mr Sapsea, at last remembering the inner door, and hoping for some help for his helplessness behind it, rushes to that door, forgets his official dignity, and hammers and shouts, then the matronly figure of Mrs. Tope replies by coming into the room, and the matronly voice says,—

"Whatever is the matter? Mr. Jasper took bad again? Dear heart! what will be the end of it all, if he do go on?"

But Mr. Jasper is better now—so much better that he has a wan smile and a word for his friends, and they know that the worst is over—for the time. Yes—the impression of the two is correct, and he will live. Great *unexpected pleasure* does not kill, always.

Mr. Datchery overtakes the renegade, Mr. Philpits, not far beyond the foot of the stairs—still under the shadow of the Gate House archway. He finds this man, who pretends to have been an engineer, and who thus may be presumed to have seen adventure, and known hardship—finds him leaning against the archway, shivering a little, and in such a mood of disturbance that he, too, might have enjoyed an unexpected pleasure. He lays his hand on the shoulder of the recusant and says,—

"Well, old fellow, why did you run away?"

"Dick, I could not bear it!" answers the other, almost piteously. "Remember what has been, Dick, then recollect what is, and think whether I could stay. No—you may call me a coward, if you like, but no!"

"I am glad that you came, at all events," replies the man of the white hair. "I think that what you have seen may do you good by-and-bye, if not at this moment."

"But, Dick, shall I have strength to go on?"

"You must have strength, old fellow."

"Yes, I suppose that I must. And so I will. Do not fear me, Dick; I shall be all right in an hour, and I must be getting away at once."

"Yes, that will be best, on all accounts. Good-bye until— let me think—yes, Thursday."

"Good-bye till Thursday."

The disreputable-looking Philpits lounges and rolls away, through the arch, down the High Street, towards the river, and some possible residence beyond it; while Mr. Datchery, looking after him for a moment, and indulging certain comments, which he does not put into words, thereafter returns to his room, and makes such a mark in his score, that, finding deficiency of space for it on the door alone, he continues it at either end for appreciable distances on the floor and ceiling.

CHAPTER VI.

DR. CHIPPERCOYNE'S BRACE OF VISITORS.

RAT—TAT—TAT ! — by the heavy lion's-head knocker of a correspondingly heavy door, of a quite equally heavy-looking house in Gerrard-street, Soho—that ambiguous quarter, forming a sort of doubtful centre of the triangle of which Oxford-street, Regent-street, and Great George-street, Westminster, each with its different and well-ascertained characteristics, form the sides. The house very old, and yet severely respectable, spite of certain surroundings, worse than doubtful. Some suspicion that the last shower might have done its duty better, in washing away the blacks and grime from the dingy brick front, and its yellow window and door-copings; but none whatever of the efficiency of the domestic who had last performed hers of polishing the creamy stone of the door-steps : none of the cleanness of that knocker, or the brightness of the four-by-six brass plate on the door, on which was displayed a certain legend blending a name and a very learned profession.

The door of a surgery, in point of fact. The surgery that of Dr. Freeth Chippercoyne, M. R. C. S., if any dependence could be placed upon the brass plate before-mentioned—its well-kept appearance being at once its guarantee of respectability and candor.

Two persons alighting from a four-wheeler, and that four-wheeler remaining in waiting while the vigorous application to the knocker was made, as well as during other and subsequent operations about to be chronicled. One of those two persons,

Mr. Grewgious, looking less Angular than usual, owing to a certain droop of the shoulders and unerect carriage of the head, as also to a corresponding softening and want of assertion of the muscles of the face, suggesting that the worthy legal gentleman was being forced bodily into some movement of the propriety of which he was more than doubtful, and of the end of which his impressions were decidedly unfavorable; the second person, Helena Landless, seeming the antipodes of her companion, not only in those details of age and sex in which she could not be expected to assimilate him very closely— but in another and not less important detail, the spirit and will manifested in step and carriage. Never had the bright dark face seemed more alive and alert, winning and commanding; never had the trim lithe figure seemed more erect, springy, and suggestive of the animal and meteorological surroundings of the land that gave her birth. If Mr. Grewgious was, so to speak, for the moment under a cloud, it was beyond a doubt that the young East India girl was moving in the clear, bright tropical sunshine of a firm purpose—and that she was as much happier and more at ease, in pursuing that purpose, than she could have been in any imaginable repose—as the stream always is brighter, noiser, and more enjoyant, as well as more enjoyable, when rippling and laughing its active way towards the main, than when it lies dormant, under however pleasant a sky, and seems to have lost force as well as direction.

Possibly the domestic had over-fatigued herself in the polishing of that unimpeachable door-plate, and was not, on that account, so active as usual; for quite a moment elapsed between that decided knock, which must have been heard from attic to cellar, and the opening of the door thus vigorously assailed. And that brief space seemed to give opportunity for a few "last words" on the part of each, which may have been as important, in the connection, as those which dear lovers come back once and again to say as they part—or as those which the condemned utters as he takes his last look at the living and active nature of which he is no longer to form an atom.

"Are you quite sure, my dear young lady, that what you are doing is for the best?—that something may not result from it, leading to lasting regret on the part of both?" Mr. Grewgious asked, very anxiously, in that pause. "If you have any doubt, it is not yet too late."

"It is for *me* to ask whether *you* have any doubt of the propriety of assisting me," the young girl replied. "If so, it is for *me* to say to *you* that it is not yet too late to draw back, and that I must look for assistance in some other direction."

"No—no, Miss Landless!" the lawyer rejoined, with the face that had been Angular a little flushed. "You know that I did not mean *that!* It was of yourself that I spoke, though I suppose that I managed in some way to drag my insignificant self into the calculation. If you are to go on——"

"And I *am* to go on, dear sir, be sure of it, in whatever direction I find assistance."

"Then *I* go on, you may be equally sure of that. You are a little young, either for drying up in prison, or having that pretty neck (I hope that you do not mind my calling it pretty, under the circumstances?)—stretched by a rope in the hands of Jack Ketch; that was all that I thought of, my dear young lady."

Helena Landless laughed outright. There are temperaments to which, in the pursuance of a line of duty or impulse, the presentation of the black shadow of the scaffold in sober earnest instead of half-jest, would prove no more hindrance than the threat of tooth-ache or a lost supper; and hers, there is reason to believe, may have been one of them. She might possibly have given words to her amusement at the lawyer's lugubrious suggestion, but that at that moment the latter said,—

"Ah, there is some one coming to the door at last. You have decided: now to go on."

The belated domestic opened the heavy door with a mumbled apology.

"Dr. Chippercoyne: is he in? Yes. Then be good

enough to give him my card. We will wait here in the surgery. I have been here before; and you need not be afraid,
my good girl, of our devouring any of the contents of the
bottles: I know too well how disgusting they are. Ugh!—
for an Angular man, who should possess no delicacy of perception, Miss Landless, I have a most unreasonable nose; and
all the foul smells of a doctor's shop seem to come out at me
through the sides of the bottles, as if they were determined to
physic me, whether or no."

The servant had gone to call the Doctor from some retreat
in the upper portion of the building, where he, too, may have
been lying in wait, like his medicines, to spring out upon un-
wary visitors, and enforce the taking of the proper quantity
of offensive mixtures, without which human life might be too
easily endurable, and the chances of our seeking for a better
world correspondingly diminished.

They were in the surgery, where two heavy chairs proclaimed, in so many words, "Never more than two visitors at a
time, under any circumstances." Around them stared down
rows of labelled bottles and jars, all more or less unhealthy in
complexion, as if some sort of jaundice from their contents
had eaten into their very glass; and the abbreviated Latin of
their labels highly suggestive, to an imaginative mind, of the
sudden chopping off of and putting periods to lives with
which they came in contact. Then there was a row of drawers
similarly labelled, where might be supposed confined the less
dangerous occupants of the room — those not capable, like
their companions above, of gnawing away wood, and thus
breaking out, like so many ferocious animals in a menagerie,
to the immediate destruction of the unlucky visitor. Mr.
Grewgious, in their moment of secondary waiting, took occasion to remark so much, and to add that he should not like to
guarantee the correspondingly harmless effect on the human
system of the gentlest of them. Then there was a small table,
bearing a pair of minute scales, of which Helena, more cheerful as to the pharmacopœia, remarked that he, as a lawyer,

should be pleased with *them* at least, as the traditional appurtenances of Justice. But the lawyer destroyed this hopeful
view by reminding her that they were really employed, like
only the severer and more unpleasant branch of that Justice,
in weighing out human lives : as, so many drachms of this,
the patient may live one week; five grains of that, the mortal
career may be expected to close within two days; half an
ounce of the other, death to ensue in half an hour, and in
great agony; &c. &c.

Dr. Freeth Chippercoyne presently ended all this, and possibly relieved poor Helena from never being able to take
another physician's prescription while she lived, by making his
appearance and a bow at the same instant. A short old man,
with a good face, and white hair and whiskers, who took snuff
and grimaced like a Frenchman, but in whose presence, without one's quite knowing why, the dangerous animals in the
bottles and boxes seemed to recognize their keeper and to be
infinitely less formidable. He possessed a hearty, expansive
manner, much oftener found than expected (oddly enough)
among those who alternately dispense health and illness to
their suffering or hypochondriac fellow-mortals—with a tendency to fall off from this, at unexpected and apparently
unreasonable times, into fits of total silence, as notable if
not so celebrated as those " eloquent flashes " starring the
conversation of the Great Talker.

" Ah ! " he said, recognizing an old friend in Mr. Grewgious,
" very happy to see you after so long a time—that is, provided
you are not ill, as I do not think you are. Proud and happy
to know Miss Candless—ah, Miss Landless !" in response to
the introduction, " but sorry that *she* is to be the patient you
decline to be. Patient? why, God bless me ! now that I look
at the young lady, she is no more ill than you are, and I do
not know where to look for my—yes, call it *victim.*"

"No, doctor, neither Miss Landless nor myself is unwell,"
answered Mr. Grewgious, on the verge of laughing at what he
held to be the peculiarly felicitous word chosen by the other.

" But the fact is, that I have brought Miss Landless here, at her earnest solicitation, to consult you on a matter of some importance, with reference to the health of others, and that I must refer you to *her* for any explanation of what I may professionally call the particulars of the case."

" Ah! the young lady, then, is what you would call ' my client,' and what I cannot call ' my patient.' Well, mademoiselle—quite at your service, I am sure."

" Thanks for your courtesy; but I shall be obliged to ask to speak with you alone—that is, I believe that Mr. Grewgious does not wish——"

" Eh, what ? "

" Certainly not—not in the least degree. I never have anything to do with medicine, when I can avoid it; possibly because I am an Angular man, and pills, pestles, plasters, potion-bottles, and nearly everything that medical men handle, are round; not to mention that you, doctor, are a little round, yourself. The truth is, that Miss Landless, if I understand it (and she will allow me, so to speak, to appear in the case, as her spokesman) wishes to consult you with reference to certain preparations about which I know nothing, and *wish* to know nothing, but which she believes to involve very important interests. She needed a physician familiar with the plants and practices of the East Indies; and I——"

" With the East Indies, eh ? " the Doctor asked the question in a tone of voice best characterized as startled; and he stole a glance at the handsome dark-faced girl with the splendid, dangerous eyes, and then at the old lawyer, whom he had known so long and as so respectable; thinking—what? For one moment there is no doubt that there swept over his mind a few of the thousand stories of the ascendency gained by beautiful and designing women over weak and loving men, with the result of fearful crime, degradation, and punishment. Could this be one of the instances ? Was this young and beautiful girl a budding Brinvilliers ? Had his old friend Grewgious, so long proof against all temptation, fallen at

last into the toils? Was the requirement an East Indian
poison, to remove some person having the misfortune to be
in the way? Good heaven! if so, to what was the world
coming?

All these reflections occupied only a moment; and the
glance accompanying into the handsome face of Helena
Landless, and then round at the unhandsome but reliable
one of Mr. Grewgious, told him that he had become anxious
without cause. Crime? no! — mystery? very improbably.
But what of that? and what class of men, of all the earth,
had more to do with mystery, of right, than those who professionally dealt with the hidden and doubtful in the human
body—not to mention the more closely hidden, and much
more doubtful, in the human mind? So the Doctor was
quite prepared, when the lawyer went on with the reply to
his half-startled question, to listen with due equanimity.

"Yes, I happened to mention your name, Doctor, as that
of one whom I had known for many years, and who had
passed a considerable portion of your middle life on the Cor-
omandel coast, and afterwards in Ceylon; and Miss Landless
requested me to bring her and introduce her to you; that
is all."

"And I am pleased and flattered by the introduction, I am
sure," said the Doctor, making a supplementary bow that
included both. "Ah, did I understand you to say that mademoiselle wished to confer with me alone?"

"Yes, Doctor, that was my wish; and my good friend, Mr.
Grewgious, quite understands why I wish to do so," suggested
Helena.

"Quite so," assented the Angular man. "In point of fact,
Doctor, I am as anxious not to muddle my moderate amount
of brains, which are exclusively legal, with anything that the
young lady may need to confer with you about, as she can be
to waive my company. And I may as well say that I came
with her and introduced her, principally because I believed
that you had some reason to know my character and reputa-

tion, and that my endorsement might be worth something in
the event of her making any suggestions to you, which you
might otherwise consider a shade dangerous."

"Eh? Yes — oh, quite!" answered the Doctor, a little
absently, taking an illuminatory pinch of snuff, in that one
instant of the return of his suspicion.

"I have only to say further," Mr. Grewgious continued,
"that I fully vouch for the character and standing of Miss
Landless, and for the rectitude of the intentions with which
she seeks your aid; though I am by no means prepared to
express any opinion on the wisdom of something about which,
as I before said, I know nothing and wish to know nothing.
I remember that you have a consultation-room yonder; perhaps you will be kind enough to confer with the young lady
there, while I wait here. You will probably not be very
long; and I will endeavor to master my terror of all those
dreadful things on your shelves, enough to remain alone with
them without screaming, unless one of them should actually
come out from the bottle and attack me."

"Ah, very good," answered Doctor Chippercoyne, laughing
a little at the oddity of the lawyer's conception, and the corresponding fact that he had known some ludicrous horror of
the same character to beset simple-minded persons suddenly
left for the first time alone before the formidable array of
books in a lawyer's office. "If you can make yourself temporarily comfortable, then, without attempting to compound
any abstruse prescription while I am gone—and if mademoiselle will do me the honor to accompany me."

He led the way, taking what he believed to be a surrep-
tious pinch of snuff as he did so, through the door leading
into the consultation-room, leaving Mr. Grewgious staring
composedly at the dangerous bottles, and gradually falling
into an odd fancy for harmonizing the medical Latin of their
labels with the law jargon of his own profession—with a
result, it need not be said, pointing to headache, if not to
mild insanity.

Helena Landless found herself, the moment after, alone with the Doctor, in a room of smaller proportions than that just quitted, whereof the principal belongings were two or three chairs, and a sofa of heavy dark wood, doubly dark with age ; a large bookcase, in which the books looked ponderous and formidable, if not so dangerous as the bottles and boxes without ; and a table, on which lay scattered a few magazines, which seemed to have done duty under the fumbling fingers of preoccupied visitors for at least half a dozen years.

"Now, mademoiselle," said the Doctor, waving to a seat with the grace of an accomplished courtier, and only taking one himself when the young lady was duly installed, "be kind enough to explain what, I own, seems a little mysterious from the manner of your friend—and to tell me in what way I can serve you."

"Thanks for the permission," replied the young girl, hesitating, however, a moment in what followed. "I want a certain amount of *canabis indica*, which I could, no doubt, procure elsewhere in London, but scarcely in so pure a state as you would be likely to have it, after residence in India, and above all in Ceylon ; and I want a certain proportion each of the extract of three other herbs, not very likely to be asked for in London, and probably not in the possession of any other person than yourself in the city—possibly in England."

Dr. Chippercoyne looked very closely at the speaking dark face of the girl before he answered, as he did, slowly.

"Humph ! I fancy that I could name the other three herbs without much trouble. But I doubt whether I should be justified in doing so, or in supplying them to you if in my possession. Do you know, mademoiselle, what would be the name of the preparation compounded of the drug you have named, and the three unnamed ? "

Helena Landless laughed a little maliciously.

"How shall I give it to you, Doctor ? In the English o' the Pali ? "

"What, mademoiselle ! You know the Pali ? "

"I should know it well, though I have been for some time out of the habit of speaking it, even occasionally. Perhaps it will be enough if I mention the single word '*bangue*,' and say that that is *not* what I wish to compound, but the same preparation with the difference of one herb rendering it fit for smoking, and like opium to the taste, instead of in that shape in which its proper administration would be by swallowing."

Doctor Chippercoyne's face, as she began speaking, expressed extreme surprise; but before she finished he had been reading something in her countenance and contour, before unnoticed or not duly weighed; and when she paused, he said, more in statement than inquiry,—

"You are Ceylonese, mademoiselle?"

"Yes, I am Ceylonese by birth, though of English parentage. I was born and orphaned not many miles in the hills back of Trincomalee, where my father was engaged in business. I was nursed by a Singhali woman, and lived in communication with the race during all my childhood."

"Humph! I know Trincomalee and the country around it very well, though when in Ceylon I practised principally at Colombo. I should probably have remained there, and been by this time a wealthier man than I am, but that I had the misfortune to offer an unintentional insult to the mighty Buddha one day, and so fell under the ban of the rich natives, who were my best paying patients. Dear old Ceylon! I remember its bright skies and pleasant breezes with delight even yet, and I think that I would like to see a native elephant once more, instead of the miserable apologies for that king of animals that they lead around, and insult, and torture in the menageries."

"*I* have no pleasant memories of Ceylon," the young girl replied. "My life there was misery; but I would be happy sometimes to see an elephant once more, or a buffalo, or a tiger; and I sometimes dream, even yet, of eating bread-fruit and pines, and sleeping under the palm trees."

"But this is all away from business—not so much what you

have been saying, mademoiselle, as my suggestion that led to it." The Doctor recalled himself and his visitor by remarking, "Now to a closer point of that business, which, I may tell you, by the way, I would not pursue a step further except that you have come to me under introduction from my good friend Mr. Grewgious, and which I *must* tell you that I will not pursue a step further now, except under satisfactory answers to two or three questions."

" The requirement is quite reasonable.   Leaving aside names, which I will *not* give, I am quite ready to satisfy you on any point that you may consider doubtful."

" First, then, mademoiselle, do you know how deadly a poison is the preparation you require?   As a Ceylonese you should do so, if you know anything whatever of it; but have you that knowledge, in point of fact ? "

" I have.   I know the nature of the Indian *bangue* thoroughly—in both the forms of preparation, as you might have guessed from some words already spoken."

" Humph! Yes, those words would convey such an idea, always supposing that you had not been reading up or taking instructions to meet the emergency. From whom did you acquire that knowledge?—not very proper for a young lady, if you will permit me the liberty of saying so."

" I recognize the impropriety, Doctor, from any ordinary point of view; and I answer the question. From my nurse, a woman skilled in native medical preparations, and I sometimes fear in something worse."

" You mean poisoning, mademoiselle."

" I do."

" Satisfactory, in a most unsatisfactory way, so far.   Second, then: have you knowledge sufficient to take the risk of administering it to some one whose life you value ?—confident that you know the exact length to which the stupefaction may be allowed to go, without paralyzing the nerves of the brain to such an extent that they fail to set in operation the relieving muscles of the throat, and thus allow strangulation ? "

7

" I have that knowledge."

" From personal experiments, mademoiselle ? "

" No; from close observation under experiments made by others."

" Would you stake your own life upon possessing that knowledge and being able to put it to practical use ? "

" I would. I have no fear and no hesitation."

Doctor Chippercoyne, taking another pinch of snuff, not at all surreptitious, glanced again closely at his visitor, and his confirmed impression, deduced from that glance, was, that the young lady could at least be trusted in the detail of nerve—that she would, as she stated, neither fear nor hesitate ! Perhaps some other apprehensions, however, grew out of the very assurance.

" Humph ! Am I to understand you, then, mademoiselle, as being quite ready to stake the life of the patient upon knowing the exact moment at which to cease the administration ? "

His glance now was a gaze—a gaze under the brows of half-shut eyes.

" By no means, Doctor," was the reply, ignoring the gaze. " Perhaps I need only say three words, without any connection, to show that my knowledge does not stop at that dangerous point."

" Three words ?   Ah, let me hear them, please."

" Water—syringe—crown."

Dr. Chippercoyne indulged in one of his most notable " flashes of silence " before answering, though (between two pinches of snuff, one hidden and the other ostentatiously open) he heaved a sort of sigh, that may have been one of relief, quite a moment before he said :

" You certainly show yourself an adept, mademoiselle. You might almost be trusted, I think, with the preparation, *if I had the ingredients for making it*—so far as the Physical question goes. Suppose that we fall back upon the Moral. Why and for what do you want anything of the sort ? You wish to *make talkee,* if you will pardon my using the Indian-English formula; so much I can easily understand. But why, and to what end?"

"I have promised to answer your questions, Doctor, except in so far as they may involve names; and I will do so. A great crime has been committed—murder—nothing more nor less—upon—upon a dear friend." Her voice was a little broken, here, and the Doctor recognized the fact, but made no comment; and after a moment she mastered the emotion and went on. "I know his murderer, who is at large and almost unsuspected. He is endeavoring to throw the crime on another."

"Good God!"—this was rather an aside than an interruption of the Doctor, who thereupon solaced himself with the largest and most-openly displayed pinch of the whole interview.

"That 'other' is a near relative of my own. The whole affair is wrapped in a mystery that nothing seems able to dispel: the mode of murder, place, disposition of the body"—voice broken again, and tears in the dusky eyes, if the Doctor could only have seen far enough to note them—"everything except the *fact,* and that only clear to myself and one or two others, including Mr. Grewgious. For the protection of my—my relative, and the punishment of a human tiger—no, I will not insult the noble beast by the comparison!—a human *serpent,* whose ways are dark and his bite deadly—I mean to know all, and know it from his own bad lips."

She paused. The doctor, much impressed, and a shade frightened, indulged again in one of his intervals of silence before answering. At length he asked:

"But how—allow me to ask, mademoiselle—how are you to reach this man—this murderer? How are you to subject him to the test, all the rest being admitted?"

"He smokes opium—is gradually destroying himself with it. I have had him tracked to his lair—no, his *nest,* and I have the means to control those who supply him with the drug. There—have I not told you enough? It seems to me that

nothing more remains to be said. Can you, and will you,
supply me with the means of bringing this man to justice, by
his own mouth ? "

"On your oath, mademoiselle—no, on something more
sacred than any oath—on your word of honor as a lady, are the
statements of these circumstances strictly true ?—and would
you use the preparation, if you possessed it, for this purpose
and no other ? "

For just one instant the expression in the tawny eyes was
even more dangerous than themselves. There may be too
many questions asked for reassurance, especially with such
natures as that of Helena Landless. But the angry flash
passed away, suddenly as it had come, leaving only a slight
color on the brown cheek, as she replied :

"On my word of honor as a lady, Doctor, since you think
proper to require this repetition—I have told you the whole
truth except the names involved ; and I have the motive I
have named to you, and no other."

One moment more of silence on the part of Doctor Chippercoyne, punctuated by a pinch of snuff of extraordinary size,
and only a partial attempt at concealment. Then he said,
speaking rapidly and nervously :

"Upon my word, Miss Landless, you are an extraordinary
person, and I use the expression in a complimentary sense.
You are a brave girl, and a determined one. I can trust you,
I believe, as I could few persons in England ; and I *will*. I
have the ingredients you desire, though I little thought that I
should ever find occasion to use them. I know the whole
secret of making the compound you wish : it is at your service.
And pray pardon me if I seem to have asked you too many
questions : I have really not asked you one more than my professional duty demands."

"Oh, thanks !—a thousand thanks !—and never mind the
questions asked, if I have been so fortunate as to command
your confidence at last," answered the young girl, rising, her
face all one flush of satisfaction, and the expectation growing

out of it. "When may I hope that you will put me in possession of what I need?"

"Not to-morrow, mademoiselle—no, that would not give sufficient time for the drying after amalgamation. Say the day after: if you will honor me with another call then, it shall be at your service, as well as any additional hints that I can give you. And now for our good friend Mr. Grewgious," he added, helping himself to a concluding pinch, and really laughing all over at the idea. "Sad, would it not be, if we should find that he had been dabbling in the fearsome drugs after all, and either poisoned himself or some one else?"

That apprehension, it is pleasant to say, was not fully realized, on their re-emergence into the surgery. They only found the lawyer, with an expression of pained disgust upon his face, which made the Angularity a trifle in comparison, holding the cage of one of the apparently least dangerous animals in his hand, attentively studying its character and movements, through the glass, in the harmless-looking nuts of a jar of *nux vomica!*

CHAPTER VII.

THE DISCOVERY OF THE RIVER-BANK.

THERE is a fisherman's hut, of small size and the most unpromising appearance, not far back from the edge of the river, on the grassy bank, at a point a few hundreds of yards below that at which the small tributary stream empties into it, forming, shortly before it debouches, that timber-impeded and stone-regulated fall known as Cloisterham Weir. Before it, beyond the grassy bank sloping down to the shelving sandy beach, the broad river runs by, at times pleasant, bright, and sunny, as if it flowed down from some mountain-land where the contaminations of trade had never yet affected the purity

of its head-springs or defiled its quiet source; at others dark,
turbid, speckled, and unattractive-looking, as if it bore away
on its bosom the foulnesses of some great city sewered into it,
with no small proportion of the unnameable nuisances insepar-
able from such localities; and at still others wild, rough, and
threatening, as if it felt in advance certain stirrings of that
demoniac nature which would become part of its very life
when incorporated with the great sea,—and as if it would
willingly prove its line of descent, so to speak, in advance, by
foundering vessels, and drowning those on board them,—after
the manner of the young savage of legendary lore, who sig-
nalizes the approach of manhood, without waiting for its
actual coming, and wins the plaudits of the mighty warriors
of his tribe, by practising cruelties upon helpless prisoners,
women, and others falling into his power, hopefully indicative
of the full fiendishness which may be looked for when he
takes his destined place in age and rank.   Up and down this
broad river, from the door of the hut, low as it stands, can be
seen passing the dun sails of the boats carrying on commercial pursuits upon it, and at irregular intervals the smoke of
the one small steamer, insignificant as to size and wheezy as
to the character of her motive-power, which has been spared
to Cloisterham by the setting of traffic into other channels.
Half a mile away, eastward, the gazer from the window of
the hut on that side (if there was such a window, capable of
allowing the protrusion of his head) could see the roofs and
chimneys of Cloisterham, clustering about the river at that
point, with the square tower of the Cathedral carrying the
otherwise insignificant view to a certain culmination of gran-
deur in height, as, no doubt, the Cathedral and the things belonging to it were originally intended to form a corresponding
nucleus for the commonness of every-day life and traffic, by
which a certain spiritual elevation should be eventually
attained.   Lower, and yet higher than the roofs of the houses
of Cloisterham, might also be seen the rugged line of the
ruined monastery, standing between the point of view and

the Cathedral, though much nearer to the latter. And on the other side (the same privilege of window being assumed) would be viewed the slight promontory formed by the debouching of the tributary, with the white flashing of the waters below the ever-restless Weir behind it and riverward.

This fisherman's hut, holding, as will be remarked, a position that might be envied by many a structure of greater pretensions, is not of such a height as to suggest heart-disease for the occupants, from frequent and long ascents of stairways; and it lacks that comprehensive sweep of outer walls, implying that the builder owned all the country round, and wished to enclose as much of it as possible. There is a certain lavishness, however, not to say positive wastefulness, in its architecture; for the thickness of its rough walls is such as to create the suspicion that some other building has once fallen in the neighborhood, the debris thereafter costing nothing more than the labor of removal; and Mr. Sapsea, if he should apply to it his fine sense of derivation, and his habit of travelling by atmospheres, would unquestionably say, picking up a fragment of the reddish stone : "Old monastery —ruins—carried away—used to build this : that is how *I* put it." Similarly the roof has a certain lavishness, in workmanship if not in material; for it seems to lie in sections, over-lapping each other, and fastened down by an amalgamation of the vegetable and mineral in the shapes of ropes and spikes; and some of the sections bear odd shapes and curves, reminding one of the roofs of sea-going deck-cabooses, and leading to at least a suspicion that vessels may have been either wrecked or dismantled in the neighborhood. A chimney there is, of breadth shaming the height, the thick sides making it a miniature hut on top of the other, wherefrom smoke arises, heavily perfumed with fish-oil, at irregular periods; and windows and a door there are, though the former are small, and so very dirty, at all times, as to make seeing into them impossible, and seeing out of them unlikely, —and though the latter, refractory as to the trivial use to which it has been put, in comparison with the staid and respectable occupation of other and immovable materials, has a habit of refusing to do duty, and always hanging open by one leathern hinge.

Out of this hut emerges, also irregularly but usually of a morning when the weather will allow such visits to be paid to the outer air, Crawshe the fisherman, bullet-headed, red-bearded, round-hatted, heavy-booted, tarry-trousered, pea-jacketed ofttimes sou'—westered, and always bearing with him the atmosphere of a mud-bank with fish trimmings. He is the proprietor of a boat on the river below, and of some nets, which seem to divide their time equally and miserably between being soakingly wetted in the river, and cracklingly dried on a diminutive net-reel near the hut. The boat, which is often to be discovered lying bottom upward on the bank and receiving tarry lubrication at the hands (also tarry) of the owner, from a kettle steaming with hot pitch and a fire burning thereunder, as if in some odd way it was an animal requiring frequent food and always taking it in by cuticular absorption,—this boat is sometimes accessory to the due immersion and dragging out of the nets of which it constitutes the natural enemy; to the abduction from the waters of fish so small that the baby-act might be pleaded against their employment in any branch of industry; and to the purpose of taking out on the river as fares, and rowing aimlessly about, of persons who suppose that they are thus humoring one portion of the sporting British mind by fishing. At which and at all times when permitted by the proprieties, or in spite of them, Crawshe, a man of many humble cares and but few enjoyments, but with a heart as brave and a spirit as indomitable as they may exist in bosoms much better clothed (even *decorated*), whistles away those cares and doubles those enjoyments, with a constancy which would make his music highly artistic and valuable if a part of that quality could be transmuted into time and tune.

There is another Crawshe, the female, who makes many of

those cares of the male, and yet is by far the worse sufferer
of the two. *She* does not emerge from the hut, if emerging
consists in passing entirely beyond it—except at such rare
intervals that her last previous time of leaving may at any
moment be dated from as an era. She may be seen, however,
very often, when the day is pleasant and sunny, standing in
the doorway, leaning against one of the posts, and looking out
on the world of which she forms no part—possibly even wishing (sad pass to reach !) that she could change sex, give up all
the comparative freedom from toil of her situation, and assume
the hardest labor of her husband or others, only to be out once
more in that world, no longer *house-ridden*. For she is a
helpless invalid, without having suffered any physical injury
to bring her to that state : the incapacitating development
being constitutional headache, from which she is never exempt
as is her brow never freed from the yellow handkerchief binding it and forming her flag of quarantine. Years ago the con-
tinual recurrence destroyed her modicum of brain, and left her
only so much as suffices to fulfil the most ordinary offices of
daily life—not enough to allow her unassisted egress from that
always-open door.

They have a daughter—the fisherman and she, who emerges
from the door only less seldom than her mother, her chain
being a double one—toil and *shame*. She has been pretty,
not so many years ago; has been at service, in a family not
far from Cloisterham, in a stately house, of which the tall grey
turrets may be seen from the bridge, down the river. She has
been wronged, dishonored, cast out, to come home to the hut
and show what even wrecked humanity may be worth in the
way of a drudge. She is " dreeing her wierd," as the hard
old Scot would say ; working out her penance, as another
school of disciples of the Unmerciful might suggest ; bearing
a hard lot, at all events, in the endless and hopeless labor
which has already hardened her once fair hands to horn, and
the hopeless confinement which has already withered her
young beauty like a frosted leaf. Let us hope that, if it is a

penance, Exty Crawshe will work it out in *this* life, and have
an equal chance with her sisters for the sunlight in the life
beyond !

And there is yet another, known to more than the idle and
careless buffer Datchery, and pitied by them in that non-
helpful way. in which most brotherly pity falls upon broken
humanity. It is the hand of Wrong that has stricken the
girl; it is that of Accident (so-called) which has fallen upon
him whom the visitors to the river-side and the rough fishermen
along the banks know as Little Crawshe, without any regard
to his having or lacking another name. Three years ago,
when the boy was approaching twelve, they were busy repair-
ing Cloisterham Weir, a spring flood having swept away a
part of the timbers, and disarranged the stonework of the bed.
The labor lasted for many days; and naturally among that
large body of spectators which seems necessary to accompany
any job in civilized lands, the fisherman's children played no
unimportant part on that occasion. They sprang and
crawled over and through the heavy timbers, equally when
being removed as when lying untouched. A cross-beam
slipped from the men's hold during one of those removals;
Little Crawshe's head was half under it as it fell; the blow
on the back of the head was just sufficient, sparing the skull,
which it would otherwise have crushed like an egg-shell, to
break away some of the muscles of the back of the neck; the
head fell forward helplessly, and has never since been raised,
except by the hand of the wearer or some other. Crippled for
life, and in the most hopeless manner, unless supplied by some
unexpected dispensation with a few of the extra hands of
Briareus—for two hands are necessary for profitable labor in
this exigent world; and one of the ordinary two must not be
employed in holding up the head that would otherwise bow
like a broken bulrush. From that day Little Crawshe, once
expected to be a help to the poor fisherman, has been a burthen—a patient, uncomplaining one, it is true, and the recipient of many a small favor from pseudo-fishermen of the

Datchery type; but still helpless, a burthen and an anxiety to the poor fisherman, who might before have been supposed to possess quite enough of either.

And still one other member of the household inhabiting the little hut on the river-bank—of the household, if not of the family; and quite possibly of the latter, if words are to be allowed their true meaning. Black Tomboy—so called in defiance of the large splash of white commencing at the nose, and making the left side a mottle, thence to the middle of the body. Of the Newfoundland breed, in the main, though with a cross in his blood, which has shortened his hair, and added a slight ferocity to his aspect, while failing to deprive him of the heavy bushed tail, or to diminish his propensity for water-practice. The only member of the Crawshe household, it may be said, who literally causes no anxiety to the fisherman, as he possesses enough of thrift (some malicious persons would spell it differently, and call it *theft*) to provide substantially for his own subsistence without seriously burthening the narrow larder of his keepers (*Mem.*: He is not fond of fish!); and as he always acts as a guard of honor to the poor crippled boy, when permitted, expressing amiability and the reverse at two opposite ends, by the wag of his bushy tail and the drawing back of the red lips from his formidable teeth; but habitually saying, as he accompanies his helpless charge along the river-bank or up to the Weir, in silent language that boasted human knowledge ought to be ashamed not to understand:

"I say!—for some cause or other, not mentioned in canine books of surgery, this young master of mine has only one hand that is of any practical use. The other is always busy, under his chin. But don't let any one presume upon that! Let any one insult or impose upon him, when I am in his company—or let him only fall into the river, in which latter case I have observed that people generally want the use of two hands, and have quite enough to do with both to keep their stupid heads from going under water—then you shall see what Black Tomboy is worth, as you may not do for many a long day if you do not give him an opportunity."

There is a small bench, made of a bit of wreck-plank with
four sprawling legs driven into the bottom side of it in auger-
holes, standing at one side of the always-open-door of the hut
—sometimes occupied by one of Exty's to-be-cleaned cooking-
pots, and quite as often (without scrubbing between) by Little
Crawshe, in those hours of weary idleness, when no one has
allowed him to go in the boat and his feeble limbs have grown
weary of aimless walking along the river-bank.   He occupies,
on such occasions, nearly the whole of the bench; and Black
Tomboy exactly fills the space between the four legs, *under* the
bench, thus completing a group of singularly picturesque character, except when the dog chances to stand up, and thus
causes some confusion as to the two quatrains of legs, leading
the possible observer to look for another quadruped to fill up
space below *him,* and so on at discretion.   There is another
fact which the possible observer does not realize quite so readily—that then, even more than at other times, though always
to a remarkable degree, the noble brute is in such a state of
understanding (no pun intended, on the part of the dog) with
the crippled boy, that a mere motion will communicate an order
commonly requiring many words.

The three—boy, dog, and bench—chance to be grouped in
that wise at a certain hour of a certain evening nearly coin-
cident with the visit of Helena Landless to the surgery of
Doctor Chippercoyne.   The bench may be supposed in good
health, as it stands firmly on its *legs* and maintains its *heart-
of-oak* in usual vigor.   So of the dog, who is in fine spirits, as
shown by certain forcible waggings and beatings of the bushy
tail, indicating a desire for a debarred promenade, but reasonable satisfaction with anything else that may be offered.   So
with the boy, who, if a cripple, has learned to carry a burthen
which might have made Atlas sink at the moment when he
had shown his capacity to upbear the globe—the burthen of
helplessness and deformity in early years.   He has learned, let
us hope—poor little fellow! to thank God in his childish way,
that he *has* a hand to support the incapable head—nay, even

that he has not been so injured by his accident as to be broken-backed and too weak to crawl out into the sunshine, or blind, and thus unable to see those beautiful things in nature, fortu-ately visible to the eyes of the poor and suffering as to those of the proudest and happiest.

Mr. Datchery comes up the river bank, from the direction of the town. For an idle buffer, living on his means, and so sup-posably with no errand whatever in the world, he is walking somewhat rapidly; and his white hair floats a trifle away from his uncovered head in the evening breeze coming down the river. Little Crawshe observes him as he sits with his head on his hand, fortunately looking in the right direction; and his sad, patient little face lights up with a joy which speaks of past sympathy and kindness from the man who is approaching, and (so the sense of gratitude is compounded, there is reason to believe, in others than Little Crawshe) of past shillings and half-crowns. Black Tomboy, too, has a recognition of the coming man of this period; for a pat on the head, and a "fine dog! good Tomboy!" may have been to him that currency passing for the full worth of silver coinage; and a short bark of satisfaction and some pretence of rushing out and tearing him hilariously to pieces, make up the signs of that favorable recognition.

Mr. Datchery comes up to the bench, looking into the open door as he passes, to observe whether the sick woman of the yellow handkerchief, or even poor drudge Exty, may chance to be within hearing. Little Crawshe slides down from his bench, with his head still in his hand—still in his hand, as he seems likely to be obliged always to hold it, whenever erect, until they lay him out at length between staunch boards affording unyielding support till the Day of Cured Deformi-ties and Healed Diseases; and Black Tomboy, with another satisfied grunt, comes out from under his bench, swings his heavy tail against Mr. Datchery's legs with force enough to topple a man of weak knees, and observes, in his own peculiar vernacular, compounded of the clown and the public porter: "Here we are again, sir!—what can we do for you?"

"How are you, this evening, Crawshey?" (Mr. Datchery's own affectionate diminutive, and copyright.) "Well enough to do a little job for me, and earn a bright new shilling? Eh? And how are *you*, old Tomboy Bigfellow?" the latter greeting with a pat on the head accompanying.

"Very well, master, thank you. Oh, yes, my knees do not tremble so badly to-day, and I can do anything you wish, for *you*," is the grateful reply of the boy; while Black Tomboy answers, in his own pleasedly-growling language: "I? Oh, my health is beautiful, and I have on hand a large amount of unexpended energy. Just let some one annoy my young Master, here, who continues to have one hand grown fast to his head—or let somebody tumble into the water—then you shall see what you shall see!"

Mr. Datchery look backs along the river-bank pathway by which he has come, and seems to extend his long gaze to the very town beyond, at the point where that pathway begins. Then he asks,—

"He has not been up the river this evening?" No name used, there would seem to be only one person of the male sex in the neighborhood, to these two; for the boy appears to understand the personality, and answers at once,—

"No, master. I have not been out of sight of the door for a moment, these two hours, and he has not gone by."

"Is it not a little late?"

"A little late, master; but he sometimes comes later. He seldom misses this fine weather, except when he has gone away—up to London, they say."

"He is not away to-day; so much I know, for I saw him only an hour since, when he did not see *me*. He will come, no doubt, and at all events we will be ready for him. Now, Crawshey, there is something to do, very special, and about which there must not be any blunder. Not that I am afraid of you: the wallet business was capitally done, and you can do so well when you try. But Tomboy: can we always depend upon Tomboy, do you think?"

Black Tomboy, who undoubtedly understands the language of this unreasonable suspicion, answers it with a low growl of not the best temper; and that utterance reassures Mr. Datchery quite as much as the reply of the boy.

"Oh, yes, master: we can trust Black Tomboy, always. He is listening to you, as well as I, don't you see ? Go on, please, for he may be coming."

" Quite so, you are right, Crawshey. Well, then," and Mr. Datchery extracts from an inner pocket, where it has laid bulkily, a dark mass, of which the shape and texture cannot be at first discovered; though it eventually resolves itself into a black scarf. He looks back along the path again, and then forces it, with some difficulty, into the pocket of Little Craw-she's jacket, where the late bulky appearance in his own garment is immediately so duplicated, that if the poor boy should happen at the moment under the eye of the police, he would be incontinently searched as a suspected thief of loose-hanging articles in door-ways.

" Now, then—ah, did that shilling get into your hand, or has Tomboy got it away and swallowed it ? In your hand ? All right, then. Now then, you are to keep snug until he goes up towards the Weir, this evening, or the next time he comes; then, when he is well up in that direction and you are sure that his back is still towards you, request Tomboy to run up the path to the point I named before, and leave it there so that he will be sure to happen upon it as he comes back. Do you quite understand ? "

" Yes, master, and so does Tomboy, I think : please to look at his eyes, and see whether he does not know what you say."

" Humph ! well, perhaps he does; but Crawshey, I depend most upon *you*. Don't have any blunder made ; for you understand that he is a great friend of mine, and that I am very anxious to make him a present in this odd way, and very privately. So that if he should happen to stop and make any inquiries about it—though I do not think that he will— you are to know nothing, and Tomboy is to hold his tongue."

"I understand, master, and Tomboy and I will do what you wish. Thankee for the shilling : you are very kind to a poor boy, always."

At this moment Mr. Datchery, who may be an impressible buffer, as well as an idle and an odd one, wipes something from his eyes ; and the next moment, with only the single additional word, accompanied by a warning shake of the fore-finger, "Mind!" he passes on up the river-path for a short distance, then turns suddenly to the left and immediately dis-appears, the waving of his white hair being the last object visible, behind a rise leading to a near range of chalk-pits ; to which, indeed, he may be making his way, in order to provide himself with additional material for the Rune Marks on his closet-door.

Little Crawshe, thus left alone with his dumb companion, applies himself with assiduity to what the English pickets did on the night before Waterloo, and the Guards for a time on the day of that memorable battle—*watching and waiting.*

Black Tomboy waits, too, again retired under his bench where he pants heavily as if with much exertion, and whether or not possessing any knowledge of the personality waited for, it will need some one more learned than Buffon or Cuvier to decide.

Not long before another figure comes up the river-side path from the direction of the town. The two at the bench see him, as they saw the other. The face of Little Crawshe takes on a painful mingling of fear and dislike ; and Tom-boy, his attention drawn in the same direction, indulges in a single low growl that would not be pleasant to listen to in the event of man and dog being confronted. Then the boy slides down from the bench, and makes a motion and says, "Come!" to the dog, who thereupon follows with certain symptoms that he would prefer maintaining his position ; and the two disappear, not into the hut, but behind it—into the covert of a miserable little cooking-shed, with abundant loop-holes at the rear.

The figure approaches nearer, and it then becomes evident that the personality alluded to by Mr. Datchery and Little Crawshe, under the single word "he," must have been that of Mr. John Jasper. For he it is, easily recognizable at a considerable distance, in spite of a certain haggardness of the face and a certain hollowness of eye, not visible in either seven months before, though even then that evil tree was planted, now bearing the fruit of Sodom. There are to be discovered, too, by a close observer, a little stoop in the shoulders, and a certain dropping forward of the head, as if the man is not able to walk quite so erect before his fellow-men; but only the close observer could see so much, and to most whom he chances to meet he seems ordinarily hearty and vigorous.

He comes still nearer, walking at easy gait and with the air of one used to the pathway and susceptible to the pleasant influences of the summer evening; though occasionally he glances round him a little uneasily, as one might do who had suspicions of being followed or too closely observed. This, until he passes the line of the hut, when the head seems to rise more erect, the step to become firmer, and the gait to be noticeably faster, while the nervous glances around cease altogether. And so he passes on beyond the hut, only the black-clothed back now exposed to view, and begins to disappear behind the foot of the same rise which has so lately hidden Mr. Datchery, bending up to the left, between the Weir and the chalk-pits.

Then occurs something marking another phase in the relations between Little Crawshe and the man with the white hair, but quite as forcibly illustrating that debatable line in intelligence separating the human and the animal. The fisherman's boy, the dog at his side, peeps from the covert of the shed to see that "he" is disappearing behind the rise. Only "his" head is visible: "he" is out of sight altogether. He speaks: "Tomboy, pay attention!" and the white spotted black statue starts into vigorous life, wag-

8

ging his heavy tail and throwing up his nose in expectation. Little Crawshe takes from his pocket, with his single hand, the scarf placed there by Mr. Datchery, and holds it for a moment, with "See this, and smell it!" The dog lays his nose against the pendant woven silk, and utters a growl of rage as he does so, at the same time looking up into his master's eyes with an expression needing at least two natural histories to define. "Take this up the path, there, t'other side the reel, leave it, and come back to me!" The dog turns aside his head, and opens his jaws to receive the parcel, as a carrier, into that peculiar dog-pocket with no visible bottom, constructed by freaksome nature—but shivers all over, as if with a sudden chill; sniffs it, growls angrily, and seems to refuse the commission. "Naughty dog! Bad Tomboy! Tomboy must be whipped, and have no supper!" The dog, with another shiver and a whimper, again turns aside his head, and opens his mouth, takes into it the scarf in the four folds arranged by the hand of the boy, and moves away in the direction for which he has received orders.

But he is no longer, for the present, as Little Crawshe stands at the corner of the shed and watches him—no longer, for the time, Black Tomboy, of the generous breed and the noble instincts. Something in that which he carries in his mouth, unguessed by the less intelligent human brutes who touch it, influences him and his whole dog-being. He does not walk erect, with the long swinging stride of his race: he rather crawls, with every leg at tension, and the body bent low to the ground. But he goes on, very swiftly in spite of his altered gait, to the spot indicated, some two hundred yards beyond the hut. He drops his burthen there, with a growl which the boy rather imagines than hears at that distance,—and becomes Black Tomboy again instantly, in his fullest development. If there are avenging furies in dog-mythology, and if they have the unpleasant habit of pursuing members of the canine race at quadruple the speed of the Limited Mail, their chances of overtaking Tomboy before he reaches the shelter of his young master's presence, would be slight indeed. His legs seem to be four wings, and his tail has become a rudder for a flying-machine. He leaps, bounds, literally flies; and only an instant elapses before he is back with Little Crawshe behind the hut, growling his late terror, shivering a little, again, and only half compensated for what has evidently been the most unpleasant duty of his whole dog-life, by the smile of his master, the approving pat of his one unoccupied hand, and the pleasant reversal of the late conditional sentence, which may have been held as a virtual "suspension of judgment," pending after behavior. "Good dog! Fine old Tomboy! He *shall* have supper."

It would seem that among the arrangements made between Mr. Datchery and Little Crawshe, preceding the brief meeting at the door of the hut, there must have been some order incorporated, to watch the fate of the scarf after its deposit on the path; and possibly the spot at which it was to be deposited may have had some reference to keeping it in view; for the fisherman's boy does not leave his post of observation with the return of the dog, but watches—watches—watches, this time the up-river way of the path, by which " he " has disappeared, and by which he may be expected to return.

His watch is broken by an unheeded call from drudge Exty, from the interior of the hut, to come in to supper—and again by a momentary disappearance into the hut, to possess himself of an old sea-glass, long ago given to fisherman Crawshe by a captain whom he had served, and who had been presented with a better. It seems doubtful whether, with his single hand, he can either arrange this cumbrous aid to vision, or hold it in position at the moment when its aid may be needed; but that point can be better decided after witnessing the experiment.

And his watch certainly lasts longer than might have been expected. Possibly, Mr. John Jasper may have been feeding his love of nature with the music of falling waters at the Weir, or making that spot, where the watch and breast-pin of his dear boy were discovered, a perpetual new point of departure in his quest after the murderer. At all events, he does not come back too soon for purposes of close observation ; for the first faint shadows of dusk, even in the long summer twilight, are falling when Little Crawshe sees him emerge from behind the foot of the rise, and walk rapidly on towards the town.

Black Tomboy, perhaps fatigued by the mental and physical strain of his late exertions, or dreamily musing on the inferiority of men to dogs as a race, lies with his big head between his great paws, his eyes closed, and supposably unaware of the returning presence.

Suddenly the boy-watcher, who *has* managed to bring the old sea-glass into focus and range, with the one hand displaying almost the dexterity of two—sees John Jasper pause, as one might do who saw either a serpent or a jewel in his path —stopped by either Danger or Temptation. Then he sees him, after a moment, make a dash forward and hurriedly pick up the scarf, running it immediately thereafter through his fingers, and bringing one of the ends close to his eyes, as if in search of some mark capable of identifying it. Then he sees him half drop it from his hands and stagger back, as one who has received a sudden blow in the face. Then he observes that he staggers against the net-reel, which stands not far from the path, and appears to be suffering from some convulsion which shakes him like an ague. Then he seems to recover from the worst phase of his spasm, by a violent effort, which brings his hands to his throat—the scarf falling to the ground meanwhile. Then he picks it up; looks at it with apparent hesitation ; at last crams it into one of the pockets of his coat, with an energy like that of anger ; then removes his hat, and draws his hand across his brow, with the motion of one wiping away heavy perspiration in that uncleanly manner ; then staggers away from the net-reel and resumes the path towards the town, with his head bent much lower than when he came, and certain stumblings which denote that the eyes are not looking at the way he is traversing—rather gazing into space, the future, the terrible, and the unknown.

And well they may do so — those eyes. For who can measure that undescribed horror, the Rising of the Buried? What torture had Macbeth, in a mentality which we must believe to have been keen and sensitive, like that of the unbidden sitting of Banquo at his table? And what, for John Jasper — what have these mute witnesses of a deed more carefully and calculatingly committed than any other in all the long annals of crime, to do with the outer world from which they were once so effectually buried? Two days since, the wallet with the very name of the "dear boy!" to-day the scarf, damnably the same, as the initials give only too certain evidence! If these are loose in the world, what else may not be? What a farce is closest concealment, what a mockery the very name of security! And whence and how all this? Has nature—dreadful thought!—in some convulsion broken through all laws that held the hidden and the secret close, so that to-morrow — or, why not to-night? — the folly of past ages may become the awful wisdom of the present day, and spectres haunt all places where the hand of crime has done its undiscovered work? Or is human malice—thought no less dreadful!—playing even more cunningly than the hand of crime itself? Is suspicion abroad, with material proof in its hand? Is justice aroused? Which way to turn, in a labyrinth become too thick for sight or judgment? How to know the truth—be it that miserable *best* which yet remains, or that unnamed *worst* which every new development renders more probable? Ah, there remains one refuge still—the drug. Opium—its blackest dreams are paradise to that accursed world of real life, which always opens at some foredoomed hour to guilt!

Certainly Mr. Datchery, if, instead of being a single buffer of easy disposition and idle habits, living on his means, and merely seeking Cloisterham for its antique picturesqueness and inconvenience, he was the most acute, the most persis-

tent, and the most unscrupulous of revengeful foes — could
scarcely invent a more exquisite torture of punishment for
his victim, than that upon which he appears to be stumbling
in the mere development of his indolent but somewhat med-
dlesome good-nature!

But what is this which John Jasper sees, through the gathering dusk, when he is well down the river, opposite the ruined
monastery, and entering the town?   He seems to feel it, as
he rather totteringly reels and plunges forward than walks
with his usual step.   It seems black, and it bears, through
the obscurity, something like the shape of a dog.   It keeps
a certain distance behind him, on the path and afterwards in
the street—a certain distance : no more, no less.   He pauses :
it stops.   He goes on : it follows.   Once he musters courage
to pick up a stone against which he has touched his foot, and
to throw it at the shape of fear : it utters no sound, gives no
token of molestation—only stops when he pauses, and follows
when he goes on.   He sees it—or thinks that he sees it—
following him, at the same certain distance, to the very archway of the Gate House.   He is doubtful, as he goes up the
postern stair, enters and shuts the door, whether he shall find
that he has left it behind him ; but he seems to have done
so, for it is not in the room.   No—it is not—it cannot be ;
for, looking from the window, towards the Close, as he draws
the curtain that now shuts away so little, he sees it dimly
through the thickening dusk, apparently at the same distance
from him as before, sitting erect and looking at that window!

What is it? he asks himself, as he strikes a light and falls
half-fainting into his chair.   What is it?—a dog of actual
life, thus following him?—a mere phantom of the imagination, conjured by that fearful something equally black in his
pocket?—or *a ban dog of hell, hunting him silently to his
doom?*

CHAPTER VIII.

ALL THE DAUGHTERS OF HER FATHER'S HOUSE.

AMONG the ills most difficult to bear, of the long catalogue
to which the holding of affection subjects us, most surely may
be counted that which sees a loved one pained in body or in
mind, and yet lacks power to counteract disheartening influences, except as physical disease, beyond the doctor's skill,
may be alleviated hour by hour. To many a man—and all
the more because the heart was tender to the faintest touch
of sympathy — the task of sitting by some loved one's bed,
witnessing pain there was no power to soothe, has been a
sorer trial of the courage than marching up to any battery or
daring elements in wildest strife. And if, as is certain, this
is true of bodily disease, a thousand times more painful must
it always be to sit beside the sick-bed of the soul, and have
no power to still its murmurings. For doing this so better far
than man has power to do—for being ever and again that
ministering angel who has courage to flee away when only
fiercest ravings or most weak complaints repay the efforts of
unwearied care—for these, if nothing more stood to her credit
in the great account, would woman be superior far to man,
and worthy of the crown of Love as matched against his
diadem of Strength.

Helena Landless, though she may scarcely have thrown into
so many words the reflections connected with her situation at
this period, cannot well have avoided becoming aware how
circumstances had placed her in one of the most difficult of
positions, little suited to her young life and inexperience,—
and how most difficult of all must be the task of winning back
her brother to the hope and strength which seemed to have
gone out of him like a lost quality.

It might have seemed to be enough, surely, that the young
girl, so lately without a care beyond those connected with the

unfortunate circumstances of her early life, should have come,
in so brief a space, to carrying in her bosom the heart of a
widow, who had not only never been wedded, but had not even
been wooed; enough, yet more surely, that with this should
have been combined that fearful duty to which in the exercise
of her highest conscientiousness she had set herself—at once
to avenge the man she had loved, and protect the one remaining dearest to her; it seemed more than enough that at this
period, she should be called upon to meet and combat, in its
worst form, the mental disease of that remaining dearest one
whom she was changing sexes to protect.

For Neville Landless was, at this time, utterly and
thoroughly broken down, in spite of the efforts made to prevent that issue of his wrongs, by both Mr. Grewgious and Mr.
Crisparkle, and in spite of the untiring devotion of his sister,
which seemed to subordinate all other thoughts and wishes
to his will.   That constitutional irascibility, of which the
clenched hand had given Mr. Crisparkle even better evidence
than his words, had been rather supplemented than replaced
by the melancholy and discouragement succeeding his arrest
and disgrace.   He followed, with almost painful assiduity, the
course of reading marked out for him by the clergyman and
superintended by the lawyer; but he did so more than half
mechanically, and with the very slightest influence produced
upon his mentality.   He held the same invincible objection as
at first to appearing in the light of day, even when there could
be no probability of his meeting any person who had previously known him—so that only occasionally at night, and
then under the urgent persuasion of his sister, he quitted at
all his place under the roof, where he may be said to have
nested like a wounded bird of the eaves.

He was subject to long fits of moody abstraction, during
which not a word could be won from him, for hours, by the
most tender solicitude; and these were varied, not seldom, by
other fits bearing something of the character of paroxysms,
and marked by restless stridings of his little room, his face

dark, troubled, and threatening, his hands often beating
together in what seemed impotent rage, and his whole action
that of a caged animal blending unconquerable impatience at
its confinement with fear of anything lying beyond it.

What had become, now, of that silent sympathy between
the twin brother and sister, spoken of, as a harmless boast, in
those first days at Cloisterham, and of which only the truth
has been told in stating that through its means each divided
the thought of the other, nearly always, without the utterance
of a word? Alas!—another truth must be told of this
tenderest of all the relations of life—that *there are certain
conditions under which only the twin-beings can retain their
full intimacy of communion*—and that the first of those
conditions, in their instance, had been broken. No other and
dearer tie, however different, must come between the two
persons of this pre-natal compact, or both are changed thenceforth. And such an interposition had come to each ; both
Helena Landless and her brother *loved.*

Loved, how unfortunately, what words can say? It had
been the fate of the sister to conceive a passion for a man
already betrothed, that betrothal only broken the very hour
before his murder. It had been the fate of the brother to
conceive a similar passion for a woman standing in the same
relation, and from whom, when released by that murder, he
neither dared to look on nor ask for one answering throb.
His shame had come in the accusation of his committing that
very murder in jealous rage for *her;* and if love between
them could thenceforth be possible, would he not seem to be
trampling upon the dead in breathing a word of that love, at
whatever distance of time? Truly, it did not seem easy to
conceive of two who had more signally wrecked themselves in
a few weeks and a first venture, than the occupants of the two
rooms under the roof at Staple Inn !

What words had she, self-appointed the comforter, with
which to comfort him, the discouraged and the disconsolate ?
Fewer even than she might have found at the day of his first

coming. Was there not a possibility, then, that some day in the far future would arrive in which she would have at least the privilege of showing to him in darker and worst discouraged hours, Rosa, recovered at last from the shock of Edwin Drood's death, freed from her lingering apprehension of John Jasper, and remembering the unfortunate engagement as only one of the episodes of a school-girl's life, learning to love her brother, and come to be so much better a companion and consoler than herself ? And had she not really hoped to be able to use that argument for patience—that proof of so much yet remaining and being worth striving for ? But of this, what was left now ? That had happened, complained of so often in another shape, by fathers and mothers who have surrounded darling daughters with the utmost wealth of parental love, to find each of them swept away, almost beyond their knowledge and quite beyond their control, in some fateful hour, by the coming of a *mere stranger*. The anxious sister had suspected—she knew only too well, now : Tartar had come, brown as some tropical fruit of which the outside gave only the least promise of the luscious feast within ; fresh and reviving in character and conversation, as she remembered some of the breezes of the very tropics of which he would speak : Tartar had come ; the empty heart was empty no longer ; Neville Landless' chances of winning her, if any he had ever possessed, were beyond recall ; and on that one possible ray of light in the future, darkness had closed down for ever. Really there seemed little left with which to cheer and comfort the discouraged ; and it needed no less than one of the Florence Nightingales of the hospitals of daily life, to remain by that figurative bedside of a wounded spirit.

So stood affairs between the young man, his sister and his narrow world, when they returned, late one evening, from a walk into which she had succeeded in persuading him—that walk, taking, oddly enough, not the Oxford and Regent Street directions, into which she was in the habit of drawing him whenever possible, but leading them through the doubtful neighborhoods of Soho and the Seven Dials. Perhaps the poor young fellow felt that he faltered less, moving among scenes of poverty and misery, than where more of luxury and enjoyment met his view : perhaps he was being led by paths which he did not understand, towards that eventually to form his life-work and lift him above all which then seemed so cruel in the providence of God.

He had been unusually silent, even for him, during their absence from the house; and when they returned to his own room, and Helena bent herself to amuse and interest him there, the same tendency continued until chased away by something quite as alarming. For many moments he sat, in the most hopeless of postures, his head upon his hand and apparently heedless altogether of the pitying face so near his own ; then a quick shudder ran over his frame, he dashed away the hair that had fallen over his eyes, sprang to his feet with something half uttered, that Helena trembled to believe a curse—and commenced striding rather than walking the floor of his apartment, with that right hand clenched as Mr. Crisparkle had seen and reprobated it, months before, and with all the more dangerous elements of his character evident in set lip and lowering brow.

"Neville ! — brother ! what excites you so fearfully ? and why will you not speak to me ?" at length asked the sister, after this angry stride of the room had continued for many moments.

"Because I am not fit to speak to you, or to any one," was the answer, coming apparently through clenched teeth. "Because there is murder in my heart, and I think I only need opportunity to prove that the worst they have said of me is true."

"Neville !—brother !" the sister repeated, in a tone that now blended alarm with her anxiety. "What do you—what can you mean ? Are you tired of *me*, and is it *me* whom you wish to kill by becoming so unlike yourself ?"

"To kill *you?* No!" he answered, for that one moment softened by the word. "No, you know that I would give my life for yours, if there was the least occasion for the sacrifice. But how do you know"—and he still kept on with clenching hand, and striding foot—"how do you know that I am 'becoming so unlike myself,' as you call it? What if I should be merely becoming *myself?*—throwing off all the shame and pretensions in which I have been wrapped even from *you*, and merely showing you the combination of weak fool and incarnate devil that I really am? They have accused me of being a murderer—if they have not put the brand of Cain on my brow, they have at least made me feel something like it burning there; and I look in the glass, sometimes when you do not see me, and wonder whether there is not a stain that will by-and-bye become visible to all eyes!"

"Oh, Neville! Neville!—my brother!"

But still he did not heed her, and went on, unceasing alike in his walk and in the torrent of mad words accompanying.

"Hush! do not interrupt me, for I know what I am saying, better than you. What if they were right after all!"

"Neville!"

The word did not come, as the preceding ones had done, as expressive of mere alarm and anxiety: it came out hardly and with a fearful effort, through lips that seemed to be frozen with horror. She repeated it, with an addition which at last arrested the foot of the reckless promenader. "Neville!— my God!—what do you mean?"

He saw, as he turned, the wild expression of her eyes: that compounding of ferocity and dread which might so easily amalgamate to Hate. He saw her clutch at the back of the chair by which she was standing: she, who never before, in all his life with her, had faltered in nerve or given sign of being moved quite beyond herself. Great fires, they say, extinguish little ones: the agony on that face recalled the half-mad man to himself in a moment; and as he caught her in his arms he said:

"Helena! Sister! What is it? What have I said or done, to move you so?"

"*What if they were right, after all!*" She repeated the words that he had used only the moment before, and with the same indefinable hardness in the intonation, as if the lips that uttered them were really stiffened by some overwhelming revulsion that could only be horror. And she did not come into his embrace, as he attempted to draw her—for the first time since they had been old enough to know the endearing names of brother and sister.

"Helena! Sister! what is it?"

She did not reply, again: she leaned back against the wall near which they were standing, closed her eyes and tried to think, while the reckless and half-unconscious cause of that agony watched her with a horrified fear only second to her own.

What was it? Simply this—nothing more nor less. For that one moment, the brother of Helena Landless, uttering words for which he had neither necessity nor warrant—dangerous and irresponsible as any madman—had stricken her to the heart with a fear that he had indeed been the murderer of Edwin Drood!

Impossible!—let no man say. There are no impossibilities in the career of madness, or in that of its kin, reckless imprudence. Nor from this hour until the Day of Doom, let any dream of characters so pure — of places in the world's esteem so high—of love so perfect in the dearest hearts as should inspire implicit confidence, that the holder may not weaken or destroy the one or the other by his own word or deed. If the worst foes of a man are those of his own household, so his worst and most dangerous manifestations may be those of his own lips—lips for which the command: "Thou shalt not bear false witness!" have an application as important, if not as general, to false witness against one's self as against a fellow-man. The world is old enough to have done with the hideous masks with which cruel boys start out from

doorways and frighten their sisters or some group of younger
children ; and it may be old enough to learn another and not-
less-needed lesson of that *property in manhood* which no one
has a right to profit, even temporarily, either in braggadocio,
passion, recklessness, or mock-humility.

Incredible that the sister could even for one moment have
doubted ? Perhaps not—all things considered. What guarantee had she, more than others, of his innocence ?   The
knowledge of what she believed to be his disposition—and his
own words of horror and loathing of the crime ? Ah ! here
were the very words of his own mouth—why not as possible
to believe as the others ?—proclaiming the fact that he had
no horror or loathing of the crime—that he had, as he himself phrased it, " murder in his heart; " that his real self was
not his better self, but that ungovernable and savage animal
impulse ; that those " might have been right, after all," who
laid the weight of blood upon his head !

This not for long : it could not be for long, without something occurring to one or both, for which no time could ever
yield a compensation.   Helena Landless, still standing and
still half out of that offered embrace, opened the eyes that had
been closed in that interval of miserable thought, and looked
into the face of her brother.   Then she came nearer, while he
stood silent and surprised—put both her hands on his two
shoulders, and looked deep into the eyes that had been a study
to her own faithful orbs since childhood.   And as she looked,
the great horror rolled away.   No—the brother of her love
might be mad, but he could not be—*was* not, a murderer, even
with his own fearful words as his accusers !   No—she had
wronged him beyond forgiveness, even in that momentary
thought !   Had she before been devoted to him ?—she must
be doubly devoted now, after having done him a wrong, of
which she almost thought—uncalculating and generous soul !
—that instead of merely entertaining it for one lightning
instant in her own mind, she had thrown it out into the world
and done him injury beyond recall !

So it was that the handsome tawny eyes changed back from their expression of doubt and terror, to one of affection unutterable. And so it was that she went into the embrace before half-refused, kissed him fondly, and said with more than all her past tenderness,—

" Poor old boy ! how weak and nervous you have grown ! and how you almost frighten me sometimes, when you fall into these dreadful moods ! "

And *he !* What was the effect upon *him,* of this culmination of morbid passion, and its result ? Diseases of the mind, more than any others afflicting humanity, often require violent remedies—as maniacs have been found restored to reason under shocks that might have been sufficient to dement the same. And such a shock had Neville Landless experienced, whether he had or had not read tho whole awful truth for one moment revealed by his sister's eyes. He had terribly shocked and pained her—that was quite enough to know. He had seemed for one instant on the verge of losing her love—of becoming to her a thing of fear and distrust : that was more than enough to probe him to the very bottom of his being, and to throw into shape and form resolutions of endurance before only too crude and general.

" Forgive me, sister, as you have forgiven me so often ! and I will try never again to pain you so much by my wild words and my mad actions." This he said, and this was all that he could say, as his arms closed around the lithe waist in that answering embrace ; and then, as the young girl disengaged herself, after a few words more of fondness and reassurance, he walked away to the window and looked out upon the summer night, leaving her to busy herself with some detail of his apartment that needed setting in order before leaving it for her own. He looked around, after a few moments, and she was gone—strangely enough, without having said good night. So he resumed his watch from the window, over the dusky roofs and the scattered lights of the great city—portions and details of a labyrinth which fitly seemed to typify his own life, that

had neither object nor prospect—but realizing more closely
than he had ever done before, the besotted folly of that man
who, lost in such a labyrinth, should merely moan and make
no effort at finding his way, or of failing to make use of those
lights, blind and confused at first, but the most intelligible of
guiding stars to the careful and the initiated. Then he heard
what he supposed her returning step, after a few additional
minutes, looked around again, and found an unbidden and unannounced stranger, who had taken that opportunity of intruding himself, in spite of the locked doors leading to the
hall-way !

He was of spare figure and middle height, with handsome
dark face and intelligent expression ; and he wore dark clothes
bespeaking him that cross between the gentleman and the
young man employed in some description of trade, the most
difficult of all classes to " place " beyond doubt. He had not
shown the courtesy, on entering the room, of removing his
round-crowned hat, which showed the peculiarity of sitting a
little high on his head; while the hair hanging beneath it
seemed a little thick and, so to speak, bunchy. Take him all
in all, he was one of those handsome young fellows, of whom
one may meet with an hundred during a day's walk, about the
better portions of London, and whom one would be likely to
pass without a second glance, unless enough at leisure and unoccupied to bestow a moment of reflection on the fact that fine
eyes and a certain feminine tidiness of manner are not monopolized by the female sex of England.

Of course Neville Landless did not need more than a second
glance to recognize his sister, though a stranger would certainly have been driven to at least a third, and even then hesitated
before speaking; and as a consequence the masquerading
young lady lost that special triumph which would have been
found in momentarily confusing and forcing the wrong word
from one who knew her best. It was not the first time, by any
means, that the brother had seen her in a corresponding disguise, though a long time had then elapsed since the last in-

stance. Seas as well as years rolled between the latest previous masquerade of that character, and the present; and he had never before seen her half so well disguised, whether for his own eyes or those of indifferent spectators. For, as he noticed at his second glance, the vest had been so skilfully "made-up," by some expert tailor or practical costumier, that the woman's shape was entirely concealed, and only the too-diminutive size of the hands and feet remained to make betrayal likely.

His first words showed the recollection of previous disguises, with which he associated the present; 'those next following gave evidence that he had no idea of any necessity for this change of personality.

"Ah, my handsome boy, again!" he said, in a lighter mood than that of any portion of the late conversation. "What name was it that you figured under, dear, the last time that we tried it, and when we made the run to Colombo, and thought that we had at last succeeded—'Joe Gilfert,' was it not?"

"Yes, 'Joe Gilfert,' and you were 'Tom Gilfert,' and we had just heard that our father was very ill in England, and were anxious to get home at once—don't you remember? But, tell me, in spite of your cruelty in knowing me at once —how well am I 'got up.' Isn't that what they call it? Would any one else recognize me readily?"

"Upon my honor, no!" he answered. "I do not believe that any other person living than myself, without a closer examination, could suspect you. How very well the figure is concealed! But tell me two things. When did you come into possession of these clothes, as I have never seen them before? and if they are new, as I think, why have you gone to the expense of procuring them? I hope not merely to amuse me!"

"No, brother, not merely to amuse you, though that might be object enough, dull and lonely as you are. I have a use for them; I have something to do in them. You see that I am answering your last question first. I need to go where I

9

cannot go in my own sex or dress, and where I can send no one to act for me; that is why your 'handsome boy, Joe Gilfert,' has come back."

"Helena, dear!" The brother had been examining her face, as she spoke, and saw that under the playful air she had assumed, there was an expression of determination, almost threatening in its earnestness. Very different to the wild, startled gaze that had met him half an hour before—the glance of her eyes, now deepening to something very like fierceness, told the intimate associate of her life that no holiday frolic was involved in this temporary unsexing of herself; that there was work of fearful earnest to be done, and that she would do it, bar her way what might.

"Helena, dear!" he repeated, "you are wiser than I am, as well as braver. No—do not stop me: I know what I am saying now, if I did not when I was speaking, only a little while ago. I shudder to see you wear that dress, wherever you may have procured it. You are going into *danger* more for me than for yourself. Can you think to what a position that reduces *me?*"

"Danger? no, brother, I do not believe that I am going into any danger whatever!" and the face of the young girl, high, hopeful, and determined, showed that she was only speaking what she believed to be the truth.

"You are going into something that may lead to meeting and collision with *him:* I know so much, quite as well as if you told me: is there no danger in that?"

"Danger, brother? No! You are right, however, in one thing. I am going into conflict with *him*, but it will not be one to involve danger worth the name—only a visit or two to an unpleasant neighborhood, and a little repulsive company, so far as I have any reason to believe."

"But—I say it again—do you realize in what a position this places *me?* Suppose that it may have been so throughout childhood, and that I endured it—what then? Is it to be so always? Our father left two children, a boy and a girl:

is the sister always to play the part of the man, to defend the
brother? and is the brother always to allow the sacrifice to be
made for him? I tell you, no, Helena. I may not understand so well what needs to be done, but you can certainly instruct me, and I have yet to learn that I am deficient in animal
courage, whatever may be my mental infirmities. You were
endeavoring to incite my true manhood, half an hour since:
will you do it by usurping the place and credit of what manhood belongs to our family? You are 'all the daughters of
our father's house:' do you wish to be 'all the sons too,' for
my sake, while I am living and with quite the average of
health and nerve? No, thank you! this must not and shall
not be!"

Helena Landless looked proudly on the speaker, as he concluded: even if there was a shade of pettishness and dissatisfaction in his words, they were nevertheless healthy and hopeful. Still there was nothing to which *she* could bow, as her
reply soon told him, with the addition of a startling item of
knowledge which almost induced him to look upon her again
in a certain doubt as to the personality.

"Stop, Neville, dear!" she said. "Before you say another
word, *I* have something to tell you which may change the
position of affairs in your mind, and show you that you do not
stand half so dependent upon me as you would persuade
yourself. Answer me one question, please. Do you believe
that in dealing with you I speak the truth entirely and
always?"

"Always and unconditionally—yes."

"That I make no reservations, mental or other?"

"I have always believed so, sister, as I know that I have
always so dealt with *you*. But why ask the question?"

"Because I have something to say, at this moment, which
may surprise you and almost lead you to believe me guilty of
subterfuge. Stay, have we not been standing long enough?
and can you not oblige Joe Gilfert, whose trousers you have
now studied to full advantage, with one chair, and yourself

with another? Thanks! You believe, Neville, seeing me in
this disguise, that I am engaged in some enterprise threatening to *him*. I acknowledge that so much is true. You
believe, next, that I am proceeding to extreme measures
against him, principally because he is threatening you more
closely,—that I am acting chiefly and in the first instance for
your protection. You need not answer: I know that you
think so. *Upon my word of honor, such is not the truth:*
I have another and a personal motive, stronger even than my
desire to keep you safe from his hands."

"Another and a *personal* motive, sister!" The tone in
which he emphasized the fourth word showed that the young
girl had been wise in recalling to his mind the habitual candor
of their intercourse.

"Yes—another and a *personal* motive, with which you can
have nothing to do, and for which you cannot be in any manner held accountable."

"What — what has HE done to *you*?" There seemed a
whole world of possibilities in that broad, eager questioning.

"HE HAS KILLED THE ONE I LOVED; and I am going to
rid, not only you, but all the world of him."

"Helena! you thought me mad, awhile ago: are *you* mad
now?"

"Mad? no—why should I be, for saying so much? I have
no reason to conceal the truth now, and from *you*. I loved
Edwin Drood—loved him at the moment when you and he
were in deadly quarrel. He did not know it—perhaps he
knows it now—farther away than Ceylon! I am going to
convict his murderer, from his own lips, before I have done
with him. That is all, but it is enough to show you, I think,
that I am not moved entirely by anxiety for *you*, and that
there are portions of my duty which I could not delegate even
to the brother I love and trust."

"You loved Edwin Drood, Helena, and I hated him!"
Neville said, after a moment, and more as if musingly than
addressing his sister. Then he sat silent for a brief space;

and then he added: "But what matter now? He is gone, and the only result is that *your* heart is broken as well as mine. But I cannot allow you to go into danger, as you probably will do, without at least demanding to *share* that danger. Let it be as you will, in other regards; but wherever you go, and whatever you do, let me go with you."

"No!" Helena spoke strongly and decisively; then pausing a moment before she went on. "No, wherever I go I am not going alone. Let that satisfy and reassure you, brother."

"I have at least a right to ask, then, who will accompany you—have I not? You will tell me so much?"

"I will tell you everything, Neville—so far as I have the right to do so. Where I am going, I have no right to tell even *you*, as yet. As to who accompanies me—it is Mr. Tartar."

"Mr. Tartar! Ah! I understand. You have answered more questions than one in that name. Mr. Tartar it is, who has procured you these clothes—I am sure of it."

"Well read, brother mine. It is indeed Mr. Tartar who has played furnishing-clothier to Her Majesty, and who will be delighted to know that His Royal Highness approves the excellent selections."

Again Neville Landless sat silent for a moment, moving one foot nervously the while, as if the limb was expressing something that the tongue yet restrained. Then he said:

"Yes, I like Mr. Tartar, as I do not every man on first acquaintance. I believe him to be a thoroughly good fellow, and that I can trust even *you* with him. Perhaps I like him the better because the same tropical sun has shone on the cheeks and warmed the blood of both of us. But, Helena— one word more. You have just told me of a heart buried in the grave of—one whom we need not again name. You are very lovely: who does not know it that comes near you? Pray take care, if you have no love to bestow upon this new friend, that you do not allow him to misconstrue your dependence upon him. A word, a glance, may do the deed; and then——"

"There is no danger, brother; Mr. Tartar's heart is already filled, and by one much more attractive than your brown-cheeked sister!" Helena hurriedly exclaimed, anxious to reassure him, and saying words that the moment after she would have given anything within her power to be able to recall.

"Ah! He has an attachment? You know the lady then, sister?"

Why did he ask the question so close upon the heels of his exclamation? Why were his tones so intense and earnest, as if the welfare of a life was involved in the words? Why were his eyes troubled and startled, again, as Helena had so often seen them since their first coming to Cloisterham? Why, but that Nature, wiser than her boasting interpreters, may have some means of conveying instantaneous warning signals, in advance of any great impending calamity—shaming the telegraph and outrunning even the beams of light: to be understood or misapprehended by the subject of the coming visitation, as he is or fails to be in that state of mind rendering such quick recognition possible? If such warnings exist, as most believe, surely here was a marked instance of the lightning conveyance of one.

The sister's voice, unknown to herself, contained it: the brother's quick sense caught it without being for the instant able to analyze it.

"You know the lady, then, sister?"

"I? No. What did I say? Oh, what an unfortunate tongue I have, to utter just what I should avoid, and give pain to those I love best! What are Mr. Tartar and his heart affairs to me?"

"That only answers one part of my question, Helena. You *do* know the lady. Who is it?"

The tender sister hesitated. How could she give that finishing blow to all still remaining of distant hope?—how destroy that one charméd spot on which to build the deficient fortitude? Very low and broken was her voice, as at last she said, after causing innumerable agonies by the useless delay:

" It is Miss Bud—Rosa."

" Ah !" This was a veritable groan, coming from the heart
of Neville Landless.   He sank back in his chair, covering his
face with both hands, as if to shut away the world and all
that it contained.   And the voice was hoarse, not now with
passion, but misery, in which, after moments that seemed
centuries to the sympathising sister, he continued :

" Tell me all, sister.   I think that I can hear it now.   All ?
Why should I ask, when I know already?   He loves her.
You are his confidante, and hers, no doubt.   Does *she* love
HIM ?"

" Heaven pity and keep us both, Neville !   No matter how
I know so much—I do know it.   She who never before knew
the meaning of the word, loves at last ; and Mr. Tartar, the
stranger whom she knew but yesterday—*he* has what cost
Edwin Drood his life, and what I would almost have given
my life to see in your possession.   She loves him dearly, and
will love him all her life."

The sister had approached the chair of her brother as she
spoke, and the two were in each other's arms as she concluded
—an appropriate but deceptive group, that seemed to be formed
of two twin brothers ; and the groan that burst from Neville's
overcharged heart, with no attempt at restraining or concealing its character, was breathed upon the bosom that no other
love had power to wean from him.

Then followed a second act in that strange drama of curative shocks, of which the first took place immediately after the
culminating moment of Neville's madness.   The Known
Worst is nothing to the Dreaded Unknown.   " I cannot bear
it," utters many a man, when the lash is descending and before it has touched the quivering flesh—many a man who, when
the moment of actual agony comes, proves that he *can* bear
nearly any torture devised by malevolent fate.   David seemed
to be moaning helplessly, while the life of the child that had
cost him and the nation so much, hung trembling in the balance : it might have been expected that he would sink entirely

in despair, forgetting all the blessings that still remained, when the servant came to him with the last formal announcement. But he rose up, then, girded himself, washed his face from the ashes that had fallen over it from the bowed head, and was a man again, with hopes, fears, duties, and a recognition of all.

So Neville Landless—far away in time as in position from the King of Israel, but heir like him to a nature that could better bear the Worst than the Dreaded,—after a moment of his pitying sister's embrace, went out of it, so to speak—put her arms gently from about him, rose from his chair, straightened the bowed shoulders with a gesture like that of throwing off a weight too long borne, and said, with a voice much firmer than had marked his utterance for many a preceding day. —

"'Thank God that it is over! She never could have been mine, after what has already occurred; and yet I was weak enough to hope against hope. Now let her love and marry a good man, as she will; and I shall live to prove to her, and to you, sister, that a *man*, who has the true meaning of the word in him, may lose Love, and suffer Wrong, and almost reach Despair, and yet rise above all and do his Life-Work bravely. Do not think that I mean to boast, dear; there will be dark hours, and many of them; and you must forget your own sorrows, to help me through them. But I will try to burthen you as little as possible; and who knows but the day may come when I may even sustain *you!*"

"My brave, noble brother, now!" exclaimed Helena, with something like a cry of joy. "Sustain me? Why, you are worth fifty of poor me, already—the moment that you *will.* Not my brother only, now: my *hero!* Kiss me good night, and promise to believe in me, and allow me to have my own way for a little while longer, before you show me how strong you really are by becoming a tyrant. For 'Joe Gilfert' must run away, now, to change himself again into your brown berry of a sister, and then to put that berry in its basket that they call a 'bed,' though I wish it was a hammock, and swinging under a palm-tree out yonder in the quadrangle!"

CHAPTER IX.

MR. TOPE'S TRIBULATION.

MR. TOPE, verger of Cloisterham Cathedral, is in trouble. Perhaps, in justice to his connection with an ecclesiastical edifice of remote antiquity, the severer form should be adopted, in speaking of his abnormal frame of mind—designating it as tribulation. Troubles, as no one could be more likely to understand than Mr. Tope himself, are vulgar—of the world, worldly. They may be suffered by the most ordinary of mortals, even down to the level of smock-frocks and hobnails. Tribulations have something clerically refined in their designation —something characterizing afflictions within the pale ecclesiastical, and even requiring a certain dignity within that pale, before they can be borne with propriety. Mr. Tope is severely within that pale ; Mr. Tope has a certain dignity, not likely to be overlooked by those who fall into his hands ; therefore Mr. Tope's discomforts shall not be troubles but tribulations.

As there are many more negatives than affirmatives in this unfortunate world, which many of us believe to have either sprung into existence wrong-end foremost, or been upheaved and misplaced by some rascally Archimedes who *did* find his lever—Mr. Tope's mental state may be more readily indicated by first mentioning what has *not* happened to disquiet him, than what has really tended to produce that effect.

Nothing has occurred during the summer to disturb Mr. Tope's proprietorship of the Cathedral—that proprietorship, unclaimed but well understood, in which all the other officials, from the Dean downwards, are mere subordinates, whatever high-sounding names they may assume—after the manner of London's famed historical Abbey, whereof only the uninitiated believe the tombs of the great to be the property of the nation, with the Dean and Chapter as virtual trustees ; while the instructed thoroughly understand that the whole gray old pile with all it contains, is the personal possession of the grave-faced and somewhat monotonous men with the black gowns and the sticks, especially of those with the sticks that are gilt-headed.   After the manner, too, if one may descend so far into the domestic relation underlying the ecclesiastical and the historic, of certain private mansions of great elegance, and fitted with "all the modern improvements," whereof the governing powers are believed to be, by many thousands of ignorant outsiders (including the poor wretches who starvingly sing Christmas Carols under the windows, and look up to those windows for slow-descending pence), the grand persons who are at intervals seen riding out from those mansions, with much state of James and John, and who are not always seen paying the bills connected with that state—instead of the real masters being James and John aforesaid, with Thomas at the door of the butler's pantry, and various and sundry Williams, Josephs, Bettys, Susans, and Marys, in those more-eclectic lower regions hidden from the eyes of permitted visitors.

Mr. Tope, to repeat the remark, has not been in any way dispossessed of his proprietorship in the Cathedral, and, re-flectedly, in the visitors who temporarily become his property, while meditatively strolling through the same to be warned from this, directed to that, impressed with the other, and stunnedly brought to a moral and physical standstill in the presence of yet another.   He has enjoyed unlimited privilege of instructing, patronizing, correcting, historically informing, covertly sneering at, and occasionally badgering in a skilful way, not to mention depleting of foreign purses and adding correspondingly to his own modest store ; for the season thus far has been a favorable one at the Cathedral (as might have been said of the same period at some watering-place).   It has enjoyed actual plethora of visitors compared with other years—whether because more men have been growing old, and thus freshly anxious to visit and inspect something yet older than themselves,—or because certain rumors and half particulars getting about of the tragedy enacted there or in

the neighborhood last Christmas-eve, there has been a little
scent of blood, so to speak, touching the human nostril at a
distance, and attracting to the place.   As an institution,
Cloisterham Cathedral has never stood so enviably before the
public eye as at this moment; and correspondingly Mr. Tope
has never before enjoyed so wide as well as undisputed an
absolute monarchy.

Nor has there been any failure in the succession of those
"discoveries," without which any old religious house must
eventually become more or less *fadé*, and lacking brilliancy of
attraction.   Thanks to the pick and hammer of Durdles,
never more recklessly employed, and never before so intelligently (for reasons which may at some future period develop
themselves), the number of Old 'Uns Unearthed, or more
properly unlimed and unmortared, has been unusually large
and interesting.   Not only have there been discoveries of
three—two mitred abbots and a knight of the shire—less deficient than usual in the details of nose and fingers, in those
closed niches of the choir and chancel where the careful seem
to have hidden everything valuable, before the coming of the
ubiquitous Cromwell and his hard-fisted Ironsides,—but older
and more remarkable discoveries, not liable to the sneers of
the Didymuses of non-ecclesiastical life, that they have been
" put there, so that they could be dug out again, and make a
new stir ; " older and more remarkable discoveries have been
made, of those whose warlike fame may have dated back to
the Crusades (judging from the mold and dilapidation of
their effigies), in that narrow space between the outer and
inner walls of the Cathedral, in the supplementary construction of which latter—a sort of ceiling—the worshippers of
something less than an hundred years ago seem to have anti-
cipated the modern professors of ventilation, and sacrificed
space to sanitary considerations, in the way of guarding ·
against the inevitable dampness of single walls.   Oddly
enough, the knowledge of such a supplementary construction
is nearly a new thing in Cloisterham ; and the merit of the

discovery, made a few months before, would seem to be nearly
equally divided between the Verger and Durdles—the latter
of whom made the first inroad with his hammer, after suspicious soundings and long speculations,—and the former of
whom very soon after discovered an entry in the expense-book
of the Cathedral, kept in the vestry, pointing to a time, late
in the eighteenth century, when large amounts were paid out
for that purpose, to stone-masons and laborers, in connection
with other sums to carpenters for the supplying and laying of
heavy timbers as the foundation for the then reconstructed
roof. So that Cloisterham Cathedral has a slight new celebrity in that regard ; though even the instructed visitor can do
little else than stare at the supplementary wall, with the
knowledge that compressed air, much darkness, and many
rats, may exist behind it, repairs to the invaded wall having
been as many and immediate as the openings.

Nor is Mr. Tope rendered unutterably wretched by the temporary absence of the Dean. His Reverence, born near the
sea-coast, and naturally anxious for his native air at enervating
periods—the latter end of summer, to wit—has betaken himself, his comely gaiters, his mild manner of repetition, Mrs.
Dean, his personal foot-bath, and other appurtenances and
belongings, easily movable, to one of the quiet sea-side resorts
of the east coast, where he has already preached twice in the
Chapel-of-ease, smoothed down the tone of society, and become
a welcome feature. Mr. Crisparkle, *his* sea-side resort lying
no farther away than the river, and his health an assured
thing while he maintains his present habits of regular exercise and equable temper,—has as little thought as opportunity
for removing the China Shepherdess and himself from the
pleasant air of Cloisterham, during the absence of the Dean—
even if the two difficulties did not exist, of packing china so
as to be removed with safety, and of carrying along to any
chosen resort, two closets and their contents, held equally indispensable. So the Dignity of the Minor Canon is by no
means diminished by the temporary removal of the greater

light; nor is that of Mr. Tope, who, perhaps, loses certain opportunities of conciliatory and deprecatory action (laughter at
very mild witticisms included), but who certainly gains in the
new necessity of so carefully arranging words that may be
good enough for any lower member of the church polity, but
will scarcely do without revisal, before the Dean. So that the
absence of His Reverence can scarcely be the grievance entitling the worthy Verger to quarter the painful arms of
Tribulation.

Nor has Mr. Tope met with domestic or pecuniary affliction
calculated to disturb his equanimity. Mrs. Tope is buxom
and active as of old, managing her somewhat extended household (divided, though not in the worst sense) with the skill of
thrift and experience. Mr. Jasper (over whose failing health
she worries in her mild way) necessarily still retains her services as purveyor and attendant; and Mr. Datchery seems so
attached to the picturesque inconvenience of Cloisterham, that
he has retained the lodgings so long window-billed and unlet,
paying his weekly liabilities with that regularity indicative of
a buffer whose means are certain, if not liberal. Once more
the Mordecai sitting in Mr. Tope's gate fails to be discovered,
and another effort is necessary to decypher that personality.

Perhaps, after all, the oppressed Verger himself may be the
proper person to whom to appeal for information ; and he may
be allowed to detail that grievance, grown to the solemnity of
a tribulation, in a conversation with Mr. Crisparkle, occurring
at that period when the Unpleasant has simply become the
Unendurable.

The Minor Canon is in conversation with his mother over an
egg and a muffin, at that hour in the summer morning when
the most golden of all lights touches the roofs and chimneys
visible across the Close from Minor Canon Corner ; and when
the birds, not yet done with the duties of the season, though
a little sobered from their exuberant voice and action of spring,
are trying to decide in their own favor the vexed question
whether flower-incense or bird-music best typifies the blest

celestial influences of which they seem to form a part. It is early; not so early, however, but that Mr. Crisparkle has enjoyed his header in the bright water in the vicinity of the Weir, and his brisk walk homeward afterwards; so that all the cheery and hopeful tendencies of his nature are in full play as he chips the shell of his egg, inhales the fragrance of his Hyson (one of his few unhealthy weaknesses—the green being always coppery, and poisonous, and inferior to the black on the score of hygiene—as any old woman can demonstrate), and looks at the browned muffin with some doubt whether it does not intend to exhale before he can come to it, in an aroma of wheat fields and the dairy.

The China Shepherdess is not quite so cheery: as how could she be? seeing that a single adoption of the morning practices, which have so invigorated her darling Sept, would unquestionably have put her beyond the remedial powers of the closet on the upper stair. And she is disposed, in her own quiet way, to tone down the spirits, to say the least, of that beloved son, who may be quite as dear to her, for all we know to the contrary, as an object on which to exercise her waning parental authority and mild captiousness, as for any and all other reasons together.

"Must you positively go to town to-day?" she asks, after a slight pause, which has only been broken by the delicate metallic sound of the chipping of the egg.

"Scarcely must, in the absolute sense, ma, dear," the Minor Canon replies, taking a spoonful of the egg with much evident enjoyment. "Only that I think I had *better* go to-day, as I do not know of anything to prevent. Is there any reason why you wish me to remain?—anything I can do for *you*, if I defer going until to-morrow?"

"No, Sept," she answers, sipping her tea; "if you are really going, either day, I do not know any difference."

Mr. Crisparkle pauses a moment, with a second spoonful of egg half-way to his mouth, before he asks, with a shade of surprise in his tone,—

"Ma, dear, do you know that there is something in your manner of speaking, though possibly you may not be aware of it—leading to the idea that you would rather I should not go to town *at all*—at present?"

"Is there, Sept, dear?" the shepherdess replies, her dear old eyes all meekness and innocent cunning. "Why, how odd! as if I could have any objection to my son, the Canon, going where he pleased!"

The Reverend Septimus Crisparkle feels that this is uncandidness, not to say a subterfuge, on the part of his parent; and he is one of those straightforward men in whom the emotional has never conquered the rational—going at once to an end which he sees before him. So he sets down the egg-cup, lays down the spoon, wipes his well-formed lips very carefully on the napkin at the edge of his plate, then rises, goes round the table behind the lady of the celestial cognomen (who of course sees nothing of all this preparation), catches her head between both hands, and draws it back, so that he can kiss her, in a sort of boyish and upside-down fashion, without any serious disarrangement of the becoming head-gear.

"There! and there! and there!" he says, between the affectionate salutations. "I thought that there was something I had forgotten this morning, and now I have it. I had only kissed you *once*, and do not remember that you kissed me back at all. Stop, please—do not attempt pulling away, for you know that would be of no use. I do not intend to release my naughty child until she behaves better, and tells me what is the real reason for her not wishing me to go to town, either to-day or to-morrow."

"Sept, dear, you are very rude,—very rude indeed! My cap will look a fright—I know it!" replies the assaulted mother, very proud and happy in her son, in spite of that indefensible violence. "There!" with two or three return kisses, soft, gentle, and apparently from lips as unwithered as when they were laid, dewy rose-leaves, on the brow of her boy, when a boy indeed—"there! Now go back to your chair, and your breakfast, like a good Sept, and I will tell you what I mean, if you *must* know."

"I *must* know, ma, dear, for the Dean is gone, and I am the highest ecclesiastical authority in Cloisterham, at the present moment," replies the clergyman, pleasantly obeying the maternal injunction, and extending it by attacking the muffin, which has taken the opportunity to cool from its late everheating.

"Every time that you go to town, Sept, my dear, you call upon that unfortunate young man, whom you will persist in designating as your 'pupil,' though he is nothing of the kind. I think I am right; I do not recollect your coming back, without making some remark with reference to him or his studies."

"Well, ma! is there anything extraordinary in that?" queries the Minor Canon, as she pauses. "I know that you had very serious objections to the young man, last winter, at the time when the—the unfortunate circumstance of poor young Drood occurred; but I had no idea that you held the same objection to him now that he is out of your sight, and at such a distance. Do you believe that he can corrupt or contaminate me in any way, even if the worst of the suspicions against him should be true, as I am quite confident as ever that they are not?"

There is a little additional flush of red on that portion of divine pottery forming the cheek of the China Shepherdess, as its owner replied, after a moment, lying back in her chair with a grace shaming that of the young, and making no pretence at emulating her son, and continuing the breakfast with the conversation :—

"I do not like the young man, Sept, my dear, as you know. I do not see how I have had any cause to change my unfavorable opinion. He had a terrible temper; that even *you* must admit; indeed I have heard you speak of it quite freely, and with reprobation."

"Yes, ma, he had a most violent temper; but I hope and

believe that we have seen the worst of that," interpolated Mr. Crisparkle, with his utterance not at the moment clear enough for the sacred desk, owing to the presence of the muffin.

"I am sure that I hope so, Sept—very sure that I hope so," the old lady goes on. "We should not only work for, but hope for, every reformation in the characters of those who— who give us any cause to fear for their future, either on their own behalf or that of others. Still, I am not likely to be highly pleased with the young man, I think; and I must tell you candidly, my dear son, that I am not likely to be better pleased with *his sister*."

The Reverend Septimus Crisparkle is a man in whom all the faculties are held under good control—those of the body as well as the mind; but the slight flush on the face of his mother is nothing to the blazing red which at the moment invades his whole countenance, coming up with the suddenness of the Aurora flaming over the Northern sky, and only reaching its zenith beneath the roots of his hair. No school-boy, detected in one of the high crimes or misdemeanors of juvenility, could more ingenuously supply evidence against himself at the moment of accusation.

He is aware of the inglorious fact—as no man can very well be ignorant where a stream of hot blood plays up and down his face with the force of a torrent! And the China Shepherdess is aware of the *triumphant* fact, even though her eyes may not be so young or so keen as they were five-and-forty years ago. She is almost sorry that she has spoken, seeing the effect produced, and possibly misapprehending its meaning, to the extent common with the keenest-eyed mothers (not to mention the fathers) of any age; and he—But he is, as he lately remarked, the highest ecclesiastical authority in Cloisterham, in the absence of the Dean; and he may well be allowed to answer for his own sensations.

"I understand you, ma, dear," he says, after a moment, when the hot blood has flowed back a little towards the heart, temporarily deserted, and when his utterance, for the time em-

10

barrassed, has again become clear. "I understand you, from your emphasis, without your saying another word! You believe that in my visits to Neville Landless I am in the habit of meeting his sister?"

"Yes, Sept, dear, I do believe so."

"You go farther, ma—you believe that I seek such meetings quite as eagerly and anxiously as those with her brother?"

"I do, Sept, dear; I do."

"You believe, ma—for you see that I must put your suspicions in plain words—that I am in love with Helena Landless?"

The mother pauses a moment looking, as close as age will permit, into the eyes of her son. Then she answers, almost as concisely as she has before answered the other questions :—

"Yes, Sept, dear; I am sorry to believe so, but I do."

The Minor Canon has ended his breakfast, now; though there stands a neglected egg in the second egg-cup, and he has only finished a single dish of tea. There are such things as chokings in the throat, during the reign of which there is not much more chance of swallowing than of enjoying after deglutition; and the clergyman has come to one of those periods —happily for health and digestion, very rare with him. He leans back in his chair, as his mother is still doing, and addresses her with much calmness and gravity, and without any suspicion in the face of the late flush :—

"Ma, dear," he says; "you have just placed me in a strange position for a grown man of my years; and in doing so you have made it necessary for me to say a few words that might never have been said under other circumstances. Do not interrupt me, please, while I say them; and do not think that you know all, at any moment, until I have quite done."

"Sept, dear, have I given you pain? If so, forgive me; for what I said, I said for the best, and I will never again refer to the subject, if you do not wish."

The mother's face is very tender and anxious, now. It may be very set, in its own ways and fancies, sometimes, but it is

a dear old face, full of a true mother's love, after all ! And
for that something may be forgiven, as well as much for
Mary !

"No, ma, dear," the Minor Canon replies. "Do not make
any apologies, whatever you may have driven me to say. It
is best that it should be so. I have never had a secret from
you before, and this shall be one no longer. You are equally
right and wrong. I seldom, almost never, meet Miss Landless when I call upon her brother; so that she has nothing
whatever to do with my visits to town. So much for that.
Now for the next. I love Helena Landless, with all the heart
that I can allow myself to hold for any earthly object; or,
rather, I should say, perhaps, that I *did* love her with that
intensity—for the passion, please God, is under my feet, after
a long struggle, and it will never rise to trouble me again,
unless I grow weaker than I believe. You saw the red flush
on my face : it was not that of shame—only one of sudden
agitation and surprise."

"You *must* let me interrupt you *so* much, Sept, dear," the
mother says, "I knew it was surprise, not shame, on the face
of my dear son."

"Thank you, ma, dear; though I might have known so
much. I have only to tell you, further, that I more love and
admire Miss Landless, both in person and character, than I
have words to express—more than any other person whom I
have ever seen. And then I have to add, what my words
may already have conveyed—that she does not know of what
I may call my past regard for her, and will never know ; that
we will never be more to each other than we are to-day; and
that I only ask one favor of you, with reference to her, never
to speak of her, or if you do so at all, only in terms of that
respect which is the due of a noble woman."

The Minor Canon ceases ; the mother, almost stricken
dumb by this avowal, and by the feeling that it is for *her*
her son has made such a renunciation, reverses the action of
a few moments before, rises from her chair, comes round

behind him, throws the dear old arms about his neck, and
kisses him repeatedly, while her words are a loving murmur
of admiration and (yes, let the practical truth be added!)
gratification—such as the possessor of the costly new bracelet *does* feel in the ownership of that desired ornament, in
addition to any unselfish love for the donor.

" My dear Sept! my good, thoughtful son! can you ever
forgive your poor old mother for the pain she has caused you?
and can *she* ever repay you for the sacrifice you have made
for *her?*"

Mr. Crisparkle is very nearly himself again, already—very
nearly his own bright, cheery self, oblivious of personal discomfort and on the alert for any duty or any employment
promising a new and harmless sensation. He kisses his
mother again, with almost the same effusion she herself
exhibits, then clears himself from the entangling arms by a
little gentle force, setting the China Shepherdess safely in the
middle of the floor by the act, and asks, pulling out his watch
with habitual vivacity,—

" May I go to London, now, ma, dear? Yes? Then I
shall not have much more than time enough to catch the
half-past ten train. Here is my coat—reach me my hat,
there, like a good old darling, as you are, and so away we go.
Good-bye, until I return."

He assumes the hat with a haste which seems unclerical,
but which never has the effect of making him untidy, throws
on the coat with corresponding speed, grasps his umbrella,
gives the parting kiss to his mother, and is out of the door
and into the temporarily bright sunlight of Minor Canon
Corner, all within the space of less than a minute.

Where he is confronted by Mr. Tope, whose customary
black, no darker than his own, would not be likely to affect
the general appearance of the whole Cathedral vicinage, but
whose face, heavy, downcast and discouraged-looking, with a
soupçon of that expression graphically designated as " injured
innocence," certainly does produce a darkening effect on the
whole cluster of surroundings.

"Good morning, Mr. Crisparkle. Proud to see you looking so well, sir."

(Mr. Tope does not look as if " proud " of anything; but his word must be taken—at least with the " not-at-homes " and " pleased-to-see-yous " of polite society.)

" Ah, Tope—good morning. But you are scarcely looking your best—are you, Tope ? " (Mr. Crisparkle has just emerged from a severe exercise of candor, and is still quite under the influence of the action). " Ill in any way ?—I hope not. The weather is certainly oppressive — at least I hear some, who feel it more than myself, saying so. Anything from the Dean, Tope ? "

Mr. Crisparkle says all this briskly and a little hurriedly, as one who has not many minutes left in which to catch the ten-thirty train ; and his motion is towards the High Street, where he will be obliged to make a long leg, now, or forfeit an omnibus sixpence.

" No—nothing from His Reverence, sir, since day before yesterday," answers Mr. Tope. " He was very well, then, as you know. As for myself—you were good enough to inquire about me—I am not sick, thank you ; but I am that worried, Mr. Crisparkle."

" Worried? I am sorry, Tope. But you must excuse me if I hurry away. I am going to catch the train."

" The train ? oh, certainly, sir. Excuse my stopping you ; and what I have to say to you—"

" Oh, you have something to say to me ? What say, then, to walking with me to the station ? Not far, and splendid exercise. Come, the walk will do you good ; and you can say what you wish as we go easily along."

Mr. Tope is " in for it," and quite aware of the fact. The steady and unlaboring stride of the Minor Canon is a proverb about Cloisterham, where few men take their constitutionals with the same regularity, and where possibly there are few of the same vigorous natural constitution, unimpaired by the least mental or bodily excess. The Verger's tendencies,

though he is by no means a plethoric man, are towards moderate motion, with many pauses, as becomes one in the habit
of making very slow tours about the Cathedral, putting in a
perambulatory comma at short intervals, and a semicolon, or
even a colon, at no considerable distances apart.   He is, however, as already said, in for accompanying the rapid walker, at
whatever peril to his breathing apparatus; and he submits
with what grace he may.   The brief conversation following,
as the two measure their way down the High-street towards
and over the bridge at a rate indicating that they are scan-
dalizing the Cathedral town by walking for a wager, is consequently somewhat interjectory in its character; and that part
of it contributed by the Verger may be said to lack full breath
at intervals — of course, without the least suspicion on the
part of the Minor Canon that he is proceeding at a rate to
distress a mere invalid.

"Now then, Tope, what is the subject of your worry?   Out
with it, man, or we shall be at the station before you have
concluded, if the matter is at all important.   Anything wrong
about the Cathedral, Tope?"

"Not about the Cathedral, Mr. Crisparkle; and yet I am
not that sure but it has some connection with it.   Have you
noticed, sir, that Durdles is drunk less of the time than usual
of late?"

"Humph! why certainly, Tope; you do not consider *that*
a matter to worry about, do you?   *I* could bear it, I think,
if he should remain sober all the time; and so should you do,
if you have not grown to consider him a part of the Cathedral,
to be exhibited slyly to visitors, and the more tipsy the better.
Perhaps Durdles may be following a little more closely than
before that 'work of art' about which you and I know so
well.   Why not?"

"It is not Durdles being soberer than he used to be as
makes me think that there is something wrong, sir," puffs
the Verger, already beginning to labor in wind at the rate of
climbing a long stair, "but his having more money than he

seems to earn — gold, sometimes, as has been seen at the Queen's Head, and being in the employment, evidently, of persons that nobody in Cloisterham knows nothing about."

"Knows *anything* about, you probably mean, Tope," corrects the clergyman, momentarily forgetting the absence of the Dean, for whose delicate ears the lingual roughness of the Verger are principally smoothed. "But who gives Durdles money that he does not earn?—and what stranger employs him in a way to make *you* uncomfortable?"

"You know my lodger, Mr. Datchery, sir," Mr. Tope rather asserts than asks.

"Mr. Datchery—yes, I have seen him, several times," Mr. Crisparkle assents. "A pleasant, odd sort of person, so far as I have observed—quite a regular attendant at service, and with a droll practice—has he not?—of going into the street without his hat, as if he had once been in the habit of living in bare-headed Ireland?"

"The same, sir," puffs Mr. Tope, "though you may not have observed quite so much of him as others. There is nobody in Cloisterham as knows anything about him, and he strikes me all of a heap, sometimes, acting that suspicious—"

"Pays for his room, and — his other bills, does he not, Tope? If not, why keep him?" interrupts the Minor Canon, talking as he is walking, quite at his ease.

"Oh, yes, excellent pay, sir; but that isn't what is so suspicious. You must know, sir, that as the lodgings are mine— that is, Mrs. Tope's, and immediately below where we live ourselves——"

"You enjoy excellent opportunities for knowing what he does: in fact, keep a little delicate observation over him— what some persons would call 'peeping' in a moderate degree!"

"Mr. Crisparkle is kind enough to complete the sentence, which seems to lack breath of itself.

"Not 'peeping,' exactly, sir," answers the Verger, his breath recovered by the relief, but evidently not flattered by the mode in which it has been supplied, "only observing of things as cannot very well have the go-by."

"Umph! well?" assents Mr. Crisparkle.

"Now, what I put that and that together, and make out that something is going on in Cloisterham, as the Dean and Chapter ought to know, and don't—is that Durdles and this Mr. Datchery is thick as two thieves."

"A rather coarse simile, and not a very charitable one: I would not use it, Tope—at least I would not at any time when the Dean happened to be present."

Mr. Crisparkle again corrects, having breath to spare, and falling again into the old habit.

"Well, sir, under correction," Mr. Tope tries to assume the dignified—not to say the injured, but with moderate success, from the lack of force to throw out the words with the proper readiness, "it stands to reason that a man living on his means, like Mr. Datchery, as must *have* means to live on 'em, wouldn't take up, for company, with such riff-raff as Durdles——"

"Riff-raff — an inelegant phrase always, Tope, besides being a collective noun, when used, and so implying more than one—I would not use it for Durdles alone, who is only one, unless you include his bundle," again pleasantly corrects Mr. Crisparkle.

"That he wouldn't take up with such as Durdles, and have him with him for hours on hours, whether drinking or not, or doing worse, nobody can say—not to mention giving him money that free—if there wasn't something between 'em as is dangerous."

Mr. Tope, ignoring the last interruption, manages this long sentence with much dexterity—really seems to be getting what the athletes call his "second wind."

"And does he do so, Tope? I mean, does he do so to your own personal knowledge, or do you only speak from a certain suspicion, founded on knowledge of Durdles and dislike of Mr. Datchery?" asks the Minor Canon, with more show of absolute interest than he has before displayed since the commencement.

"They are together that frequent, Mr. Crisparkle, and that sly, that the Dean and Chapter ought to know it, before the worst comes to the worst," Mr. Tope asserts, strongly and conclusively. "And at nights—I wouldn't believe it, sir, if I hadn't heard it with my own ears—but Durdles has been in Mr. Datchery's room, up to past midnight, a matter of three hours at a time, and they a-talking, talking, talking all the time, as if there was a plot to burn down the town, or do something to——"

"The Cathedral." Mr. Crisparkle kindly concludes this sentence, which is again a little laboring for breath.

"Yes, sir, the Cathedral, which cannot be too much thought of, in my opinion," supplements Mr. Tope, with real dignity, and again recruited wind.

"Of course not, Tope; the Cathedral cannot be too much thought of. And there may be a mystery here, as you say. I am glad that you have told me, though I do not think that there is any great cause for anxiety. If I was you, Tope, I would not say anything of this to any one else,—except Mrs. Tope—of course, except Mrs. Tope. I will speak of it to the Dean, when I see him; and I scarcely believe that they can do any serious damage to the town before His Reverence returns. Thank you very much for your confidence, Tope. By the way, how is Mr. Jasper? for the last twenty-four hours I have not seen him; and I am sure that he has not been looking well of late."

"Mr. Jasper was quite well, sir, last night; and he went out early this morning. Possibly *he* may have gone to town already."

"Ah! Happy to hear that he is so well. But here we are, Tope, and I must bid you good morning. So much pleased to have had your company, and hope that the little walk has done you good."

Mr. Crisparkle, who has caught something vindictive in the

hiss of the steam from the engine-pipe—as if that harnessed
motive-power had borne the restraint nearly as long as it intends to do, and is about to go off independently, if no one is
ready to accompany,—Mr. Crisparkle, not frequently enough
a traveller to require a season-ticket, takes a header into the
booking-office only less pronounced than his late one into the
river, and emerges thence, in an inconceivably short space of
time for a man who has forced out a ticket through the small
hole in the interim. He comes out; not too soon, however—
just in time to spring into a carriage commencing to move,
without subjecting himself to the penalties of the forty-shil-
lings rule, which the Boxing Compass Railway Company, naturally jealous of the forms of carrying out any homicidal rights
in it inherent, rigidly enforces against all offenders who presume to peril their lives out of due course.

Mr. Tope, remembering that he is away from the Cathedral,
and therefore at liberty to unbend, is leaning against a post
of the station, without the least pretence at dignity, recovering his full breath after his late exhausting performance on
the field of Captain Barclay, and feeling less oppressed with
his tribulation, now that he has made the Dean and Chapter
prospective sharers in it.

The Minor Canon, recovering no breath whatever, and only
in the pleasant glow of a man who has taken the briefest of
morning walks at a brisk pace—indeed, momentarily hum-
ming a bit of refrain, as if to show how little breathed he is—
leans back in his seat as the train rolls away, and muses for a
moment on the oddity of the white-headed man, oblivious of
his hat, and the folly of Tope's story, which is likely to have
no better foundation than some one of the freaks of that oddity.
But this reflection fades away ; the late conversation over the
breakfast table is not one to be forgotten in half an hour.
And somehow there grows and assumes shape, on the seat
opposite to him, the pliant and graceful figure of a woman—
young, tawny, Oriental—with dusky brown eyes that seem
capable of infinite love, as well as infinite fierceness, and sweet

firm lips that have once been laid on a hand which has never forgotten the pressure, or lost the pleasant warmth on one favored spot. And across the whole figure—blurred in indistinct lines of soft light, like a phosphorescence—he reads one single fateful word, (and bows his head thereto with a thought of silent prayer for that strength not to be found on the path or in the river) : " LOST ! "

CHAPTER X.

CARRIED AWAY.

Rosa has occasion, one afternoon, for some of those small indispensables of the female work-table, more intricate and foreign to the coarse male mind than ever were the famed Eleusinian mysteries to those outside the pale of that especial worship. Something—who may guess what?—has gone astray with the spools, the skeins, the dainty bits with which the still daintier little fingers busy themselves, during so many hours that cannot be devoted to intellectual occupation even of the lightest form. Something is missing, without which life would become temporarily a burthen, and the sending for which, by a domestic, would almost inevitably result in the bringing home of articles bearing the same relation to the actual things needed that the ceremonious delivery of, say a prize turkey, or six brace of partridges, would bear to the reception of the pet canary carefully ordered. Result, Rosa has no choice but to exhibit the pretty school-girlish form and habit in the streets, by going out personally on the all-important errand.

It is approaching evening; but the summer twilight is still long, though the extreme afterglow of June is some weeks gone by. Rosa (once away from Cloisterham and a certain fear connected with that place of mystery) has still remaining a little of the school-girl fancy for freedom and unaccompanied

wandering; and she does not ask Miss Twinkleton, as she
might so properly do, to lay aside the crochet out of which
some wonderful monster in coarse worsteds is arising to torture
an unfortunate chair, and accompany her on her quest that
will only occupy half an hour.

So Rosebud goes out alone, very little before the evening
lamps are lighted—down the little distance into Holborn, and
thence eastward towards the shop of that fortunate draper
who has succeeded in securing the Appointment to supply
small-wares to this peculiar Small Majesty. Oddly enough, as
she trips, she pays little attention to her actual surroundings,
and does not even speculate at length on the purchases which
it may be proper to make when arrived at Bolding's—being
engaged, mentally, on one of those longer and more important
tours which Youth and love sometimes go out to make, together, assuming the length of a voyage, and altogether inde-
pendent of bad carriages and cabins, mixed connections, railway accidents, storms and wrecks at sea, and all the other
thousand-and-one disagreeables which beset travellers by the
usual humdrum earthly modes. She has—dear little atom of
incarnate girlhood !—just now a companion whose bodily presence is not visible to the passers on the streets : indeed, she is
only dreamily conscious, herself, of his accompanying her ; but
she floats, and sails, and skims many millions of miles with
him, over the sea and the mountains of Fancy-Land, and only
comes down to the lower earth when a baker's small boy, with
a belated board of steaming and fragrant edibles, nearly knocks
off her mite of bonnet, and clumsily apologises for the accident
which her own abstraction has principally occasioned.

Thereafter she is a shade more cognizant of the earth, the
bipeds crawling upon it, and the clumsy erections with which
builders have disfigured while they fancied that they were
ornamenting .it. She goes on quite steadily, now—manages to
cross the street, between four cabs going in four different directions, with an impunity which a bulkier person than the little
beam of light might fail in finding,—and soon thereafter is

dispensing delight and trouble throughout the whole domain of small-waredom. Three shopmen wait upon her, under helpless but happy protest, to the neglect of other and more important customers (amounts of purchase considered) ; spools roll towards her, on the counter, with an apparent desire of forcing themselves into her infinitesimal reticule, to the no small danger of her being arrested, on going out, for a very cheap species of shop-lifting ; light goods get into hopeless tangles and snarls of unrolled condition, for the same or similar causes ; and when at last she trips out of the draper's with a few ounces added to the weight of her reticule, and a shilling or two correspondingly subtracted from the avoirdupois of a purse which might have been made by the skilled artificers of Lilliput—then the draper and all his assistants draw long sighs of mingled regret and relief, and the business of the establishment once more resumes its natural conditions.

It is nearly dusk when the purchaser, thus heavily burthened, recrosses the street, and returns up the north side of Holborn, past Furnival's and Holborn Bars. Nearly dusk, but the lamps are now alight, and for all practical purposes it is broad day. She must hurry home, however, for her promised half-hour is already overstayed, and there may be worry on account of her. Hurry home, of course—but, ah, how beautiful are those pictures in the shop-front,—and is there any charm remaining to us from childhood, so potent as that of looking in at the pictorial windows ?—possessing, for the time, all the graces and wonders in form and scenery there displayed, without the cost of purchase, or the difficulty of knowing what to do with the coveted gems if in actual ownership !

A few moments more go in this way ; the falling dusk comes closer ; and now she must really hurry, indeed. A little tremor of terror, at being in the street alone, later than ever before, creeps over her, accompanied by a half-wish that she had started earlier, or that she had asked Miss Twinkleton to accompany her. She trips, rapidly, very rapidly now ; the baker's boy, if he should chance to be returning with his empty board, would be in danger of meeting a different momentum from the same small body, in the event of a second collision.

She is just opposite the archway of Gray's Inn, when a sudden shadow seems to fall upon her path : not the night, for that is shutting down but slowly ; not any extraordinary giving out of that illuminating vapor by which the good people of London are habitually allowed to see that it has become dark, for such a change would be physically impossible. They are the face and figure of a man, throwing the sudden shadow which alike affects eyes and brain; and the man is John Jasper.

He stands at the western side of the archway, with his face in the direction from which Rosa is proceeding; and the young girl, looking up at the sudden Presence, recognizes him at once, as it is only too certain that he recognizes *her*—only too probable that he has been keeping a watch on her movements, and meeting her thus of set purpose.

It is she who first speaks—incapable of seeming not to recognize him : by no means strong enough for the sudden movement that might carry her past him in that frightened rush which comes into her mind, but does not communicate itself to the limbs. She utters in her fear, only the one exclamation—his name :

" Mr. Jasper ! "

" Miss Bud ! Rosa ! " he answers, his voice hoarse, and broken enough to be himself under the influence of a fear corresponding to hers, or some other emotion quite as powerful.

" Excuse me, pray !—and good night. It is late, and I must be at home."

The brain has communicated its will to the limbs, now, and she attempts to walk past him. Without allowing her to come into collision with him, he yet steps before and bars her away.

" Excuse *me*, Rosa !—you do not think to leave me with only a word, do you ? " he exclaims, in the same hoarse and broken voice. "No—I have something to say to you before we part—something that *must be said.*"

"Mr. Jasper, if you are a gentleman, you will allow me to pass on; for it is late, and I must not be away from my lodgings any longer," she musters strength and courage to say, though she is aware that strength and courage are both oozing away from her, in some unaccountable manner, in that Presence which seems to *compel* her like a tyranny.

"No—you must not, shall not go, until I have said what I have to say," is his reply, still standing in her way.

"Please let me go on!" she implores. Then a frightened threat with no awe in it. "If you do not, I will call for help—for the police!"

"No, you will do nothing of the sort," he answers, with that assurance in his voice which shows how well he under- stands her last words. "No—you have escaped me—run away from me; and you have been fool enough—pardon my plain words!—to suppose that you had escaped me altogether. Do not imagine it. I am a man not easily balked, where I have set my mind; and what when I have set my *heart?*"

"Oh, Mr. Jasper——" again she attempts to implore, but more feebly than before. He cuts her short, and the sentence is never finished.

"Stop! what you are about to say will be of no use—worse than of no use. Listen: do you remember the last time that I spoke to you—by the sun-dial, in the garden of the Nun's House?"

She does not answer: he does not intend or desire that she should do so; he only wishes that she should remember, and oh, how keenly and shudderingly she does that!

"You tried to get away from me, then, and you could not do so. You cannot, now. I have waited for this hour, ever since you ran away: it is mine, and I am not to be disappointed."

The young girl feels that the fearful magnetism of his will is conquering her—has conquered her. She is literally powerless, firmly as the heart may rebel against the tyranny. She is as much alone with this man, here on the pavement of one of the most frequented of London streets, as she could be in a desert. For though persons are passing and repassing, some of them almost touching her skirt as they go by, she has no more power to call for aid than if she possessed no physical tongue.

"Turn into this archway with me for a few moments," he says. "There is a Square beyond where we can converse without attracting too much attention."

"No, I cannot—I will not!" she speaks, mechanically.

"You both can and will, Rosa!" he replies. "Come—I go on; you follow."

She endeavors, with what power she has—not to obey him. She recognizes every reason why she should not and none why she should; and yet she feels that her limbs are turning in the direction he points—that she is going through that dusky archway into the Square of which she knows nothing! She summons strength to propound one condition and he accedes to it—mercifully.

"If I go in there with you, will you promise not to touch me? Will you swear?"

"You should go in, without any promise from me whatever; but I will humor one of your whims. How many of your whims would I not humor, Rosa, to have you take me, even though you hated me, trampled and even spat upon me, at the same time! Yes, I swear that you shall go into that square, and come out again, without my touching you. Is that enough?"

It *is* enough. It must be. She has no strength to make the condition otherwise than sufficient. He moves within the archway, and she follows, walking mechanically, and more as one might do, with short, jerky steps, in a somnambulic dream, than with the ordinary motion of waking life. He does not touch her, though walking very near; and yet she has no more power to go away from him, at the instant when her whole soul is moved by the extremity of mingled fear and abhorrence, than if he held her by chain or cord.

A few yards, and they are in the South Square of Gray's Inn, where the lights throw a sickly glare on the dull bricks of the Hall and Chambers, and where, even at that hour, the very spirit of dismal loneliness and sequestration from the world seems to reign.

Here he stops, she within two or three feet of him, and resumes what he has been saying in the street. The words seem indefinably very near her ears; and yet, on the other hand, she appears to be hearing them across miles of distance. They are near enough to excite helpless terror: they are far enough away to suggest that any help or deliverance is as remote as they are beyond hope or expectation.

" Rosa," he says, his voice hoarse but steady, now, as if he had conquered any tremor in it, " Rosa, look at me."

Mechanically she obeys, as she has been doing all else mechanically. For the first time, under the full light of the lamp near which they have stopped, she sees his face with the opportunity of observing it; and she feels that it would be pitiful, if she were not so cruelly in his power, to mark the inroads which even a few weeks have made in face and figure. The figure seems shrunken and a little bowed, as it was not in those other days so near in reality though seeming so very far in the past; the clothes, though scarcely shabby, are arranged with less than the old care, and have that indescribable air of belonging to one who no longer pays the full regard of his natural disposition to external appearances. But the worst change is in the face, and that she observes most closely as in the best light. That face, too, seems shrunken, like the figure; even under the lamp-light it is yellow and hard, like parchment; the lips are drawn sharply over the teeth, and have lost fulness; and the eyes are burning—burning—two coals that may contain the spark of fever or of madness.

" You have looked at me," he says, after a moment. " I feel your eyes, as I feel every pulse and faculty of you, and as

11

you—cruel girl!—do not feel *me*, except as I compel you. You see how I am changed? You do—I know that you do."

He appears to wait for an answer. She answers mechanically, after the manner of everything else that she has done.

"Yes, Mr. Jasper, you are changed."

"I am changed, I know it!" he resumes, almost fiercely. "And what has changed me? *You!* You have bewitched me. I know what the witchcraft of olden time is, now. You pretend that you have not done it—that you have not intended to do it: bah! I know what such language means, in the mouths of beautiful little fiends like yourself."

"Oh, Mr. Jasper! why, why will you say such awful things!" she begins to exclaim, a little relieved, by very fear —and horror, from her stupor. But he cuts her short again.

"I knew how it would be—you would deny everything. But it is of no use, and it is too late. You cannot escape me, as you see; and how much longer is this farce to be kept up? Your new lover, Neville Landless, has the rope around his neck, already, that *I* have placed there; and I have brought you here to-night to ask you once more, and for the last time, whether you have duly weighed what I said to you in the garden of the Nun's House, and whether you intend to make me any repayment for the ruin of body and soul that you have caused?"

For the first time, since the meeting in front of the archway, poor little Rosá breathes freely—almost shakes off the spell which has so far held her. A wonderful relief has come —yet how horrible! This man, of whom her terror has been so extreme from a widely different cause, has changed to her in a moment: he is simply *mad*—nothing more nor less; and she has far slighter fear of the mere madman than of the same evil man with his magnetic tyranny. She has even (so subtle is the principle of vanity in the human breast, forgiving that is done for love of *us!*) a certain pity for the man who seems to have been more than half-crazed for her sake, however evil and dreadful he may be in other regards.

But the difficulty of the situation is by no means removed, whether her suspicions be true or false—as she is soon to remember. For the hard-drawn lips, for one moment silent, take up the fearful refrain almost immediately.

"I repeat my inquiry, Rosa, darling, and I repeat it for the last time. I told you, before, that you might do what you would—that you might cast me off (that included running away), but that you would never be rid of me. That no one should come between us, or I would crush him as I crush this lump of gravel under my heel. That I would pursue you to the death."

The terror returns, in intensity if not altogether in kind, as he repeats the language of their last interview. How terrible is her situation! and how can she escape him, as escape him she must, and at once, at any hazard!

"Mr. Jasper," she says, in the calmest voice at command, "I hoped that you would not keep me here so long. It is so very, very wrong; and what will they say of me at my lodgings? Indeed, indeed, you must allow me to go, now!"

"What, Rosa!—without my answer? No—never think it! You hoped something else, no doubt,—that you might never see me again! Do not hope that, either! You do not leave this spot until you have answered my question—asked for the last time. Will you throw away your new lover, as you threw away the old, and be *mine?*"

It is almost a scream that bursts from the young girl's lips in reply—the utterer scarcely aware of the utterance, but moved thereto by much in the past and much more in the present—that shadowy but most real image accompanying her when she first set out on her unfortunate errand.

"Oh, no! no! no! How can you ask me again, when I have already told you that I cannot? Oh! why will you torture me so?"

He is silent for a moment; then his voice is hoarse as the very roaring of a torrent, as he says:

"I understand you, then, Rosa, to refuse me, unconditionally and always? Let there be no mistake between us, that both of us might regret, some day. You refuse to be mine, *ever?*"

"Yes! why will you make me say again what I do not like to repeat?—and why do you keep me so?"

"I will keep you no longer, Rosa—Miss Bud," he answers, very calmly, to all appearance. "Come—what we have to say here is said: you wish to *go.* Let the consequences be on your head, if you are afterwards sorry for the conclusion of this interview."

He does not touch her, as he has sworn that he would not. He turns towards the narrow archway by which they have entered—his face, whatever it expresses, hidden from her view by his turning away from the light. She follows, only a little behind and at his left—little less than astounded at the comparative calmness with which he has received her hopeless refusal, even though there is a terrible threat in that calm utterance. Only let her get out of his power, now, she thinks, and the future may take care of itself, especially as she will take that portion of the "care" involving her never again being in the street alone, under any circumstances, while *he* lives! Only let her get home now, before Miss Twinkleton and the rest have grown too much alarmed about her!

Mr. Jasper maintains his wonderful calmness, and no other word passes between them. They repass the archway, as they entered, and are once more in the street. The danger, whatever it may have been, is over.

Just then occurs something, the explanation of which may be as difficult to Rosa, twenty years hence, as at the moment. She has, if her brain is capable of taking in the philosophy of facts in an instant, another illustration of the folly of supposing that we know when absolute danger begins or ends, the term being a relative one.

There must be a cab standing at the curb—a four-wheeler, with the door open. There must be, though she does not see it, and though she may never know how it comes to be in that place at that juncture, and whether the fare so suddenly supplied is that for which the cabman has previously agreed under "Act of Parlyment." For her first knowledge is, that she is being lifted off the ground, and thrust into the cab, with such instantaneous action that she has neither the power to resist nor the thought to scream; her second, that her companion rather hurls a command to the driver than gives him a direction; her third, that he is inside the cab, beside her, and with his hand upon her mouth, almost at the same instant when she has arrived at the two previous conclusions; and her fourth, that the cab is whirling rapidly away towards Oxford Street and the Circus.

There are circumstances under which the brain of an inexperienced school-girl can manage to combine incidents with tolerable rapidity and clearness; and poor little Rosebud, in the moment or two following, springs quickly to certain most reasonable additional conclusions. She understands it all, now —why she has been taken into the Square; that she might be driven to a final answer; why she has been kept so long there : that the dusk might be deeper on coming out; beyond this, that she is being carried off by the man—mad or worse—whom she a few moments ago pitied, and for some horrible design or purpose, beyond guess as to its atrocity. Here her frightened thought stops, very naturally : more experienced persons than she might find difficulty in going further.

She struggles, of course, and attempts to cry out. The effort is vain; for one arm of her abductor is around her slight form, holding her without difficulty, and the other hand is over her mouth, using just so much force as silences her, and no more. And how, even in the worst of her terror, she shudders under the pressure of hand and arm! He would not touch her in the Square! No, he could easily swear to so much; but how cruelly he can touch, now!

But the hand over the mouth, though one of the most effectual of gags, is not one of the best, from the fact that the experimenter may find other use for the member, and that then sudden removal may be awkward. John Jasper (expert in certain details of drapery—scarfs, to wit!) may be impressed with this idea; for he very soon makes the attempt to substitute the hand by binding a handerchief over the sweet little mouth; and that attempt is—so to speak—fatal.

By some inadvertence, in this operation, the Choir-Master makes the mistake of allowing one of his fingers to slip between the two rows of pearly teeth that he has so often and so much admired. Recognizing the fact and their duty simultaneously, the teeth close upon it as if it constituted part of the most dainty morsel ever crunched—one of the true Lumps of Delight, of which the others are only faint types and shadows. The sharp pearls set into it like a vice; no jerk, short of one tearing off the finger, seeming to be capable of removing it. The abductor needs both hands in the effort, groaning, in spite of himself, under the agony. And the partial release of the body enables the young girl to swing herself nearer to the side of the cab, and to make her hitherto deferred assault on the glass of the closed window.

An assault, not with the infantile hands, which could be of no possible use, but with the small reticule (heavier for the purchases at Bolding's) which has a steel frame—and at the third blow goes crashing through the glass. "Jingle!"—out goes that brittle barrier! "Whoa!" speaks the driver, from his box, at once pulling up to ascertain why, what, and how much the damage. "Help! help!" yells (there is no other truly descriptive word for the cry) the captive, through the opening thus made, releasing the tortured hand as a compromise for being allowed to open her mouth. "Damnation!" grinds out John Jasper, between his set teeth, recognizing in an instant (mad or no) that the chance is lost, opening the opposite door and springing out and away, while the cabman is on the other side of the vehicle. And "Miss Bud's voice calling for help! What is all this, cabby?" naturally inquires Mr. Grewgious, coming up from the pavement, where, going home to his chambers, he has been made a surprised spectator of the concluding scene.

"Mr. Grewgious! oh, Mr. Grewgious! why, why did I ever come out alone, and so late?" is what the rescued young lady first finds breath to say—the sentence being, it will be observed, a direct personal question addressed to the lawyer, which he may be pardoned, under all the circumstances, not being immediately ready to answer.

"Miss Bud! my dear young lady! what does all this mean?" says the lawyer, not strictly in reply, as he accepts the invitation of the extended arms, and helps Rosa out of the cab, landing her, with awkward dexterity, in the middle of the street.

"Oh, Mr. Grewgious! oh, how fortunate it was that you chanced to be here! and oh, why, why did this ever happen? And I can't tell you, here—do please take me home!" Such are the rather confusing than explanatory exclamations following, from the lips again so happily opened.

"Certainly, my dear young lady, certainly. Not hurt, then, whatever has happened? Good!—tick that off. And cannot be frightened dangerously, or you could not talk. Good again! —tick that off, also. And now, as you suggest, I will take you home—without the cab, the distance not being a formidable one, even for *you*."

But here the cabman interferes, just as the two are leaving his physically injured vehicle, and his mentally and pecuniarily injured self, standing in the middle of the street.

"Hi! I say! ain't nobody going to pay me my fare, and the breakage of this 'ere winder?"

"Good gracious, my dear," cries Mr. Grewgious, with the lawyer's abstract sense of justice (which is, or ought to be, full of Right Angles), and turning round at once. "What is to be done about the cab? Did *you* engage it, my dear?"

"Oh, no! no!" earnestly replies Rosa. "I was thrust into it by force, as I am going to tell you—"

"Well, then, cabby, I do not see that you have any claim on the young lady, and I am sure that you have none upon *me*. Where is the person who engaged you?"

" 'E 'as run away, since this 'ere glass was broke—leastwise
it looks so, seein' that he's nowhere about," replies the cabman,
dolefully. "But, Miss," and his voice is temporarily more
cheerful—"no offence, I 'opes, wasn't it you as broke the
glass?"

"Eh, my dear young lady?" helpingly queries the lawyer.

"I? oh, yes, I broke the glass to get out—to get away from
him."

"There, I told you so—it was 'er as did it, and I wants my
money for that, any way!" triumphantly replies the cabman.

"Oh, what shall I do, Mr. Grewgious? I haven't enough
money to pay for it!" dolefully exclaims poor Rosa, thus suddenly brought to a second grief at the moment of apparent deliverance.

"Card!" suggested the elated proprietor of the vehicle,
who almost feels the money in his palms.

"Stop!" says Mr. Grewgious. "Allow me, if you please,
to apply the law to the whole case, before deciding upon any
part of it. You did not hire the cab, Miss Bud, nor was it
hired at your request or consent?"

"No—oh, no."

"You were forced into it, by some one who apparently had
hired it, and whose name is not at present essential to the
case?"

"Yes, oh, Mr. Grewgious!—"

"Pardon my interrupting you and going on, Miss Bud.
You broke the glass, if I understand correctly, as one of, and
possibly the only means of attracting attention and thus
escaping?"

"Yes, but I am very sorry——"

"Regrets, like the man's name, my dear young lady, are
not at present in the case. So far as I can at this juncture
determine the law, the cabman *may* be given in charge as
particeps criminis in an attempt at forcible abduction and outrage on the person of a minor, for which the punishment, if
convicted, would be heavy,—or you *may* decline to appear
against him."

"Give *me* in charge!" indignantly says the cabman.
"Blessed if I wouldn't like to see you do it!"

"Avoid swearing, in the presence of ladies, my good man,"
continues Mr. Grewgious. "As for the damages to the cab,
they are clearly due from the hirer, if he can be found; and
you owe him nothing, my dear young lady, unless you *do*
choose to have him arrested. Now if you will accept of an
Angular man's arm, which may not be fitted on in the most
convenient shape for a lady's use,—we will proceed."

"Well, cheek me if that isn't cool! And blessed 'ard it is
on a poor man, to go and 'ave his winder broke out like this
'ere, and no fare! Wouldn't I like to catch '*im*, though!
wouldn't I I!"

With which poor consolation, the cabman grumblingly
remounts his box, a little chaffed by a small group of idle
bystanders who do not chance to have suffered corresponding
pecuniary damage, and drives away to the stable and repair-
ing shop; while the lawyer and his ward, so opportunely met,
pursue their brief way to the lodgings of the latter at Billickins, not yet vacated, though under notice to that effect, the
original term of contract having still a certain brief period
to run.

During this walk, however, brief as it is, Rosa manages to
impart to Mr. Grewgious not only the name of the foiled
abductor, but all the circumstances of importance connected
with the first interview. To which she adds a request, for
which the reason may be readily found in the unwillingness
of the young girl to have the unfortunate adventure canvassed
even among her friends—that her guardian will consent to
keep it for the time a secret between themselves, until there
may be better occasion for revealing it. The lawyer, who has
listened with more absorbed interest to the naïve and child-
like relation, than his replies give evidence, or than Rosa will
ever know during her life upon the earth—consents to the
temporary suppression with a readiness born of the secrecy
of his calling. And so, a few minutes later, he hands her to

the door at Billickins, declining to go in on that occasion, but
waiting within view until he sees the door opened for her, after
which he plods on, in his Angular way, to his lonely chambers
under the broad ægis of P. J. T.

These letters assume, to him, an hour later, as he sits over
the concluding morsels of his lonely (even Bazzard-deserted)
supper, the aspect of Passion Judicially Tried, with more
evenness in the holding of the scales than many characterize
the examination, into litigated cases, of many of the learned
judges who make the ermine at once feared and respected.
For it is himself and his own impulses that he is trying again,
as we have seen him doing months before,—but with what he
would himself call new evidence come into court, materially
changing the aspects involved.   And the lonely old man sighs
as he reviews the last item of that evidence—sighs so deeply
that for the moment he ceases to be Angular and ungainly,
and comes close to the hearts of all those who have loved and
suffered but borne both the loving and suffering like men !

"Ah, well," he muses, ' there is no fool like an *old* fool,'—
so says the proverb, and so say *I!*   *Her* ring—I wondered
whether it would ever come back to me.   It has come : so
strangely that its coming outruns the other wonder.   And *she*
has come back : does she know it, in that far land to which
she went so many years ago ? come back in her daughter.
And I, old, ungainly, unattractive, who have no more chance
to win the love of even an ordinary woman of middle age,
than the man who carries in my coals.   I must see so much
of her mother in her, that I can scarcely avoid betraying myself in her presence.   Good God ! how much she looked like
her mother to-night, in her half-alarm !—and what it cost me
not to disgrace myself for ever, by saying what would have
sent her away from me in a worse fright and disgust than that
she feels for the other villain !

"Ah, well !" after a pause pointed by another sigh quite as
profound as that preceding his rumination.   "Hiram Grewgious, you may be a fool, but there is no obligation to become

a coward. Labor for strength, and even pray for it, old nondescript, if you have grace enough—that you may be able to
remember the nobody that you have always been, and the past
generation to which you belong—that you may see *her* wooed
and wedded, as you saw her mother, and claim neither love
nor pity, as you deserve none."

This while, what of Rosa, the subject of a suppressed passion of which she as little dreams as she could do anything
else than childishly weep over it if she knew of its existence?

Ah, if the old lawyer's glance were but keen enough to
pierce through distance and obstacle, between Staple Inn and
Bloomsbury Square, the sight might be deeper, even if no
more hopeless, because the dreaded end would show nearer.
For the drama of Othello and Desdemona is being acted over
again, in its earlier and more innocent portions, with no other
audience than Miss Twinkleton, who may be accepted in her
usual *rôle* of Propriety, but who may be simply a Chorus not
yet come to voice.

Rosa, coming in from her adventure, somewhat anxiously
looked for, but all inquiries and explanations avoided by her
making her appearance under the safe convoy of Mr. Grewgious,—has found Mr. Tartar just on the point of leaving,
after calling to pay his respects; and for some cause, then,
the intention of immediately returning to the Admiral's
Cabin and calling all hands to holystone decks and tidy her
up a bit, would seem to have been abandoned. The handsome,
breezy, and brown-faced man of the wide experience has
dropped into a chair, with endurance if not satisfaction in that
article of furniture, though it might better answer its purpose,
certainly, if a capstan or a corner of the binnacle; and Rosa
just enough reminiscent of her late terror to be more keenly
alive to the fact that in this company she had no terror whatever. Rosa had rather floated than dropped into another, too
near for a naval engagement at long range—too close even for
the Benbow and Anson theory of yard-arm and yard-arm—
almost near enough for boarders ahoy! and grapplins ready!

And he is telling her, not boastfully, for that would destroy more than half the charm, but with that quiet, half-technical commonplace of expression which seems to fit every interesting subject as with a garment especially belonging to it, and with an air of personal indifference to the marvels related, which claims no share and so receives the larger—telling her some of those stories of adventure by sea and land, in storm and calm, through danger and ludicrous mishap, which have no more power to grow old or lose interest than the very scenes among which they are laid.   And the young girl listens so attentively that the narrator may well be satisfied without any additional audience than herself at the front, and quiet-crocheting Miss Twinkleton (who has not yet finished the woollen monster) in the background.

He tells of elephant-hunting or boar-spearing in Ceylon, or of tiger-shooting when on long leave in Bengal; and his listener follows him with lips as well as eyes, seeming to think that he may be even yet possibly in danger—merely throwing in a not-too-brilliant word at long intervals, to remember that Ceylon is Helena Landless' native island, or to say: " Oh, why, why, why did you act so rashly ? " He paints her the typhoon of the China Seas, with the heavens a pall and the sea a black yawning tomb; and she seems to be buried with his stout ship there, until the peril passes and the merry life on shipboard begins once more.   He grapples with pirates on junk or proa, and she seems to feel that knife or creese is yet at his throat, and to try to shield him with her poor little hands, till that danger, too, passes, and she helps him (a little vindictively, it is to be feared, though severely frightened) to blow the piratical craft out of water, or hang 'em to the yard-arm with a long rope and a short shrift.

Ah, Rosa—dear little Rosa of that bewitching, dangerous girlhood which seems to have sent Edwin Drood to his murdered doom; which John Jasper arraigns as driving him mad and making his life an unendurable burthen; which Hiram Grewgious does not arraign but worships, as that which

makes him a grey-headed idiot deserving of the school-boy's
rod—ah, Rosa, this, as even your untutored young heart feels
and confesses—this is the end of all. You have learned to
understand and appreciate an experience and a power beyond
your own; and so the chain is woven that must either grace
or gall. The merest girl yourself, the *boy* was not for you;
the man is here, and you are his. Othello comes, Desdemona
listens; and the drama of her life, whether for good or ill, is
thenceforth written, beyond the skill of the veriest playwright
to change scene or sentence.

CHAPTER XI.

JOE GILFERT'S FIRST JOURNEY.

NIGHT is falling on the dark and dismal streets of a portion
of the City lying not far from the Tower, with a tendency
towards the London Docks and Wapping. Streets that show
the claim of antiquity to respect, and very little else capable
of securing that appreciation—as may be said of some tottering sot or wrinkled harridan, thoroughly disreputable, but
with years enough to write the prefix " old." Streets that may
have been laid out by those nearly omnipresent people, the
Romans, for anything that modern convenience or modern
cleanliness can indicate to the contrary. Streets that might
have belonged to one of the Cities of the Plain, lying under
water for the comfortable period elapsing since the destruction
of Sodom, and only lately and slimily dried out to view,
through the use of improved drainage—such a deposit of mud,
damp, and all the elements of watery discomfort, may be seen,
like a dull leprosy, on mouldy house-front, and more fully
developed on slippery uneven pavement. Streets into which
the daylight seems to come unwillingly and of cruel compul-
sion, even in those often quoted and rarely appearing

"brightest days of summer"—as knowing the forcible opposing influences with which it must contend, and the general
rough treatment which it is sure to encounter before getting
away again in a state of feeble half-extinguishment. Streets
in which the most frequent of wheeled vehicles is the coster-
monger's barrow, with fruit or vegetables arrived at the due
state of ripe rottenness for that peculiar consumption; varied
by an occasional cab, only presuming to enter the precincts
when become sufficiently shabby in general appearance of
trap, horse, and harness, not to affront the inhabitants by any
mocking display of splendor. Streets where the few females
appearing are always slip-shod as to feet, frowsy as to hair,
and fugitives as to the dropping away of clothes — nearly
always carrying home pennyworths, stopping to talk to equally unclean and dowdy cronies, or screaming after barefoot
children of such uniform dirt in face and semi-covering, that
there must be difficulty in distinguishment by the fondest
maternal eye. Streets where the open market shops show
flabby fish, damaged meats, and abhorrent vegetables, with
small heaps of coals in foul recesses, indicating purchase by
the ha'porth; and where those with closed doors seem to display the same unappetising wares, in the unwashed windows,
that they have shown to the past half-century of deficient
means, and will show to the next half-century of means still
more incapable for purchase. Streets intersected by narrow
alleys and narrower courts, in which all possible of the
previously named conditions are intensified,—and pierced by
the openings of yet dingier and more gloomy archings, over
any one of which Dante might have written his famous farewell to Hope, without risking entrance into the dismal and
dangerous gloom within.

Night is falling, in a mode entirely consonant with the character of the streets it is visiting. For it comes down with a
hot and steaming sultriness, choking the breath, and making
the clothing adhere to the person with a tenacity suggesting
that the last ablution has been performed in glue-water. It

renders well-aired rooms half-untenable, and close dens, Black
Holes of Calcutta in miniature; and it sends the tenants of
attics broiled all day under the misted sun, out into miserable
alleys, courts, and doorways, with something of the feeble joy
that might be predicted of a doomed joint temporarily escaped
from the oven or the spit.

It is on such a night, so early that the hour may yet be
called evening, that two persons pass down one of the moul-
diest, closest, and most forbidding of those streets, going on
from bad to worse with a steadiness indicating that they do
not intend to falter at any ordinary development of the disreputable. If the evidence of clothing can be depended upon,
they are both of that stronger sex to whom it is understood
that the rougher labors of life are to be entrusted; and an additional guarantee to the same effect will be found in the names
they bear—one styling himself, when he takes that unusual
trouble with his own personality, Robert Tartar, or sometimes
Bob Tartar, late lieutenant in Her Majesty's Service; and the
other bearing the easily spoken cognomen of Joe Gilfert.

Tartar has rummaged, from some one of the sea-chests or
lockers of the Admiral's Cabin, wherein is stowed dunnage of
a highly miscellaneous character, and an amount making the
place a small rival of Portsmouth—a rig of toggery reducing
him, in its comparative shabbiness and evidences of long
use, below Luff or Powder-monkey, and leaving him scarcely
respectable enough for a foretopman; though not even dress
can change the brown comely jollity of eye and face, the neat
waving curls of his thick hair, or the general expression of
being the hearty, active, companionable fellow combined with
the gentleman.

Something different from this must be said of "Joe Gilfert,"
for whom no other name is at present necessary. He looks
the stripling, but a very slight, young and handsome one—
brown in cheek, keen in eye, and lithe in every movement;
while if his feet and hands are a trifle too small for what Mr.
Tartar would require in an able-seaman, no undue notice need

be taken of them in the night-time. Better-dressed than
Tartar, he appears, as we may have seen him on another
occasion, a shopkeeper's lad of more than the usual good looks
and ease of manner ; and he appears nothing more under any
ordinary observation. Nothing that he wears sits upon him
as if it belonged to some one else ; no uneasy movement indi-
cates that he has ever borne another name, or been at home in
different habiliments.

"Oh, no, you need fear nothing for *me*," he says, evidently
in response to some suggestion with reference to the sultry
heat of the evening. "It is a dreadful old place, I have no
doubt. Such people could not carry on their business in more
respectable places, you know, even if they could afford them.
But you must remember that I, as well as yourself, have been
used to heat, making the worst of London weather very tem-
perate indeed. And it is only for a while, now ; by-and-bye we
shall have something, taking much longer time, if we are not
both mistaken."

"What a brave g——"

"Take care, sir !" Joe interrupted him, suddenly. "Remember where we are, and what an awkwardness we might be
plunging into by some one overhearing."

"I beg pardon, and I quite understand, and will be more
careful," Mr. Tartar replies. "Sailing under orders, of course
I obey them without question, and never mutiny, except the
Old Man is too sharp. Umph !—I was going to remark what
a brave little fellow you were (how do you like *that ?*).
and how much I should like to have you with me, some time,
in a nice little job of cutting out !"

. "Cutting-out ? What's that?—anything to do with the
ship's tailor ? " laughs Joe, maliciously. "However, you can
explain another time, if you please. Do not let us talk of
other things until we pass the place, and find ourselves down
at the river. Are you sure that you remember ? "

"Oh, yes, quite sure. And, by-the-bye, here we are. It is
not nice, I know, plunging into this hole, but how can we

help it ?   But before we go a step farther, are *you* quite sure ?
Not of your courage—I do not doubt that, but of your knowing how to manage ? "

" Yes, quite sure, thanks.   Under heaven's favor, I do not
expect either to be frightened or make a blunder."

" As for the former," the ex-Lieutenant replies, " if that
should happen, as I do not believe that it will, remember that
I shall be very near you.   I have beaten up the quarters
pretty thoroughly; and I may be looking in at you, through
the window, any moment.   Well, last orders given and received.   Boarders away !   Here we go ! "

They turn down the narrow alley, miserably lighted, with
out further word.   A turn, a winding, and they are at the
wretched door of the house, where John Jasper has so often
enjoyed temporary transport to elysium, with longer-during
.eturn to the infernal regions.

They have no occasion to knock, even if the door is in the
habit of demanding that extreme courtesy of civilized life;
for a coarse-faced man, his bleared eyes just visible in the
dim light of the court, is coming out, and regards them with
the suspicious stare of not believing them to be either thieves
or cut-throats.   But he passes on, looking back in continued
suspicion; and they are free to enter.

Only one does so, however—Joe Gilfert.   Mr. Tartar says,
in a low voice :

" Remember what I told you—three-pair-back.   When you
come down I shall be here, for I shall know when you leave
the old caboose.   Take care of yourself, like a good boy, and
don't be long, please ! "

Then, as Joe enters the door, he disappears from before the
doorway—where, his late companion has no more idea than
of the intricate topography of the many-roomed old rookery
that he is himself entering.   We, of later days, may be better
informed, in the statement that he immediately relapses into
his element, by applying some of the knowledge of locations
obtained in previous reconnaissances, scaling two rear-walls,

12

climbing a spout in the most approved Reefer style, and
perching himself where, with his foot on a projecting ledge,
and his left arm rove through a convenient gutter-sling of
iron, he can secure an unbroken view into a certain half-
opened window, just now of peculiar interest, as well as attain
something of that supreme felicity found in standing in the
foot-ropes, and holding on by the yard-arm, in a stiff gale and
a beam-sea.

Joe Gilfert has an interval of climbing too, of very different
character—less difficult, but scarcely less dangerous, in the
absence of light and the probability of some serious collision.
Fortunately, there is a ray of light from a room emitting
villanous smells and more villanous words, at the second landing ; and again, fortunately, the current of travel does not
seem to be setting downward, for he accomplishes the three,
by aid of that peculiar sense of feeling, belonging to the foot,
and of the broken banister, without meeting any one descending.

At the third landing he feels and fumbles for a door—finds
one that opens with the touch of his attempted knock, and
follows that door, as it swings, into the room.   There is no
sound, except a slight crackling, and the apartment is almost
entirely dark—so dark that only three objects can be distinguished.   One is the window, half-open, through which the
faintest of reflected rays comes in from the court ; and the two
others are both lights of a different sort.   The more important proceeds from a small mass of coals burning in what appears to be a furnace or brazier, in the grate ; and the smaller
is only a spark, higher up, fading and brightening as if with
the drawing of human breath.

"Halloa !"

This salutation of Joe Gilfert's may not be strictly polite,
on entering, uninvited, the residence of a person of distinction ; but really there are occasions when only this, or its
equivalent of " Look here ! " or " I say ! " can be found at
command of the intruder.   In the present instance it produces

the desired effect; for there came a reply, in a hoarse, cracked, rattling voice, which indefinably seems to express the possession of all the miseries of humanity, and more than half the vices and crimes :

"Who are ye, deary? and what do ye want?"

"Oh, there you are, aunty!" exclaims the visitor, cheerily, and striking, at a venture, into a mode of address fitted to one whose name he does not know, but whose age he understands.

"Yes, but who are ye? I can't see ye, till I light a match, and my lungs is so bad and my breath is so short—how am I to find it, deary?"

But Joe Gilfert seems to have come provided for just such an emergency; unless we assume the other hypothesis, that the handsome stripling is in the habit of indulging in dainty cigarettes and carries lucifers to that end! He strikes a match on his boot sole (it does not betray, as it might do, how small is that sole!); and it flares up into light enough to show his face and figure, the ensemble of the miserable apartment— broken bed; tottering arm-chair; small table with a short bit of unlighted candle standing upon it; grate with the charcoal brazier; and the old woman, smoking, shaking, and occasionally coughing, as she attempts to convey, among other suggestions, her impression of the visitor.

"Why, bless ye, deary! did I ever see ye afore? Ye're a boy, and how handsome! Here's the candle—light it like a good handsome young gentleman as ye are. O me, my lungs is weak and my head is bad. Whatever's to become of us all? Yes, light the candle, deary!"

Joe Gilfert has not been waiting for the exordium, to make that additional and more satisfactory light. Before the old woman has repeated it, the candle is lighted and he replaces it on the table; while the owner, trembling, coughing and very decrepit, is attempting to rise from her rickety chair.

"Now then, aunty, here we are, and we can look at one another to a little better advantage!" he exclaims pleasantly, as he deposits the candle and assists the miserable figure from the chair.

"Why, ye're handsomer yet than I thought ye was, deary!" the decrepit crone goes on,—some spark of what should have been long defunct in the woman's nature, apparently flaring into light more lurid than that of the match had been, at sight of that exquisite beauty of the opposite sex, possibly long denied to her besotted eyes. "But why do ye come here?—though I'm glad enough to see ye? What's yer name, deary, and where do ye belong? O me, my lungs is dreffle bad," coughing, "and my head is so weak. Ye won't mind tellin' the old woman what's yer name and where ye live, will ye, deary?"

"Mind? no, aunty, not in the least. Name is Joe Gilfert, with people who care anything for me: Joseph, with some who don't mind wasting breath. Places where I live—two of them—here in London, Tottenham Court Road; and in the East Indies."

"In the East Injees! Bless ye, deary—that's where the stuff for the mixter grows, isn't it? And maybe ye know something about it, though ye're so young and so handsome. Is that what you come for, deary—a little smoke? Have they been bad to ye, so young, and do ye have the all-overs? If ye have, this is the place to cure 'em, and ye did right to come to the old woman. Jack Chinaman, over the way—he makes believe and don't do no good when ye're sufferin', 'cause he doesn't know how to mix it! Do ye want a little smoke, deary?—and have ye money for the poor old soul?—for the market price is dreffle high, and ye must pay according!"

It seems incredible how many words the old woman manages to utter, in a given space of time, between the rattling coughs that seem shaking her miserable frame to pieces; and the mingled glare of curiosity, admiration, and cupidity, in her bleared and sodden eyes, is one of the most instructive and melancholy of spectacles, to at least one observer.

"No, I do not wish for any 'little smoke,' aunty—not just now, at any rate," says the visitor, when she has ceased, from pure exhaustion and coughing. "Sit down again: it is easier for you, and let me sit on the side of the bed, here," half-pushing the uncomely hostess down into her chair, and suiting the other action to the word, with a shudder of disgust that there is no fear of the other recognizing. "No—I have some other business with you, aunty, that'll do you much more good."

" There isn't no good for the poor old soul with the bad lungs, and rent so dreffle high up here, but money, deary ! " She whines, picking up the pipe that has been temporarily laid down, and fumblingly lighting it from the brazier within reach, to the filling of the room with a pungent, sickly odor.

" But listen to me, aunty. I have money, and you are to get it if you do as I wish," says Joe Gilfert, from the side of the bed.

" Oh, bless ye, deary, for sayin' so ; for trade is so dull, and the market price is so high ! " comes the whine, mingled with coughing and attempts at the pipe.

" Money ? Yes. See here—and all for *you*, for a very little trouble." And with the words, the handsome boy thrusts one of the small hands into his pocket, and withdraws it with a sovereign glittering in the palm. In an instant the old face of the woman is demoniac with greed, and she makes a clutch at the coin, as marked, and forcible as if she had thirty years less of wasting vice resting on her head.

" Ah ! no—don't try that, aunty ! " exclaims the handsome boy, dropping the coin back into his pocket, and in the very next instant showing the short hilt and glittering blade of a poniard, which he half-draws from its concealment within his vest. " See, I do not mean this for *you*, especially, but for any one who lays hand on me or what I carry."

" O me, to think ye could believe that of the poor old soul, and she admirin' of ye so, deary ; and she with her lungs so bad, and her head so weak ! " comes the rattling whine of the crone, dropping helplessly back into her chair.

" See—let us quite understand each other, aunty," resumes the visitor, who evidently carries at least two of the metals. " I show you the piece of gold, and tell you that it is for *you*, if you do what I wish; then I show you this other thing; which is of steel, and very sharp, to inform you that I am not to be *robbed*. Do you quite take my meaning, think?"

"What is it ye want, deary? Ye that's so handsome and yet so hard with the old woman! I never seed ye afore, and yet I'd do anything in life for ye! Don't keep me waitin'; it makes my lungs worse and worse, and nothin' but rags and strainers."

"There is a man named John Jasper—maybe you know him by that name, or maybe some other—a well-looking dark man, with fine hair and whiskers—who comes here sometimes, for a 'little smoke,' as you call it?"

Instantly the thought flashes across the suspicious mind of the old woman. "Crime—a man after him—punishment— dragging up for participation or knowledge!" and the conjunction shows in the wild terror of the eyes, that age has by no means robbed of all expression,—as she coughs hurriedly:

"No, deary, no; ye're in the wrong place. It must be Jack Chinaman's over the way, that he goes to. Not here, deary!"

"Oh, then of course I must take my money to Jack Chinaman, over the way. Sorry!" This remark of Joe Gilfert's is made in the most matter-of-fact manner imaginable. Indeed he could not be more at his ease, if he was a detective of the keenest scent, worming out by nonchalance some secret destined to cost a life.

"Oh, no, deary—oh, no, ye wouldn't do *that* with the poor old soul, and her lungs so weak and she so dreffle low!" whines and rattles the crone, with a pitiful rubbing of the hands, that is half-wringing them. "The money for *me*, deary, for tellin' ye where to find him. John Chinaman—he is rich, along of mixin' so much of it, and so bad; and he don't need it, like the poor old soul."

"Stop, aunty!" says the handsome boy, very sternly. "We have had enough of this, and we will not have any more. I know that John Jasper comes here: I have had him tracked to this door!"

"O me, my lungs is ribbons and strings!" she coughs, as the only comment on this threatening announcement, which corroborates her worst fears and yet leaves her defenceless.

"Yes, no falsehoods, for they will do no good," Joe Gilfert proceeds. "You have no reason to suppose that I wish to hurt *him* ; and I give you my word that I do not wish to hurt You. But he has a secret; and I want it, from his own lips. Only help me to get *that*, and you have the money!"

Joy, surprise, and a certain terror, all seem to commingle in the wretched face, as the old woman manages to straighten herself from the chair with sudden vigor.

"A secret, deary? and you want to make him talk, when he has the 'smoke' on him! Only that, deary? But ye can't do it! Oh, if ye only could! The old woman has tried it, more'n twice or three times, and he won't say a word that does any good. No, deary, ye're very handsome, but ye can't make *him* talk!"

"Do not be too sure," the handsome boy replies, as the old woman settles back into her chair and coughs with renewed rattle. "You do not have the right mixture. *I do!*"

"Ye, deary?—and ye are so young and handsome? No—there's nobody has the true secret of mixin' it, like the old woman. Ye can't do it, deary! Oh, if ye only could!"

"Did I not tell you that I lived a part of the time in the East Indies, aunty?" Joe Gilfert rejoins, bringing up his reserves. "You do not think that you know, here, all that *we* know, do you? What I want of you, to earn the money, is that you will inform me when this man comes next, and allow me to give him his 'little smoke'—that is all."

The calculation is not misplaced. The mention again of the "East Indies" brings up in the mind of the naturally superstitious associate of criminals and outcasts, a little of that awe with which the Orient is always associated in the thoughts of the vulgar; and thenceforth her visitor has her at advantage.

She only puts in, now, her stereotype parenthesis of recalling the melancholy condition of her lungs and head; the face, meanwhile, strangely blending the expressions of admiration, fear, and compelled respect, which have successively grown out of the looks, words, and actions of the other.

"Now listen, for my time is nearly up, and you may have other visitors. If you wish this gold, and possibly twice as much——"

"Oh, bless ye, deary!"

"Then remember what I tell you, and obey me. Mr. Jasper, as I know, always comes here in the daytime of late to arrange for the night—so that he may not have too many companions."

"O, my lungs is too bad! How do you know, my handsome one?"

"Never mind how I know that or many other things : only obey my directions, or not a penny in your purse. The very next time that he comes—no matter what day—the moment that he has gone, to come again, send this card, by any boy that you can pick up in the court, to Mr. Tartar—you can read the name on it? Yes? Well—to Mr. Tartar, at Staple Inn. Tell him to hurry, and there will be half-a-crown for him. Mark as many strokes on the back of the card as will tell at what hour he is to come, in the evening. Say nothing to make him understand that his 'little smoke' will be different to what you have given him before. Half an hour before the time named on the card, I will be here."

"And then, deary? What then?"

"Then, while we are waiting, I will prepare his pipe. Leave all to me. But time enough for all that, *then*. Do you understand me?"

"Yes! O me, my lungs is so dreffle bad! But are ye sure, deary, that yer not goin' to pison him and leave his dead body to hang the poor old soul? Think of that deary!—ye're not goin' to pison him, are ye?"

"No—on my honor. But perhaps you will not believe in

that. I swear to you, then, that what I do shall not affect his life. Besides, if I wished to kill him, why could I not do it somewhere else as well as here ? "

" So ye could, deary,—so ye could. And ye'll give me the money, sure, then ?—the whole piece that ye had in yer handsome hand? Swear to that, too, deary."

" I will do nothing of the sort ! " replies Joe Gilfert, with an indignant gesture making the old woman sink back into her chair and resume coughing to the verge of strangling. " I promise you — that is enough. Stop — I will give you something on account, now ; and the sovereign shall all come to you, besides, when you have done what I require."

" O, bless ye, deary !—how handsome ye are, and how good ye are to the poor old soul ! " coughs and sputters the crone, as the visitor hands her two half-crowns that make a pleasant jingle to her greedy ears when they fall into her clutching palm. " And ye are sure, deary, that ye can make him talk ? Oh, if ye only can ! "

Joe Gilfert, as may be imagined, has enjoyed nearly enough of the atmosphere of the miserable apartment, in which the dead fumes of opium combine with the rankness of foul clothes to revolt the senses. And, the arrangement as definitely made as he has power to make it with such a personality on the other side of the contract, he merely repeats instructions on two or three of the more important points ; says a good night, which meets with the coughing whine : " Bless ye, deary !—and ye so handsome ! " leaves the old woman in her chair, with the short candle burning low in its socket ; and gropes his way again down the dangerous stairways, to find at the door Mr. Tartar, who has tumbled overboard from the yard-arm, or descended the back-stay head foremost, at precisely the right moment.

" I said that I wouldn't miss ye, deary ! " the old woman coughingly and rattlingly apostrophizes some unseen being, rubbing her withered hands, and chuckling hoarsely, when she is alone. " Ye said ' unintelligible,' and so ye was, like

the rest of 'em, *then*. But *he* is from the Injees, deary, and
he will make ye talk ! Maybe ye'll say something for the
poor old soul that'll be larnin' a new art o' mixin' it at the
same time ; and not all for *him !* And then the old woman'll
know whether ye've always been John Jasper, or somebody
else that she's a bigger account to settle with than ye think,
deary ! "

CHAPTER XII.

THE MISSION OF THE STONE-MASON.

CLOISTERHAM, or so much of it as cared to do so, saw, one
morning, not many days after the long conference held by Mr.
Crisparkle and Durdles over the unfinished and never-to-be-
finished bust, a spectacle capable of astonishing that respectable old city, if the faculty of astonishment had not literally
gone out of it under the influences of time and change. This
was nothing more nor less than the appearance of Stony
Durdles in the High Street, proceeding on a journey and
bearing all those marks of unaccustomed care and preparation which always do so much towards making the subjects
uncomfortable.

To say that Mr. Durdles, bent on an important mission,
had arrayed himself in holiday attire, in the sense of putting
on other outer raiment than that usually worn—would be to
take even worse liberties with the language, than those in
which the stone-mason was himself in the habit of playfully
indulging. For there is no reason to believe that he kept in
useless idleness a part of the material wealth of England, by
possessing garments which he could not wear—*id est*, more
than a single suit : all that he could conveniently assume at
once, except in Arctic weather. And long use had so accustomed that suit to the dusty grey and grime of the stone-yard,

that it would have consented to turn into rags before parting with the color at any bidding of the severest of brushes.

But there had been certain ameliorations, internal and cuticular. More nearly than at any previous time in popular memory, Durdles had washed himself; and there was a preponderance of limp dirty-white shirt-collar dominating the whole of the garment of which it formed the outward and visible sign, and suggesting that some great occasion had arisen, long waited for by that special shirt, in a state of aristocratic exemption. Of the untidy shoes, naturally nothing could be said, they having long before passed into that state in which Day and Martin would have bankrupted their stock in filling an order to supply them with blacking to the extent of polish; and the hat is equally beyond reach, all the figures of geometry being already represented in its curves and angles, so that the force of ornamentation could literally go no further. The big horn-buttons of the coat may have been rubbed clear of lime, and even polished on the cuff thereof: such things have been, and even Durdles (as witness the shirt) was not entirely proof against the blandishments of the syren Vanity.

What need to say that he bore his bundle? Does the elephant peripatate without his trunk, except under the most extraordinary circumstances of the loss of that convenience at the hands (presumably) of his railway-porters? Does the peacock flaunt without his rainbow of tail, except under deprivation by human peacocks, who believe in the old adage that "fine feathers make fine birds"? No—on the contrary, Durdles, bent upon a tour of marked extent (to London, and return) had evidently labored under the impression that the metropolis was in a state of starvation, rendering sustenance there unattainable, or that divers and sundry accidents and detentions were likely to be met with on the road, rendering extensive provisioning as necessary as for a cruise on the African station. So that his bundle, in point of fact, presented even a more notable appearance of extraordinary preparation than himself; and it might have been not difficult to believe that he was accompanying *it* instead of its accompanying him.

Durdles, embarking after the long preliminary journey of the Cloisterham people in those days, was a shade difficult, too, with reference to the carriage which he patronized; avoiding two in which the compartments had been (accidentally) cushioned,—with some apparent objection to sitting upon anything less solid and substantial than stone, or its next substitute, wood; or else impressed with the belief that in any of more effeminate construction he might be lulled into slumber, lose his personal luggage, or incapacitate himself for the stern realities of his errand to the metropolis.

His errand—aye, let it not be supposed that the stone-mason was going Londonward without an errand,—indeed, that he was going without some errand of enough importance to be called a mission. What was the errand, no one knew, when he left Cloisterham, except himself—not even Mr. Crisparkle, whom he had admitted, under circumstances easily recalled, to knowledge hidden from all his world besides. That it was not an amiable one, calculated to make the object of his visit materially happier, might be judged from the sullen set of the heavy jaw and the lowering expression of the coarse, beetling brows. It might be benevolent, like most of the pursuits of the Rev. Luke Honeythunder; but if so, it seemed likely to go even beyond the requirements of that forcible person, and to assume, not merely the characteristics of the Aggressive but the Violent in Philanthropy.

And it seemed likely—suggestive enough the fact—that Mr. Honeythunder would enjoy the opportunity of comparing notes on the great systems of the Angry in Benevolence; for the course of the Cloisterham stone-mason, on arrival, was threateningly in the direction of that Haven which could not always be certified as one of peace. Dropping overboard, so to speak, from the train which had borne him so far, into the great Sea of London, whereof the ripples were human beings and the larger waves cabs, drays, vans, and 'busses, he rather floundered than swam his way in the direction of the head-office of the United British and Foreign Universal Philanthropists, appropriately situated in a certain quarter within stone's-throw of Leicester Square, where as much philanthropy seemed to be needed, as in any other spot of the broad earth, and where the original location had no doubt been made from prudential considerations, looking to the managers being able to show contributing visitors Legitimate Objects from the windows, upon the same wise principle which induces thrifty Life Assurance Companies to choose buildings that give view upon churchyards.

Not a very long journey, or a very difficult search, fortunately; for there was neither much patience nor much skill in the man who was pursuing both. Whelmed and lost, a few times, in the great sea, then fished up by a less than usually gruff passer-by, or a more than ordinarily useful policeman, he floundered and drifted in the right direction; the scowl on the grey brows growing darker, the mouth more set and sullen, and the latent combativeness in the sluggish heart more and more dangerous. And then he stood, at last, at the portal of the Head Haven, which might be considered a mouldy old huge stone pier, thrusting itself out into the sea he had been buffeting, and promising that it would either shelter or crush all craft closely approaching it, as the case might be.

Fresh difficulties began to beset Mr. Durdles, even at the moment when he had floundered alongside this dusky and mouldy stone breakwater stretching out into the great dangerous Sea of London. If it was a pier, it may have partaken something the character of those London and Liverpool docks which excite the admiration of the world, not less by their difficulty of admission than their costliness and solidity. They have gates, and they can only be entered at a certain height of tide. Wealth being the tide at the Head Haven, undoubtedly a rated amount was necessary to float into it;

and it may be said confidently, that in the Durdles calender water was invariably low.

To drop the figure, he was not well enough habited, in spite of the distinguished shirt-collar, to indicate to the powers, however subordinate, giving and barring admission to the Haven, that the U. B. F. U. P. would be benefited by his entrance. Most commercial men know, and others than commercial men may form shrewd guesses, of the different eyes with which an evidently intending purchaser may be viewed, at the door of the shop, and one who gives corresponding evidence that he is only prepared to *sell*, in the small way of a pedlar, or to BEG! That Mr. Durdles did not come to the Haven, to announce a munificent bequest, or to bring a heavy donation, was quite evident, even to the bleared eyes of the Underpaid at the door: much more likely that he came on one of those Illegitimate and Inadmissible demands (those involving the paying out of money in a practical and unostentatious way), which supplied one of the chief sources of torment to the society of many initials.

So when Durdles, unwisely removing his hat even when without the half-opened door, and worse crumpling that head-covering than before, in the effort to make it do duty for fumbling purposes, instead of the horn buttons, — momentarily brought back the swimming simile by making a plunge into the very midst of his demands, *à la* Crisparkle, with :

"Durdles wants to see your big man, Mr. Honeythunder!"

Then the Underpaid, though he may well have recognized the propriety of the description, as applying to the physical size of the person inquired after, may also have been excusable in the superciliousness of the glance with which he first stared at the abrupt applicant, and then looked around for "Durdles," who, spoken of in the third person, might be supposed to be in hiding somewhere behind the heavy door-post. Besides, the Underpaid, habitually bullied within, doubtless understood the necessity, as a sort of mental pabulum correspondent with his daily bread, of bullying all those who looked humble enough for that exercise, without; and so he merely performed a part of his duty (to himself) in the return gruffness of his reply :

"Durdles? Who's Durdles, and *where's* Durdles?"

To which the stone-mason, giving the hat another crush and indenting into it at once Embarrassment and Ill-usage :

"Who's Durdles and where's Durdles, stupid? Durdles is here, and isn't ashamed of his name!—leastways he doesn't know it, if he is!"

Then thus the Underpaid, naturally irritated by the objectionable epithet, but not quite free, as a subaltern, to give his indignation full indulgence :

"Oh, then *you* are Durdles! Didn't know but it was My Lord Durdles, or Archbishop Durdles, or——"

"In which case," interrupted Durdles, severely, "you would ha' let him in at once, 'stead o' keeping him at the door! I want to see Mr. Honeythunder."

"Oh, you do, do you? Then all I can say is, that you cannot see him. Just go away, my man, and allow me to shut the door."

"Oh, then, that is what you're up to, in this here place with the big name : keepin' people out as has business of importance!" gruffly replied Durdles, making a forcible shove past the doorkeeper, the ponderous bundle doing good service as a forward protrusion, not to call it a battering-ram, and the impetus being such as to carry the stone-mason quite past the Underpaid (who may also have been the Underfed) and to set that person spinning like a teetotum as he whirled against the door and closed it.

By this time Durdles, energetically pursuing his momentary advantage, after the manner of skilful tacticians in offensive warfare, had crossed a gloomy vestibule, penetrated beneath a line of obstructing and otherwise useless columns, and was in the presence of the chief clerical force of the establishment,—still scribbling, folding and directing unlimited thousands of circulars, beneath hazy gas-lights, and with a faith-

ful rapidity which indicated belief that the true mission of
Philanthropy was to distribute written and printed papers,
and that they were rapidly advancing the Millennium by
hastening the day when no human being should be without
an Appeal.

To this vantage-ground he was at once pursued by the
Underpaid, but too late for any practical result. It is not
only "the first step which costs," often, but which *gains*.
Durdles, thus far arrived, and at once flushed with indignation at the attempted exclusion, and with a sense of victory
over it—Durdles, observing that all the clerical force looked
up from their work at his advent, lost no time in throwing
himself into oratorical position, with the bundle now doing
duty as a wand or paper-roll to mark emphasis, and commenced the delivery of a gruff address to all and singular
the clerical force thus aforesaid, in which his loud demand for
Mr. Honeythunder to be at once forthcoming, was blended
with an amount of denunciation of the door-keeper, and,
indeed, the whole establishment and all concerned, entitling
him to immediate engagement as one of the higher stipen-
diaries, had sufficient intellect presided over the scene.

Yet he might have waited until. doomsday, there is
reason to believe, no one being specially addressed, and no
one ever taking to himself a speech addressed in the general
(notably when extra exertion is to be involved)—had not the
loud tone of his voice created a certain sensation in other
apartments adjoining, and suggested a temporary lack of that
silent subordination requisite in the U. B. F. U. P. Penetrated, peculiarly, to the private room of the Manager, then
engaged in jubilant and hilarious reading of a long statement
of starvations, trade depressions, and doleful prospects, in a
philanthropic journal of his patronizing — to which enjoyment he naturally wished to devote undivided attention, as
more forcible Appeals and more thundering Denunciations
would necessarily grow out of this pleasant painfulness of
general situation.   With the effect—this inopportune break-

ing in, of drawing the Manager to the door, armed with a frown of much intensity, and a voice fitted for early manufacture into speaking-trumpets.

"Gentlemen!" he began, thunderously, "what is the meaning of this unseemly noise in a place which should be devoted to quiet and conscientious labor in The Cause? If I hear any more of it, there will be a general reckoning of the severest character——"

The effect of this exordium, uttered and about to be uttered, was materially marred by an interruption at this solemn and breathless moment. Durdles, feeling the necessity of remarking, very gruffly and yet with a certain air of loud satisfaction at the smoothing away of threatening difficulties:

"There he is, now! That's him! Durdles knows him!"

The sensation caused by this outburst can only be computed under a full knowledge of the horror with which all the subordinates regarded the idea of interrupting the Manager. They may be said to have glared at each other, in the presence of such an enormity—except one or two who surreptitiously tittered, but would have expected death in being discovered. The Manager himself did not glare, in the vulgar sense of the word: he rather gloomed loftily, as he thundered, after one instant of surprised silence:

"Who is that man? and what does he want here?"

At which, before Durdles could himself reply, one of the clerks nearest the Manager took the liberty of explaining, in a very low and conciliatory voice, that "none of them knew who the man was, but it was he who had made the noise which they all regretted, muttering something about wishing to see Mr. Honeythunder and would not take no for an answer."

"Ah! what? wishes to see me, this person?" replied the Manager, sonorously, with the air of one who should add: "Has Philanthropy come to this pass, that such wretches dare intrude upon the sacred time of the Manager of the

13

United British and Foreign Universal Philanthropists, in his very Head Haven ? "

" Yes, Durdles wants to see *you*, Mr. Honeythunder; and what's more, to speak with you, and the sooner the better ! " was the reply of the stone-mason, ostensibly made to the uttered words of the Manager, but really to the others as well.

It is probable that only the first part of this was heard by the person addressed ; as it is scarcely credible that if he had heard the whole he would not have resented it by an immediate order of expulsion. His action was really an unbending, of the most notable character, for *him*. He did nothing less than to step forward from the door, with what he intended as amiability.

" Well, my good man, if you wish to speak to me, what is it ? "

Durdles waved around his bundle, at the force of assistants, as if it had been an index-finger, and said :

" Not here, afore all *them*. Durdles must speak with you alone. Go back into the room as you come out of, if it's a private one ; and Durdles 'll follow."

" No, my good man," replied Mr. Honeythunder, with an oppressive loftiness, in his most overwhelming of fair-weather voices (intended for the ears of all the clerical force), and waving his large hand with a round sweep, which expressed proprietorship of the whole Haven and all it contained. " No— I have no secrets from my assistants. " If you have anything to say, go on with it."

" No secrets, eh ? Don't you be too sure of that ! Confidence is a bad habit, and it may grow on you ! " replied Durdles, in his gruffest voice, " better do as I ask you, Mr. Honeythunder, afore I take you at your word."

This was insolent—there was no denying the fact. And Mr. Honeythunder, the man who professionally impressed people as well as *op*pressed them, was not much in the habit of allowing *himself* to be either directed or impressed. Yet something in the manner and words of the rough stone-mason,

while it offended him, had the wonderful effect of inducing
him to change his original intention and submit to what was
literally an order. He turned towards the door of his private
room with:

"Well, you may come in for a moment—only a moment:
my time is valuable!" and Durdles shambled after him,
banging the door as he passed, with his impracticable bundle.

"Now, we are alone. What is it that you want, of so
much consequence?"

The Manager spoke roundly now. Durdles took a brief
survey of the luxuriously fitted but dusky room, with its
Manager's private table, its large cushioned chairs, and the
Map of the World hanging on a side wall, heavily dotted in
red for the stations and boundaries of Universal Philanthropy,
—before he answered the imperative demand.

"Yes, I wanted to see you alone, for you mightn't like all
them to know your business."

"*My* business? What do you mean, fellow?" (not "my
good man," now!)

"Yes, *your* business, Mr. Honeythunder—the *Reverend*
Mr. Honeythunder, I've heard say. You're in a hurry, are
you? Werry well! Then Durdles won't keep you long, and
you can think about what he tells you, arterwards. I want
you to come down to Cloisterham—you know where it is, for I
seed you there not long ago,—*and take charge of* YOUR SON.
That's all, and it don't take long a tellin', does it?"

"*My son?*—you disreputable old wretch, who ought to be
put in the stocks, or the pillory, if they had had sense enough
to keep such things! *My son?* Are you crazy? or what
swindle are you attempting?"

"Softly, don't speak so loud, or *they* may hear you, which
would not be a good thing for *you!*" calmly replied the un-
awed stone-mason. "Your son: Durdles said it, and he
means what he says. *Your son*, and SARY LEWT'S."

"Ha! what do you know?"—the surprised Manager began,
though in a much lower voice; but he stopped as if uncertain
what to say, and Durdles filled up the space.

"Durdles knows a great deal, Mr. Honeythunder—*Reverend* Mr. Honeythunder,—that wouldn't read nicely in the papers, if, so be it should get there : and you'd better be still while he tells you the rest. I know the boy; I knowed his mother; she was Sary Lewt, and she lived at Newcastle. A psalm-singin' chap disgraced her—maybe you know his name : *I* do ! She bore that boy, and died."

He paused a moment, wiping either his brow or his eyes (who shall say which ?) with his cuff. And in that moment Mr. Honeythunder rather hoarsely hissed than roared in his usual tone,—

"It is a lie, you old impostor ! I will have you kicked out."

"No you won't; and it *isn't* a lie, and you know it. You'll come down and attend to him now that you know where he is. He's a credit to his father. Durdles seed you a-whoppin' him, pounding your own flesh and blood, as it deserved, t'other day, when you was down at Cloisterham."

"Will you go, before I have you kicked out, lying old scoundrel !" the Manager rather hoarsely whispered, again, than roared, though at the last words his broad bulk had dropped into one of the wide arm-chairs.

"He is a perfect young devil, but maybe you wouldn't like to be the father of a gallows-bird, as you *will* be, if you do not take care of him," the stone-mason went on, without the least sign of having heard the enraged words of the other. "Name is 'Deputy'—leastwise that's what they call him, for want of any name from his father; and you can find him, when you want him, at the 'Travellers' Twopenny,' in Gasworks Garding. Better write 'em down, afore you forget 'em; and better take care of the young willain afore long, or the story may get into them papers, and not do you any good."

His mission accomplished, in his own peculiar way—shambling out as he had shambled in, and this time unopposed by the Underpaid,—Stony Durdles left the Haven, and drifted and floundered back through the great sea, on his return to

Cloisterham,—stopping covertly, in a convenient arching, to lighten his dinner-bundle, which was thereafter of a little less formidable proportions; and leaving the Rev. Mr. Honey-thunder the wiser for his visit, and no doubt all the better pre-pared for anything Aggressive and Denunciatory, which might present itself in the world of Philanthropy—if not absolutely better content with himself and the world.

It was dusk when Durdles reached Cloisterham; but not too dusky, as he shambled along towards his Hole in the Wall —for him to observe Deputy vigorously cannonading an unfor-tunate cat, that he had succeeded in driving to the shelter of one of the tree-tops near the old monastery, after disposing of her family by various pleasant and ingenious modes of extin-guishment.

"Ha! you young devil!—what is it, up that tree?" Mr. Durdles accosted the commander of the investing force, in the pause between two volleys.

"Old Boxley's tortoise-shell! Hi! Wasn't it sport with her kittens, yesterday? See—that's the time that I nearly fetched her! There goes a piece of her tail! Hi!"

"Deputy!" said Durdles, solemnly, "what will you say, if I tell you that I have been out, to-day, looking for a place for you—better than the Travellers' Twopenny?"

"Yer lie—ye've been drunk, and dreamed it! Give me the three ha'pence you owe me, or I'll smash you next, after I finish this cat!" was the amiable response of this type of the rising (gallows high), generation, as he turned again from the less-exciting diversions of the ribald tongue to the nobler sports of the cruel hand, and hunted the last of the poor tortoise-shell's nine-lives with a vigor promising certain and early capture.

Durdles ventured no more, but shambled away to his hut. As he did so, he shook his head so widely, that the expansive shirt-collar gave way beneath the pressure,—with a gesture that may have indicated a certain amount of sorrow, and that may have been merely expressive of discouragement, with a problem past solution, by the aid of either measuring rule or hammer—a Young 'Un throwing all the Old 'Uns into complete insignificance.

———————

CHAPTER XIII.

REVISITING THE GLIMPSES.

MORE visitors have come to John Jasper in the brief space of time elapsing since the two discoveries, apparently accidents, placing in his hands the pocket-wallet and the black scarf, than have ever before visited the choir-master during a corresponding period. Not that he has become more popular, as a man or a professional: on the contrary, the practices to which he has surrendered himself, and something deeper in his life and brain, neither known nor suspected by the body of those meeting him, have begun to tell upon face and manner—so that his company is less sought than of old, from the very natural reason that we do not willingly force ourselves into companionship inflicting pain or awaking sorrow, when the alternative is open to us of only visiting or entertaining the pleasant and enjoyant. Haggard face; sunken eye, with occasional gleams that seem to blend fear and ferocity; hands shaking to an extent that would be pitiable even in age; and the frequent recurrence of those spasms which, for the time, threaten life and indicate the early extinguishment of reason —these are not elements of increased or even continued popularity, in Cloisterham, any more than elsewhere; and the choir-master may be aware of the unpleasant fact.

Mr. Crisparkle calls seldomer than was his wont at the Gate House, to refresh his musical sympathies or ask after the heal.h of the man who is much oftener than of old absent from the Cathedral-service. Mr. Tope, so very near a neighbor, does not fail him; but it cannot always be said that the company of Mr. Tope is exhilarating, and it might almost be averred

that it is at times depressing—especially since the coming of
his tribulation, which he has *not*, however, confided to Mr.
Jasper, or to any one else than the Minor Canon and his Reverence the Dean.   Mayor Sapsea pays occasional visits, of
course, exclusive of the meetings which take place between
the two at the Mansion House and elsewhere—the pompous
old donkey finding few others, failing the obsequious Datchery,
to pay him such adulatory court as the Energetic Man whom
he believes that he has so characterized.   Besides these, Mr.
Jasper has certain regular visitors connected with the Cathedral service and his profession as a music-teacher, not to mention some remains of social life ; but all those have certainly
not increased in number or frequency of call, and they may
even be said to have declined in both, since the day when his
dear boy came home to him, and then went away so suddenly
and mysteriously, last Christmas-eve.

And yet John Jasper has many visitors—may be said to be
actually burthened with them.   The pounds avoirdupois of
many of them, might be expressed in the most minute of frac-
tions or even by the arithmetical 0, while their weight upon
the spirits could scarcely be set down in any aggregation
of tons.   They have colors enough to delight a painter search-
ing after the lost tints of Titian,—shapes enough to give a new
impression of form to Euclid,—and powers of motion rendering
the mysteries of the Abracadabra things of everyday belief.
They are frequent as duns, importunate as beggars, inconstant
as lovers, unexpected as blessings, unwelcome as deserved misfortunes, mysterious as the realm from which we come and the
land to which we go.

Some of them, Oriental in their character, may have accompanied him home, unobserved, from his opium-dreams in the
miserable court in the London bye-street—lain *perdu* until
the proper time for torture, to glide out and present themselves before his eyes at a moment when he has no spell with
which to exorcise them.   Some of them — milder and more
sorrowful—may have their derivation in certain bars of music,

or in the recollections of childhood, lost loves, and perished friendships. Some of them—who can say?—may be shadows from past crimes and endured punishments, with evil faces and suffering forms bearing the manacle, wasting toil without a hope, hunger, and the lash. And some of them—dark, fearful, frequent, and horrent — may be remembrances of that blackest of shadow-lands, whereof the earth is dismal quicksands and fatal pitfalls, and the waters are gurgling flows of black blood — lying, geographically, half-way between the realms of Evil Passion and Madness.

They had been few in number and comparatively innocuous in character, before the day of the delivery of the pocket wallet by Mayor Sapsea; more frequent and worse thereafter; but increasing a thousandfold since the picking up of the black scarf on the river-bank. Before these things, they had been merely the phantom shapes of Remorse, surrounding a shadowy figure, with pitiful face and upstretched pleading arms, like that of his dear boy in death-extremity : since then, they have not only increased in number, but varied and darkened in form, bearing the mingled features of that same Remorse combined with Horrible Fear.

Not all impalpable or of ghostly shape, these visitors, either, though many of them have at once that double and that lesser alarm. There are some, bearing human form, not to be mistaken in their humanity or their profession. There is one, a dog, of late coming, that can scarcely be called a visitor, as it has never come nearer to the Gate House than a certain distance from the window, where he has seen it, once and again, sitting erect and black, unmistakably gazing towards that window—silent, grim, terrible, and always leaving the same doubt, as he has removed and replaced the curtain, whether it is a veritable beast, with claws and teeth to tear and throttle ; a phantom form of some fierce dog that has been, such as might follow the Wild Huntsman in that Demon Chase through the Black Forest ; or a shape from the Lower World, sent to haunt him till the appointed day, and then drag him downwards with the awful metamorphosis of the Faust.

Perhaps the visitors bearing the human impress are the most terrible of all—coming nearest, as they do, to representing that awful Possibility hanging over him from the hour of the delivery of the pocket-wallet : representing as they do, not Remorse, but Discovery, Detection, Arrest, Imprisonment, Trial, Conviction, Sentence, The Gallows ! For among them are so evidently the shapes of those whom he has seen when they were bearing corresponding relations to others—officers of the law, in pursuit, armed, and sometimes with gyves showing in their hands or clanking horribly in the pockets where they lie concealed for human wrists ; criers commanding attention for the most solemn of duties, in the midst of crowds whose upturned faces have an interest sickening to the beholder ; stern judges, black-robed and severe-faced, opening close-set mouths to deal out vengeance only less severe than that denounced against red-handed Cain.   And one figure there is, accompanied by a double voice, which belongs to another invisible, which returns so often, that he has come to know the features of the one and to recognize the sound of the other—though all besides seems hidden in a whelming dark, smoky mist, beneath which there may be, for all that he can tell, that same awful sea of upturned faces.   How much of this is from past recollection of scenes where men have been on trial for their lives, or how much of it may be an omen of some dreadful future soon to be—how can the bewildered, opium-soddened, guilt-appalled brain be capable of measuring ?   He only knows that he has seen that black-capped grim judge's face so often, during the last unendurable days, that he has even learned by rote the words of the Clerk of Arraigns, and of the Crier, announcing that the verdict has been given, and that only the one dread formality remains for the Court that commissions the Hangman. Strange blendings of the past and present realities of a life ! ever as this recurs, as recur it does, now, at such brief intervals as to indicate that by-and-by it will be only one long procession of dreadful sight and sound—ever as this recurs,

the passion and habit of his profession come up with it, and
the voice of the doomster becomes blended with the sound of
a chorus of thousand voices sweeping and rolling through the
arches of a cathedral so many scores of times larger and
gayer than his own, that it seems to span the whole round
globe; and these are the words that so over and over again he
hears, half-said, half-sung, until there is nothing else in
earth or heaven, nay, nothing else in hell, than that one awful
formula:

"Prisoner at the bar! After a prolonged investigation,
conducted with a patience and care which leave nothing to be
desired on the part of a jury of your countrymen, you are pronounced guilty of *murder*—a verdict in which I entirely con-
cur. If anything has been said or omitted which can be explained in your favor, the law gives you one more chance.
What have you to say that sentence of DEATH should not be
passed upon you?"

There comes a pause, broken only by the muttering thunder of the long echo under the arches; and in that pause
(sometimes this is in sleep) he feels himself struggling to give
utterance to words of denial—to protestations of love for his
dear boy, too tender to allow his laying hands upon him—of
accusations of another, on whom will be found some of the
property of the murdered. But he cannot succeed, be it
night or day, in giving utterance; and after a moment he
hears another key of the double voice go on, in tones only
less rolling and sonorous, and yet more awful to the quailing
sense:

"*Oh, you! Oh, you! Oh, you! My lords, the Queen's
justices, do strictly charge and command all persons to preserve silence while sentence of death is passed upon the prisoner at the bar, upon pain of imprisonment. God save the
Queen!*"

And then he listens, still, although the thunder-tone has
ceased and that grave face is fading from his sight—listens
and looks as well, to see the set lips move and hear them

speak, in yet another voice, those solemnest of all mere
human words which give a living man to dust and worms,
yet calling on the God whose privilege of life and death is
thus perforce usurped to hold the hand of violence from scat-
tering murder broadcast through the land—calling on Him
to show that mercy to the perilled soul which mortal justice
is not strong enough to hazard all the future by declaring to
the forfeit life. He listens so, but never seems to hear. The
grave face fades away, entirely, now; the echoes heralding the
words of doom grow still; all changes to the nothing that it
was; to be again recalled at any hour, and shake with awful
tremors soul and body, as if for one at least has come the
Judgment Day so looked for and so dreaded by the Ages.

So much has been, and is. But how much more may come,
at any hour—whether in imagination or reality! What, if
in the first, the fancy should change to that one yet more
horrible, and the face of the hangman take the place of th
of the judge! What, if he shall begin to see, in advance
of any possible actual rehearsal of the same scene, the coming of the dread official into his prison cell, ascend the scaffold, see that sea of faces without any smoky mist to hide
them, hear the howls of execration bursting from ten thousand throats, feel the rope around his neck, the drop falling
away beneath his feet—feel—oh, God!—Death while yet a
living man! What, if among that crowd he should see *her*
face—that face for which he has given up time and eternity,
and for which, yet, if he could only call it *his*, he would give
up as many of each as could be crowded into imagination!
Could the brain bear this? and would he not end all, at some
moment more mad than others, by leaping into that Presence
so impossible to meet—so certain to blast the slayer of his own
blood, and the false witness, with consuming fire!

And what, beyond even this, of fearful reality? What is
it that hangs above his head, in terrible earnest? Whence
these things which should not exist in the outer world—that
should be hidden as closely as the crime? How much is

known—how much guessed—how much suspected? Is he merely harassed with his own self-created fears, like a fool?— or is he being played with, deliberately and cruelly, by that Power which only gives him respite for agony — the tiger dallying with the prey that nothing can prevent its crunching? Question above all—where is IT? What has happened to IT? What has been taken from IT, and what remains? Horror to know, but double horror to continue in doubt, and that incapacity for defence which ignorance involves! And so——

So John Jasper passes silently out from the Gate House, late one night, when this torture has grown unendurable. Going towards a spot than which he would rather visit any other on the broad earth, and to do that which is only less terrible than the phantoms haunting him and the shameful death menacing him. The night is a moonlight one, reminding him of another, when he made his explorations of the Cathedral, under the guidance of Durdles, and certain other explorations by no means within the knowledge of the stonemason.

The hour is so late that not many persons are likely to be abroad in sleepy old Cloisterham, guiltless of many routs or revels, and proverbially going to bed with the rooks. And yet he goes out displaying as much care, as to certain details of his equipment, as if he was sure to encounter many eyes and needed to be careful in concealment. He wears a larger top-coat than the warmth of the season demands, especially for so short a distance as that he is about to traverse; and both the large pockets of this large coat are bulky, to the point of being ungracefully protrusive in day-light.

But his way of proceeding towards his destination makes the distance much longer than it need be; for he passes out from the archway into the High Street, goes up it for a certain distance, towards the Nun's House, then turns to the right, down a narrow side-street and emerges, after two or three turnings, but without encountering a solitary promenader, as there is reason to believe that he fears, from many and furtive glances on either side. Thus he approaches the Cathedral from the opposite side to the Gate House, and also reaches it in deep shadow.

Pausing for a moment, he takes something from one of his overfilled pockets, which proves to be a large Key—though certainly not the key with which Durdles gave him admission on a former occasion. Whatever its identity, it serves to unlock the low door leading into the crypt, which operation he performs, as also the opening of that door and closing of it when he has passed within, so carefully that an observer of superstitious tendencies might doubt whether he was not the dark-robed ghost of one of the Old 'Uns within the Cathedral, opening the portal with a phantom key held by a phantom hand, and returning to durance after a nightly promenade in the free air.

Once within the crypt and the door locked on the inside, the contents of one of the loaded pockets became apparent. He takes therefrom a bull's-eye dark-lantern, from another pocket a box of matches; and very soon thereafter the glare of light from the bull's-eye flashes among the damp and mouldy columns of the half-under ground and now disused vault, in which, perchance, religious ceremonies of peculiar solemnity may have been held in the days when Rome, addicted to subterranean splendors, held control over the old religious house. It shows, in bright relief at the focus of its radiance, mouldering tombs with dim inscriptions at the circumference of the crypt, and throws others, out of this focus, into that half-lighted gloom which suggests so much more of impressiveness than broad glare; and it makes the mouldy old arches seem sinking lower and coming down upon the head—what time the bearer of the lantern, apparently with the least distasteful portion of his task accomplished, leans against one of the columns, drops his head forward on his breast, and trembles and shivers as if the sudden chill of the vault had struck into his frame and rendered him half helpless.

This only for a moment or two, however. He shakes off the
weakness, after a time, crosses the crypt, approaches the door
leading up to the main floor, takes from his pocket another
key, with so little fumbling or hesitation as to indicate fre
quency of use—unlocks, ascends the narrow stair to the iron
gate at the top, unbolts it (through from the inner side), and
is in the body of the Cathedral.

Here, unaccountably enough, he seems more affected by the
surrounding influences, than in the deeper gloom below ; for
he looks around him with evidences of absolute terror in his
face, and seems chained to the spot where he stands, as if all
the strength of body and mind had suddenly deserted him.
On one side, the moonlight streams in through the stained-
glass of the transept windows, most weirdly and dismally ; and
this, blending with the cross-lights of his lantern, may affect
him by the combination of ghastly hues which it imparts to
some of the old prelate and warrior figures lying on their altar-
tombs in the line of light, with palmed hands pointing upward
helplessly, and seeming to ask to be forgiven the pride and
glory which gave them place. Crime is always more or less
superstitious : this man might be shuddering at the thought—
no farther from reason than many of his vaticinations—that
something of the life so represented yet lives in those gray and
often-mutilated figures, and that at any hour, recognizing the
presence of one against whose hidden practices they must
have sworn when binding knightly spur on heel or sitting
mitre on priestly brow, they may start up from their stony
sleep, seize sword or crozier as it lies beside them, and brain
the guilty midnight intruder where he stands ! He may even
go further and believe, bent upon the unholy errand on which
he goes, that before it is ended there will ring shriek after
shriek through the old Cathedral, compelled from those stony
throats, by an enormity greater than the worst perjured
knight or forsworn priest among them ever committed, and
that before and around him will stand, if he lives to descend,
a serried line of mortal foes, more terrible than flesh and
ghastly as his conjured phantoms.

This may be in his thought, unnerving him for many minutes; or something nearer to the present time may affect him only. Whatever the influence, it sets him to trembling again, brings wild terror to the eyes, and beaded drops to the brow; but whatever it is, on the other hand, he shakes it off, eventually, as it is to be believed that he has before shaken off many a fear more reasonable,—and staggers across the choir to the low door leading up, first to the organ loft and then to the tower.

For this door, too, the last locked one on his course, he finds a key in his pocket, with the same facility which has so quickly found the others; and opening this, he avoids the curve of the narrow stone stairway turning away to the organ-loft on the left, and keeping the main stair-case, black with age, and foul with the dampness of many fogs that have crept in thither and never been expelled, comes at last to the end of that stairway and the level of the roof, beyond which, into the tower itself, another leads, of wood and of much less antiquity in construction.

His errand does not seem to be in the tower or farther towards it; for, pausing here, he extracts yet another key from his pocket, with the same ready facility, and inserts it into a low black wooden door at the level of the stair-head. But he does not open it with the same readiness shown in finding the key. Another of those fearful shudderings seizes him — so strong and powerful, that it becomes a veritable spasm, sending the beaded drops from his brow, almost like rain, causing him to set down the lantern in very great fear of extinguishing it, and wringing from him absolute groans of agony. Behind that door!—what can there be behind that door, thus concentrating all the pained capacities of his nature, and threatening to send him headlong to the floor still as a corpse, or dashing out his brains as a maniac? IT? Who knows, save God and himself?

But this spasm, too, passed; for John Jasper, even yet, is a strong man, in that sense involving the recovery of self-command. He sweeps away the beaded drops from his forehead, with a gesture of such shame as if some one had beheld him in unmanly weakness; takes up the lantern from the floor, and dashes his hand upon the key in the door, with what can only be described as *trembling fierceness*. This door, too, opens, and he passes into that floored space, between the beams of the ceiling below and the rafters of the roof above, for which the architects have neglected to supply any technical name to the lay-world, but the outer or gabled end of which, in the Greek orders, would be called the tympan of the pediment. A place seldom visited, as may be supposed—nothing less than a conflagration or the bursting in of the roof by water, being likely to send any one thither in the space of a dozen years.

John Jasper is staggering a little, now, spite of his remains of fine bodily strength, and his undeniable nerve; and his face, in its blended fierce determination, horror, and terror, is something awful to behold. But he sets down the lantern, with another groan of agony not easy to designate in character—and applies to the other pocket of the large coat, from which he takes several yards of a stout soft rope, knotted at distances of about a foot each. Then he throws off the coat, and follows that movement by throwing off his remaining or body-coat, standing in his shirt-sleeves, as if something is about to be done, demanding freedom of arm and involving severe labor. What can that something be? Has it anything to do with IT?

The heavy rafters, with the stout planks resting upon them and supporting the outer roof, are dark and discolored with age and leakage. So is the planked floor; but it is notable that in one direction from the door, leading away to where the rafters lower to the eaves, there are little spots and flecks of white, as if mould or fungus of that color may have grown in the long years of dampness. He moves the lantern, so that its rays fall in that direction, shuddering and shivering all the while, as if with a more moderate recurrence of the spasm, wı ıch has lately so nearly prostrated him. He sees the small white spots, goes to his coat, lying in a heap on the floor, takes a handkerchief from the pocket, and rubs out the brightest of them with that handkerchief dampened with moisture from his mouth ! How careful ! How neat !—far past the verge of cleanliness ! And for *what ?*

Then he takes up the rope, and passes down under the rafters nearly to the side-wall and close to the point of intersection at the joint of the cross. Shivering, now, even worse than before, and the great drops standing thickly on his forehead, while his eyes are fearful in the agony of mind they express—but going on bravely with whatever he has to do. He stoops, and then puts down his hand with an obvious effort and a momentary turning away of his head as from something that cannot be borne. The hand lifts a trap-door, some three feet square, that under closer examination would show sufficient roughness in shaping to prove that it has never known the carpenter's hand ; while the same inspection would show that space for it has been made by cutting away the planks of the flooring with a chisel, in hands correspondingly unused to the craft of the wood-worker. There are hinges to the trap, but they are merely pieces of stout harness-leather, nailed on, to complete a job as unworkmanlike as ingenious and persistent. What next ? Is it here that IT is to be looked for, by eyes only too well instructed ?

Some answer to these and other questions seems probable, now ; for the next moment makes it almost certain that the suffering hero of crime is about to descend into that dark and noisome hole of blackness to which the trap gives access ! Descend !—and for what ? and to what unimagined horror of place and occupancy ? Is IT there ?—and has the need at last grown imperative, that the hidden shall be explored and the marvellous explained, at once and for all ?

He *is* about to descend, so much is plain, shivering as under an ague fit, as he may be, and evidently suffering tortures to which the rack of old time would be ordinary pain. For he

14

stands with set lips, at the edge of the black hole, and ties the knotted rope, with hand careful and strong, even if shaking, to the rafter immediately over it. It would be easy to believe, looking at rope and rafter, and ignoring the black aperture below, that he was about to close all questions, and life with it, in the quick leap of the suicide, but very different is to be his exit from an existence grown quite miserable enough to warrant the worst. He steps back towards the spot where the lantern is still standing; takes from the pocket of the top coat, still lying near, another and shorter bit of rope; takes up the lantern and commences fastening it to his waist with the rope, after the manner of a miner about to go down his shaft. A few moments more will see some solution of the mystery of all those strange preparations. Will they give the key to the place where IT may have been lying for more than half a year, undiscovered, because concealed with such demoniac ingenuity and carefulness?

Crash! Jingle! and a Yell! There must be something in this man's life and fate, connected with the breaking of glass and the scream of the human voice. For a broken pane and a woman's cry of terror have blended, not many days before, in bringing about the rescue of Rosebud from his hands; and now, at the very moment when the lantern is loosely held for tying to his body, a stone comes crashing through the round window in the pediment, accompanied by a shrill yell, of which he can plainly hear the sound, and recognize a human voice, without being able to distinguish any word at that distance.

How much he does distinguish or understand, none may know. Does he recognize it as being mortal, and so understand that the light has been seen, and dread human discovery? — or does some momentary horror of the supernatural overcome him, acting like the sudden and unaccountable panic which sends a brave and veteran army flying like a herd of frightened deer?

For the lantern drops from the busy, shaking hand, extin-

guished in the fall; and with a cry of mortal terror he feels
for his clothes, grasps them, feels for the door, opens and flees.
Down the stair, in the darkness, except as the struggling
moon-rays through the small windows give him a trifle of
light. Breathing hard, like a hunted stag that has been
chased nearly to the verge of endurance and must soon suc-
cumb. Trembling in every limb; sweating cold sweat at
every pore; staggering, stumbling, nearly falling, once and
again. He pauses to close and lock the doors behind him,
and this seems to exhaust at once thought and nerve.
Through the body of the Cathedral, where the light is
better, but where he does not see the recumbent statues,
now, or think of them as rising to judgment — with that
greater terror behind. Down into the crypt, again; out into
the open air on the shadowy side of the Cathedral; and the
flight not stayed even then—not until he is in his own apartment in the Gate House, sinking in the last stage of mental
and bodily exhaustion, and older by half-a-score of years, if
the grey hair of to-morrow can give any true evidence, than
he was when he left the same apartment, less than an hour
ago.

John Jasper has heard nothing more than the crash of the
window, and the yell too distant to distinguish words. One
at that moment nearer, would be aware that a limited bom-
bardment of the Cathedral, to fierce martial music, has been
in progress, consequent upon the discovery of the light in
the pediment window by the wandering Deputy, on his way
homeward (or elsewhere) from some Bedouin excursion,—and
that the practices of the most warlike nations of the barbaric
world have been duly carried out, in the fitting of the words
of the national hymn to a special occasion, with high poetic
power and fervor—the Yell, so important in its results, being
nothing more than one of the louder bars of:

> " Widdy widdy wen,
> I sees—a—light—arter—ton ;
> Widdy widdy way,
> I—takes—the—old—windy—in—the—eye!
> Widdy widdy wakecock warning."

CHAPTER XIV.

RASH MR. GREWGIOUS.

THE remark may not be strictly new, that the heroism of non-combatants often throw into the shade those of the recognized fighting fraternity; but at the worst it may be repeated without danger of working serious demoralization among those who are to be depended upon for resisting that long-coming Invasion. If trite, it is true; and perhaps none more fully comprehend the fact than those who have oftenest dared bodily peril by land and sea, and thus discovered that there are so many things to be more dreaded. Certainly that distinguished Field Marshal, the dare-devil admiration of two armies, who could never meet his Xantippe little wife without something approaching to serious bodily fear—he, if yet alive, may endorse the statement; even if that other and scarcely-less noted commander, who came home covered with glory from the fiercest battles of the Flemish campaign, to mount a chair in mortal terror of the scampering of a mouse around his feet,—has ceased to be humanly available as a witness.

This is not intended to be especially a record of heroisms; and yet something of the kind may have crept into it, without reckoning the uncalculating devotion of Helena Landless. Something of the chivalric may have made its unexpected appearance among baser and more ordinary elements; it being a consoling fact that nature has the same habit of dashing unhoped-for lights into many a dark picture, which she often balances by blurring and blotting those that might otherwise be too satisfactorily brilliant.

Fortunately, perhaps, the Bar and the Pulpit only, of the three leading professions, have been represented in the present instance; unless Mr. Tartar, lately come, may be held to have introduced the combative element in the direction of the Naval arm. But it happens that Mr. Tartar is precisely the

person who has no sacrifices whatever to make—rather that he
has seemed to be the Lucky Prince arriving late, after the
surmounting of most of the dangers by others, and at once
becoming the prospective possessor, for scarcely the asking, of
that divine Princess for whose sake all the blood has been
fruitlessly shed by the earlier combatants. So he must stand,
at last, out of the calculation; and between the Bar and the
Pulpit must be adjudged the palm of heroic sacrifice.

It was certainly no ordinary development of the emotion of
generosity (the true foundation of the heroic), which could
induce Mr. Crisparkle, profoundly loving Helena Landless,
and believing that in her possession would be found the best
good of a life,—to forego any pursuit of her, without a word
to indicate his passion, with no belief that she had formed
any conflicting attachment, and only moved by the two
thoughts, that he owned a mother who must fill to him all
dear relations combined, and that possibly his usefulness in
the service of his Master might be impaired by the distraction
of marriage. But Mr. Crisparkle, as we have seen, was warily
wise in carrying out his difficult renunciation. He had no
absolute duty which could lead him often into the presence
of the woman whom he loved almost to the verge of adoration; and his discipline of mind (nearly perfect, like that of
his body) was too good, not to make him aware how much he
would avoid suffering by making her already little more
than a memory. True wisdom, this, beyond a doubt; as it
will always be for any one who utters with a personal application the prayer: " Lead us not into temptation ! " to avoid
leading *himself* in that direction oftener than is inevitable.

This of the Pulpit. Very different was the action of the
Bar in the person of Hiram Grewgious, Esq., of Staple Inn,
whose status, as another of the hopelessly loving, has been
already established to melancholy satisfaction; and it is with
reference to his action that the question of comparative heroism arises, however that of wisdom may determine itself, once
for all.

"Hiram Grewgious, you may be a fool, but there is no obligation to become a coward! Labor for strength, and even pray for it * * * that you may see *her* wooed and wedded, as you saw her mother, and claim neither love nor pity, as you deserve none!" So the old lawyer had said, sitting in his lonely chambers, on that eveuing following the rescue from the attempted abduction; and upon that faith and that resolution he had acted during the little time elapsiug between that night and another following it very closely, in which his imprudence seemed to culminate—in which possibly his heroism also culminated temporarily, only to reach a still higher point at one not distant day already foreshadowed.

Rosa had never seemed to find so much necessity for him, or so many errands with him, since that eventful visit to Cloisterham which immediately preceded the tragedy, as during that brief period. Perhaps an added feeling of gratitude for the rescue towards the one guardian who remained so faithful to her, may in some degree have conduced to this; perhaps the increasingly gritty state of the domestic affairs at Billickin's, in which speaking hostility had been succeeded by silent ill-treatment, gave her more necessity than might otherwise have existed for seeking the counsel of the man who had unwittingly placed Miss Twinkleton and herself in that mild purgatory. At all events, her visits to the quiet gloom of the chambers, which she always seemed to brighten like a stray beam of dancing sunlight, were even more frequent, at about this time, than would have been demanded by her occasional calls upon Helena Landless in such near proximity; and the tiny notes, in the intervals of the visits, which called Mr. Grewgious to Southampton Street, were correspondingly and unusually numerous.

And how bravely — aye, how heroically — he bore it all, when the self-defence of avoiding her would have seemed a simple duty which he owed his own peace of mind, and when every step of the light foot and every tone of the girlish voice must have fallen like a blow upon the brave old heart, with a

pain which the inflictor could no more understand than avoid
giving! How calmly he schooled himself to meet the frequent touch of her atom of hand, which he felt to be given to
him with no more tender tremor than would have characterized it when laid on the head of a faithful old dog that she
might be patting,—and which had yet the power to move
every pulse of his being with an intensity generally credited
only to the young, while the young ordinarily know no more
of it than of grey hairs or sciatica! And how he said over
and over again, in action, what even the brave and self-deny-
ing Minor Canon would have lacked courage to say, under
corresponding circumstances :

"Every time that I see her, I love her more and more
dearly, with that love which has come back to me from her
drowned mother, especially to be expended again upon *her.*
Every time that I meet her, I know only the more surely how
hopeless is the distance between us—how I, the Angular old
man, could not win, if I would, this darling child who might
have been my daughter—and would not, if I could. It might
be some men's privilege to run away; it is not mine. My
folly has been criminal, and it is only just that I should bear
this as my punishment."

The present culmination to all this, came in the manner now
to be indicated.

We have, when young (perhaps we have the same when old
—only lack that delicacy of perception which instructs us *after*
wrong-doing), an enviable faculty of performing acts of positive cruelty, with the very kindest intentions, and not the least
thought in the world that we are doing anything else than
making people cherubically, or seraphically happy—as the sex
may be. Rosa carried out this trait, by taking into her
charming little rattle-pate an idea which could not be otherwise disposed of than indulged. And one evening, very few
days after the cab-adventure, she assailed the Angular man
with a suggestion growing out of it.

"Do you know what I look back upon—not very long, of

course, but long enough to look back—as the happiest hour of my trifling little life ? "

The question so naïvely asked, surprised Mr. Grewgious in so great a degree that it actually set him blushing a little, and quite put him out of any power of considering it rationally which he might naturally have possessed. He plunged into the sea of necessary speculation, however, manfully if awkwardly.

"The happiest hour, my dear ? The question is a trifle embarrassing, because I have reason to suppose that nearly all your hours have been happy—not of course, every moment—such as those in—yes, say in cabs in which you did not wish to ride, for instance. I think if you gave me a wider field, and asked me what I believed to have been the happiest time for all concerned, connected with yourself, I might be disposed to answer—the hour when you were born."

"Oh, please do not say that !" she exclaimed, with more than ordinary feeling manifest in face and voice. " I am sure that I am such a worthless little thing, and make so much trouble for every one, that the very opposite might be said, with more truth."

"Trouble, my dear ? " he echoed, with the air of one to whom some astounding proposition, not before reckoned as even a remote possibility, had suddenly been thrust forward.

" Yes, trouble, and worse ! Think how much I cost poor Eddy, who did not love me at all, and think what I *should* cost any one who did love me."

The Angular man did not groan, as he had more than a temptation to do. Perhaps it was the very age that he re-gretted which saved him that exhibition of weakness. For the thrust so little intended, was sharp, and it went home. What should she not cost, indeed, to one who loved her !—what was she not costing, day by day, to one who had been unwise enough to assume the two antagonists, Love and Hopelessness, at the same moment !

But what a hero of heroes was this unromantic and very commonplace man, who would not only force himself to endure the agonizing presence of the woman he loved without one thought of hope, but who would not even avoid saying or receiving those words naturally calculated to try him to the utmost! What besotted folly was it to reply, following her self-depreciation:

"Umps! I am an Angular man, as I have before told you, I think; and a bachelor, beginning to wear the prefix 'old' before that name,—so I cannot be expected to judge the passion very intelligently. Indeed, my dear, I do not remember ever having seen any one worth loving, in what I suppose to be the true sense of the word, except—your mother. But I should say——"

"My mother! my poor mother! and she was drowned! Oh, why, why, why did they allow her to drown!" exclaimed Rosebud, breaking in a little inconsequently, and thus making what might be called a temporary change in the channel of the conversation——"

"I cannot say, I am sure, not having been present at the moment when the accident occurred; but I was assured that everything was done——"

Another interruption, not quite so inconsequent as the preceding.

"Oh, why, why was not Mr. Tartar there, to save my poor mother!"

"Mr. Tartar, my dear!" Mr. Grewgious accepted the change of channel, enough to say. "Of course I am ignorant, too, why he should not have happened to be on the spot; but you must realize the impossibility of any one person being present at the same moment at all the places in the world, where other persons might be liable to fall into the water. Still——"

"*He* would have saved her, I know! He saved Mr. Crisparkle, you remember, and I believe he is strong enough to save any one, anywhere!" came the third interruption, followed by a sudden silence, and a blush which might have caught the attention of eyes younger than those of Mr. Grewgious. Then the course of the channel of conversation seemed to be turned back in its original direction, with a suddenness indicating that the preceding had grown either dangerous or distasteful.

"But why do you make me think of so many things, when I am trying to say something else? Next I shall forget all about it myself! You have not told me, yet, when you believe that I was happiest in all my life."

"Certainly I have not, my dear," he replied, "for the very good reason—though I believe that no lady is bound to consider it conclusive—that I do not know."

"You might, then!" pouted Rosebud. "You certainly ought, as it is all about *you*. Do, do, do think twice, and tell me!"

Mr. Grewgious could not have told her, at that moment, had he known, and had life depended on the exercise of his enunciatory faculties. For the unfortunate combination of the young girl's words—blending her greatest pleasure, and *him*—may be easily understood, as well as partially the effect produced. For one instant a mad, delicious thought ran through him, making every pulse tingle, sending the blood like a torrent to cheek and brow, and lifting the sad, patient old heart so high as to choke utterance. What if——. The other words of the mental sentence were never supplied, for before they could be shaped, came the one crushing word, forming a sentence in itself: Impossible! and behind it rang out two others, used so many times before, and forming another pregnant sentence: Old Fool! Then the rebellious heart sank back to its proper place, the momentary madness passed from face and frame, the throat ceased choking, and the voice returned.

"Really, my dear young lady," he said, when the voice was clear enough for that exercise, "I am stupid enough not to know what time you refer to, unless it may possibly be the visit that I had the honor to pay you at the Nun's House, to make arrangements for terminating my guardianship. That prospect, and certain other things connected, may have had the effect——"

Fourth interruption, with the pout very decided, though even under such circumstances the little face was the reverse of formidable.

"Why, what a dear stupid old guardy you are, to be sure!" stopping to emphasize with an impatient pat of one small foot hidden somewhere near the floor. "What other time *could* I mean, than the evening when I first came to your dear dismal old rooms in the Inn, yonder, and when you gave me—oh, such a very, very, very nice supper!"

"Umps! ah, yes, my dear—I understand, now," said the lawyer very quickly—quite reduced, we may be sure, from his mental inflammation of a few minutes earlier. "I remember, of course, that *I* enjoyed that first visit very much; and I think I may have remarked, on that occasion, that your coming saved very heavy expense in the way of painting, paper, gilding, and otherwise beautifying the room which certainly needed renovating. But Lord bless me! I had no idea that *you* could have been so pleased with the *supper.*"

"With the *supper?* oh, why, why, why will you misunderstand me so, or tease me so if you do not mistake what I mean! Just as if I cared for a supper!—and just as if I didn't mean that it was so nice and jolly to feel safe and to be where I suppose that young ladies are not in the habit of taking their suppers, and to sit on the opposite side of the table to you."

Another suggestion of the Impossible, that without the preparation of the previous crisis, might have produced scarcely less effect on the hearer. For no dearer thought fills the mind of the expectant lover, than that some day the form so dear will sit opposite to him at his household table, giving him a feast of the heart from her loving eyes and pleasant lips, at the same moment when he pampers the body with more substantial viands; and there are few pictures drawn by pen or pencil, more sweetly appealing to all that is domestic in the

love-nature, than those which exhibit the opposite companion-
ships of the Table and the Ingle-Side. But this unfortunate
suggestion, too, was neutralized after one more exertion of the
patient will, and he was enabled to answer with the same outward calmness of simplicity:

"Ah, I see, as I should have done at first: there were other
things than those brought by this person from Furnival's contributing to the pleasant result; and I need not say that you
make me proud and happy by referring to the occasion."

"Do I? Thanks, then, for you make it easy to say what I
wish to say so very, very much! Did I paint the old bookcases, and paper the walls, and make the whole place look so
jolly, just by laughing like the poor little chit that I am?
Take care, sir—don't tell stories, mind!" and she held up a
terrible warning forefinger of less than two inches in length—
"for you have no idea what will happen to you if you do. If
one girl's face made the old place so jolly, you will have it all
ablaze some evening; for I am going to ask you to give me
another supper, just like that, and allow me to bring some one
else with me who is worthy of being called a visitor."

"Lord bless me, my dear young lady!" the surprised lawyer exclaimed, his brain all in a whirl at the suggestion, and
yet a wild, imprudent joy overmastering surprise. "Another
supper? Certainly. Tick that off, as already arranged.
When shall it be? Say to-morrow evening? You approve—
excellent. Tick that off, as the time. And for how many—
remembering that the place is small as well as mean, and that
there would scarcely be room for more than a dozen?"

"A dozen! why, good gracious, you dear old willing guardy!
What can you be thinking about? It is only Helena, who
has heard me speak, so often, about our wonderful supper,
which seems to me to have been the nicest that ever, ever was
laid,—and who has promised that if you will permit her to
come with me and make all the dry old law-books angry by
eating among them, she will thank you *so* much!"

"Helena?—Miss Landless? Certainly, with the greatest

pleasure!" exclaimed the old lawyer, literally wild with delight at the prospect, forgetting any danger or pain that might
be involved, and springing up with an alacrity marvellous in
so Angular a man,—under some sort of idea that he must
rush around to Staple's at once, inform P. J. T. of the double
honor about to be done him, in the presence of the Precious
Jewel Two, and of the Peculiar Junketing Triumph certain to
be achieved under his auspices,—besides employing a small
army of persons to make war upon accumulated dust, rearrange
everything in the dingy old rooms, and generally reduce them
to a condition of splendid propriety, such as might be considered necessary in one of the great feudal mansions when under
expectation of the Sovereign's arrival in the course of a Royal
Progress.

He checked himself, however, before actually rushing out to
the street to put the royal preparations in progress—and added
a suggestion which bore immediate fruit.

"Now that I think of it, my dear, why be selfish, even if I
should be quite as glad to have the company of Miss Landless
and yourself as all St. Giles' and St. George's?   There is room
for more than three, even at my small table; and the hotel at
Furnival's is running over with good things that are very jealous at not being consumed more rapidly.   What say to one or
two more—Miss Helena's brother, for instance?   He is very
lonely and goes out so seldom ; and perhaps *you* could induce
him, even if I failed."

"Oh, yes, if you would be so very, very good!" was the
pleased assent, with clapping hands as the accompaniment,
leading Miss Twinkleton, who entered at the moment, to believe that the Billickin had intruded and been ignominiously
routed, and that this was a demonstration of joy at her discom-
fiture.

"And now that I think of it again," the Angular man went
on, "there is another.   Why not have four?—making five
with myself (Mr. Bazzard has not returned—so that he will
not need to be consulted)."

"Oh, who? who?" inquired the young lady, who may or may not have been entirely in the dark with reference to the next suggestion, taking into account the sparkling eyes and the slightly-flushed cheeks accompanying the inquiry.

"Well, the truth is, my dear," replied Mr. Grewgious, feeling that possibly a little apology might be necessary in this instance, for—so to speak—intruding the other person of the party—"the young man of Naval antecedents, who swims so well and is so strong, as you did him the honor to remember a little while ago."

"Oh!" interjected Rosebud, though whether in mere surprise or gratification, the lawyer might have been puzzled to decide as he certainly did not.

"Mr. Tartar," he went on, "is scarcely so confined or lonely in his habits as his young neighbor, as you are no doubt aware, as I think he sometimes calls upon you——"

"Yes, sometimes!"

(Oh, Rosa!)

—"But possibly he might consider the little attention a pleasant one, without being at all in the way; and then in the event of any music being considered proper, I believe that these marine people always sing, and he might be able to accompany *you*, as I think that our young friends, the Landlesses, are not melodious."

Yes, Rosa thought, taking all in all, that there could be no objection to adding Neville Landless to the original three, and no insuperable difficulty as to Mr. Tartar, though she did not speak very enthusiastically (little half-unconscious hypocrite!) of the prospect of the latter's presence. And Mr. Grewgious, feeling that a privilege had really been conferred upon him, in permitting him to make those additions to the company first-named, manifested (grey-headed and Angular old noodle!) something of that pronounced delight in the prospect of the *soirée* of limited proportions, likely to be exhibited by a schoolboy in whose favor a child's party has been kindly arranged by his parents or guardians. It was to give Rosa

pleasure—dear little Rosebud, the daughter of her mother;
no consideration of peace to himself, or prudence for the future,
could have weighed for one moment against her expressed
wish, in the mind of the ultra-heroic and most unwise and
Utopian old lawyer of Staple Inn.

CHAPTER XV.

SUPPER AND MUSIC FOR FOUR.

IT need scarcely be said that the single day intervening
between the evening of making the arrangement, and the
Appointed Festal Night, was all too short for the needs and
requirements of that day—and that Staple Inn, jealous of the
honors of the Middle Temple, which boasts a tradition of
Oliver Goldsmith having kept up a singing revel in his chambers there, until complained of by the tenants of the apartments below,—notes this event in its humdrum history, with
that mingling of pride and indignation very often bred of the
Unaccustomed. The substitute for Bazzard, under orders
from his employers below to supply the place of that gentleman in light attendance upon Mr. Grewgious, found his situation anything else than a sinecure during that special day, so
many removals and re-arrangements needed to be made in
what was before quite sufficiently in order; and the entire
culinary force of the hotel in Furnival's may have believed
that Staple was about to undergo a siege, and heavily provisioning to that end, from the amount and variety of food
ordered to be ready at a certain hour of the evening.

Staple himself may have been astounded, and no doubt
P. J. T., date 1747, was so, at the coming in, in the hands of
two porters, of a sofa of very peculiar and incongruous construction, long viewed by Mr. Grewgious with interest, on
account of its rare oddity, at a shop in Oxford-street, but

never achieving the triumph of purchase until this day; and language must fail in the attempt to convey the scandalization of both Staple and P. J. T., when a light van sat down an upright piano, and the men managed to convey it up the stairs with such skill in navigation, on their own behalf, that they should at once have been enrolled as pilots for difficult navigation—and the piano itself, from the extent of its wanderings and the improbability of its ever reaching the place actually achieved, deserved place among the Eminent Travellers of the Geographical Society.

The chandler, too, was placed under severe requisition during the afternoon, for various and sundry pounds and packages of candles, fortunately of wax, as had they been of tallow, and seen to enter any one doorway, the impression would undoubtedly have got abroad on Holborn, and supplied a legend for all future time—that a party of Russians at that period held a grand banquet at Staple, consuming unlimited fried-candles as the crowning delicacy of their feast. For these, the ironmonger was obliged to supply candlesticks and sconces, to the extent of depleting his shelves devoted to those articles, and putting him in immediate correspondence with Birmingham for a fresh supply, and also of suggesting a doubt, they being intended to hold the all-prevailing candles, what place in the limited space at command was to hold *them*.

It will always remain a question whether Mr. Grewgious, in this extraordinary provision of lights, was merely following the tradition of the old royal gatherings at the palaces now gone to decay, that the radiance of wax-tapers was the only one fit to be allowed to show on the cheek of beauty, but could not, being perfect in kind, be excessive in quantity, to reveal the softened beauties of the fairest of the fair, or whether he was merely expressing the general joy of Staples, in the way of an illumination in honor of the coming of distinguished guests; but really the moot is no serious one, the patent fact being established that in one way or the other he was performing what he believed to be the highest duty of loyalty and chivalry.

Not the only one of those highest duties, however. Personally, his sacrifices at the same shrine were little less than tremendous.

There are secrets of the male toilet only less impenetrable than those of the female, so that it may be difficult to throw any clear light (like that of the multitudinous wax-candles) upon this point.

His coat, for instance, had cost him hours of anxious thought and study. He had drawn sketches of it; and, as to his waistcoat, all the colors of the rainbow had been passed under supervision, and compared with the wonderful coat, and the effect upon the trowsers carefully and mathematically calculated. These latter articles, we should say, were the least successful part of the dress, to unprejudiced observers, though eminently satisfactory to the amiable, if unfashionable, Grewgious himself.

But certain it is that Rosebud, could she have seen her guardian, under observant and unembarrassed circumstances, as arrayed *en grande tenue*, an hour before her coming, and had she applied to him her peculiar formula of girlish wondering inquiry, would have said:

"Oh! where, where, where, Mr. Grewgious, did you get that coat with the collar sawing off your ears, and the skirts narrow enough for a pair of pen-wipers—like some of the prints that I have seen, of beaux who flourished immediately after the naughty, dear, dreadful Prince Regent? How, how is it, that the vest has been laid away so long that it is yellow? or was it originally yellow and has it faded? And why, oh why, did they not make your trowsers the least tiny bit in the world longer, so that you would show a little less of your dear old stockings, and make us fancy that your precious old varnished shoes were the least trifle smaller?"

But Rosa, as may be imagined, was not present at the proper moment for any such good-natured animadversions; and the good old lawyer, whatever trouble he had taken with his personal adornment—even to the procurement of fragrant

15

Maccassar for the straight hair, making it even less manage-
able than ordinary—was not likely to observe either the
perfections or imperfections at which he had arrived ; merely
congratulating himself, probably, that the unwonted refine-
ments of dress had made him a trifle less Angular and so less
obnoxious to the eyes of the Pretty Jilts Twain about to pass
under the escutcheon of P. J. T.

Angular as was Mr. Grewgious, there were some of the
details of good living by no means unknown to him—as his
own private store of wines, darkly imprisoned below by a legal
power which they had no means of calling in question, and
only released at the last moment of existence—may already
have given evidence to the careful observer.   And there were
certain maxims which he must have imbibed, other than legal,
and going beyond that cardinal one which sends the consumer
to his cellar for wine, and to that of the dealer for vinegar.
Among these was one pointing to the folly of receiving festal
visitors at any moment before the meal should be ready for
service ; and the wisdom of preventing, for himself and them,
that dreariest of half-hours preceding the taking of places at
table.   As a consequence, in this instance, the supper came
over from Furnival's almost at the very moment when the
guests were arriving,—brought by the Flying Waiter who had
served him on the occasion of poor Edwin Drood's unexpected
supper, assisted by two others, subordinate and only less active
than himself, and not tyrannized over by the Immovable of
that occasion, who was understood to have been driven out of
his immobility and " moved on " by the inexorable policeman
of the Hadeian district, immediately after a dinner rendered
indigestible from gradual stagnation of all the vital powers.
The wines, retaining yet the flash of the ruby, the glow of
pale gold, and the glint of yellow harvest straw, in spite of
that long imprisonment which might have proved quite sufficient to bleach the complexions of their human imbibers—had
already found their way to perilous light and fatal freedom,
under the care of the Substitute, who seemed to be mar-

vellously well pleased with his task, and who may have divided
cargo, after the manner of stevedores loading ships, putting
part on decks and the remainder below, to much additional
convenience. Mr. Grewgious had overlooked all, with much
rubbing of the long hands, and much screwing of the Angular
face into expressions of peculiar anxiety, gradually smoothing
a way to satisfaction; he had opened and closed the piano at
least half a score of times, dusting the keys repeatedly with
his handkerchief, and studying them in their stupid silence, as
if something of their musical capacities might be caught by
the eye as well as the ear, with sufficient patient attention.
All was ready, and even the numerous company pertaining to
the household of the host, standing ready and silent for the
reception of youth and beauty.

There may be some who would not have recognized the
presence of these waiting retainers, from their very silence.
Far be it from us, however, to ignore them especially as they
had been dusted and even rearranged for the great occasion.
Did not stout Henricus de Bracton stand calmly in a conspic-
uous place, in his quarto coat of yellowy-white parchment,
holding out to uninstructed to-day *De Legibus et Consuetu-*
dinibus Angliæ Libri of the time of the Third Henry, and
showing that our forefathers of six hundred years ago were
equally blessed with Latin and Law, and all the Lore leading
to Litigation?   And was not Bellewe near him, in antique
calf, quarto, but tawdry in heavy gilding, opposing to the
experience of Lincoln's Inn the *Cases*, preserved by a
Bencher of that legal temple, of *Les Ans du Roy Richard*
le Second?   And near him, again, was not stout old Sir
John Fortescue, literally bulging with the round Latin of
de Laudibus Legum Angliæ, defying translation, and looking
scornfully down on an attempt thereat lying at his feet?
And was not here even richer and prouder legal antiquity,
in eclectic Cumin, classically fragrant with the Twelve Tables
of Justinian and the Fragments of Ulpian?   And here did
there not loom the mighty bulk of Domesday Book, most

interesting of British records, and invaluable to-day as it was
when it first told the story of how many broad acres had
passed into the possession of the followers of Duke William?
— and the slighter form of indispensable Kelham, bridging
that else broad gulf between the compatriots of the same
Duke William, and those whom he came to conquer?—and
the thin, attenuated but attractive presence of that brave and
Learned Lawyer, Judge Jenkins, Prisoner in Newgate, upon
Divers Statutes concerning the Liberty and Freedom of the
Subject—about which it would seem natural enough that the
grave and learned judge should then and there have been
concerned?—and a goodly row and array of others, the companions and followers of those men weighty in the law, forming the peculiar treasures of the scholarly old man who could
no more be thoroughly modern in his library than the fashion
of his coat for special occasions?

Dry company, these!—and especially as assisting at the
reception of three or four young persons who could be expected to know no more of their scope or value than of so
many Hebrew tables or Egyptian obelisks similarly placed!
But they had been, many of them since the day when there
were fewer grey hairs on his head and fewer Angular cranks
in his body, the peculiar treasures of Hiram Grewgious, Esq.,
of Staple Inn; and who can wonder at the pride with which
he ranked them even above the unequalled sofa and the wonderful piano, in imparting a certain dignity to the dull old
place that had now become a reception chamber.

An extensive and elaborate framing, perhaps, for a picture
of only moderate consequence; for really, as the guests
arrived, at that lucky moment which rendered waiting on
the part of the viands or the consumers equally unnecessary
—they seemed scarcely notable enough for all this preparation. Only three of them, when they came, in one charming
group of incongruity — the difference in sex, between Mr.
Tartar, navally reminiscent in costume, in honor of the occasion, and his two companions, scarcely more marked than that

in appearance and temperament, showing in the splendid dark
beauty of Helena and the radiant girlish English loveliness
of the Rosebud.

They were received by Mr. Grewgious, at the moment of
reaching his landing, with that alacrity which showed that he
must have been in waiting expectancy—and with that *empressement*, of an old-fashioned and ceremonious sort, which
conveyed a high sense of the honor conferred. There was a
disappointment, of course, to be commented upon and apologized for, in the non-appearance of Neville, whose health and
spirits, as Helena informed the host, were not such, that day,
as to allow of his accepting the invitation for which he was
none the less grateful. Mr. Grewgious, who knew no reason
(how should he?) why the young man should be indisposed
on that particular occasion, was thereupon about to disarrange
the whole order of proceedings by going up to his apartment,
accompanied by the Substitute, and gently forcing him down,
after the manner of an officer bringing a refractory witness
into court, but was restrained by Helena, who barred the
movement by the happy statement that her brother, suffering
from headache was at that moment in bed !

" Save the man !—can that be possible ! " the host exclaimed, under that extraordinary information. " Umps ! then it
would *not* be convenient to bring him down, would it ? and
all that we can do is to send him up such portions of the supper—say a fowl and a bottle of wine—as will not interfere
with the headache, and try to make the fifth at table out of
regrets for his absence."

It needs no messenger from the upper portions of the dusky
old tenements of Staple Inn, to tell us that Helena Landless
was in that instance—doing whatever may most midly express, in deference to a lady, deliberate falsification of fact !
Neville Landless was not in bed. Headache he may have
suffered, but his faithful and careful sister knew only too well
that the worst ache was in the *heart*—that he sat at that
moment, in an unlighted room, staring into blank darkness or

looking out on the night, with no more power to wean his thoughts entirely away from the little gathering below, than he possessed of courage to join it, and thus enjoy an hour of paradise at the expense of an afterweek of purgatory. No— the young man, at once warned and strengthened by the late conversation with his sister, was fighting the battle of renunciation more manfully than could have been believed from former weakness; but in that fight he needed, and *knew* that he needed all the aids to fortitude—absence from temptation not the least among them. Rosa was lost to him, he knew it now, and was conning that most difficult of lessons—*learning to submit*. But he could not do this and meet her often. He could not allow himself to come into her presence, except perhaps accidentally and unavoidably. To sit at table with her, for a whole evening would be little less than mental suicide: to sit with her thus, and glance from her to *the man who had now won her*, that would be madness.

There had been a conversation between the brother and sister on the subject, of course; and Helena had faintly urged him to meet his incarnated fate and be strong. But she had known, even while speaking, that he was right—that good could scarcely result and evil might follow; and she had left him with a tender kiss, thanking heaven, silently, that whatever of grief lay in any love-relation with herself, had been given *her* to bear—that there was no man sighing away his life for *her*, or wearily struggling for that negative good found in indifference or forgetfulness. Thinking this—saying this —in the generosity of her brave spirit, and little dreaming that at that very hour, perhaps, only a few score of miles away, by the shaded lamp of his study in Minor Canon Corner, or baring his brow to the celestial influences, under the stars looking down on the old Cathedral—one of the noblest and truest of men was passing through the same fiery ordeal for her sake!

But the supper!—which did not wait for these reflections, happily for the appetite and digestion of all concerned. The

supper, at which no Gurney, scribe of the closet, took surreptitious notes, even had the good things, solid and imaginative,
been equal to those of each of the Noctes Ambrosianæ—so
that the spirit of the one is necessarily lost with the aroma of
the other. The supper, at which Mr. Grewgious presided
with suave dignity, the very reverse of Angular, and at some
of the more appetising details of which pretty Rosebud
clapped her hands, repaying him a thousand times over for all
outlay and anxiety, with her exuberant admiration :

"Oh, where, where, where, you dear old guardy ! did you
find anything to please us all so much ! "

Perhaps the highest of compliments is paid to the courteous
skill of the host on that occasion, in saying that he refrained,
under innumerable temptations, from sending to Rosa, who sat
at his right hand, one and another of the various tit-bits by
which he might have marked her as the favorite among his
guests, at the same time carrying out his private belief that
she should close her dainty lips over nothing coarser than
celestial ambrosia. So that Helena was *not* neglected, as she
might so easily have been—and that Mr. Tartar was *not*
defrauded of his opportunity to pay insensible court to his
divinity through the medium of the pampered appetite.

But the hour came — all too soon yet inevitably—when
nature sank under the burthen laid upon her, and when even
the marvellous supper from Furnival's arrived at the incapable
stage of *toujours perdrix*. When Helena, marking the last
laboring efforts of the host to stimulate his guests by his own
activity, roguishly doubted whether he had not laid himself
liable to a closer acquaintance than that of the day of their
visit with the dangerous chemicals in the jars of Dr. Chippercoyne ; and Rosa said:

"Oh, don't, don't, don't ask me to eat any more, unless you
wish to kill me at once !"—which no one did, to that cruel
extent; and Mr. Tartar breezily suggested that four such
members among a ship's company would put all hands on
allowance before the cruise was half ended, if they did not
finish by eating the cabin-boy on the first banyan day.

At which astounding possibility, knives and forks were dropped by mutual consent, and the memorable supper was a thing of the past, so far as solids were concerned. But not so with those vinous prisoners from below, who became free and victims at the same moment, with the result of smoothing out almost the last Angular wrinkle from the face of Mr. Grewgious; and causing Mr. Tartar to go off with a free wind, steering large, on a cruise of adventurous narration, in which, however, he never seemed to grade higher than Second Luff, and was often no more than a Powder Monkey; and making even the bright eyes sparkle more brightly than their wont— not to mention the possible bringing out to view of certain characteristics ordinarily a little more closely hidden.

It was then that, for the first time, the old lawyer caught a dim perception of the reason why, in the inscrutable orderings of Providence, he had been led to gather the young people together in the dim old room of Staple Inn. It was then that the scene from "Othello" became re-enacted, less at length than on the evening of the abduction, at Billickin's, but still sufficient to have warned the grave old Senator of Venice, had he kept his eyes about him, and to instruct other eyes than his, once accustomed to the close reading of faces in the criminal-dock and the witness-box. It was with a sharp pang, which almost made him groan aloud, and which quite made him spill his wine in the effort at a quick gulp—that Mr. Grewgious saw and recognized what a less simple-minded man might have read an hour before—the absorbing attention with which the young girl devoured with her eyes the narrator, ever and anon evincing by a quick shudder or some girlish exclamation the terror, even in things of the past, so easy to feel for *him* — the unconscious air with which, frank, innocent, and knowing no reason why she should do otherwise, she seemed to gaze up to him as to the one prevailing master and lord, set apart from all other men, and to be received unquestioningly and completely.

The Angular man did *not* groan : so much has been said

already. He did not even spill his wine, a second time, but sipped, with a hand as steady as the staunch heart deserved to second it. And yet, in that moment, he better knew than he had believed that he could ever do, the difference between the feelings of the condemned criminal, day by day when the inevitable is as yet unreached,— and on one fatal morning when the jailer enters his cell with more than the usual pitying respect, knocks off his heavier irons, and introduces the priest who is to aid him, within an hour, in setting out on his last journey.

He had thought of her as to be wooed, won and wedded— some day, and by some one. That had been the Indefinite. He saw, now, the man ; and he could almost mark the hour. This was the Certain. A week—a month—six months—what matter how long since it was to be he ?—and she would disappear, as her mother had done, and he would be again alone —alone—alone ! as only wifeless, childless, broken old men can be !

Which of his three guests saw what must have been written on the old lawyer's face, in characters however indistinct, if he was not more than mortal ? Not one—to read and understand it as of any strong significance. Perhaps the keener eyes of Helena Landless saw something that seemed a shadow of pain, and that that was the reason why she rallied him cheerfully, the moment after, on the dangerous old fellows in the bookcases, worse than the wild animals in the doctor's bottles, who might at any moment stalk out and overwhelm them with a pitiless assault of Law, leaving each doubtful (civilly) whether they possessed everything or nothing, and (criminally) whether they had committed all the crimes in the calendar or only suffered them. But even if she saw enough to excite one moment of suspicion, that suspicion never grew to a certainty, and her tongue would have been the last to utter what could benefit none, and must cause regret to some whom she loved so dearly. As for the others— what could *they* see ? What could they be expected to see, except each other ?

Nor was there more of pained intelligence on any of those faces, let us believe, when, half an hour later, they were in the midst of a rubber at whist, in which Helena could not avoid feeling that she was but feebly supported by Mr. Grewgious as her partner — he seeming to play with something more of attention to the interests of at least one of their opponents. Nor when he exhibited the wonderful new sofa, upholstered at the two ends in different materials, cloth and leather, so as to allow what he called " first and second class " among his visitors—absolutely placing the little Queen of the occasion in the very post of honor at the first-class cushion.

Nor when the upright piano found its mission, and school-girl Rosa dashed and rattled away a dozen of beautiful nothings, which must have startled the old worthies in the bookcases from their little remaining propriety, by the intro-duction not only of music but light-hearted frivolity, into the staid domain of Law. Nor when Helena, modestly doubtful of her few and late accomplishments, but gifted with a clear voice and an excellent natural method, yielded to gentle pressing and sang, to Rosa's accompaniment, the " Last Rose of Summer," sweetly enough to bring tears into the eyes of at least two of her hearers—so full was it of the very feeling of winter snows coming down on sunny lands, of true hearts broken by neglect, and happy lives left lonely. Then there came a weird little chant of the Ceylonese, monotonous, and scarcely more than an incantation in the musical Pali, to which the bass keys of the instrument so well supplied the tap of the calabash - drum in the performances of the worshippers of Buddha. It made the blood run chill, slightly, in the veins of sensitive Rosa, to whom new worlds opened so readily ; the sailor listened, and went back in the sound to his far-away wanderings among coral rocks and orange groves ; and Mr. Grewgious, listening, remembered the visit to the doctor in Gerrard Street, thought of the errand which had carried the young girl thither, and mused over the strange combination, bodily and mental, which could make th s splendid young creature at once a thing to be loved to the death and feared with equal intensity.

Then, after a time, Mr. Tartar rather drifted than dropped into the chair which Helena had vacated, and his rich, unrestrained, and half-cultured baritone voice rang out — fresh, breezy, and conveying the irresistible impression of brown ripeness, like himself. But it made no allusion, oddly enough, to the Wooden Walls of England, which might have been expected to rise on the ear at any moment, nor repeated the consolatory truism that "Britons Never Will Be Slaves," nor even dealt with the Black Eyes of Susan, and the troubles brought upon affectionate William by a certain traditional disrespect to his superior officer, nor the nautical accomplishments of Thomas Bowline, captain of the foretop on board His Majesty's Ship the Thunderer. Instead of these he sang sea-song after sea-song, pleasantly new to his hearers, as they undoubtedly would have been to those who ordinarily provide for the marine fancies of the musical ear, sang them, roundly and feelingly, to his own simple accompaniment, which seemed rather the inspiration of the moment than any written score. Such songs, with salt air and sea foam in their every word, as had no doubt beguiled many an hour on deck in the night-watches, or in the mess-room, on those far-away seas and lonely coasts of which he had been telling so graphically—the summer breezes of the tropics sighing through them, alternated with the roaring of fierce tempests, the wails of the perilled and perishing, and the thunder crash of great guns fighting England's battles on the deep.

His skill was simple, but wondrously effective; and his auditors bowed to it as they had little expected to do when he began. Helena Landless's tawny eyes grew alternately sad and fierce, as something was to be borne, or something to be done. Little Rose clasped hands and devoured this new master of her destiny even more ravenously than she had lately been doing at table. And the old lawyer, sitting "second class" and bending forward, first craned his neck as if to come nearer to what pleased him so well, then sank back upon his seat, and leaned his head upon a hand that gradually covered more and more of his face.

Then there came a change—inspired by what, who can tell? The rich baritone voice broke out in the words and air of that plaintive old melody which our mothers must have monopolized, as their daughters know nothing of it—"Alice Gray." Mr. Grewgious's long hand was completely over his face now, though none noticed the fact. The singer went on, with the first two stanzas, and there seemed no breath in the room except his own—older and younger alike rapt with the spell. Then came the conclusion, so blending hopeless love and declining life:

> " I've sunk beneath the summer sun,
>   I've trembled in the blast:
> My pilgrimage is nearly done—
>   My life-sands nearly past.
> And when the green sod wraps my grave,
>   May pity kindly say:
> ' Ah, his heart—his heart was broken
>   For the love of Alice Gray ! ' "

What blind force was it, driving on the singer from one step to another of the sadly pathetic, and each with a pang that he could not know, to at least one listener? He knew as little as the others, we may be sure. It is enough to know that he went on, taking up a refrain much more modern but equally sad and wonderfully appropriate to his appearance and past calling. Neither of the young girls saw their host, so absorbed were they with the singer and his words. And still the lawyer sat, as they could not know—one hand over his eyes, as before, and the other pressed close upon the brave old heart that was suffering an agony never to be duplicated on this side the Dark Valley.

The first lines of the last song rang out, in the full rich baritone that seemed literally to revel in its power:

> " Don't you remember sweet Alice, Ben Bolt?
>   Sweet Alice, whose hair was so brown?
> Who wept with delight when you gave her a smile,
>   And trembled with fear at your frown?
> In the old churchyard in the valley, Ben Bolt,
>   In a corner, obscure and alone——"

"Lord bless me! Please stop, Mr. Tartar, if you don't mind! Lord bless me!—what is this?—"

The hand had come down from the lawyer's face, now: both hands were pressed close upon the heart so near to bursting. He tried to utter the words, but they came so low and faint that only Helena caught a sound of them, and neither Rosa nor Mr. Tartar distinguished them at all. So that the concluding lines were heard, in their full burst of sad melody:

> "They have fitted a slab of the granite so grey,
> And Alice lies under the stone."

Helena had started forward as she saw the gesture of suffering and half caught the words of alarm. But it was only when the last note had ceased, that the two young girls, seeing the sufferer drop yet farther forward, sprang to his assistance, followed by the startled singer, who turned as he saw the hurried movements of the others.

Mr. Grewgious was not fainting—rather choking with that rising of the heart to which over-agitation may subject even the most Angular. Leaning upon Mr. Tartar's arm, he rose to his feet, after only a moment, apologizing, in a low voice, for the alarm he had caused, and anxious to dissipate it. He had an excuse ready, too—brave old undecorated chevalier!—not the less worthy because it contained only half the truth: credited all to "Ben Bolt" and nothing to "Alice.Gray."

"Dear me!" he said, his voice very low but tolerably distinct—"Dear me!—this is very extraordinary. I assure you, if you will kindly believe me, that this has never happened before, and that I will take care it shall never happen again. The room is rather warm, is it not? And that last song, my dear," to Rosa—"I am afraid that it may have affected me a little, reminding me so much of Your Mother."

CHAPTER XVI.

THE BABBLING OF A SECRET.

THE Hour has come, and the Man.

Not many days have elapsed—bringing the Hour—since the visit paid by Joe Gilfert to the noisome and dangerous abode of the disreputable woman in the East. No doubt the phantoms have been pressing numerously and closely around the harassed man, especially since that defeated attempt at the Cathedral—rendering every hour some new variety of torture, suggesting that any distraction from their presence must be again untold, and making the Man ready for that event already foredoomed.

There have been two days of constant rain, not foretold by Zadkiel in his most comprehensive speculations; but possibly brought about ·by something done or omitted to be done by that damp apostle, St. Swithin, on his appropriate day of mid-summer. To say that London streets have been flooded, during the two miserable days, would by no means do justice to a rain-fall reaching the verge of a phenomenon : perhaps a better idea may be conveyed by saying that the oiled capes of the cab-men, after enduringly resisting the down-pour, have at last become flaccid and flabby, slinking around their figures like so many mantles of soaked muslin, and depressing their spirits to such a degree as even to make them incapable of vigorous lying over distances (to strangers), or whiningly squabbling for an additional sixpence (with all and sundry their sopped and steaming fares). The morning journals of the day, temporarily deficient in topics of thrilling interest from a dearth of Appalling Accidents, Extensive Robberies, and Great National Grievances, have found refuge in suggest-ing the organization of an Umbrella Lending Company (Limited), with principal stations at the Bank, Charing Cross, Regent Circus, &c., and sub-stations at every corner of prominence, thus rendering the world of transit less tributary to the cabmen at such periods, besides guarding against sudden and irremediable accidents to new hats and unimpeachable coats beyond the reach of the most effective cab-remedy.

But this drippy condition of affairs generally, alternating with the gritty one of previous weeks, and substituting damp for dust in the town-residences of Her Majesty's lieges, has not prevented, at an hour approaching dusk on this special day, the progress, from a well-known district, E. C., to a correspondingly well-known one W. C., of a small boy, villanously grimy-faced and perpetually dodging from expected cuffs; less than three feet in height and clothed in the turned-up and cut-off habiliments of six feet, additionally falling into the ragged strings of their warp; known to an extensive, if not a highly respectable clientele, in his own special precinct, as Nuts—possibly from some precedent possession of certain delicacies of that name surreptitiously obtained, or from an expressed inclination in that direction as yet lacking fruition.

The pluvial condition of the atmosphere, and the correspondingly watery one of the streets, as already stated, has not prevented the progress of this energetic person, on a certain Mission, with credentials in the shape of a card, pulpy by long holding in a wet hand, but still decypherable as to its legend—the vigorous pushing forward of the small bundle of rags and street-vice, through puddles assuming the depth of rivers to his short legs, and among a multitude of spattering cabs calculated to grind him up between them like the toothed cylinders of a rag-mill, being stimulated by the promise, which it must be owned that up to the moment of reception he has only half-credited, of a bright silver half-crown, capable of depleting the stalls of his bailiwick, of shelled delicacies more numerous than the sands of the sea-shore. But the half-confidence has not been misplaced.

Nuts has reached Staple Inn; he has exhibited his card, after the manner of polite society; he has been pointed gruffly to a stairway, and ascended it, with horrible suspicions of being there, then and thus entrapped into life-long imprisonment for some crime of which he may be better aware than others; he has delivered his credentials to a brown man who laughed instead of arresting him at the companion-way of the Admiral's Cabin; he has received his guerdon, tried it with his teeth before believing in the possibility of its being genuine, at last succumbed to the delirious certainty of possessing untold wealth, capable of making him thenceforth an envied wonder to Pups, and Ginger, and Creamy Joe, and other feudal barons, his peers; and then he has fled away eastward, the wondrous coin tightly gripped in the hand lately holding the card,—from the double motive of increased security and the possession of no pocket capable of retaining smaller objects than a paving-stone or a cigar-box.

There have been eleven strokes of a stubby pencil, very unsteadily made but recognizable, on the back of the card. The hour indicated is to be late, no doubt for additional security against the presence of others, difficult to eject and dangerous to retain, in the possibility of the word "unintelligible" losing a syllable. At eleven. At ten, Joe Gilfert has made his appearance in the Admiral's Cabin, waterproofed in addition to previous costume. He has been immediately joined by the Ex-Lieutenant, also waterproofed, but not to such an extent as to impair his necessary agility. Within ten minutes thereafter they have left Staple nodding and P. J. T. quite unconscious that there is any occasion to Protect Jasper's Tongue against imprudent revelations which may tend to Punish Jasper Terribly; and they have astounded a four-wheeler autocrat by promising him sixpence extra for speed and full time-rate for waiting their return at a certain locality where he knows of the existence of Meux and Co.'s Entire, suspects pipes, and can therefore pass his waiting not unpleasantly. They have reached, again, the dark and dismal streets of their previous visit— now the drowned-out and the sloppy, with apologetic feeble gas-lights flaring in the wind and winking in the drip of leaky lamps. They have left the cab; they have taken their way again, into the miserable court; they have again exchanged last inquiries and instructions; they have again separated at the door. Mr. Tartar has once more gone aloft, taking in topsails in thick and blowy weather, off Cape Finistère, or is in the tops, keeping a sharp look-out for land to leeward, in equally thick weather and half a gale going Round the Horn. And Joe Gilfert has once more put his handsome stripling face and figure, no doubt his limited amount of gold, and almost certainly his poniard, into the repulsive presence of the woman whose lungs have passed through such stages of deterioration that there are left no more adverbs and adverbial adjectives with which to describe them.

Needless to say that he has been received with whining admiration, deeply touched with greed and not free from suspicion. That in the half-hour intervening since his arrival, the handsome boy has heard the epithet "deary," and the plural noun-substantive (in that case alleged unsubstantial) "lungs," so often, in addition to previous repetitions, that he would be very willing to have them blotted out from the language during the remainder of his natural life. That there have been renewed inquiries after the promised money, only satisfied by its exhibition, — and greedy clutches, then and thereupon, making it necessary to re-exhibit another metal, in a different form. That threats as well as directions, have needed to be employed, in making the alterations in the arrangement of the miserable apartment, necessary to secure a place of temporary concealment. That the greedy old eyes have gloated, and the withered old hands worked convulsively, while the new comer has laid out, also in concealment, a small glass syringe, and a small porcelain box containing the preparation which is to do so much in other hands and may be made to do even more *in hers*. That the same greedy old eyes have watched, as if life and death hung on the issue (perhaps they do—who can say?) the process of cleaning the pipe from all previous defilements, and showing precisely the

16

proper blended quantities of the preparation so skilfully made
by Dr. Chippercoyne. That the whole atmosphere of the place
has seemed to Joe Gilfert during that half-hour of preliminaries and waiting—weird, devilish, unfit for the stay of any
Christian man or woman, except under the compelling of some
high purpose — nearer to certain fearful things remembered
among the poisoning followers of Buddha, in a far-away
island of the sea, than anything that he had ever again expected to meet during mortal life.

But the Hour and the Man. The Hour is here, and the
Man is coming; for John Jasper, whatever his faults, vices,
crimes, lacks that one besetting sin giving birth to all others
—Unpunctuality. He would keep an appointment, at the
named hour, there is reason to believe, with the Prince of
Darkness, once committed to a rendezvous with that person
of the unenviable name. Eleven strikes from some one of
the dingy old church-towers of the precinct; and the sound
comes faintly in through the wind and falling rain. Almost
at the same moment there is a step on the stair, and the
old woman says, in her hoarse whisper, too low to be heard
outside the door:

"That's his step, deary! I knows it, hearin' it so many
times afore. Get away, deary, get away, if you don't want
to kill the poor old soul with fear for ye."

Joe Gilfert hears, and though his share in the fear may be
a moderate one, he disappears, without a word, into the place
of concealment in the far-corner of the room, arranged behind
the bed-head and in the additional shelter of a line of ragged
dirty white clothing that may or may not be estimated as
washed, stretched on a cord leading from the window to that
portion of the room. He may be a cool youngster; and possibly reason has been given to believe that he is so: but he
must be something more than even this would indicate, if he
can hear that advancing step at the top of the stair, stumbling up as his own has come so lately—without remembering
the warning of the Doctor, his own early education, and the

important interests involved—and feeling some tremor at the approach of the moment of trial.

The step comes nearer — the door opens, without a knock or any other notice (as warranted by the previous arrange-ment of the hour); and John Jasper enters. Joe Gilfert sees him, in the dim candle-light, through the loophole con-trived for that purpose between the hanging clothes: sees him well enough, even though the light is dim, to note certain particulars inducing astonishment and almost pity. His hat and garments are heavily dashed with rain, as if he has been coming on foot through at least some portion of his journey from Aldersgate Street; and as he removes his hat with a swing throwing the clinging drops from it, the evidence of what he *is* comes up to confront the memory of what he WAS, only so little while ago.

The face is haggard in its lines and leathern in the color and texture of the skin. The eyes seem bloodshot, and there is a supernatural fire in the pupils, giving the impression of hot coals from the brazier on the hob—of combining fever and madness. The whole contour of the face seems changed —thinned, sharpened, and lacking all grace and roundness. But there is yet another change more important than either of the others named, and all the more marked because in this regard the subject of it has been notable for the attractiveness of his appearance. His hair, so abundant, dark, glossy and well-kept, in those better days which seem so long ago and are really but yesterday, when Helena Landless first came with her brother to Cloisterham and first saw John Jasper there at the house of Mr. Crisparkle—his hair, so dark and glossy, if neither so abundant nor so well-kept, only a few days since— is heavily greyed, and in sections literally wealed with thick stripes of white, as if five-and-twenty years had suddenly fallen on the dark head and left its impress in that remark-able manner. Such a change, in this one particular — Joe Gilfert recognizes the fact, with something like a shudder but with no faltering of determination—such a change could

scarcely have occurred to him in a dozen years of sickness or
imprisonment. What must the terror or agony have been, to
produce that extreme symptom of premature age thus suddenly ! And what must it be, indeed, to endure the rack of
Fear and the thumb-screw of Remorse, at one and the same
moment, in a refinement on all the cruelty of the best-
appointed old torture-chambers !

"Ye have come at yer time, deary ; and the old woman is
very glad to see ye again," the crone coughs hoarsely, rising
with an effort from her chair and making a feeble motion to
assist him to lay aside his wet outer clothes. "Why, how
soaked ye are! and where's yer umbereller? But never
mind, the poor old soul—O me, my lungs is so bad, and this
cough shakes me into fragments — the poor old soul, as
thought ye had deserted her and gone over to Jack Chinaman's there,—or gone to taking it yer own way, as is dangerous, werry—she has the art of mixin' it as it ought to be,
and ye'll soon get clear of them shakes as punishes ye. But
mercy, deary, however did yer hair get so white in this little
while, like as if ye was old ? But ye didn't answer me, when
I told ye so to-day, did ye, deary ? O me, where's my ink-
bottle, and where's my spoon ? "

"Never you mind about the color of my hair, which may
have been dyed when you first knew me, and the dye simply
gone off it now ! " is the gruff reply, as Mr. Jasper throws
off his waterproof, and then divests himself of his body coat,
as if, all preliminaries having been arranged in advance, he is
not disposed to waste further time in the world of reality
where that of dreams is so easily attainable.

"O, we are short and snappish again to-night, all because
we want a little smoke so badly ! O me, my lungs is dreffle
bad, and my poor old head is going to split. But here's the
pipe, deary, and here is the spoon, and the mixter's all ready
for ye ! " So she coughs and splutters, while hobbling to the
little table, under the window, where stands the "mixter," in
its new shape—as prepared by Dr. Chippercoyne and brought
by Joe Gilfert.

"Listen," he says, as she is preparing it. "I have an idea, lately, that you are using mere trash instead of opium. It does me no good, or next to none. No more of this—no foisting of miserable stuff on me, instead of the true article for which I pay you,—or you have seen the last of my money! I shall go back to taking it in my own way, which you don't seem to like. Do you hear me?" He has dropped into a chair, with all the symptoms of intense weariness and weakness, though he speaks with his usual determination.

"Oh, no!—never take it your own way, deary—it isn't good for trade, and it isn't good for *you !*" she mumbles and coughs, repeating an old formula found very effective in former interviews. "And don't ye be hard on the old woman, deary, that's got the true art of mixing it to cure the all-overs! Find fault, do ye, because it doesn't seem so strong to ye now as it did when ye was a babby to it! O, me! that's because ye are so strong now, and it takes so much to send ye off."

"Well, all I can say is, that if you lose your power, I go elsewhere, or serve myself!" is the querulous reply, with the addition, "How much longer am I to wait? Is it not almost ready?"

"O me, my lungs is dreffle bad, and my head's like to split! Yes, deary, its a'most ready, and better than ye ever had it afore, becausé I've been a makin' of it a little stronger, so that ye would be sure to go off easy," is the reply, coughed and rattled like the preceding, but with the crone still at the table.

Mr. Jasper may have cause to be a shade impatient at the delay of his infernal happiness, or his celestial misery—whichever phrase may be held best to describe opium intoxication! For the old woman, fumbling with her shaking hands, is doing more than either John Jasper is likely to know, looking at her from behind, or Joe Gilfert, in his place of hiding, and with his attention principally concentrated upon the other visitor. She is ostensibly filling the pipe and arranging it so that just the proper quantity of air for steady combustion will be drawn through the drug. She is really taking out something more than twice the proper quantity for the pipe, from the box of Dr. Chippercoyne's preparation, and concealing all not needed for that one "little smoke," in a scrap of paper, and in the bosom of her gown! Is she not learning the art of administering *this*, which is to make the subject "talk" as nothing of hers can do?—and, the business of this evening over, will she not be fully competent to do a little on her own account, if she can only secure a sufficient quantity of the new "mixter," as she has no hope of being able to do through any communication or benevolence of the handsome but imperious boy? So she accomplishes her theft, with the remaining dexterity of fingers that have no doubt slipped cards, or even picked pockets, before they became so old and shaking; and neither of the others, keen observers though they may be, have the least idea of what is occurring. How surely, in the event of a closer knowledge of that instant and the future, the hand of John Jasper would be at her throat, even if the poniard of Joe Gilfert did not point itself at a portion of her old anatomy only a little lower! But this is not to be; enough that we know what is.

"There—it's just ready for you, deary; and sweeter and stronger than ever afore—just a little stronger, so that ye'll be sure to go off easy."

She brings it to him, nearly dropping it on the way, in one of her accessions of rattling cough. It is lighted, and the faintest aromatic perfume creeps into the room. He catches the aroma, and rises from his chair, the fiery eyes alight with a new pleasure.

"Ah," he says, as he seats himself on the side of the bed and takes the pipe from her hands. "Yes, I catch the odor, already. It *is* better and stronger than you have made it for me, in a long time—more as it was when I first began; and you *have* been swindling me of late. Don't do it again, now that you see I am in earnest. Let me have *this* whenever I come, or no more of my money."

He has inhaled a few whiffs, and becomes deliciously over-powered within a space of time equally short as compared with his own calculations or those of the old woman. For he merely says: "It is very fine—charming. I see flowers of all colors, and hear music from dozens of instruments at once. Ah—delicious—heaven—ah!—ah!" Already he sinks down upon the bed, with the pipe-stick between his teeth, his eyes closed, but the inhalation continued and steady with the breath coming in through his set teeth. Not another word—not another motion; he might be an infant in its first dream-less slumber; or, save for the light breath that is seen to heave his breast and heard softly to sigh from his lips, he might be sleeping that still calmer sleep which needs no watching by any below the heavens.

The old woman is frightened—as well she may be—at some-thing so beyond her knowledge. No occasion, now, to sit be-side the sleeper, stir the contents of his pipe with her needle, and prepare for refilling it at any moment when the signs of complete stupefaction cease. A few whiffs, a few words, and this man is literally senseless. And think of his "talking!" Make *him* talk, while under this influence! As well make the attempt with the rickety chair, or the askew bed-post! No, ye can't do it, deary!

Now the handsome boy, who may be presumed to have seen, heard, and noted all the proceedings of the past few minutes —comes from his concealment, behind the bed, with the single warning sound "Hist!" to attract the woman's attention and prevent any dangerous movement of surprise. He leans over the bed and the sleeper, studying the face and the respiration for a few seconds; then he says, in a whisper, close to her ear: "It will do, now. Say not a word. If he moves un-easily, stir the mixture in the pipe for a moment—nothing more." Then the old woman, as much racked with painful curiosity and a certain sort of fear, as if she was a young girl paying her first visit of horrified delight to the seventh daughter of a seventh daughter—sees the handsome boy reach down and lay the palm of one hand close upon the palm of one of the sleeper's, lying unnerved and open,—applying the palm of the other hand, pressed close, the next moment, to that slight depression in the exact top of the head believed to have nearest access to the brain. What he had accomplished now, it might be difficult for any one, lacking his peculiar Oriental experience, to guess; possibly subjugation of the bodily powers, through the influence of the drug, and enforced communication with and command over the mentality, through this bodily contact at peculiar nervous centres, bearing the character of simple natural magnetism. Something even of the formality may be more a remembrance than a belief— mild charlatanry blending with earnest action oftener than many of us would be pleased to admit, or are even capable of recognizing at the moment when practising it.

A few minutes of this, with perfect silence, except as the old woman strangles a short rattling cough, which excites no attention, and the low breathing of the sleeper is heard in the pause. Then, at a signal, the crone stirs the contents of the pipe with her needle, and another brief interval of silence suc- ceeds. Then Joe Gilfert speaks, in a low but distinct and musical voice close to the ear of the sleeper, while the little remaining blood in the system of the one waking hearer chills with a supernatural fear, not entirely inexcusable under all the circumstances.

" Do you feel me ? "

Apparently a spasmodic effort on the part of the subject to loosen the benumbed organs of speech, the mouth working with the exertion, and the mouth-piece of the pipe dropping away from the lips as the teeth open. The old woman is about to replace it, but the other motions with his head for her to take it away as no longer wanted, and she holds it in her trembling hand. Another moment, and the power of articula- tion is regained; though it is notable, then and after, that every word coming, comes as under constraint and with a short choppy snap, as if the teeth might be cutting it off in attempting to prevent the passage. After this first reply, however, the experimenter, keeping what may be supposed the circle unbroken, by retaining his two palms on the one palm and head of the other, there is not much delay in the replies, even if something of the same struggle accompanies many of them. The first brief answer comes:

" Yes."

" Do you know me ? "

" No."

" It is not necessary that you should. Enough that I am your Master, and that you must obey me. Do you understand so much ? "

" I do."

" And hate me ? "

" Yes."

" How do you feel me ? "

" All around me—holding me—oppressing me. I would kill you to escape, if I could."

" That is well. But you cannot kill me, and you cannot escape. You have but one thing to do—to obey me. The more promptly the sooner you will be free. Do you under-stand ? "

" Yes."

" Answer every one of my questions, then and at once."

" I do not wish to. I would rather kill you. But I must."

" Where is the body ? "

A terrible struggle is for the moment evident in the sleep-ing figure; but it passes, and there are no signs of wakeful-ness. He subsides to quiet—he answers, after a much longer interval,

" Between the two walls of the Cathedral."

A spasm of pain and suffering passes over the face of Joe Gilfert, sharper than that lately convulsing John Jasper; but the bleared old eyes of the dumb and frightened woman can-not see it; and he commands himself so well that there is not one instant of withdrawal of either hand from palm or head. Then he continues his questions:

"Who placed it there ?   Yourself ? "

A slighter struggle than before, and then the answer ·

" Yes."

" Was he alive or dead then ? "

" Dead."

" What had you done to him before that ? "

Another fearful struggle in the sleeping man, but the stupor as yet too deep for freedom from the hated thrall compelling him to speak.

" I had strangled him."

" Where ? "

" On the top of the Cathedral tower."

" With what ? "

" With my scarf."

" How did you place him between the walls ? "

" Through a trap-door in the floor above."

" Who knows of that trap-door besides yourself ? "

" No one—I made it."

" What else did you do, after throwing down the body ? Anything to destroy it ? "

" Yes—I threw down lime, from the Mason's-yard."

" When did you place his watch and pin in the Weir ? "

" Next day.   I forgot it that night."

" Did Neville Landless know anything of your intention to kill him ?   Did he assist you ? "

" No—no ! "

" Why did you accuse him, and have him arrested ? "

" I hated him.   Wished to get him out of the way."

" He has a sister ; do you hate *her* ? "

" Yes.   Hate and fear her."

" Why did you kill *him* ? "

" Because he was in my way, with *her*."

The sleeping man stirs a little now, and speaks with a shade less of constraint. If Joe Gilfert had known years more of experience in that which he is conducting, he would be aware that the drug is beginning to lose its power, and that

the pipe should be reapplied to the mouth. But he is too busy
with other thoughts and interests, to be quite careful of this
detail. He goes on:

" Are you not sorry now, that you killed him ? "

" Yes. Since I know that they would never have been
married."

Less and less constrained the delivery now: nearer and
more imminent the time of waking, unless fresh fumes are
supplied to the struggling brain.

" You feel Remorse, then, do you not ? "

" Perhaps. I do not know. I suffer terribly. Cannot give
my suffering a name. It is infernal."

" Do you feel Fear—fear of detection ? "

" Yes—lately. It haunts me, night and day."

" Ah ! you say 'lately.' Since when ? What has happened to disturb you ? "

" Since two articles have been placed in my hands that I
left on *him* when I dropped him between the walls. Some
one must have seen the body. Some one must have removed
those things from him. Or else——"

" Ah! Heavens, what is this ! "

The cry comes from Joe Gilfert, and it is not addressed to
the sleeping man. Suddenly moved by what new and strange
hope, drawn from the sleeping man's words, there is no present occasion to speculate—he utters the cry, and in doing so
puts one hand to his heart, thus withdrawing it from the head
of Jasper. In an instant there is a threatening movement in
the recumbent figure ; and in the next, before the old woman,
newly alarmed, can replace the pipe at his lips, he opens his
eyes. But even that instant has sufficed the handsome boy to
retreat to his place of concealment, and when John Jasper,
sitting up the next moment and opening his eyes entirely,
though they are filmed and glassy—looks around with something of a puzzled air, no one is to be seen in the room but
the woman of the bad lungs and himself.

The poor old soul, sorely frightened, must speak, however,
and does so in a venture:

"Ye've had a nice sleep—haven't ye, deary?

"I do not know," he drowsily mutters, in reply. "I must have been asleep, I suppose, but I remember nothing, except seeming, just now, to hear other voices than yours. There has been no one here?"

"O, me! How could there be any one here, but me and you? No—ye must have been dreaming. And see ye slept so long and so well, that I let your pipe go out. Have another, deary? There is more of the mixter, and the poor old soul'll have it ready in a moment."

"No," he replies, putting his hand to his head. "No—enough for to-night. You must have made it very strong, for I seem to have had entire forgetfulness, for the first time in many months. Did I say anything at all?"

"Not a word, deary, after you fell away. I was a'most frightened when ye laid still so long, and even my cough that is so bad and my lungs so dreffle, did not trouble ye."

"Ah, well," he says, yet a little stupidly, and without anything of his ordinary imperious manner. "Help me with my coat, for I think that I am weaker than I was when I came. But I feel refreshed—so much refreshed, after all! It is so good, sometimes, to forget *everything*, and have all earth, heaven, and hell a blank!"

He lays down some silver money on the table, says that he will come again—perhaps in a week, if she will be sure to mix for him in the same manner, and so passes out of that door of which his succeeding number of entrances is already set, and goes down the dark stairway into the night and the continuing rain.

When he is gone, Joe Gilfert comes out from his hiding-place—trembling, however, and so much agitated that the old woman would scarcely recognize him as the same with the light-hearted youngster of an hour before. She attempts to cough herself into renewed conversation with him; but he checks the attempt at once, advises her that if she is wise she will say nothing of what she has done, seen done, or heard, until she is allowed to do so by *him*, unless she wishes to get into serious trouble with the police—as she does not! Then he carefully takes the remainder of Dr. Chippercoyne's preparation, wraps it and puts it into his pocket, with the unused syringe; lays the promised sovereign in the withered old palm so greedily waiting for it; says and receives a brief good-night; and so follows his late subject down the dark stairway and into the night and the rain.

To be rejoined, at once, at the door, by Mr. Tartar, who in this special tumble-overboard from the yard-arm seems to have fallen into deep water and come up one incarnated drip— so vigorously have not only the ordinary spirits of the storm but those especial water-demons presiding over his chosen gutter, been pouring the thin, cool fluid down upon him, for the past hour, in all the modes taught by world-sprinkling Aquarius.

And, to go back to the waiting cab, and to Staple Inn, with head and heart both in such a whirl that temporary insanity seems only one degree removed—burthened with the fearful success of the late experiment, and the definite knowledge of personal loss, a brother's innocence, and the guilt of the Choir-Master, thus obtained; but burthened also with a new thought which cannot be entertained for its very joy—which would not be dismissed for a crown—and which cannot be analyzed by any process of mental exertion.

The while the poor old soul takes from the bosom of her unclean garment a very small packet, unrolls it, rolls it up again, hugs it like an infinitesimal baby or a revenge, and coughingly mutters:

"Ye'r coming again, are ye, deary! So ye will, sooner than ye think; and now that the old woman knows how to mix it, and to deal with it, and *has it*—here—here!—ye'll tell *her* what she wants to know, as well as the handsome young devil—won't ye, deary!"

CHAPTER XVII.

BADGERING THE BILLICKIN.

THE term for which Miss Twinkleton and Rosa had been installed as lodgers in the house of Mrs. Billickin, through the mistaken kindness of Mr. Grewgious, was rapidly drawing to a close, without the Angular man having been made aware that other than the most cerulean sky ever overhung the domestic firmament in that portion of Southampton Street, Bloomsbury Square.

It is always graceful, when the assiduous eagerness of a friend, urging us to a cross-cut by way of abridging long and wearisome distance, has plunged us into a thorn thicket, to the laceration of flesh and raiment, or into a slough, to the discomfort of the one and defilement of the other,—to avoid showing the well-intentioned but mistaken adviser what have been the fruits of his counsel; and there is a certain wisdom in doing so, unless one is quite prepared to accept a secondary misery in the shape of too many humble apologies, regrets and self-upbraidings. Mr. Grewgious, as both the ladies knew, would have overwhelmed himself with reproaches for having been the means of leading them into any discomfort, the moment he became aware of the fact,—and the more surely so, because the lodging-house keeper chanced to be a distant relation of his own, in whose favor he might be un-generously suspected to have strained a point at the expense of others. So nothing had been said to him on the subject of the armed neutrality relations—not even after the open rupture already recorded, between the two contending powers, who might be said to have then withdrawn within their own lines of fortification, after a series of light actions causing great discomfort to the neutral power really owning the territory over which they skirmished. The time of the inflic-tion could not be long, from the double fact that the term of agreement would soon expire with liberty to make what changes they might choose at its termination—and that the close of Miss Twinkleton's vacation must soon send her back to her charge and Mrs. Fisher at the Nun's House.

Send *her* back—her only: Rosa, as already known, stood too much in fear of John Jasper, even before the attempted abduction, to dare resume residence within a stone's throw of his daily presence; and after that event it may be supposed that her resolutions on that point were even more confirmed. She would remain in London—in what portion of it she had no idea, but somewhere that might be selected by her "dear old guardy," as she delighted to designate him; and from the day of their parting at the close of their present connection, the lives of teacher and pupil were likely to have little in common. They were likely to have less, indeed, than either knew; but the foreshadowed separation was quite sufficient to place them on a different footing to that which they had ever previously occupied.

We do not usually form unconquerable antagonisms to the butcher or the baker who purveys food for our mortal bodies —unless they may chance to be peculiarly atrocious in the bad quality of their provender or the inexorable extent of their overcharges. Nay, we even consent to entertain a certain amiability of feelings toward the draper and the glover, and (femininely) towards the *marchande des modes* except under correspondingly unpleasant circumstances to those just named. Why is it, then, that the instructor is regarded as the natural enemy, to a fiercer or a milder extent, from the moment when the relation commences to that when —*it is about to end?*

Leaving aside the illustrations that might be drawn from the boy-world, commencing with tutorship in the home or grammar-school, taking in Harrow and Rugby (in spite of Dr. Arnold and Thomas Hughes, M.P.), and only ending with the last battle between the undergraduate and the don of Oxford or Cambridge—setting aside all this, and dealing only with the similar propensities of the gentler sex, the wonder will still remain, and still the same necessity for explanation.

The pupils are by no means alone in the feeling, though they may be far more affected by it than the teachers, and manifest it in a more objectionable manner. And why, why, why, as Rosa might ask—why should it be so? Why should Miss Twinkleton, in those old days at the Nuns' House, have kept a comparatively stiff and starch visage during all hours devoted to the young ladies under her charge, taking far more than the necessary unfavorable notice of the inattention of Miss Ferdinand, the antics of Miss Reynolds, and the laughter of Miss Giggle,—and only showing that underlying genial self, reminiscent of The Wells and half-regretful of Foolish Mr. Porters, in the comparative solitude of Mrs. Fisher's company, when none of the fresh young hearts could be gladdened by the knowledge that she held loves, regrets, and weaknesses? And why should Miss Ferdinand, Miss Reynolds, and Miss Giggle, respectively, have taken corresponding trouble to show themselves at their worst, during the same hours of tuition, and only manifested the qualities endearing them to their circles in both school and home when beyond the eye of the preceptress? Alas!—why should even Rosa herself, already the pet and favorite of the self-restrained spinster, have objected privately to her well-intentioned Pyramids, and called her dear old lectures Bores?

These questions are not asked to be answered—as may before this time have become apparent. Rosa could not solve them, nor could Miss Twinkleton—any more than they could foresee the events and changes, of startling importance, destined to take place before the expiration of their brief term at Mrs. Billickin's. All that either could do was possibly to make some faint recognition of that change in their relations, involving their propounding in this place.

They were about to separate; and preceptress and pupil had changed their relation—half-insensibly to both, to something like that, say, between niece and maiden-aunt of a certain age—enough of the regulating habit of age remaining on the one side, be sure, to prevent the connection becoming quite sisterly, even with the difference of years understood; and enough of the charming wheedling sauciness of youth on the other, to make the charge of the elder no sinecure, while it should continue.

Miss Twinkleton, even with the past experience of Tunbridge Wells and that Mr. Porter's whose prefix indicated the reverse of wisdom—neither was nor believed herself an expert in detecting manifestations of the tender passion. And yet she was not blind enough to ignore, after a few visits of the brown-faced and breezy Ex-Lieutenant, the fact that her pupil was in danger from another than John Jasper. She saw peril in the Tartar at an early day, and commenced certain warnings on the subject, destined to be nearly as tardy in completion as the worsted monster growing slowly under her hands. For Rosa was a young lady by no means easy to " lecture," upon any theme which did not commend itself to the small imperial judgment; and when Miss Twinkleton, at the termination of one of the more pronounced Desdemonaian demonstrations, after Mr. Tartar had bowled away, a little belated in sailing, but with a free wind, for his port in the Admiral's Cabin—said:

" Rosa, my dear: is it not possible that Mr. Tartar is paying more frequent visits to this house than propriety would allow ? "

Then Rosa merely pouted, in the most charming of infantile ways, and uttered that one word which had been found so effectual in preventing the too-close approaches of " poor Eddy."

" Absurd ! "

And when Miss Twinkleton, on a subsequent occasion, after another of those pretty exhibitions, hemmed twice (not with her crochet-needle) and recommenced the deferred warning, with :

" Rosa, my dear, is not Mr. Tartar the least in the world

17

tiresome, with his long stories of such outlandish adventures ? I think that I would scarcely encourage him, by listening with attention that must seem like being really pleased with —with those dreadful things that a young lady should scarcely care to know—though of course it is very good of you to flatter him in that manner ! "

Then Miss Rosa's eyes flashed a little, gentle and kind as they were at ordinary times ; and she concluded the conversation with the same suddenness that had marked the fate of the former, bridling (drolly, of course) instead of pouting, and only increasing the one word to five :

" Indeed ?   Thank you, very much ! "

And when Miss Twinkleton, on a third occasion, beginning to believe that if any mischief had been imminent, it was now probably done beyond recall, commenced her remark in a different tone, with :

" Rosa, my dear, I am really afraid that sailor-man means to carry you off, some day ! "

Then Rosa grew so lovely a rose-pink that she would temporarily have commanded a high price at the perfumer's, to be used in the manufacture of rich carnations, and neither pouted nor bridled, but looked bewitchingly agitated and girlishly happy, as she said :

" Oh, dear Miss Twinkleton, why, why will you tease me so about *him* ?—and don't you think he is very, very, very nice ? "

After which, there was really very little more to be said in the way of warnings ; and the time, so far as the good spinster knew, had not yet come for felicitations ; so that the conversation on that point was not resumed, and the worsted monster progressed towards shape with a rapidity at last threatening to the foredoomed chair.

It was at that precise period that a new sensation came to Southampton Street, and that Mrs. Billickin was ushered into a charming prospect of immediately re-letting the apartment so soon to be vacated.   Circumstances, easily understood, made the two ladies aware of most of the features of the occurrence, which may or may not have contributed a crowning felicity to the existence of The Billickin.

It came—the Sensation—in the shape of a most irreproachable equipage—perfectly appointed carriage, with a crest on the panel, well-groomed pair, and coachman and footman so absolute in their unimpeachability as to be literally overwhelming. It drew up at the door, at such an hour of the afternoon as would have indicated that after making a Call it intended to Drive, attracting general attention from neighboring windows and areas, and materially adding, at an instant's notice, to the standing of an entire street, whereof the lodging-houses, for some reason suggesting ill-will or indifference, was too much defrauded of its due share of visitors in carriages with crests and lacking crowns.

The knock of the powdered footman, who loftily descended from his elevation for that service, was only three times repeated, but loud enough to advise the whole street of the event — three solemn, deliberate raps, ponderous, heavy, well-measured, awful—reminiscent of some fateful summons of the Vehmgericht or other secret tribunal of the Middle Ages. After the delivery of which summons, the impressive footman, without waiting for the opening (which might be assumed, after *that*), went back to the carriage, opened the door, and held up his arm to be used as a hand-rail for the descent of a lady who at once became the Second Sensation, and threw her predecessor into comparative insignificance !

She might have been fifty-five or sixty, as Miss Twinkleton and Rosa (indefensibly peeping from window at so much magnificence) saw her descend to the pavement and advance to the door. Tall, with hair slightly grey, rich dark dress of old fashion, and all other appointments equally combining the privilege of age and the assurance of position. She moved with a step as slow and stately as had been the knocks at the door, and held her arms crossed with an appearance of rigid devotion that was beautiful to contemplate as well as slightly depressing to the observer. In her presence the street-door took on an appearance of humbly apologizing for an existence deficient in the highest respectability with an additional flavor of piety; and the house-front broke out into a sort of apologetic perspiration for the vulgarity of its plebeian bricks and mortar. It was notable, too, that she was served by persons of corresponding grave respectability; as neither the coachman on his box nor the footman who had returned to it in waiting, could be induced to turn their heads or relax their impressive countenances at any capped blandishments from the neighboring areas. She ascended the steps, and was at a dignified distance from the humbled street-door when it retired before her into the hall.

That door was opened by a servant, as became the respectability of the establishment; but arrivals in crested carriages have a habit of being telegraphed with extraordinary rapidity in mansions of the Billickin order; and, however advised, the proprietess was herself in the hall at the moment when the stately lady entered,—shawl-draped and shivery, in compliment to the hall, but with a Candor on her face which should at once have disarmed all questions, and meeting the overwhelming honor with a sweeping bow and an appendix of courtesy.

The stately lady spoke. In awful gravity, she might have been Siddons in the gloomier passages of the rôle of Lady Macbeth; in the measured monotone of her voice, and the long-drawn " Ah—h—h !" with which she began every sentence, and the expiring " Um—m—m !" with which she generally concluded, she might have been Johanna Southcote in her most interminable whine.

"Ah—h—h !   I wish to see the person of the house. Um—m—m !"

To which the Billickin, with extreme candor:

" I will not deceive you, Madam—or perhaps I should say my lady. Far from it. I am the person of this house."

"Ah—h—h !   You let apartments?   Um—m—m !"

" Madam, or my lady——"

"Ah—h—h! I am not my lady. Say Madam. Life is short and words should not be wasted. Be good enough to go on. Um—m—m!"

Thus adjured, Mrs. Billickin, shiveringly, and drawing her shawl around her with a clutch.

"To be candid with you, Madam, which I do——"

"Ah—h—h! Any rooms vacant now, Mrs.—— What is your name? Um—m—m!"

The Billickin, with stately dignity, not unmingled with hurt feelings:

"As is on the door-plate, Madam, which I am not ashamed to have any one read it as can—Billickin."

"Ah—h—h! Billickin. Married? Um—m—m!"

The Billickin, with a mute protest against being thus figuratively driven to the wall, but overpowered by the recollection of the carriage and footman:

"Which it is a question, Madam, which I never hanswer, seeing as there is difficulties in the way of a lone woman——"

"Oh—h—h!"

"—Keepin' of her name on the door, that certain against trouble, as is one who has a husband not dead and gone this many years——"

"Ah—h—h! That will do. I understand. Widow. Um—m—m!" '

The Billickin, half-choking with the oppression practised on a lone woman and an invalid:

"Not to deceive you, as I wouldn't for worlds, Madam—yes."

"Ah—h—h! Now what rooms have you? on what floor? Um—m—m!"

"Which I am not free to say that I have any to-day, Madam, but the first and second to go out in a few days, under notice give on account of improper language on the part of one as would have stayed for a twelvemonth if better tenants was not desirable for the best rooms in the 'ouse."

After which the invalid naturally paused for breath, and

one better accustomed to her would have understood that she
was narrowly escaping a series of swoons.   The grave woman
saw nothing of the kind, but proceeded, characteristically :

"Oh—h—h !   In a few days.   Um—m—m !   Perhaps
that may serve, if the apartments suit me.   That is indispensable as well as the position.   Terms are comparatively of no
consequence.   Um—m—m !"

There was no affectation, not even one of candor, in Mrs.
Billickin's making one of her heart-clutches, at that moment.
"Terms comparatively of no consequence !"—and those words
from a lady who came in her carriage and therefore could be
no doubtful patron !   When had such blessed words ever
before been spoken, in the ear of a lodging-house keeper, by
any person not an acknowledged maniac ?   Ah, the position !
—that, as the wonderful woman had just declared—that was
indispensable, and hence the explanation of the otherwise
mysterious liberality.   And would not she, Billickin (perhaps
the lady did not put the thought into precisely those phrases
but " words to that effect "), convert her into an absolute gold-
mine, and make her pay out to an extent hitherto unknown
in the annals of Bloomsbury Square, besides possibly running
her through the quartz-crusher, in the way of extras, and thus
making the extract entirely satisfactory !   Five-and-forty
shillings the week—the contemptible sum for which her relative had cajoled her into letting the rooms to that arrogant
person whose name she would not mention, even mentally—
what was that to the magnificent five pounds, or even guineas,
so easily to be drawn from a purse that must be plethoric, with
a fool for its holder !

The astounded and delighted Billickin rallied from her
mental spasm, however, before the lady with the crossed hands
had quite lost her patience, — and said, with another bow
which was more than half-curtsey, and a manner' which
denoted that she was thenceforth the slave of the impending
liberality.

"I will not conceal from you, Madam, far from it—that the

rooms as I mentioned are quite at your service to see whenever you likes and not caring the value of one ha'penny
whether the persons now in the 'ouse is pleased with it or not,
as how could you expect that——" she came very near to
mentioning the sum that Rosa paid weekly, and thus marring
her future golden expectations—but luckily checked herself
in time, under cover of a slight paroxysm which failed to
elicit any notice from the other—" that them as is going
away and mercy knows deservin' of the notice to go out could
shut doors that is not their own and prevent any other persons
from coming in—I say again, how could you expect it ? "

" Oh—h—h ! "   The grave lady wisely avoiding any
attempt to answer the last question.   " Then I will look at
the apartments, at once.   Um—m—m ! "

" Certainly, Madam, you may do so, free as the air, and
nothin' to conceal except it belongs to them as is in the way
and what do I care for that? "

Whereupon Mrs. Billickin led the way up the stair to the
first-floor landing, taking opportunity to remark breathlessly
on the way, that steps as was as much used would wear and
how could you help it ?—she defied you to try if you was
stone yourself as goodness knows some people was and better
that than flesh-and-blood with no feeling and no breeding as
no doubt Madam knowed to her cost."

To which the appreciative answer was very brief, a colophon
being for that occasion inserted in place of the head-piece :

" Um—m—m ! "

The long utterance of this single word in its disjointed
state, was sufficient to bring both to the door of the drawing-
room, whereat Mrs. Billickin knocked, loudly and boldly, with
perhaps more of a sensation of absolute joy than had visited
her widowed bosom since the more or less lamented departure
of B.   Debarred from entering any apartment occupied by
Miss Twinkleton, since the day of the explicit understanding
between them—she was now about to resume her privilege, in
a manner best calculated to annoy that lady, at the same time

that immemorial custom gave her the right to do so without question, as exhibitor of rooms soon to be vacated. The style of knock, based upon this understanding of her rights and privileges instead of saying, with timid respect: " May I intrude upon you for a moment?—and will you kindly overlook any inconvenience that my coming may cause you?" roared, with the force of a brazen trumpet or a Bull of Bashan: " Open, you, at once! I have a right to come in, and woe to any one who attempts to hinder me! The more annoyance the better!"

Miss Twinkleton opened the assaulted door with quite as much alacrity as could be expected. Rosa was still at the window. Mrs. Billickin favored the elder lady with a scowl that would have become a fainting swoon upon any proper occasion, and introduced her business with as little ceremony as she had bestowed upon her summons for admission.

" A lady to look at the apartments, Miss," she said, ignoring Miss Twinkleton after the old fashion, which had been found so convenient; " and I 'opes there will not be any objection to my 'avin' my rights in my own 'ouse, on the part of hany one in this room."

" Um—m—m," threw in the grave lady, as a sort of appendix to Mrs. Billickin's remark, which might have been inadvertently omitted.

" Certainly, Miss Billickin—come in, if you wish. I am sure that dear Miss Twinkleton will have no objection," said Rosa, very pleasantly.

" Oh—h—h!" interpolated the grave lady.

" If the person of the house wishes to enter these rooms, Rosa, dear, for any business purposes, we can have no objection, certainly," replied Miss Twinkleton, with frigid politeness towards Mrs. Billickin expressing itself at every point of face and figure.

" Ah—h—h!" punctuated the grave lady.

" Very good, Miss, which I will not conceal from you that it saves trouble," acknowledged the Billickin, thereupon turn-

ing to the lady in quest of apartments, who might have been
blind, so far as any proof was given that she had noticed
either of the occupants.   " This is the drawing-room, Madam,
and a sweet room, though I am obliged to say it before persons
as have very little respect for any hopinions but their hown.
The view across the street, too, Madam, is that pleasing as
many people would think themselves very 'appy to get, and no
impertinent minxes of nursemaids and other servants looking
in every time that the windows is opened."

" Ah—h—h ! " lucidly remarked the grave lady, refusing
the chair to which she had been motioned by hospitable Miss
Twinkleton, who said at that moment :

" Rosa, my dear, was I mistaken, then—you should know
best, with your young eyes—in thinking that two of the servants across the street have been in the habit of troubling us
very much ?—staring over, so that we scarcely dared open the
windows at all ? "

" Oh—h—h ! " absently commented the grave lady, while
the face of Mrs. Billickin would have seemed enraged if in the
possession of a more robust woman.

" No, dear Miss Twinkleton," Rosa rejoined, in her manner of most charming innocence.   " You were not mistaken.
They *have* troubled us very, very, very much nearly every day,
and sometimes a dreadful man with them, with an opera-glass."

" Um—m—m ! "

Mrs. Billickin felt the necessity of fortifying her position,
thereupon, and did it with promptness and great candor.

" If I was to tell you, Madam, that there was no persons in
this 'ouse as would say malicious things about the werry best
rooms in it, I should be deceiving you, as I will NOT.   Consequent, as you have seen the room, and there is no stoppin' of
tongues as ought to be ashamed if there was any shame in the
world and will be some day, we will look at the others.   And
eligible apartments they are and ought to command six pounds
a week or perhaps guineas if wished though if persons whose
breeding is no higher than boarding-schools and them only

second-rate will be wenomous as tabby cats what can you expect, try how you may !"

"Rosa, my dear," calmly observed Miss Twinkleton, without the least appearance of having heard a word of the late resumé,—"how much was it that they asked for those very pleasant rooms higher up the street and larger than these ? Was it two-and-thirty shillings, or did the person mention one pound ten ?"

The reply of Rosa, to this, was inaudible, so that the exact figures of the proposed transaction cannot be given. Nor is there data for deciding whether the grave and respectable lady caught the remarks, though the belief may be hazarded that Mrs. Billickin heard, "marked and inwardly digested."

"Ah—h—h !" said the lady of the crossed hands, at this juncture for the first time abandoning that disposition of those members, to take a carpenter's two-foot rule from her pocket and open it out—as also for the first time using her vocal organs to any extent, since entering the drawing-room. "Ah—h—h ! No, we will not yet leave the apartments of these—these persons. Um—m—m !—Mrs. ah—Billickin. The room seems well enough, but small. As I need to bring my grand piano, my sofa, a large chest of drawers, an *étagère*, a book-case for devotional books (I read no others—Um—m—m !) a table and several other articles requiring space, it will be necessary to know its exact dimensions. Um—m—m !"

The next ten minutes, during which Mrs. Billickin looked on with deferential surprise, and both Miss Twinkleton and Rosa with what seemed quiet amusement, were devoted by the lady to measuring the size of the room on every side, as well as the space between the walls and chimney, with occasional variations of stopping to examine a spot of the size of a coffee-bean or a pin-head, on the wall-paper. Each of these measurements, and especially each of the discoveries, was accompanied by comments with the " Ah—h—h !" "Oh—h —h !" and "Um—m—m !" predominant, on the question whether her piano would consent to fit into this place, her sofa into that, her pet chest of drawers into the other (it would seem that she had three, each larger than its predecessor, but only one intended for the drawing-room) her religiously inclined bookcase into a fourth and fifth, &c.

As anxious, now, to evacuate the fortress of her enemy as she had lately been to enter it, the Billickin bore this delay and particularity with the grace of that last exhaustion precedent to swooning; but she was naturally too much impressed by the lady who not only came in her carriage but was the owner of all those valuables, to dream of opposing her measurements and comments.

Her patience (as well as that of Miss Twinkleton and Rosa) was at last rewarded by the curious person having apparently measured and commented upon the height and breadth of walls, doors, windows, chimney-piece, recesses, grate, and indeed everything capable of the application of tongue and two-foot rule. But that she had not yet finished with the apartment was evident. For she sat, now, *without* an invitatory motion from Miss Twinkleton, and commenced upon another branch of what she evidently considered indispensable in the hiring of rooms.

Ah—h—h! She had observed that there were certain spots on the wall-paper. The room might and probably would need re-papering. Would there be any objection? Um—m—m!

Reflection on the part of Mrs. Billickin, showing in her face, with reference to the gold-mine and the means of working it. Answer: No, if the rooms should be let, to *her*, this would be re-papered, if absolutely required, though before supposed in excellent condition.

Ah—h—h! She had noticed that the locks on the doors (discovery made while measuring) were not in good order. As she had many valuable articles, safety was of the first consequence. Would there be any objection, &c. &c. &c., to replacing them? Um—m—m!

Additional reflection on the part of Mrs. Billickin, embrac-

ing not only the gold-mine aforesaid, but the security of payment and probable length of occupancy on the part of one who
owned so many valuable articles, and must have so much objection to removing them.   Yes, the locks would be replaced,
if also absolutely required, though no deficiency had been previously noticed.

(Affair growing rather amusing than otherwise, to the
present occupants of the rooms, if one could judge by the content with which Miss Twinkleton continued the shaping of a
red paw of the worsted monster, on a yellow ground, under a
blue tree,—and the transparent pretence with which Rosa pursued her reading in what seemed—suggestively enough—some
book of Oriental travel and adventure.   Affair everything else
than amusing, at this stage, to Mrs. Billickin, who remained
standing, fidgeted with her shawl-of-resource, and would undoubtedly have swooned had she not been in such objectionable presence.)

Ah—h—h!   She had also observed that the cracks under
the doors were very wide.   It would soon be autumn, with cold
winds.   Life was but a bubble to those who looked beyond, as
all should do; but there was a certain duty incumbent upon
all, to avoid virtual suicide.   Draughts must be prevented.
There would be no objection, of course, to having wood placed
on the bottoms of the doors, to prevent them?   Um—m—m!

Same reflection as before, on the part of Mrs. Billickin, with
the addition that this would cost very little.   Answer as before,
with same reservation.

Ah—h—h!   That seemed nearly all.   Stay—there were no
brass rods around the cornice, with hooks to hang valuable
paintings safely.   She had valuable paintings, and must hang
them.   Would there be, &c. &c. &c.?—Um—m—m!

Same reflection, in part, as appended to the last.   Not alone.
This would be costly—quite as costly as re-papering the room
However, &c. &c., and answer as before.

Ah—h—h!   One thing more and this was positively the
last.   The grate was old-fashioned, which did not make it ob-

jectionable; but it seemed too small, which did. Autumn—cold, &c. Would there be, &c. &c. ? Um—m—m !

Reflection, that there must be an end to this, or even the gold-mine would scarcely repay the outlay. But as this was to be the last, and at five pounds the week, &c. &c. Answer favorable, with movement of impatience that could no longer be dissembled.

The grave lady arose and announced her willingness, now, to examine the other rooms. Her two-foot rule being again in pocket, for subsequent use, she crossed her hands and was ready. Mrs. Billickin, scarcely feeling that beating up the quarters of her enemy had been a thorough success, manifested much alacrity in conducting her to the remaining apartments.

They disappeared; and it is to be feared that a certain merriment thereupon broke out and reigned in the place they had just quitted, evidencing everything else rather than sympathy with the victim of the numerous requirements.

There is a shadow of mystery over the proceedings immediately succeeding, owing to the easily understood difficulty of following the gold-mine and the adventurous miner into apartments where they conversed without witnesses. From all data at command, it seems probable that the two-foot rule was used with liberality, and that the little requests—having the force of commands—for certain trifling repairs and alterations, as a condition of removing the gold-mine and other valuables into the 'ouse, must have been employed with only less liberality than that displayed in the Ah—h—hs ! Oh—h—hs ! and Um—m—ms !

Fortunately, the temporarily lost chain can be recovered, at the moment when they returned to the drawing-room, under ths allegation of the grave lady that she had omitted to ascertain the exact depth of the chimney; and the Billickin performing the knock, in this instance, with what seemed the merest ghost of her robust former summons.

Even as she knocked, a mental struggle took place within her, and she rapidly turned over in her mind the chances she would have in a physical encounter with the grave lady, for she had reached the boiling point of indignation, and her constitution panted for a safety-valve; she resolved herself into a committee of one on the subject, took the sense of the meeting, concluded that five pounds a week covered the entire humiliation, and meekly re-entered the room with the indomitable grave lady.

There had been no change, during those few minutes, in the positions or occupations of Miss Twinkleton and Rosa; and it is only justice to them to say, that they scarcely manifested the extent of annoyance which might have been expected, at the second intrusion,—and that (perhaps prepared by the late occurrences for *anything*) they failed to manifest any surprise whatever.

Mrs. Billickin, clutching at her escaping heart, stood silent while the two-foot rule again came out from the pocket, to measure the depth of the chimney; and it is possible that something like despair seized her when she saw its bearer drop into a chair—after requesting and being accorded permission, with the air of intending to close the business then and there.

"Which it would be more convenient, it seems to me, Madam, to come to my sitting-room, as is the back parlor which I cling to and never part with for I will not deceive you, it would be better there than to trouble persons who are that set in their own ways, and that shifty."

The grave lady cut her short with an alarming suavity which she lacked strength to combat, from the presence of that very characteristic.

"Ah—h—h! If these persons do not mind, we will say the few additional words that may be necessary here, as the outlook is on the street and I have an aversion to rooms at the rear. Um—m—m!"

"We have no objection to your remaining, Madam. Have we, Rosa, my dear?" very cordially said Miss Twinkleton, whose willingness to entertain, there is reason to fear, may have had its origin in the evident disinclination of Mrs. Billickin, if in no worse motive.

"Certainly not, dear Miss Twinkleton. On the contrary, we shall be so very, very glad."

After this there was nothing remaining but to submit to the inevitable—which the lodging-housekeeper did by rather flopping than dropping into a chair, wishing herself meanwhile anywhere else on earth than in that especial spot, and only consoled by distant views of the auriferous deposit.

"Ah—h—h! rather moaned than spoke the grave lady. "With the few repairs and alterations made, I may say that I like the rooms very well—and that I shall take them, if the answers to a few questions are satisfactory, as I have reason to hope—and the terms can be agreed upon, as I have no doubt. Um—m—m! What is your religion, Mrs.—ah—Billickin?— Protestant or Catholic? Um—m—m!"

"Which I will not deceive you, Madam, though the question is not one as is often asked of the person of an 'ouse, but that Protestant I am to the backbone, 'oping it may be satisfactory," responded the Billickin, not seriously troubled by this opening ordeal.

"Oh—h—h! Good, very good indeed. And of course you go to church on Sundays? Ah—h—h!"

(This chronicle is not responsible for the indefensible action of Miss Twinkleton, from whom better things might have been expected, or Rosebud, from whom almost *anything* might have been looked for,—during some portions of the catechism immediately following. If Miss Twinkleton frequently chuckled, with a certain grimness born of her mature years, and yet not so loudly or visibly that notice could be taken of the act—and if Rosa found matter for mirth in her book, without reading a word of it, and laughed oftener than a young lady should laugh, except in merry conversation: let it be understood, again, that this chronicle is by no means responsible for the actions, in this and other instances, which it is obliged to record.)

In response to the church-going question, Mrs. Billickin, slightly embarrassed and very shivery, with spasmodic indica-

tions, was understood to say that she was as open as the day
to state anything as affected her moral or religious character,
but she put it to you whether you could always go to church
of a Sunday morning with the cares of an 'ouse so heavy on
your shoulders and you not strong, and wherefore try?

Um—m—m! This involution on the part of the grave
lady was understood to indicate that the last reply had been
scarcely satisfactory, but must be considered allowable under
the circumstances. Ah—h—h! Were there any babies in
the house?—or would there be any? Um—m—m!

(Something very nearly approaching to an explosion, on the
other side of the room, the particulars of which cannot be
entered into, for obvious reasons.)

Mrs. Billickin was understood to reply, with heightened
color and some agitation, that she did not wish to deceive but
which she never 'eard the like before in all her born days and
she a lady—but No!

Oh—h—h! Any pianos, with young ladies practising
upon them, in the house? Um—m—m!

Mrs. Billickin, partially recovering, answered that question
also in the favorable negative.

Ah—h—h! Any noisy boys of, say from six to twelve or
fourteen, always on the stairs, and with very thick shoes,
generally muddy and invariably loud? Um—m—m!

Response comparatively calm and equable—No!

Ah—h—h! At what hour was the house always closed
and secured at night? The reason for requiring an answer to
this being the expected presence of the before-mentioned
valuables, the safety of which must be secured. Um—m—m!

Response, with evident returning cheerfulness, under reminder of the valuables—that lodgers was that difficult to
manage as no one could depend on 'em and latch-keys stipu-
lated but she would be candid twelve o'clock and sometimes
much earlier but never later the 'ouse was closed and she defied
you to get inside after that hour do what you might even the
Lord Mayor.

Ah—h—h! Only one more question then. Could the attendance in the house always be depended upon as genteel and respectable, so that any of her visitors, most of whom would be persons of quality, might receive that quick and courteous attention which they had reason to expect? Um—m—m!

To which Mrs. Billickin, much revived under the prospect of soon concluding the negotiation, now, and becoming the proprietor of the gold-mine, with reversion of the other valuables,—replies with characteristic candor, with the assurance of always two and oftentimes three 'ighly respectful and dealt with that liberal as never give reason for neglect or fault-finding and she 'oped that now enough had been said and that Madam was quite satisfied.

Ah—h—h! Um—m—m! The grave lady had yet one more question to ask—possibly two—no more. Oh—h—h! Um—m—m! Could Mrs.—ah—Billickin put her in communication with the person receiving the rents, so that she might confer with him and satisfy herself that those rents were paid with regularity? — as she had much valuable property that might be seized upon, being found in the rooms belonging to *her* — Mrs. — ah — Billickin, in the event of any default being made in that payment; besides which, it was always unpleasant and discreditable to have officers in the house. Um—m—m!

(At this juncture, for what cause there is no data to explain, both Miss Twinkleton and Rosa rose hurriedly and left the room; so that the brief remainder of the conversation, if heard by them at all, must have been heard in that discreditable manner to which reference has already been made on more than one occasion.)

Mrs. Billickin rose also, with the lately-banished color coming back into her face, and indications of a belief that even gold-mines might be too costly in their working. There were recurrent symptoms of a swoon, too, that might have taken the place of the indignant protest which she had never been

18

so insulted in her life before and defied even persons whom she would not name but wenomous as serpents though thank goodness they had no power to sting, to say that she had ever been behind with her rent for one day and the landlord that sharp——

When the grave lady obviated the necessity of her concluding the somewhat-long sentence, by accepting all mooted points as disposed of in a satisfactory manner, and bringing the negotiation down to those financial terms of the liberality of which she had already given earnest.

Ah—h—h! Waiving all further inquiries, as she was by no means a difficult person, she would consider everything as meeting her wishes, and agree to take the rooms that day two weeks—her figures, which could not be otherwise than liberal, as she always avoided bargaining and never made second prices—being agreed to.

"Which you mean to make 'em, Madam, five pounds a week, in course, with all the improvements and dirt cheap at that by the month and lights and coals extra as is a rule I have never departed from and never mean to if you should ask me till doomsday and wherefore try?" said Mrs. Billickin, making a single stroke, with the verbal pick, into the gold-mine, though she felt that she had been, so to speak, exhausted in the preliminaries and was more or less feeble at the moment when she should have been strongest.

"Oh—h—h! as I was saying, Mrs.—ah—Billickin, I will take the rooms, this day two weeks, all the other conditions being kept, at—well, I will strain a point, as life is short and we all owe duties to each other — at, we will say *five-and-thirty shillings a week*, WITHOUT coals and candles. Um —m—m!"

The grave lady, whose hands were still piously crossed, looked the very incarnation of benevolence as she made the proposal; and it could not be that she felt herself other than the Lady Bountiful of her time. As for the Billickin—her gold-mine thus suddenly changed into the veriest dust-heap, her time worse than wasted, and herself humiliated before one whom she so disliked to the very verge of abhorrence, as Miss Twinkleton,—there are scarcely words to describe the threatening blaze of her face, where apoplexy seemed for the moment much more probable than swoons,—and the scream of veritable rage with which she hurled back the words at the calm utterer.

"*Five-and-thirty shillings a week!* What do you take me for, Ma'am, and who are you, I should like to know, to keep me trapesin' and travellin' up and down stairs for half a day to make me an offer which I was never so insulted in all my born days besides talking of persons of quality and of valuables that is more likely to be deal-tables and pewter spoons than anything else if anything you have and goodness knows!"

"Oh—h—h! So, Mrs.—ah—Billickin, you do not think proper to accept my offer, to-day? No matter; life is short, but it is long enough for reconsiderations. I will call to-morrow or the next day, and make one or two of my little measurements over again; and perhaps by that time you will be prepared to think better of my liberal offer—more than the rooms are strictly worth, Mrs.—ah—Billickin. Um—m—m!"

With the same slow and stately step so notable when she ascended the stairs, the grave and pious lady, undisturbed by the rage so visible in the other, moved again to the landing, and passed down to the hall, towards her waiting carriage-of-state, which must have been detained somewhat more than an hour from the intended Drive.

She may have heard, and she may not have heard, the actual scream assailing her as she descended the stair and passed along the hall—the voice pitched in the Billickin's shrillest key, and the manner the least in the world like that of any woman contemplating an early separation from her heart.

"Come again, to-morrow or next day, will you, with your fine carriage as is hired from a livery on credit, you old owdacions! Which you daren't do for your eyes, and you know it! Such imperence! and to me as has kept this house all these years and knows the worth of them rooms to a ha'-penny! *Five-and-thirty shillings!*—Jane! Jane! where are you, Jane? If I call you again, out of the 'ouse you go without warning mind that! *Five-and-thirty shillings!*"

Most of the concluding portions of this was addressed to the now-appearing attendant, who might be called the shawl-bearer, in emulation of the East—the Billickin being at that moment at the landing, on her way down to her own private back-parlor, where the long deferred swoon was to be indulged —and needing assistance, in her prostrate condition, even to become insensible with due attention to details.

But we have much more endurance—many of us, than could be supposed before the moment of trial. Mrs. Billickin might clutch at the escaping heart, but there were still a few beats in that indispensable portion of her anatomy—as shown in the instant following, when now-silent rage may be believed to have culminated at the crowning insult of the grave lady's visit.

For the servant-maid, opening the street-door for her egress when the Billickin had not yet left the landing, attracted the pious attention, and gave opportunity for sowing a few more of those remaining seeds of good for which the world cannot be too grateful.

"Ah—h—h! You are one of the servants, here? Um—m—m!"

"Yes, mam," with a bobbing curtsey that may have expected threepence—if so, how marked an illustration of the vanity of all human calculations!

"Ah—h—h! Do you always keep your caps clean? Are your morals strictly looked after? Do you keep the policemen out of the area? Um—m—m!"

"Clean caps, mum? Morals, mum? Pleeseman, mum!". The girl's assaulted cap shook with indignation, but she found no opportunity to express it in words, for the grave lady continued at once:

"Ah—h—h! Does Mrs.—ah—Billickin allow you to go to
Church on Sundays?—*every* Sunday? Oh—h—h!"

"Which I wouldn't hev time, mum, with the knives and the
boots, and us only keepin' two," explained the girl, a little
mollified. "But I 'as my outs in the arternoon, in course,
when Mary Hann and me, over the way——"

"Oh—h—h! Vanity, child, vanity!" interrupting. "Go
out? where should you 'go out,' if not to Church? Life is
short, oh—h—h!—and remember that you have a soul! You
must go to Church every Sunday—twice if possible. Tell
Mrs.—ah—Billickin that I say so. Um—m—m!"

The door was open, and the grave lady swept away to her
carriage, possibly without hearing all the half-indignant and
altogether puzzled reply of the maid—that "she might have
a soul, but she didn't believe *they* would be 'ard on a poor girl
as worked day and night, and did the best she could, even if
she didn't go to Church twicet of a Sunday, and sometimes
went somewhere else for a mouthful of fresh hair." The impressive footman descended from his perch, the lady took her
place in the carriage, and Southampton Street, Bloomsbury
Square, was relieved of that overshadowing respectability with
a tinge of piety superadded.

Miss Twinkleton and Rosa came back into the drawing-
room, at about the period when the enraged Mrs. Billickin
finally reached her recumbency in the back parlor. They
were laughing, to an extent scarcely warranted by anything
which had occurred; and dear little Rosa was actually holding
her mite of waist together with her two mites of hands, as if
there was danger of her falling into the traditional explosion
of fat men. And she was saying—what time Miss Twinkleton, only less amused than herself, though much less riotous
in the demonstration, labored to restore her to comparative
equanimity.

"Oh, wasn't it all too, too absurd! And how, how, how
could *he* punish her in that manner! And how could *she* do
it, ugly and cross old thing as Mrs. Billickin has been to
you!"

Of which last words no authoritative explanation can be given; though something may be hazarded, possibly not farther away from the truth than explanations are generally found to be. As that, the grave lady never coming back to discover whether Mrs. Billickin had thought better of her proposition, the question remained an open one with at least some of the parties cognizant of the leading facts—whether the visitor had been a *bona fide* one, type of a class of apartment seekers not yet entirely extinct in London or elsewhere, who ask everything and offer nothing—and so the most proper of persons to have chanced upon the cantankerous Billickin and revenged all her victims upon her at once; or whether she may not have been a person employed for the occasion—possibly an actress — her appointments procured, and the salient points of her rôle set down, in the combined interests of Rosa, Justice, and Mischief, by the brown, breezy, pranksome, and dangerously-unemployed incumbent of the Admiral's Cabin !

CHAPTER XVIII.

MR. HONEYTHUNDER PURSUES A SPECIAL OBJECT.

MR. HONEYTHUNDER is uncomfortable. The statement may seem rash in itself, and derogatory to one who should stand so high above the reach of mundane discomforts; but such things have been, and why should the respected manager of the United British and Foreign Universal Philanthropists, high in power at the Head Haven, and mighty in influence, not to say in terror, at the innumerable Tributary Havens with which the benevolent coasts of the British Islands are indented—why should not even *he* find a crumpled rose-leaf in his couch of sublime content ?

Not that anything has gone wrong with the Gigantic System which certain irreverent persons have been found capa-

ble of designating a Gigantic Fraud, making more evils than
it ever cured, and using ninety per centum of all moneys
passing through its hands, in salaries, fees and perquisites to
the Honeythunders, the Cringeloughs, and the Bleademfre-
leighs of the organization, to ten per centum used in recognized
objects—besides obstructing the course of true benevolence by
disgusting the whole body of liberal givers.

Not that there has been any decrease in its ramifications,
any falling off in the number of its compelled contributors, or
any failure in that crop of tangible miseries out of which the
wordy capital is drawn for new appeals and more forcible denunciations of all opposers and recreants. No—the world—
Mr. Honeythunder's world, at least—is hopefully improvident:
gratifyingly mean, narrow, obtuse and arrogant; ravishingly
prone to do those things which invite abusive circulars,
declamatory addresses, stormy personal interviews, and explanatory (generally defamatory) cards in the public journals.
No one has acted, so far as current report can be trusted, precisely as he or she should have acted ; no one, if rumor can be
credited, has thrown oil on the waters of dissension or lost
opportunity for re-kindling the half-extinguished fires of sec-
tarian or sectional difference : Wrong is all-prevailing, Right
powerless ; and the whole universe, outside of the United
· British and Foreign, is going to Moral Wreck and Spiritual
Ruin in a manner most exhilarating to forcible temperaments.
So that now, if ever, those who wield the forces therein incarnated, should be in that jubilant state ascribed to the critic at
the moment when a hecatomb of enemies' books is lying
around him ready for slaughter.

And yet Mr. Honeythunder is uncomfortable. Infinitely
above Mr. Tope in status, he would not dream of admitting
that his discomfort is a Tribulation—he would be much more
certain to think of it (he is not likely to *speak* of it, with
that overwhelming voice whose least whisper is a roar) as a
Thorn in the Flesh, sent for the express purpose of reminding
him of his mortality. And he would no more be likely to

feel, under the severest self-examination (supposing that he ever Honeythundered himself instead of others) that *he* had any part or lot in the growth of that Thorn, than the most inveterate lover of old port and heavy dinners could imagine that his gout at fifty did not come from some distant and unjust world of ill-natured dispensations, instead of from bottle and tureen.   Why should this thing be ?—he roars, mentally.   Am I not at once a man of mark and usefulness ? Am I not necessary, and indeed indispensable in carrying out ends and objects in which the Divine Powers may be supposed interested ?   And is not the whole force and energy of my nature necessary to carry out those ends and objects ?   And if I am troubled and vexed, how can I carry out those ends and objects with full vigor ?   And if I do not carry out those ends and objects in full vigor, will not the Divine Powers be more or less the losers ?   Then why do the Divine Powers permit me to be troubled and vexed ?   Why this Thorn in the Flesh ? —from which it is consolatory to know, however, that even the saintly Paul was not free.

Perhaps, meanwhile, if any man has ever devoted his arboricultural energies to the growing of a Thorn, with more assiduity than another, that man will be found in Mr. Honeythunder, now of so ultra-benevolent and notable a character. Planted it many years ago—ah, true : we hold, many of us, whatever of excuse may lie in the fact that we planted long ago and have not been pursuing the same course at a very late period.   But it unfortunately happens that time does not inevitably wear away Wrong or its consequences,—that it is quite as likely to widen and deepen those consequences,—and only ameliorate the original act by a sort of ostrich-hiding of the head in the sand—that trees grow larger and stronger as they increase in years, instead of considerately shriveling away at the moment when we choose to wish that they might cease to exist.

A certain number of years ago, when the Philanthropist was only budding, and then resident at one of the Northern towns

of the Empire—there fell into his way a young woman.
Name Sarah Lewt. Family, the reverse of respectable, not to
say low—working-people, in point of fact. Education of the
girl, so limited as to have no effect in moulding her character.
Disposition, slightly vain and frivolous, with a tendency to
harmless flirtation of a certain girlish sort, not intended to
reach serious action. Appearance, somewhat attractive—indeed, enough so to make her an object of contention among
young male persons of her own rank in life.

It would be difficult to characterize (in the words of Mr.
Honeythunder at this later period) what chanced between the
young woman and himself at that earlier time in the North.
It was understood that she had been under engagement of
marriage (such an "engagement" as people of that condition
are capable of forming) with a young man of her own condition, or a shade removed for the better, whose name, if the budding Philanthropist ever knew it, he had not closely remembered through those after years in which so many names
sounded in his ears, and his own sounded (loudly enough) in
the ears of so many. For some cause that engagement became
broken off, and the young man grew indignant, sore-hearted,
and went away—where, the budding Philanthropist, again, had
no idea. For this rupture of the engagement, a certain impression in the mind of the silly girl, that he intended to
marry her, may or may not have been responsible. If such
an impression existed, he remembered no words that could
have given rise to them—therefore, as a practical fact, there
could have been no such words.

Some things, following, were even more difficult to characterize. They involved unpleasantnesses: they might almost
be said to involve guilt, only that such a thing in such a connection, was simply incredible. That he, Mr. Honeythunder,
training for a life of energetic and active Evangelical Benevolence, could have been guilty of the seduction of a working-
man's daughter—that was simply one of those things not to
be mentioned, because out of the range of possibility. That

he might have allowed himself to drift, through fault more
than half that of the woman, into a certain intimacy involving unpleasant consequences — that might be possible : he
might even know that something of the sort had occurred.
He might go so far as to credit the fact (not known to him
from any personal presence with the mother) that a child had
been born, alleged to be the fruit of that intimacy ; and dimly
might be admitted the possibility (again outside of his personal knowledge) of the mother having died, even more
thoroughly broken-hearted than her cast-off lover, and the
child having been thrown out on the world, uncared-for, liable
to starve, to rob or murder as the consequence of want and
ignorance, to go to ruin in any way that might be found most
convenient. So much might be admitted as having been
within the bounds of possibility, in the early career of the
Manager of the United British and Foreign Universal ; and
certain reflections and memories, bearing shapes analogous to
these, may possibly have visited his waking dreams, not to
say his nightly visions, in those days when the voice of an
applauding public had not quite drowned the last echoes of
the "still small voice" within.

But it has been said, aforetime, that "of all things in this
world success is the most successful;" and the Rev. Luke
Honeythunder, M. U. B. F. U. P., had every reason to
realize the truth of the axiom. He had the public voice,
at an early day; and eke his own, all the while. When
the public voice failed to carry him sufficiently high on the
wave of applauding sound, he could always rely on his own,
equally loud physically and morally, and entirely relieved from
that embarrassing modesty which has been the life-long hindrance and eventual ruin of so many. The world, fortunately
for him, was a combative world ; there were plenty of opponents
at whom to hurl fierce invectives and opprobrious epithets;
his auditory was large, not only at the Head Haven and elsewhere, where he carried on the operations of Aggressive and
Subjugatory Philanthropy, but at the Conventicle in which

on Sunday mornings he vented what amount of unexpended sound had accumulated during the secular days; and it was no difficult task, we may believe, to forget the mere penny-whistle squeak of conscience (perhaps a very little and modest conscience, for so large a physique), amid the blare of oratorical trumpets, the crash of philanthropic kettledrums, and the hoarse roar of the sea represented by thousands of voices engaged in the most ardent of all worships, if the blindest.

It may be doubtful whether, twice in a somewhat long public life, Mr. Honeythunder found an antagonist who galled him so much as Mr. Crisparkle, in that little affair of Neville Landless, whose guardianship he was nearly as glad to relinquish as was the poor young man to feel himself fairly out of the power of that rude manner and blustering voice. There was that in the demeanor of the clergyman, at the last interview held at the Head Haven, more annoying to the coarsely impervious Philanthropist than would have been almost any other form of assault—it being simply evident that the Minor Canon of Cloisterham thoroughly despised him ;—and it being correspondingly difficult for persons of a certain temperament to avoid despising themselves a *little*, under angry protest, when made aware how very low they stand in the estimation of others whom they are compelled to respect. And no doubt the bitterest pill of humiliation ever swallowed by the Manager, was gulped on the day already noted, when he went down to Cloisterham, to put himself again into communication with the Minor Canon and rectify an error in the Landless accounts, which certainly seemed to need an explanation as well as the more substantial justice.

That visit, as we have seen, bore fruit not originally expected, in the glimpse of the broad philanthropic personality accidentally afforded to Durdles ; and the secondary effect of that visit, as also already shown, was to induce a return visit on the part of the stone-mason, the reverse of gratifying to the recipient, to use the mildest phrase capable of conveying the fact.

And here we reach, by two circuitous roads meeting at the

same point, the secret of Mr. Honeythunder's disquiet, not less pronounced than that of Mr. Tope, and by no means so easy to remove by any simple process. The little wretch at Cloisterham, with whom he had begun his acquaintance by receiving a stoning verging towards the painful honor of martyrdom, and continued it by administering a flogging equally undignified and deserved—the worse-than-untrained whelp, with every evil propensity apparently full-developed, any better possibilities lying as dormant as seeds in frozen earth—the infant Arab whom he had threatened with arrest and confinement in a Reformatory (which even *he* knew to be the severest of punishments), as the only probable means of saving him from the gallows or the state-prison,—this to be *his son !* His, the Rev. Luke Honeythunder! A leading light in the evangelical world, burdened with a child whom he dared not acknowledge, with the possibility that at any hour he might be made to do worse than acknowledge it, by having it thrust upon him in a public accusation, through the threatened hostility of Durdles (whose intelligence and dislike he knew), and the co-operation of the Minor Canon (whose dislike he also knew, and whose information he feared)! *The* leading light in the philanthropic world, father of a certain small mass of filth, rags, and vice, his neglect of which might be at any moment exposed, through the same instrumentalities, and the hollowness of all his loud-mouthed adjurations to others, thus made apparent to the most obtuse of intellects!

It is really not strange, all things considered, that this Thorn in the Flesh, commencing its definite pain with the visit of Durdles, should have increased in discomfort instead of diminishing, as days went by and became weeks. That the Haven of Philanthropy should have ceased to be a complete refuge, such as it had been in days not long gone by. That there should have ceased to be the same unalloyed satisfaction in showing himself in crowds or on the rostrum, and hearing the smothered exclamations of admiring applause: "There! that's him !" "That's Mr. Honeythunder, the great philanthropist!" Makes everybody give to everybody else, whether they will or no!" "Oh, such a good man!" "Wonderful man!—what would the benevolent world do without him?" &c., &c., *ad inflnitum*, though never (to one special stomach) *ad nauseam*. That he should even have found himself, on one miserable day, declining to preside at one of those great occasions which was to see ten thousand persons verbally belabored primarily, and millions belabored secondarily; and a general field-day indulged in against all ranks, classes, and conditions of men, not content to put a particular prison-stripe on the objects of their benevolence; and much current coin of the realm (bank-notes not excluded) added to the conveniences for further gatherings and belaborings; and necessarily the presiding genius for the time little less than a demigod. Whether the chief cause of this renunciation of honors was to be found in some faint suspicion that he might not be quite worthy of them (first step towards regaining any lost quality) —or whether the idea of his outcast and reprobate son had grown upon him, until he half-expected him, on some one of those grand occasions, to start up from the outer circle of the crowd, break out into a demoniac chorus:—

> " Widdy widdy wen!
> I sees—my—old—dad—again
> Widdy—widdy wy!
> If—E—don't—acknowledge—me—I—let—fly.
> Widdy widdy wake cock, warning!"

—Salute him with a shower of flints, and manifest his joy at the opportunity by a war-dance of unusual vigor and atrocity, —which of these considerations may most have moved the Manager in his singular self-abnegation, must remain a mystery with no chance for solution whatever, except as we practice the mercy recommended by His Lordship to the gentleman of the criminal panel, and give the accused the benefit of any doubt.

Let the doubt be a little influenced in his favor, too, by a knowledge of the resolution at which the Manager arrives, after an indefinite number of days of this growing discomfort, and upon which he acts with that vigor which cannot be denied him whatever the measure of his other claims to respect.

He will go down to Cloisterham, while he would rather go anywhere else on the round earth. He will find this juvenile demon of his past raising. He will discover, at least, what opportunity there may be, without serious peril of compromise, to " do something for him." (Indefinite phrase, which may mean, to kill, to succor, to pension off, to put out of the way. With Mr. Honeythunder it simply means "something — according to circumstances.")

So the underpaid, overworked, and over-badgered clerical force of the Head Haven, and the less-worked and better-paid assistants in the higher ramifications, are duly advised, on the day of the resolution, that the Manager will be absent on the following day, and perhaps that succeeding, being called a short distance into the rural districts by an Object of Benevolence which demands his immediate attention. And let us hope that the candor of this statement, and the purity of his intentions towards that special Object, are not detracted from by a little occurrence which takes place within the half-hour following this announcement, and when the sycophantic undertones of compliment to the zeal and energy of their superior in The Cause (intended to be overheard) have not yet died on the subordinate lips.

The occurrence comes in the shape of an application from a gentleman of limited means, but many active and unobtrusive charities, who has heard very favorably of the British and Foreign Universal, as carrying on a great work of systematic beneficence, and who asks the aid of that society towards a small fund for the immediate relief of the widows and children of two-score poor fellows just killed by a fire-damp explosion in a coal-mine. For the moment, in the reception of this request, Mr. Honeythunder, however oppressed by other cares, is his best self again; and the round, convincing phrases with which he rebuffs the application, explaining that the rules of the association, and the heavy pressure upon it for means to meet Special and Legitimate Objects, render such a contribution entirely out of the question and on the verge of being preposterous. These should have been sufficient to win him overwhelming applause, even at the gathering of declined honor, besides covering the applicant for aid to an Object, thus demonstrated to be General and Illegitimate, with the due amount of regret, disappointment and chagrin at having ventured to make the suggestion.

Then follows an interval of nightly rest (its snores undoubtedly pitched upon the same sonorous key as the daily voice), sandwiched between the Good Action already done, in sending away the coal-mine advocate empty, and the remaining good action which is to be done—much more, as he persists in feeling, in the interests of others than in his own.

And then he goes down to Cloisterham, on the following day, a little hazy as to what he is to do when arrived there, but with the name of "Durdles" in recollection, and with some dreadful thought that he may be driven, in finding his Object, to present himself in that disreputable and unevangelical place, the "Traveller's Twopenny," of the name of which he also retains a recollection through the unwelcome instruction of the stone-mason. There is one thing clear in his mind, however: he may intend to do something for the young wretch, but it will go hard with himself if he does not do so without leaving any impression about the old town dishonored by the young wretch's abode, that the Rev. Luke Honeythunder is extending to him the bounty of the United British and Foreign Universal, from any other motive than his duty as a Philanthropist, obliged to turn his attention, when called upon, to the most objectional cases.

He reaches Cloisterham without taxing the patience of Joe, driver of the Cloisterham omnibus, from the distant station to the town. Somewhat contrary to his usual wont, he strides over the bridge, as if taking a constitutional *à la* Crisparkle, and emerges upon the town, having attracted little attention, and seeming to wish to attract no more (so unusual for him!) than may suffice to lead him to the object of his unwilling search.

He makes a few inquiries, full-voiced as usual, and even a little additionally pompous, as one who should say, in the very act: "Good people, recognize in me, Incarnate Benevolence, seeking out an Object of Pity, and do not mistake me for any other person, with any other motive!" He asks for the boy under the name of "Deputy," again remembered from Durdles; and once he appends the information that he has heard of him as at some low place of resort called the "Traveller's Twopenny." But the amount of information received is by no means extensive; only one of those from whom he inquires, has ever heard of such an objectionable personality; and *he* suggests that looking for him would be worse than fox-hunting on foot, as he is here, there, everywhere and nowhere, nearly at the same time, and always in some villany or other. Adds this person, that if he will go to Cathedral Yard, not far from the city wall, there he may find the mason, Durdles, somewhere among the stone-work, and *he* will be more likely to discover the interesting young person for him than any one else whom he knows.

Mr. Honeythunder would rather not meet Durdles, remembering him (only) as the messenger bearing that intelligence which has grown to be the Thorn in the Flesh. But there seems no avoidance of his doing so, if he does not intend to spend the whole day wandering about the dull old town, which is doubly distasteful just now on account of some of its inhabitants.

Another inquiry or two brings him to the spot, among the monuments and stone-chips, where he remembers the humiliation of being set upon by a juvenile fiend (then unknown), and the triumph of beating a part of that juvenile fiend (physical) very nearly to a pulp. Then he sees before him the tumble-down stone hut which he saw on that occasion

when accosting Mr. Crisparkle,—and enters: He sees a low
middle door, to pass beneath which he will be obliged to stoop
his high head ; and he hears beyond the door, the chip ! chip !
chip ! of what he has no doubt is the work of the stone-mason
whom he is seeking under protest. He stoops his high head,
with a smothered malediction (of an evangelical pattern) on all
persons who construct such miserably low doorways, who ought
at once to be arrested and forced to build higher, under high
pains and penalties ; and then he is within, in the presence of
the man who not long ago visited him so unwelcomely at the
Head Haven.

Durdles is chipping away at his life-work, coat removed,
sweat on the stolid brow, and making so much noise, naturally,
that he does not hear the entrance of the other, or know of
his coming in, until turning to walk back and catch a better
view of his progress, after the manner of sculptors.   Then,
when he sees the visitor, and recognizes him, the heavy face
becoming darker and worse-tempered than any one who only
ordinarily saw the slouching, half-drunken man, could believe
possible ; and he backs up, so to speak, covering the unfinished
bust, as if the intruding eyes could not be allowed to look
upon *that*, at any hazard,—casting a look, meanwhile, towards
the curtained niche, which would tell Mr. Crisparkle, if present, that the movement is part of the current anxiety for concealing everything in connection with the work on the block.

" Oh, it is you, is it ? " he says, very gruffly, after a moment,
and when he evidently judges that he has quite covered the
bust with his broad ungainly person.

" Yes—you are the man that called upon me at the Head
Haven, in town, some weeks ago, with information about a
boy. You recognize me, I believe—if not, my name is
Honeythunder—Rev. Luke Honeythunder."

The Manager of the United British and Foreign Universal
scarcely speaks with that overwhelming force which ordinarily
makes the renegades of the philanthropic cause (all who differ
with him in idea or mode) quake in their high-lows, proclaim-

19

ing that a veritable Son of Jove is banging away at their ear-drums. For some cause, here and now, he is a mere mortal, nothing more; and for some cause, at the same time, the ungainly man with the mallet and chisel seems unaccountably the more commanding of the two in position.

"Oh, yes, Durdles knows you!" he replies. "You said you wouldn't come down, and Durdles said you would! You said Durdles lied—there, among your scribbling dummies that you handles like tools—same as Durdles does this chisel, but may be not so well. You knowed it *wasn't* a lie, then; but you stayed away as long as you dared, for fear of Durdles splittin' on you, and then you come! A nice 'Reverend,' *you* are!"

Mr. Honeythunder has not often been addressed with such force, and certainly not often with what a Quaker would call the same "plain language," from the day when he over-whelmed a certain local world with his colossal size and power-ful lungs, at birth. And he is not disposed to accept the new status too calmly—the denouncer to allow denunciation of himself: the verbal engineer holding the same objection or-dinarily ascribed to the mechanical, against being "hoist with his own petard."

"How dare you, low fellow!" he thunders, recovering the lost voice. "If there was any law in this miserable place, I would have you set in the stocks for filthy language to a person of condition, or sent to some reformatory prison, where you might learn better manners."

"Oh, you would, would you!" answers Durdles, with some-thing very like a sneer—something that would be quite a sneer if we did not know that only people of a certain standing can employ that weapon of polished offence. "You would like to frighten Durdles, wouldn't you, with your big voice and bluster? Don't try it, master, for it wouldn't do; and the habit might grow on you!"

"Insolent scoundrel!" again begins Mr. Honeythunder; but he is silenced, instantly, as no assembly has ever had power to silence him.

"Better save your reverend breath to cool your reverend porridge!" palpably sneers the stone-mason; but with the words his voice deepens, and his face—that face ordinarily so dull, stolid, uninteresting—becomes something not pleasant to look at, from other characteristics—dark, fierce, dangerous. "See here!" he says, in intense passion, which for the time gives him a position above himself—"don't go too far, if it's all the same to *you!* Durdles don't want to brain you with this mallet; so be keerful! You come down here to look arter that young devil. Wery well. You shall have a peep at your crib; but Durdles wants to tell you something, first, that may-be you'd like to remember. Please to turn them eyes that's looked on so many great folks, onto a poor feller that's got no money for you to wheedle out of him—and say, if you know *me!*"

"Know you, fellow?" Mr. Honeythunder echoes, with angry contempt. "No, and I do not wish to, for you seem to be below even the efforts of Philanthropy. You seem to sup- pose that my errand at Cloisterham is to look after that boy; if so, show me where he is, take the money that I shall pay you for the service, and then never let me see your bad face, or hear your vile tongue again."

"Don't know me—don't you! Don't know Durdles! Why, that's bad o' *you*, as ought to know everybody that's poor and miserable! Praps you might remember, then, one Samuel Dustin, as was a going to marry Sary Lewt, when you took her away from me, like a psalm-singin' willain as you was, left her with that brat, broke her heart, and mine!"

There is terrible impressiveness, if not pathos, in the words of the ungainly stone-mason, as he thus reveals the buried secret of years in the very face of the wronger. And the words have force to the ears that hear, for they literally end the conflict. The Manager of the U. B. F. U. P. bows his head, with a gesture nearer to manly humility and submission than any living man could remember of him, and does not speak for a moment after the other has ceased. The Thorn in

the Flesh has a new rankle, evidently; but it is not beyond
the mercy of God that it may rankle beneficially now, and
assist in the eventual remoulding of that which so needs to
change form as well as substance!

"Samuel Dustin! You?" is all that he utters, after that
moment of silence. And this is followed by another moment's
restraint, and then by a groan, much more earnest in character, there is reason to believe, than many that he may have
vented over Legitimate Objects, at one period or another of
his successful philanthropic career.

"Yes, Samuel Dustin as *was ;* drunken old Stony Durdles
as *is ;* and all along o' *you,* psalm-singin' Luke Honeythunder! That's what Durdles means, and he hopes you likes
it, and 'll tell about it at your next preachin'!"

"I am sorry—Dustin—Durdles—whatever you choose to
call yourself, now. I wish that I had never done what was so
wrong *to her* and so sad to you. I *did* know that you were
telling the truth, the other day; though I did not know *you*
then. And I *have* come to do what I can for—for—my poor
little wretch of a son. There: what can I do more? And
will not this satisfy you, without saying more rough words *to*
me or *of* me?"

Undoubtedly, Luke Honeythunder has not spoken so candidly or feelingly half a score of times during all his career of
philanthropic charlatanry. The candor and true feeling even
affect Durdles, who dashes his rough left hand across his eyes,
throws down the mallet still remaining in his right, draws on
the clumsy coat with its big horn buttons, and assumes his
dinner-bundle, all without one word of reply. Then he throws
an old potato-sack over the unnoticed bust, and says, with all
the sneer gone out of his harsh voice, though the gruffness can
no more be extracted than the squeak from saw-filing :—

"Yes, that'll do for Durdles, and it'll do for *him :* leastwise
it will do better nor nothing. I haven't seen the young brat
for the last two hours, but I seed him then, going up towards
the Weir, and I think that we can find him. Come along, if
you mean what you say."

"Stop — Dustin — Durdles! one word! You will not destroy my usefulness by telling others——"

"What are you afeard on, Luke Honeythunder?" the stone-mason interrupts. "Of Durdles telling on you? No! —not if you take keer of *her boy*. But don't you talk no more about 'that, for I don't like it; and it isn't no use, is it? Come along!"

Durdles acting as guide, they leave the hut, pass up a narrow and miserable alley, near that Travellers' Twopenny with which the Manager has now no business whatever, and are soon emerging on the river-bank, on some portion of which, in some ramification of villany or trouble in connection with the fishermen or their boats, he expects to find the by-no-means desired though wanted Deputy.

The two have not so great a distance to proceed, however, as Durdles imagined. For they have scarcely opened the view upon the path, when they become aware of a group of four or five, on the edge of the bank and in evident commotion. Something unusual has certainly occurred, for as they come nearer they recognize the garb of fishermen and hear words of pity and alarm.

Then they reach the group, and as the details of the scene burst upon them, they not only see what they are not likely soon to forget, but what explains itself so well as scarcely to need an additional word.

On the grass of the river bank lies Deputy, or what remains of him—a mass of rags, torn flesh, and clotted blood—more nearly "eaten up," in that sense attempted to be conveyed by the story-books, than often chances to others than those who fall into the jaws of lions or tigers. The right hand will never shy stones any more, even if life is spared to the body, for it seems to have been in a fanged mouth and is literally crunched—bones, flesh and sinews. The throat, too, is lacerated; though the worst effect, there, is partially hidden by a thick black scarf, of netted silk, now soaked in blood, hanging around it. The eyes are closed, in death or insensibility:

the former seems by far the more hopeful guess of the two, under all the circumstances.

Close beside him is poor Little Crawshe, on his knees, crying bitterly, his left hand supporting the incapable head, and his right pitifully trying to do what could only be done by both—to *wring itself.* Crawshe, the fisherman, is bending over the mangled little wretch, with his rough face full of pity and sorrow, and his own hands covered with blood from an evident attempt at rescue. There are two other fishermen, and one of them is holding, with a vice-like grip on the loose skin and firm hair of the neck, Black Tomboy, whose gory fangs and flaming eyes only too well explain what might else only be guessed.

There is only one to explain, in words—poor Little Crawshe, who answers the eager horrified inquiries of the Manager and Durdles, between his sobs and ineffectual attempts at wringing a single hand.

It would seem that Deputy had on more than one occasion stoned Black Tomboy, at safe distance, awaking unpleasant suggestions in the canine mind, if producing no worse effect. Returning down the bank, that day, only a few minutes earlier, from a predatory excursion among the fishing-boats, the expert had hurled a few stones through a net hanging to dry on the reel, been mildly remonstrated with by Little Crawshe, flung at the latter a few epithets (sharper and more cruel than any stone in his loaded pockets) touching the shame of poor Exty, and ended (more than he knew) by knocking down and beating the poor helpless cripple.

Beyond that, even Little Crawshe himself knows very little, and is too horrified to be very explicit. He only realizes that Black Tomboy, who had been lying under his bench, and must have seen the assault at some distance, came flying upon Deputy, bearing him to the ground before he could himself rise from it; and that then a terrible clench and fight took place between Deputy and the dog, with the former kicking, striking and yelling, and no words of his

availing to call him off—until the cries of the two brought
his father and two others of the fishermen, and the dog was
torn by main force from his prey. He attempts to add, but
thinks better of it, and resolves to tell only Mr. Datchery—
that the scarf around Deputy's neck is the same, he thinks,
which came into the hands of Mr. Jasper only a few days
before—at a time of which only themselves and Black Tomboy know. When he does so, the man of the white hair will
probably speculate a little,—whether Jasper, haunted by the
re-possession, gave it away to Deputy, as a means of ridding
himself of it most effectually ; or whether Deputy had simply
stolen it, as a professional duty ; and whether its presence
around the neck of the drowned boy was not the principal
cause of the fearful laceration, from the hatred which the dog
had already shown towards the scarf and its wearer.

Mr. Honeythunder returns to London, the same afternoon,
in a fly from the town to the inconvenient station, and thence
by rail,—bringing back with him, in a close carriage in which
there are also a bed and a surgeon—an Object. He has discovered it, something too late, perhaps, but, while it still
contains life ; and one of the metropolitan hospitals and a
world of difficult experiences may aid him in making it, in
time, something else than a mangled mass—possibly something else than a hopeless cripple or a boy-fiend—even possibly a Man ; just as some day there may pass out of his own
mind, through actual benefits conferred upon humanity by
unostentatious practical benevolence, or under the renewed
benumbing influences of a sounding sham-philanthropy, the
most humiliating of the recollections connected with his
Thorn in the Flesh.

And Durdles, in a sort of stupid grief which is half joy,
lounges and shambles back to his Hole in the Wall. He will
be stoned home o' nights no more, and will never again hear
that Flibbertigibbet chorus, and so feels, stupidly, that there
has been a loss. But he will not be likely again to see *her*
child in rags, in crime, and travelling towards the doors of a

prison ; and who shall say that this is not, again and always in his shambling and stupid way, sufficient compensation to the Stony One ?

CHAPTER XIX.

THE DATCHERY—DURDLES STATEMENT.

STATEMENT of Samuel Durdles, stone-mason and architectural monument worker, residing and carrying on the business of his calling, at Cloisterham, Chalkshire ;—made in the presence of and taken down by Richard Datchery, Esquire, barrister-at-law (in expectancy), of Barnaby's Inn, in the city of London, in the county of Middlesex—at the lodgings of the said Datchery, at Cloisterham, on the——day of——18—.

With reference to the disappearance of the young man or person known as and called by the name of Edwin Drood, and the suspicions existing as to the supposed murder of the said Edwin Drood, at or about Cloisterham, aforesaid, on the night of December twenty-fourth, in the year of our Lord one thousand eight hundred and.....

Statement procured by Mr. Datchery, with reference to possible future use in furthering the interests of justice, by detecting the real perpetrator of the alleged crime (be the same more or less), and removing from certain person or persons improperly charged with the same, a suspicion against them which may otherwise work seriously to their disadvantage. Any concealments, of names or otherwise, made herein by Mr. Datchery, to be duly and in full explained by him, with explicit declaration of all motives which may seem ambiguous in this proceeding or others connected with the affair—whenever he may be called upon by properly constituted authority, or have the opportunity afforded him (the affair having then progressed so far as to make such explanations proper) of entering into such statement on his own account and behalf.

Statement of Mr. Durdles not made under oath, for want of opportunity on the part of the examiner to procure the administration of such oath, without placing knowledge of circumstances necessary to be kept as yet entirely secret, in the possession of officials liable to display want of reticence, from ignorance of the important interests involved.

Original intention on the part of Mr. Datchery to procure the drawing up of statement under Mr. Durdles's own hand and in the original language of that person; but serious difficulties rendering that course impossible; and this explanation made, in order, in the event of the death of Mr. Durdles or Mr. Datchery, or both, before the production and use of the statement, to make the two reasons fully apparent for failing to secure, in the manner suggested, the best written evidence.

Difficulty first : Strange perversions of language on the part of Mr. Durdles in conversation—doubtless owing to many years of objectionable association, a certain degree of intemperance, and original deficiency in education—rendering any statement embodying all his own words comparatively unintelligible and in many respects improper for public use. *Difficulty second :* Almost total loss by Mr. Durdles, through intemperance before mentioned, careless exposures of the body, benumbing influences of his coarse labor, and long disuse of the faculty except in the mere act of signing his name at intervals of years,—of the amount of chirographic skill which he may once have possessed, rendering any attempted document of that character certainly illegible.

Much care used, however (Mr. Datchery makes this supplemental explanation, at once in justice to himself, and that the document may be held to possess all possible weight and authenticity), 1st, to impress upon Mr. Durdles the solemn obligation under which every man lies, in any civilized community, to tell " the truth, the whole truth, and nothing but the truth," when bearing testimony which may affect others, —without the solemnity of an oath, as well as under that inducement; and 2nd, to obtain from Mr. Durdles, thus warned and with the understood additional inducement of good feeling and a certain amount of gratitude—precisely the meaning intended to be conveyed by him, even when many repetitions of phrases and involutions of questions have been found necessary.

Certain matters contained in the statement, in the opinion of the examiner more or less irrelevant to the issue, but retained and set down by him under doubt how far he would be justified in withholding from the future legal authority taking cognizance of the case, any fact, however apparently insignificant, which can possibly have the least bearing upon its details.   Some explanation applying to frequent retention of Mr. Durdles' own phrases, and to repetitions, rendered inevitable by the habit of mind of Mr. Durdles, and possibly occurring more frequently than they would do under more favorable circumstances.   As also, to certain explanatory notes, interpolated by Mr. Datchery.

Questioned as to his name, age, place of birth, residence and occupation.

Replies—to the first, that he does not see what that has to do with it.   Name is Durdles.   Everybody about Cloisterham knows Durdles.   Most of them do not know him by any other name.   Some of the boys [NOTE: With whom he seems to have been more or less at feud during most of his residence in Cloisterham] call him " Stony " Durdles, he supposes from his trade and the dust on his clothes ; but he does not thank the young varmints, and he does not care.   That is not his name : his real name is Samuel Durdles—Sam Durdles, if any one likes it better.   To the second, that his age is his own business, and he does not mean to tell it to any one.   He may be forty and he may be sixty—old enough, any way, not to make so great a fool of himself as he has been in the habit of doing, and not to be so poor as he is.   To the third, that he was born in the north, not far from Scotland—that is enough —he does not choose to put any person on the track of where he was or what he did, before he came to Cloisterham.   There are one or two who know already, enough, if not too much. [NOTE: From certain internal evidence in his conversation, there is reason to believe that he was born in Northumberland: may possibly have been Cumberland, however.] To the fourth, that he does not see the use of that, either: every fool in Cloisterham knows where he lives—in a dog-hole close by the city wall. To the fifth, that here again time is being wasted, as every one knows that too. But if he must tell what everybody knows, he must. His business is getting out and setting up monuments and grave-stones, taking care of the stone-work of the Cathedral, and digging out the Old' Uns that have been so long stowed away that no one remembers anything about 'em—in the walls, under the pavement and everywhere; the old shop [NOTE: His phrase, referring to the Cathedral, preserved on account of oddity—not to say originality] being about rotten with 'em.

Questioned as to his being married, a bachelor, or a widower.

Replies—that it seems that nothing can be left alone, in the life of a poor fellow! Who wants to know that about Durdles, and why? What is it to *them*? But there is *one* at Cloisterham as knows it already: the best and the worst of it. That one is Mr. Crisparkle. [NOTE: Mr. Crisparkle is a very estimable gentleman and clergyman; one of the Canons of Cloisterham Cathedral, and highly respected in all the relations of life. Was also active in the investigations following the disappearance of the young man Drood.] He is not married; never was; never intends to be. Has been engaged, once, and had enough of *that!* That was many years ago. A psalm-singin' chap ran off with his girl and broke her heart. Is not that enough? What more does anybody want to know?

Questioned as to his acquaintance with the young man Drood, disappeared.

Replies that he had no acquaintance with him before the 24th December, 18—, except that he occasionally saw him

coming to Cloisterham during the previous year, on visits to
Mr. John Jasper, at the Gate House; and sometimes saw him
walking out from what they called the "Nun's House," sort
of female school, on the High Street, where they always kept
a lot of girls—confound 'em—nigh as bad as them brats of
boys, guying any one as was old, or poor, or did not please
their dainty eyes. Where was he? Oh. He had seen Master Drood walking out from the Nun's House, with a very
pretty little thing, that seemed a mere child, and giggled a
great deal, but didn't guy anybody. Name was Miss Rosa
Bud, as he understood; and also understood that they were
somehow engaged to be married. Some nonsense of their
fathers, he believes. Married! They were about as fit to be
married as two small kittens to keep a public. [NOTE: Mr.
Durdles disposed to wander somewhat seriously, here, but
recalled.]

Questioned as to his knowledge of Mr. John Jasper, and the
length of time during which that knowledge has continued.

Replies—to the first, that he may have known Mr. Jasper
[NOTE: He pronounces the name as if spelled "Jarsper"—
which may or may not be of consequence in some possible future
question of identification] a matter of five or six years, since
Mr. Jasper first come to Cloisterham and went to singing in
the Cathedral.

Questioned as to Mr. Jasper's life, habits and practices.

Positively declines to answer. [NOTE: With signs of ill-
temper at the question, and possibly of some fear with reference to the person inquired of.] What does *he* know about
Mr. Jasper, his life, or his habits? Mr. Jasper sings in the
Cathedral: *he* does not—he digs. What is the use of getting
a poor fellow into scrapes by asking him questions that would
do no good to answer? Why not ask Mr. Jasper himself
about anything they want to know? There are some things,
he supposes, that he *must* tell, and he will tell *them*, and not
a word more, if he dies for it. Suppose that Durdles may
have a secret or so; isn't it his own, just as much as if it

belonged to the Dean? and hasn't he a 'right to keep his own?

Questioned as to alleged relationship between the disappeared person, Edwin Drood, and Mr. Jasper. As to the latter being the uncle of the former, as alleged.

Replies—how should *he* know? Has heard it said so; and it may be true or may not be. He wasn't present when young Drood came into the world—was he? and if not, how should he know whether Mr. Jasper's sister was his mother? Will anybody answer him that? If not, Durdles will be as dumb as an oyster, *till the time comes.* [NOTE: This was said with an air of mystery, indicative of concealed information of some unknown description.]

Questioned as to knowledge of the construction of Cloisterham Cathedral.

Replies—that if Durdles doesn't know that old shop, he would like to know who does. Has been in and around it, busy most of the time, a matter of ten or a dozen years—is not certain about the exact time, and doesn't know as he is bound to make hisself a almanack for anybody. Has put up more monuments, and dug out more Old 'Uns as had been stowed away until their werry names was forgot, than any other person, man or boy, who has ever been in Cloisterham. Knows pretty well nearly every stone in it that is worth knowing; and if he lives long enough, means to know them *all.* Can find his way about it, dark or light, from the crypt to the bell-tower, mostly as well as he can around his own house— which is not so big as to trouble him, even with his eyes shut.

Questioned as to whether the side-walls of the Cathedral are single or double — that is, with or without a ceiling of stone-work, leaving a space between the two walls. Knowledge to be his own, and not from hearsay.

Replies—[NOTE. With a certain sullenness, and evident disinclination to enter into the subject] that he *does* know of his own knowledge, though he does not see that he is under any call to tell, only that people, like the brats of boys, will

not let him alone. The walls are double. He has took Old
'Uns out of 'em. Isn't that enough?

Questioned as to whether he ever took out any Old 'Uns, as
he calls them, from between those walls. [NOTE. Referring
to coffins, with very old remains, and in some instances effigies,
discovered in and about many portions of the Cathedral]
previous to the time before mentioned—the 24th December.

Replies—[NOTE. Not in the best temper.] No. He
never did; but what then?

Questioned as to his ever having taken Mr. John Jasper
through the Cathedral, from the crypt to the tower, at night
and at the request of Mr. Jasper. And if so, when.

Replies—[NOTE. Very sullenly.] Has done so. Once.
He disremembers exactly, but it may have been in the latter
part of December—a few days, as he thinks, before the blamed
row that got 'em all into trouble, and no thanks to 'em for it!

Questioned as to whether, on that occasion, he, Durdles, was
entirely sober. If not, whence his liquor was procured.

Replies—[NOTE. Half-angrily.] What business is it of
anybody but himself, whether Durdles was drunk or sober,
that night? Well, if he *must* tell, drunk, likely. Remembers that he drank very little though, and must have felt the
liquor more than ordinary. But he had a right to get as
drunk as an owl, hadn't he? Liquor?—got it out of Mr.
Jasper's bottle. Where else? Does anybody think Durdles
fool enough to take people about, as a guide, finding 'em
tipple at the same time? Not often!

Questioned as to whether, at any time, and if so how long,
during that night's visit to the Cathedral, he lost sight of Mr.
Jasper.

Replies—[NOTE. Reluctantly.] Yes. Went to sleep on
the steps, for a while as who had a better right,—he should
like to know? And when he was asleep, couldn't see John
Jasper very well, or any one else, could he? How long?—
may be an hour.

Questioned as to where were the Cathedral keys, at that
time—to wit, when he was asleep.

Replies—that he had them on him and in his bundle, so far
as he remembers. Found one of them on the pavement, in
front of him, when he woke: supposes that he had dropped it.
Well, what then? Nothing would hurt the key, would there?

Questioned as to whether any person temporarily in possession of the keys carried by him, that night, could have gained
access, by their means, to the vestry, where the books of expense and other registry are kept.

Replies—[NOTE. With symptoms of surprise, at some new
thought or idea.] Yes, he supposes that they could have done
so, if they had wanted to. But what was that to do with it?
Who would want to go into the vestry at that time of night?
What are they all driving at, he would like to know?

Questioned [NOTE. After being duly informed, with a
certain necessary severity, that he is present to answer questions, not to ask them, and that not only he may be legally
forced to answer what he at present refuses, but also forfeit
any compensation intended to be given him for the time
occupied], as to any knowledge he may possess of the personality of a certain boy, age unknown, resident at Cloisterham,
and known by the name of "Deputy," as to knowledge of his
real name, that of "Deputy" being evidently a *sobriquet* or
nick-name. As to any employment of the boy "Deputy," by
himself or others.

[NOTE. Since this examination, a serious accident to the
boy about whom this inquiry is made, placing him out of the
question in any further proceedings, has made the answers
immediately following, almost or quite useless. It has been
thought a matter of duty, however, to preserve them as
possessing a certain interest to the curious.]

Replies—that he does not know any other name for the brat
who calls himself "Deputy." He may know another name
that he *ought* to be called by, but nobody dares do it, and
most of 'em don't know it, he supposes; and *he* is not going
to tell what that name is, at any price: leastwise, not *till
the time comes.* [NOTE. Repetition, as will be noticed, of

previous mysterious phrases, before applied to the disappeared
person Drood.] Employed the young varmint? Yes, he has
employed him, to stone him (Durdles) home o' nights, if anybody would call *that* employment! Engagement to that effect
about closing, owing to the young ruffian beginning to use
bigger stones, that hurt when they hit, and to some other
openings for him, that may keep him busy without stoning
anybody; and to his (Durdles) intention not to be drunk so
often—though he supposes [NOTE. Gruffly and as if with a
certain sense of shame] that that is none of anybody's business but Durdles'. As to other occupations of "Deputy,"
knows that he has vittles—some kind, not much of 'em, but
enough to keep him alive, and clothes that is mostly rags—for
services at the Traveller's Twopenny, in Gas Works Garding.
[NOTE. Place of location intended to be conveyed, the
Garden adjoining the Cloisterham Gas Works; and the
character of the house, as conveyed to the initiated by its
name, that of only charging twopence for a night's lodging,
the beds being laid upon ropes suspended to pulleys, which
ropes are violently dropped in the event of the lodger sleeping
more than his twopence worth and so late in the morning as
to cause inconvenience to the proprietor—the lodger being
thus thrown out on the floor and so effectually awoke as well
as informed of the time. This information secured with some
difficulty and a slight personal exposure without reference to
Durdles, and preserved more as a curiosity than with any certainty of its being in the case under notice.]

Questioned, (after being impressively informed that all the
preceding questions have been merely preliminary, though important, and that upon the explicit answer to the one about to
follow, depends all the value of his information) as to any and
all knowledge which he may possess, of events occurring at or
in the neighborhood of Cloisterham Cathedral, on the night of
December 24th, and the succeeding day (known as and called
Christmas Day), in any way connected with the presence or
disappearance of the young man Edwin Drood, or which he

believes to have any possible connection with the crime
alleged to have been committed against that person.

Replies—[NOTE. After some moments of silence, and much
fumbling with the large buttons of the coat] that he has
thought it all over, and he won't! Nobody can make him, as
he believes, and he is going to try it! Durdles may have
some secrets that he has the right to keep—same as other
property—and this may be one of 'em! How would *you* like
to be pumped—pumped—pumped—as if you was a blessed
old well and a spout into you? Not a word do they get out
of Durdles, about *that*, till he hears from *him!*

[NOTE. Evidence satisfactory, at this stage of the examination, that the habitual caution, not to call it sullenness, of the
man Durdles' nature, is combining with a certain rude sense
of what he considers honor, to prevent his speaking further or
entering at all upon the important point. Necessity consequently arising, to employ, at this time, means that Mr.
Datchery would have much preferred to hold in reserve, to
create confidence in the mind of Durdles and induce him to
proceed. Exhibit consequently made to him, of certain articles
from a locked drawer (numbered 1 and 2 in the schedule accompanying) with information of their character,—and also of a
letter (Exhibit A of written papers in the case, as showing
authority), with reading aloud of the letter, its place of date
and signature—Durdles being nearly as incapable, under
present physical circumstances, of reading written hand as of
making it. Following this, manifestations of great surpise on
the part of Durdles, not unmingled with a certain gratification.
Comparative willingness, thenceforward, to relate all that he
knows, on this special point; and peculiarity as well as redun-
dancy of expression quite as marked as before.]

Questioned, in repetition, on the points to which reference
has before last been made:

Replies—[NOTE. Not sullenly, as before, but evidencing a
certain sense of his being defrauded, after all, in the taking
away of his sole proprietorship in an important secret.] That,

20

now that *he* has split, he doesn't see any use in anybody's keeping it. May be it is all right to tell it now; maybe it isn't. As for himself, Durdles would have kept it as close as one of the Old 'Uns, and there wasn't much danger of *them* telling tales, even though they had lips! [NOTE. Chuckling a little grimly, and with the air of one who considers the Old 'Uns to be held at a certain gratifying disadvantage.] Howsoever—no help for it now! out with it, like a bad tooth!

Had been satisfied, for a long time, that there was an inside wall to the Cathedral, found it out by measurements and by making up his mind that there wouldn't have been stone enough wasted—leastwise by anybody but fools and them as had their own quarries and labor to hand for nothing—to make the old shop so wide outside and so narrow inside. Thinks that old Tope [NOTE. The verger, thus disrespectfully alluded to, though not an old man, and quite respectable] knowed it, too—only didn't want any one else to know it, for fear of having litter and rubbish about, if Durdles was set to looking into it a bit.

Well, there was a jolly old to-do about the Cathedral, that Christmas morning. Young Drood—so they said—had run away or been murdered, and everybody was looking for him and worriting and bothering that poor young fellow, Landless —he believes that was the name. Besides the wind had been so high the night before, as to blow off part of the roofing and let the rain into the tower; so that everybody as wasn't looking for Drood, was attending to *that*. Service in the Cathedral was very short in the morning—everybody scared, he supposes; and there was none in the afternoon, all along of the murder and the leak. So the shop was shut up close and tight.

Cannot state, explicitly, why he went into the Cathedral after dark on Christmas evening, but did so. May have been one reason, and may have been another—where's the consequence what sent him, so that he went? May be because he thought that the rain-leak from the tower might have come down to the ceiling of the choir; and may be simply because he was in the habit of spookin' about [NOTE. Latter phrase not well understood by the examiner, but supposed to refer to visiting lonely places at late hours, and to be used in the sense of " haunting."]

Had his lantern with him, at that time, and his bundle. He doesn't know that it is anybody's business what was in the bundle, or why he had it there. Suppose that there was a bit of bread and cheese and a sausage, with a drop of summat warm ;—and that he may have intended to pick a bit and wet his throat there, where he was disturbing nobody and nobody could disturb *him*—any harm in that ? If there was, he should like to know it. Had his lantern, because *you* wouldn't like to go into such a dismal old hole, in the dark, and break your shins over everything—would you ?

Well—he may as well make a clean breast of it, as he has heard the gentlefolks say, he supposes. [NOTE. Much water, and some soap, would be necessary to produce that effect on Mr. Durdles, in a strictly literal sense.] He was sitting near the side-wall of the nave, picking his bit, when he heard a cry, that he could have sworn was behind the wall. It frightened him—they might lie all they liked, and say that such things *don't* frighten people ; but they *do !* Durdles has been in a dark church, at midnight, about as often as any of 'em, and he isn't a chicken, and *knows !* Had heard the same sound afore—last Christmas, only that was Eve and this was Night. Had been frightened then, and was frightened now. Don't care who knows it. If anybody has any objections, let 'em come to Durdles !

Believed at the time that there was spirits behind the wall, and that they was keeping some kind of devil's holiday because it was Christmas—though he had no idea why spirits should choose that time, and hasn't any now. Nor does he pretend to explain how spirits can make a noise—that is none of his business, any more than some other things are other people's.

Started to run away at first, and upset his lantern, but luck-

ily (for *one* anyhow) the candle didn't go out. Just then
heard the cry again, in the same place, and somehow more like
the voice of a man and less like a spirit. Wasn't so frightened then, but that he had brains enough to go up close to the
wall and listen. Heard a man's voice, faintly saying, "Help!
help!" and some other words that he couldn't understand.
Durdles isn't a fool [NOTE. Witness's remark] always, though
some of the bigwigs think so! He can put that and that together, Durdles can, nigh as well as that old bag o' wind,
Sapsea! [NOTE. Disrespectful reference, recorded with regret,
to the worthy Mayor of Cloisterham, at whose hands Mr.
Durdles may have suffered some past indignity.] He! he!
Had heard old Sapsea do that, more than once, and thought
that *he'd* do it. Man missing—nobody can find him—man
here that nobody knows anything about—why not the same?
That's how *I* put it! He! he! [NOTE. Laughter grim, dis-
sonant, and by no means pleasant.]

Well, Durdles sot down his bundle, took his lantern, went
below, to what they call the Punishment Cell, on the crypt-
floor, and was back, with a crow and pick, [NOTE. Understood to be short for "pickaxe" and "crowbar," and to have
no reference to the bird of that name, or to what would be
properly called plucking it] before many of the young chaps
would have got to the door.

Listened, and thought that he heard the cry, once more.
Then all was still, and he was worse frightened than he had
been at first. But made up his mind to go through the wall,
and know what there *was* behind it, if he worked a month
and dug down the old rookery [NOTE. Another disrespectful
name for the Cathedral, used by Durdles, possibly on account
of the black coats of the clergy, though some other and unknown cause may exist] altogether. Flung off coat and
went to work.

Has no present idea how long he worked—what's the consequence how long? The stones was big, the mortar was
hard, and the wall seemed that thick as it had been built

to use up all the material in a hundred mile. Got a hole
through, after ever so long, and the sweat a pourin' so that
there didn't need any leak from the tower. When he felt the
cold air on his sweaty face had a new scare [NOTE "Skeer,"
as pronounced], but called out in a minute. Heard no cry,
but directly a groan. Thought, then, that it might be a
spirit dying, and that that might be something 'orrid; and
started to run away again. Durdles isn't ashamed to tell
when he is scared: maybe some of 'em as *is* would be scared
oftener! Did not run very far—not he! Come back, went
to work again, and soon rolled out two big stones that let him
through. Went in, with the lantern, a-shiverin' and a-shak-
in'. [NOTE. His peculiar expression, and preserved, as
seeming graphic, even if commonplace.] And found——.
What's the use o' going on any further after that letter?
Isn't all the rest, now, clearer than the light was in that
there hole? Yet if he must, he must; but any one that
says Durdles does it to bounce about anything he has done
—lies, that's all!

Well, *he* was there. Bruised, bloody, and half-dead —
knowin' no more how he got there than, than a babby.
Durdles didn't know him at first, spite of thinking of him
afore. Must have used up his last strength a-cryin' and
a-groanin', for he could only moan then. Durdles had a
little left in his bottle: what would *he* have done, if Durdles
had been one of those dry-bones old 'stainers, [NOTE. Supposed meaning, "abstainers") with nothing but water in his
bottle, to chill him worse and he half-dead? Not that Durdles doesn't know what an injury to him, and to everybody,
he supposes, *too much* is; and he thinks that if so many of
the people at Cloisterham hadn't looked at him out of the
corners of their eyes, and disrespected him so much, maybe
things might have been different. But then who knows?—
and who cares?

Yes—he not only managed to let a little summat down *him*,
after dragging him through the hole, but by-and-bye a few

mouthfuls of food, and then *he* could sit up and talk—very faint and low, like a child, but so that Durdles could understand him. No matter what he said—Durdles is not going to tell that, any way. Yes—Durdles did help him out, by-and-bye when he could walk; and keep him where nobody seed him that night; and help him away. Doesn't know where, and doesn't know, why, except that it seemed to be carrying out of *his* cranks. If it had been him, Durdles, he'd have made stir enough about Cloisterham, 'stead of going away—wouldn't he!

Inquiry repeated — what's the use of sayin' any more? Durdles kept his secret, like a man, he thinks, till now they come and worm it out of him! Doesn't see why he should have told all this, even with that letter and them things, as must make other people know more than himself. And now he supposes that it'll be all over, and he'll be drug up, somewhere, for goin' and doin'what he needn't. [NOTE. Assured, at this stage, that he need have no present fear on that point.] Werry well, then—Durdles don't want to be drug up, nor to say any more, if it's all the same to the big-wigs, and so he will shut trap and be as dumb as a blessed old oyster.

(Signed)

ƒDurdles

[NOTE.—No reason to believe, on the part of the examiner, that Mr. Durdles makes the above somewhat peculiar signature (the first letter seeming at once like an S, an F and a †)—with any forgetful fancy that his name is Frederick or Francis, or any desire to adopt the well-known Romish episcopal form, (as "† John"); but rather, want of habit of signing, with possibly some faint recollections of periods of peculiar incapacity at which he may have been obliged to sign with a mere mark or ✗].

Attest, as witness to both relation and signature,

RICHARD DATCHERY.

CHAPTER XX.

DOWN AMONG THE DEAD MEN.

WHAT induces Stony Durdles to invite Mr. John Jasper to
a second night-visit to the Cathedral, something after the
manner of that paid so many months ago, and yet very different in many particulars—may be set down as one of those
problems needing more than a single effort for solution.   And
the remark will almost equally apply to the inducement which
may present itself to Mr. Jasper, leading him to accept the
invitation gruffly and yet forcibly tendered by the stone-
mason.   One might suppose, with a knowledge of all circumstances, that Durdles, whose absolute fear of Mr. Jasper has
already been shown in the unwillingness with which he opens
his mouth to canvass a single action of the Choir Master, and
with his inevitable belief that on a previous visit the Choir
Master drugged him and temporarily took possession of his
keys for some purpose of doubtful legality,—possibly nothing
less than the moulding of them for duplication,—might be at
least slow to put himself into complete isolation with the man
he hears, late at night, in the old Cathedral where he has
heard ghosts of screams and screams that were not those of
ghosts.   And one would correspondingly doubt the probability
of Mr. Jasper, who might be supposed to have enjoyed quite
enough of the Cathedral, at night, placing himself again within those walls, at the ghostly hour, to please the whim of any
man—much less at the wish of a man holding no more commanding position than Stony Durdles.

Yet so it is.   Durdles, shambling up to the Choir Master,
dinner-bundle in hand and the lime and dust more than ordinarily thick on his habiliments—on a certain afternoon not
long following Mr. Jasper's balked attempt at exploration,—
has informed the latter of the result of long and patient investigation in one hitherto partially unexplored segment of the

cryptic circle, where his hammer has told him of solid in hollow and hollow in solid still within, leading to the certainty
that upon opening, which labor he intends to enter upon that
very night, when he is sure of immunity from disturbance by
them brats of boys—he will come upon one or more of Old
'Uns in such a state of remote antiquity, that there will probably be nothing remaining but the emptiest of empty stone-
boxes, with the very inscriptions crumbled away in damp and
mould. Additionally, he has invited the Choir Master to be
present at this solemn ceremony of exhumation—remarking
that some of the others would give their eyes to see the Old
'Uns come tumblin' out in that condition, only Durdles won't
let 'em, at no price,—and generally treating the opportunity
as one which he could not be induced to offer to any other
than this highly favored person, whom he seems to consider,
from past confidences on such subjects, as an expert in the
difficult line of Looking-On and a consulting authority of
great weight in estimating the present value of the Missing.

To this, Mr. Jasper has at first replied with that languor
natural to a man whose enfeebled condition and fast-greying
hair have now become matter of much pitying comment in
Cloisterham—doubting whether the dampness of the crypt may
not be more or less dangerous as likely to affect organs of the
throat; and whether the services of the following morning, in
the Cathedral, may not demand all the strength of his system,
without subtracting from it by late hours. But something in
the downcast face of Durdles, at this declination, may have
moved him to reconsider; and there may have been other
reasons, rendering him feverishly anxious as to any explanations under the perpendicular line of a certain part of the
Cathedral, and leading him to prefer being present and
actually witnessing the result. At all events, after a single
refusal he has accepted the invitation, for ten o'clock of that
night, when Mr. Durdles has considered all unfriendly influences as surest to be temporarily at rest, and the Old 'Uns,
however constitutionally averse to being disturbed in their rest

of centuries, as likely to offer less than their average of dodging, hiding and other passive resistance.

The night is a close and sultry one, calculated to make the
prospect of an hour or two in a cool vault less objectionable
than at other periods — when, at the appointed hour, Durdles stumbles up the postern-stair of the Gate House and
makes known to the occupant that he is in readiness. Mr.
Jasper is in waiting, and joins him at once—after taking the
precaution against throat-affections, to throw around his neck
a scarf hanging on the back of a chair, and buttoning around
him his surtout a little more closely than any man would be
likely to do who was not prevented feeling the heat by absolute exhaustion of the vital forces. He seems in better spirits
than of late, however, as he comes down the stair and pauses
for a moment under the archway, while Durdles makes some
exchange in the modes of carrying his dinner-bundle (refuge
against possibly long imprisonment and approaching starvation, in the vaults, and heavy now with keys and hammers),
and his unlighted lantern (unlighted until the time of use,
because he naturally does not wish to attract the attention of
them brats of boys and either surround the Cathedral with a
hooting and stone-hurling crowd or afford the Old 'Uns much
unbidden and unwelcome company.

They reach the Cathedral without the misadventure of
meeting any one—dreaded by both, from very different causes.
Durdles unlocks the door leading into the Crypt, and they
enter. Is it something of the chill of the subterranean apartment, spite of his buttoned coat and scarf, that strikes into
the frame of Mr. Jasper and makes him shiver as with an ague
the moment they are within ?—or is there remaining a frightened recollection of another and a late night when he opened
the same door, unaccompanied by Durdles, and with a different key—flying away from a Horror that had no name and
with a Fear to which he has never since been able to give
definite shape ? Possibly the latter may have more to do
with the long shudder creeping over him than the former.

But he masters it very fairly, all things considered; for he is
not alone in the Crypt now, and the terror is more or less a
thing of the past. He knows that, whatever it was affecting
him, no such second weakness can assail him: he knows that
never again within the walls of that Cathedral—come what
may—will he be found so unnerved and driven out of himself
as on that occasion. And it is exceedingly well to be sure of
this always, in places where the peculiarly painful has happened to us: recurrences bearing something of the character
of relapses in disease, and being often more fatal than the
original affliction. It is well to know that fears have so died
within us, and assurances so strengthened, and our surrounding world so changed for the better, that the once-deadly fears
and consuming remorses can never come back to us in their
past strength—never! never!

Durdles necessarily pays little attention to all this, being
occupied with the lighting of his lantern, and the various
transfers of his porterage, settings-down and takings-up of the
dinner-bundle, rendered necessary in that operation. The
lantern is in full glow, however, quite before John Jasper has
shaken off the last lingering remains of his unpleasant chill;
and the mouldy columns, the damp vaulted roof, and the dusky
monuments at the circumference of the crypt, are all thrown
once more into that dismal prominence remembered so shudderingly.

Meanwhile, Durdles makes a sudden pause, and chuckles
gratingly, as if pleased with some sudden thought.

"Lamp's lit," says he. "Lamp's shinin' beautiful! Why
shouldn't Durdles be lit? Why shouldn't Durdles shine
beautiful? Durdles shall!" and Durdles, mightily tickled,
puts the beloved bottle to his dusty lips, saying, "Here's
Durdles's oil, and wick, and light, and 'lumination, an' all!"
and then that sacred place resounds with a secular gurgle of
some seconds' duration.

"Now then, Mr. Jasper," says Durdles, when the double
illuminatory arrangements are thoroughly complete — "now

then, come along over here, where Durdles has been a-findin'
of 'em. The Old 'Uns has been waitin' for Durdles, this
long time, to be let out and aired, though they make a row,
sometimes, when he does come to 'em. Durdles has heard
'em, more times than he's fingers and toes, grumbling out
through the walls, after I'd been a-poundin' and a-hammerin'
for a matter of an hour or two, pretty near 'em : ' Durdles,—
why the devil don't you hurry along ? ' and : ' Have you any
idea, Durdles, old man, how long we've been a-lyin' here,
waitin' for you ? '   But they don't always play fair—the Old
'Uns don't ; for sometimes, just as I come to 'em, they move,
here, or there, or yonder, and give Durdles another job of
diggin' afore he gets to 'em."

Enlivened by this slightly imaginative sally,—much more
to be expected from unknown Durdles the Sculptor, than from
known and lime-dusted sottish old Durdles the Stone-Mason,
Mr. Jasper naturally recovers his spirits, shakes off his besetting chill with less difficulty than might otherwise have been
experienced, and accompanies the explorer to the scene of his
congenial labors.

"There you see how it is—just as I told you afore ! " comments Durdles recalling some of the technical information
communicated so long ago, that it may possibly have been forgotten ; and meanwhile repeating a few of those scientific taps
with the hammer, already believed to have made discovery
certain. " You hear *that*, Mr. Jasper ! The wall's solid
there, and nothing else than solid—stone, three or four feet
deep, maybe more. And here it's solid again. But here—
just you listen to that, though you mayn't have Durdles' ears
for them little twists o' sound that tells him so much ! Don't
you hear something hollow and thumpy like, with a bit of
jingle ? Durdles knows that, as if it was an organ, and he
a-touchin' of the keys. Just you hold the lantern, so, and
give Durdles a chance, and he'll show one of the blessedest
Old 'Uns as ever was, afore many minutes ! "

Thereupon, Mr. Jasper consenting to be light-holder for the

nonce, and thus a sort of apprentice to the great artificer—
the Stony One throws off the coat with the big horn buttons;
removes the dinner-bundle, lightened by the weight of his
hammer, to a safer distance, scanned and measured with a
critical eye, as if a matter of half-inches; and sets to work
with the hammer, and with a crowbar and pick, no doubt left
conveniently on the spot in waiting, at the time of his last
preliminary visit.

He makes excellent and very rapid progress, in this instance.
If Mr. Jasper was really more of an expert and less of an
apprentice, in the disentombment of Old 'Uns, he might be
aware with what singular ease the mortar seems to fall away
from between the great stones, and with what remarkable facility the stones themselves are removed. He might even doubt, in
that non-supposable case, whether the sanctuary that Durdles
is invading has not before been invaded and the once-removed
stone-work replaced : Whether it can be possible that five, or
six, or seven hundred years have done no more to cement the
mass of stone and mortar into something almost impossible to
separate.   But then, even if he should fall under such an idea,
the very natural reflection might follow, that possibly time
disintegrates quite as often as it cements—that time and stone-
work may grow weaker instead of stronger with age, after a
certain lapse—and that the Cathedral itself may tumble down,
at no remote period, from the same natural decay sending an
old man to his grave.   At all events, he gives no sign of being
dissatisfied with the style of disinterment practised in his
presence, but holds the lantern patiently, even if without
much interest; and Durdles works on, with abundant energy
and determination, aided by occasional recurrence to something mysteriously liquid and not proffered for distribution, in
the dinner-bundle.

Which energy and determination are after a time rewarded
—as they always must be, if we are to credit the assertions of
goody-goody books and copy-heads. Durdles, when no very
long time has elapsed, rolls out two or three stones of large

size, but singularly easy to extract from their bed, and then, muttering triumphantly: "Here they are, Mr. Jarsper; Durdles knows his business! Here's an Old 'Un as *is* an Old 'Un!" lunges forward with his whole body, as if having found an excellent opportunity to entomb himself in a distinguished manner, and being anxious to embrace it.

Mr. Jasper, looking in through what remains of the large hole after the rear dimensions of Durdles have filled up a part of it,—and then squeezing himself in with an unpleasant fascination which he can no more resist than endure,—at first sees literally nothing, under the dim light of the lantern, at that period held in the unscientific manner to be expected from a novice in the art of midnight torch-bearing.

Durdles, his own view no doubt obstructed by the same awkwardness, at once addresses his assistant and guest as thus :

"Hold the light down a little nearer, Mr. Jasper—and with a slope—so. Who could see in that way, Durdles would like to know? There—that is better. And now let's observe whether the Old 'Un is jolly at being wisited at this time o'night by two persons o' quality !"

Mr. Jasper, with a feeling compounded of nearly as many ingredients as those composing the hell-broth of Hecate, and not much more appetizing in their character — fulfils the request as to the light, and accompanies the service with the unwilling use of his eyes. He expects, no doubt, to see, by that dim light, a heap of dust, a few bones, or a bundle of discolored rags, and possibly a tress of hair—all that the most magnificent of us are likely to present to the prying gaze, after a few hundreds or even a few score of years, entomb us with what pomp and show they will, and wrap us with what robes and insignia of power they may ! But he sees something appreciably different; and so does Durdles, if his stupid faculties are not too slow for taking in the impressive at a glance, or too entirely stunned and overcome by the natural surprise of the revelation.

It is then that the Choir Master sees and recognizes what has occurred at the removal of the last large stone by Durdles, and what are the actual surroundings of the discovery. He sees that the recess thus disclosed, is one of considerable size, with a roof of very rough stone, but carefully enough arched to indicate that it has once been open to the crypt, as a known recess in the thick wall, or only closed by a door, as a vault. Very old, unquestionably, and dating back to the very earliest monkish times—with a shudder in the mere thought of what may have taken place within and around it, in those days when one religion made foxes of the people of another, driving them to refuge in the caves of the earth, and metamorphosing them into wolves in the very act. But this is the least; for, looking down at the bottom of the recess, he sees that the removal of the last stone, at the moment of Durdles' triumphant cry, has allowed the side of a worm-eaten coffin of dark wood to fall away outward, leaving exposed what again recalls the monkish period with most ghastly force and prominence. Durdles, benevolently anxious that his guest and neophyte shall lose nothing of a spectacle so instructive, himself assists in guiding the rays of light in the proper direction; so that no detail escapes the unwilling and horrified gazer.

Scarcely the withered old Count of Nassau-Saälberg and his child-daughter lying in their tarnished lace and jewels, with death making horrible mockery of life in faces and figures, under the glass of gray St. Thomas's in poor old battered Strasbourg, could embody more of the terrible than that which here meets the eye. For the skeleton remains of a Monk are here, some remnant of his black robe yet showing in the faded and discolored rags, and his profession made plain by the rosary and crucifix yet hanging from what has once been the waist. Some bones protrude from the mass, at the height of the breast, as if the ribs have not all given way; and at the place of the head lies a skull, grinning more horribly than Yorick's. And yet this is not all or the most notable: Murder is plain as death. For on the rags of the breast lies a discolored parchment, once charged with that dreadful message of hate, vengeance or tyranny, who shall guess?— and through that paper, and through what has been the body, between the ribs, and possibly at the very spot where once beat the heart—a long stiletto, with a red stone still reflecting lurid rays at the end of the hilt, has been driven through, so far that the point remains in the bottom of the coffin and holds it upright.

It would not be easy to describe the effect of this discovery on the two persons present. Durdles certainly cannot be in the every-day habit of exhuming Old 'Uns of this special pattern; so that *his* surprise (the stupid measure of it being understood, and it being taken for granted that he has not *seen it before, and used it under instruction*)—is a thing of course. And it is equally certain that Mr. Jasper, only in his novitiate in the line of disentombing, is by no means prepared for this somewhat startling proof of how, and above all, *why*, they buried people so profoundly at some unknown period in the past. Does he shudder, so that the lantern shakes in his grasp? Does he turn so sick, in heart and head, that he might be on the deck of a plunging ship in a gale at sea? Does he see fifty murdered monks, with the faded revelation of their doom on their breasts, lying there with poniards through their hearts, and bearing silent witness to long-past crimes of such atrocity, that the very stones of the Cathedral have been unable to hide them beyond their due period? Does the hiding away of the evidences of quiet, within the sacred precincts of the religious-house, assume a new shape, at this dread moment, to him who has so often intoned the solemn prayer, that the hearts of men may be inclined to Keep His Law? Do the feeble knees knock and the overstrained sinews nearly give way, in the presence of Mystery, Murder, and Sacrilege, so awfully combined? And even if all these, what is John Jasper more or less than mortal, that such should be the result of an ordeal passing the *peine fort et dure* in hard and cruel severity?

But Durdles speaks.

" Well," he says, surveying the rusted dagger, with stupid though very natural wonder, after removing it by a forcible pull from its adherence to the bottom of the coffin—" well, that beats Durdles, Mr. Jasper! If they haven't gone and murdered one of them Old 'Uns as was a Monk, and then hid him away here! Would you have believed *that*, Mr. Jasper —that any of 'em, as was the biggest willains on this earth, would have hid away the Monk as they had killed *here?* Durdles has seen some strange things, as he's been a-tellin' you, hereaways and thereaways; but that beats *him!*"

Mr. Jasper, stone cold as if he might be the Monk lying at the bottom of the worm-eaten coffin, with the weapon through *his* heart—yet manages to reply:

"You may have been mistaken, Durdles. The dagger may merely have been stuck down beside him, not through him; and so there may have been no crime—only an odd fancy. Don't you see?"

But this relief to the situation, which Mr. Jasper tries to impart from some dim idea that the place is rendered less terrible thereby, and the thought of an overwhelming judgment for all men thus carried farther away—this touches Durdles in a tender point, that of his knowledge of exact locations; and he gives vent to a scoff of such gruff and severe character as might unpleasantly affect a man of stronger nerves than his companion.

" Hoot! Just as if Durdles was the old fool they call him, and didn't know whether he picked up a stick or pulled it out from a matter of two foot in the ground! No—besides that parchment bit, as means something if there was any one as could read it—don't you go to teachin' Durdles his business, if it's all the same to *you!* Durdles knows, just as well as if he seen it a-doin', that Old 'Un, as was a Monk, had that dagger druv through him, and was hid away here by some willain of a murderer who didn't care whether he muggered up his wictims in a church or a hayrick. That's Durdles opinion, Mr. Jasper; and it's Durdles' opinion, and he don't care who knows it—that the devil's give him a double roastin' afore this, for mixin' up things in that way as wasn't respectable !"

Mr. Jasper makes a praiseworthy effort to command himself and to answer; but that effort is a failure. There are some things that no ordinary man, with ordinary nerves and sinews, can be expected to bear; and this may be one of them. What influence is it, possessing old stupid, blundering Durdles, to exhibit sights and run on with words calculated worst to shake the equanimity of the undetected criminal? How could he come nearer to pursuing the straight-forward course towards that end, if he had been employed by some scheming Datchery to act over again the discovery of an already exhumed remain of peculiar horror, for the very purpose of bringing the victim to the proper state of mind (if mind it can still be called !) for something more terrible yet to follow ?

Mr. Jasper is tired of this very soon. He expresses as much in words not to be mistaken.

"Durdles, I have had enough of this !" he says, rallying by a strong effort. "Take your lantern and show me the way out of this hole, and out of the crypt; and be good enough not to trouble me again with the digging out of what you call your 'Old 'Uns.'"

"What, Mr. Jarsper! not tired a'ready !" exclaims the other, in natural surprise. "Want to go, and leave Durdles all alone with such interestin' old fellers as this, and all the waluables he's a-pickin' up? Why, see this knife—its worth seven-and-six, if it's worth a ha'penny, and Durdles is the *heir* of unfortunit Holy Father deceased, name and circumstances of the cruel event unknown."

"Come, I say, show me out, and then you may come back and dig for a dozen more. I have told you that *I* have had enough of it !" repeats Mr. Jasper, sternly, even if the voice shakes a little.

Durdles, seeing that the other is thoroughly in earnest, not

21

only falls into his views, but adopts them with singular facility (as is not unfrequently the manner of men).

" Well, if you *will* go, so will Durdles," he says, taking up his pick and crow. " One of 'em, of that sort, *is* enough for one night, isn't it, Mr. Jarsper ? Wouldn't do to find all the waluables at once, would it ? "

Mr. Jasper thinks that it would not, and himself again taking the lantern, steps out from the dusky vault into the crypt. Durdles follows shouldering the two heavier tools as if for a tramp of miles, and necessarily knocking against everything around and above him.

" Seeing that he is not a-going to work any more to-night, Durdles'll put these away in the little empty cell yonder, by the door, as we go," he suggests, in explanation of the shouldering ; which might otherwise be unpleasant to his companion, under recent reminders and the idea that he was taking a promenade with a person quite prepared to bury as well as brain him at any moment.

It is to be supposed that Mr. Jasper accepts this explanation, and that he proceeds towards the door of the crypt with a certain sort of pleasure—confident that, whatever has been, the worst of it is over. Again it may be said—such confidence is very pleasant : it is so good to know that misfortunes and trials are ended and disturbing influences permanently at rest !

The door of the little cell to which Durdles has referred stands at only eight to twelve feet from the bottom of the stone steps leading up to the outer door of the Crypt. How it may have acquired the name of the Punishment Cell, no one knows with any certainty ; though the explanation is probably accepted that at some old time when formal asceticism reigned more severely than at present, specially devout brothers may have used it as a spot for administering their self-discipline, or others employed it to discipline *them* by means of confinement and a little starvation. Be this as it may, the Punishment Cell it is called ; and it is neither visited at all, except by Mr. Tope and some of his temporary queues of explorers, nor used for any purpose more important than the deposit of some small trifle of discarded material or light lumber.

It is in this cell that Durdles, no doubt in the habit of appropriating at will all the unappropriated, has declared his intention of leaving his crow and pick; and it is at the door of this cell that the stone-mason pauses with those tools, and the Choir-Master with his lantern, on the way to the Crypt entrance. There is no lock upon the heavy planks studded with rusty iron nail-heads; and Durdles—the while Mr. Jasper stands very near and kindly lifts the lantern to allow him the better to step within and drop his encumbrances—Durdles lays hand on the heavy iron fastenings and swings back the door on its creaking hinges. Thrown full in the door, the light of the lantern falls broad on the face and figure of a man standing immediately within—silent, immovable, the eyes seeming to have no more motion than the lips, and the left hand thrust into the breast of the coat. If ever spectre really came back to earth, from the confines of that dim and distant realm of which we speak most and understand least, of all the territory known to human thought—then John Jasper sees, at this moment, EDWIN DROOD, in face, figure, dress, and every appliance, precisely as he saw him last in life, except in one fearful closing-hour!

It has come at last—that dread Thing expected with a horrible expectation, feared with a sickening fear. No longer as one of many indistinct phantoms, distant even if marked in shape and individuality. IT has come to him, now, in the awful prominence of Banquo to Macbeth, though he has been prevented going to IT. He sees the bloodless cheek, marks the hollow and sunken eye, notes the dread etheriality of face, figure and clothing, through which the light seems to shine instead of merely shining upon them. His brain, already overwrought by the spectacle of the vault, and so ready for any new development of the terrible, sucks in the awful truth with instantaneous readiness. He realizes, as he has never before found occasion to do, the infinite distance, in awe, between the most ghastly detail of the charnel-house, however connected with crime, and the near presence of one who must come from the other world and hold immunity from all those natural laws defending us against beings of flesh. One who can enter through bolted doors and disappear through barred windows—who can mock the closed blind and disregard the drawn bed-curtain—who can assail without danger and terrify to madness without the knowledge of fear!

IT has come! When will IT leave him again now, except for those intervals that must always be filled with looking for its reappearance? Never until the hour of death—so much seems certain; and after that——

He has an impulse to speak—to express to his companion the horror of the phantom, as well as to ask if other eyes than his own can see it. But a single glance at the stolid face of the stone-mason, who so evidently, looking in the same direction, sees nothing beyond the common,—and the sound of his gruff voice, asking in surprise :

" Whatever's wrong with you, Mr. Jarsper?" these tend instantly to destroy the last hope of the spectre being other than a personal visitant to himself, at the same time that they recall one portion of his self-command. He may die, but he will not place himself at the mercy of others by speaking !— of so much of his fate, at least, he will be master !

Then he tries to remove his gaze, but he cannot—any more than the charméd bird can escape the eye of the basilisk. A moment of this, which seems centuries and to be occurring in some theatre large as the Cathedral of his ordinary spectre-haunting,—and then comes the relief. All the blood in his racked body flies to the head, as if in rescue of the over-wrought brain. Instantly the spectre assumes colossal dimensions, with all its details exaggerated even beyond that increase ; then Durdles, beside him and seen with his side-sight, becomes a grim monster only less large and terrible ; then a red mist surrounds both, and *him,* changing to a sea of blood that whelms and drowns him. He clasps hands to his throat —strangles—totters—falls forward.

Stony Durdles has another task than seeking for Old 'Uns, for the succeeding half-hour; and the dinner-bundle may be obliged to yield something to other lips than his own, before the next detail of his task is quite accomplished. What he has to do, however, he performs with that stupid persistence partially justifying the boast that " Durdles knows his work ; " and there is a living man supported away from the Crypt-door of the Cathedral, at the end of that half-hour,—instead of a dead one lying, as there might so easily be, uncoffined, but otherwise ready for the solemn service to roll through the gray arches above, in the morning.

CHAPTER XXI.

NEVILLE LANDLESS' VOCATION.

" You are looking better—I may say, almost well ; and you cannot think how happy it makes me to see you looking the bright, brave young man, again, that you were on the day when I first saw you ! "

Mr. Crisparkle was speaking, in his cheery and pleasant voice, the moment after entering Neville Landless' apartment at Staple Inn, on one of those calls not long before so objectionable to the China Shepherdess,—but now, it is to be presumed, after the full explanation between her son and herself, no more regarded either with the same fear or the same dislike. Some days had passed, however, since the last visit of the Minor Canon, making the event of something beyond the ordinary importance, from the understood anxiety of both.

Neville, who had sprung up to meet his friend and mentor, with a marked exhibition of the old alacrity, had his hand in

his, at the moment; and it is possible that something in the
feeling of that hand—its entire freedom from fever or nervous
trembling—may have induced Mr. Crisparkle to speak more
hopefully than he might otherwise have done.

"Ah, do you think so, sir?" the young fellow responded,
showing at once gratification with the remark and the manner
of its making. "Mentally or bodily—which do you mean,
sir?—or may I hope that you think me improved in both?"

"In both, decidedly, Neville," was the reply of Mr. Crisparkle, taking the chair that had been offered so cordially
through that best of invitations, an earnest motion of head
and hand,—and replying by making a corresponding signal
that his host should resume his own seat. "In both, certainly; though in point of fact, with you, to say the one is to say
the other. You have not been ill, in body, at all, except as the
mental distress to which you have been subjected, has naturally produced a certain effect on the physical nerves, that are
really, as you know, servants of the mental organization."

"Yes, I suppose so," replied the young man, with something
like one of his old sighs, eliciting from the Minor Canon a
good-natured warning.

"Tut! tut! none of that, my dear young fellow—none of
that!—or I may be obliged to retract my favorable opinion!"

"No, sir, I think there will be no occasion for recalling the
very kind expression. I assure you the sigh was much more
a matter of habit than one of feeling. I was merely indulging
a momentary shame over my own weakness, and on the point
of apologizing for it—nothing more."

"You need not even do that, I fancy," pursued the Minor
Canon, pleasantly as he had before spoken. "What you mean
to say, I suppose, if I had not interrupted you, was that you
were ashamed of having allowed the mental to produce such an
effect on the physical? Am I right? Yes?—As a pendant
to that, then, you would probably have gone on to say that
man, *as* a man, ought to be able to control the mental, as he
cannot always the physical—and that consequently there was

more of disgrace attached to any one allowing the mental to be
overcome, than to one in whom the physical only succumbed.
Have I stated your idea correctly ? "

"Quite correctly, sir. You are kind enough to say that you
think me very materially recovered from whatever may have
been affecting me. I am happy to believe that you do not
misjudge—that I am nearer what I should be, in every regard,
than I was one month since, and very much nearer than three
months ago. But you must allow me to be more ashamed of
having been off my balance at all, through some influence temporarily debilitating the *mind*, than if I had been merely suffering, during the same period, with a broken leg or a fever—
must you not, sir ? "

"Humph !" replied Mr. Crisparkle. "You are undoubtedly much better, Neville. Nothing proves that fact more conclusively than the very clear disposition to use your reasoning
powers—not to say your argumentative ones. No—pray do
not object to my word, or make any disclaimer. But allow me
to show you that even your argument is not without a flaw.
You are inclined, I see, still, to confound the *fact* with the
cause. Now the cause may be something to induce shame—
the fact one involving no shame whatever. Why more shame,
in a mental affection than a bodily ? Because the mental pre-
supposes the existence of some error or mistake leading to it ?
But may not the bodily ailment also reflect on the conduct that
has produced it ? You have named a broken leg: if the leg
became broken by some one throwing a slate off the roof, and
hitting your leg, or by your falling into a hole left carelessly
open by some other person, or by any other accident of the
class not involving your own personal folly or wrong-doing,
then there would be no shame to yourself in either the cause
or the fact. But supposing you had broken your leg in climbing where you had neither occasion nor absolute right to climb,
or in a struggle which you had provoked or might have avoided ! Or, suppose that even your fever, just cited, had been produced by an excess reflecting no credit on your temperance, or

by an exposure from which a moderate amount of ordinary judgment must have kept you—would there not in either of those cases be as much shame attached to the physical disorder as to a corresponding amount of mental?"

"Undoubtedly there would, sir," was the admission. "And undoubtedly I have needed just the lesson you have been reading to me, or a sharper one. I think that I am nearly or quite recovered; you are kind enough to think the same; and in five minutes of conversation I manage to demonstrate that though I may be improving, I am by no means well. A little of the morbid feeling is here yet, sir, I fear."

"And *I* fear very little on that account," returned the Minor Canon, hopefully. "No—the crisis is past—I have no doubt of the fact: the patient, with Heaven's help, will complete his recovery. He has been imprudent, as I think that I may have told him at the moment when he was contracting the disease; but there lies a world of purification in the fact that he has suffered."

"Suffered? yes—I have suffered, sir, I think," replied the young man, with some evidence on his face that the past tense did not quite cover the case. "Not half my desert, I have no doubt; but more than I would once have believed that I could consent to suffer, and *live!*"

There was deep feeling in his words and manner, and the Minor Canon recognized it, though without that hopeless pain which had at one time moved him in hearing the despairing cry of the same voice, through the darkness of his great disappointment and sorrow. He looked upon him, as he paused, with a loving interest which the object of it little understood; and he did not break the pause until Neville resumed:

"I hope that you will not misjudge me, sir, if I say a few words more, that perhaps I ought to say, in justice *r* myself. No: that is not the phrase—*in justice to your opinon of me,* sir, which I value so highly. So far as I know myself, the weakness is over, and the worst of the suffering with it. I know my fate, and I hope and believe that I am prepared to meet it like a man."

"With the help of One stronger than yourself, Neville!—with His help, remember!"

"Thanks for the reminder, sir, though I may be able to show you that I did not leave that first of elements out of the calculation. I was about to say that probably I have been playing the hypocrite, much of the time since—since my misfortune; though perhaps hypocrisy is not the proper word for a deception practised more than half on myself, and at least a portion of it unconscious."

"Candidly, my dear Neville," said the Minor Canon, "your commencement is a little misty, whatever may come after it!"

"Pardon me, sir—so it is—I know it!" confessed the young fellow, with a healthier color on his cheek, in the slight blush of embarrassment thus arising—than his friend had seen there for many a day. "The fact is, I fancy that I am merely trifling with words, and that I must abandon the habit, which does not sit well on me. Once more—then. *You* have believed, I have no doubt, and I have half-believed, myself, that my melancholy was principally induced by shame at the false accusation made against me. In reality, it had a different origin. I was sick with love for——one whom we need not name; and half-crazed by the circumstances, making it impossible that I could ever say so much to—to the woman I adore, much less hope to win her. The other feeling—I know it now—was entirely secondary, if not half a pretext. Had the other *only* existed, I should have flung it off, with scorn if not with anger: as it was, I was overweighted before that came, and the little additional weight was therefore sufficient to prostrate me."

"So I more than half believed, Neville—with a little experience in our natural tendencies towards deceiving ourselves on some point where our self-love has been touched: but pray pardon my interrupting you!" mildly spoke Mr. Crisparkle; and the other continued:

"Do you quite understand me, now, sir? Do you quite see how heavy the burthen I have been bearing? I do not expect

you to *feel* it: Heaven spare your good and kind heart, Mr.
Crisparkle, from ever knowing what it is to have set all the
earthly affections in a place where they can have no hold!—
from ever turning the eyes of your heart in a direction in
which you have no right to look, or in which they can only see
suffering and disappointment! I do not wish you, sir, at that
cost, to know what it is, to go astray, *there !* "

Again the Minor Canon was silent, marking the deep
earnest in the tone of the other, and perhaps stilled—who can
say?—by something very different to any contemplation of
him or his fortunes! When he replied, as he did after a
moment, his voice was very low and sweet, as if, insensibly, it
flowed with the blood from somewhere near the true, rich,
warm heart, and was softened and mellowed thereby. Yet
when he spoke, he played the hypocrite quite as pronouncedly
as Neville Landless had just accused himself of doing: let
the question of the guilt involved be settled how it may,
between his own conscience, the good Bishop of the Diocese,
and those Powers equitably holding the destinies of both !

"No—Neville !" he said. "No—my dear young friend.
I quite join you in hoping that it may never be my fate to
know, any more than I know at this day, what may be the
pangs of hopeless and disappointed love ! But I trust that I
have enough of human sympathy as well as true friendship,
quite to understand and feel for—did I not hear you say—I
believe that I did not misunderstand you ?—your *past* suffering and melancholy ? "

" Yes, I certainly did use that expression, sir, and I did not
use it unmeaningly !" answered the young man, drawing
himself up with a certain pride. " Suffer I may, and must, I
suppose, more or less—always; but I thank God that the day
has come when the worst is over—when I can speak of myself
as being—yes, there is no other than the common and physical
word to express it—*cured !* "

" And with the cure of your mind, the cure of your body
has come—as I hoped, and as I thought. That is well—how

well, you scarcely know, as yet, I think; but I can fervently join you in thanking the Almighty for this, not among the least of His deliverances. Do I trespass too far, in asking: have your studies done so much to change the direction of your mind, and improve you so remarkably, within the few days since I last saw you?"

"You do not trespass at all, sir, and perhaps I am rather glad than otherwise to have a necessity for answering you!" replied Neville, bravely, though it was evident that now, at least, he did not speak without emotion. "No—my studies have not done all, sir, nor nearly all. Do not condemn me until you know what I mean, when I say that I owe much to that passion which we are always so warned against—Pride!"

"Pride? Indeed?" echoed the Minor Canon.

"Yes—Pride. Re-awakened, perhaps; and perhaps new-born. At all events, that feeling which would not allow me to continue loving the woman who loved and was about to marry another."

"Loving?—Miss Bud?—pardon my mentioning the name, as I did not intend to do!—she, loving and about to marry! Neville, I am by no means a plethoric or short-breathed man, but you are making me breathe a little less easily than usual!" Undoubtedly the man of long constitutionals and fine physical training *was* catching his breath, as a header into the river in November would scarcely have forced him to do.

"Yes, sir, I have no right to betray the secrets of others, unless I am obliged to do so in self-defence or unavoidable explanation; but perhaps one of the two excuses may have been afforded me. I need but mention one name, and you will know as much as myself—possibly more. Mr. Tartar."

"Mr. Tartar! And you know this, beyond a doubt?"

Neville Landless was about to respond, in corroboration of the words just uttered, when that occurred which delayed the reply, and before it found opportunity for utterance so changed its character as to render it unrecognizable.

There came a light tap at the door—a woman's, by the clear delicacy of the touch.   Neville sprang from his chair, went to the door, and opened, and Helena Landless came into the room.   Possibly she had not heard the voices of the two: it was sure that she did not know of Mr. Crisparkle's presence. She was dressed for walking; and the gauzy material of her bonnet harmonized wonderfully well with the rich brown of her cheek and the splendid brightness of her tawny eyes, while her close-fitting costume showed her lithe waist and the tall erectness of her figure to equal advantage.   Indefinably, the eyes were both softer and nearer to smiling than their wont: she would have seemed to a close observer, less than usual, at that moment of the keen, self-possessed, dangerously lovely girl of the tropics—more of the perfecting woman, with a thousand needs and capacities for happiness, only to be supplied by *one,* and he the happiest of all mankind to be so permitted.   There was a change, since Mr. Crisparkle had last before looked upon her; and what had caused it ?   Could it be, that all before remaining of the tiger-blood —only a drop, in comparison with the full tide of her woman's heart; however powerful in moving her to fierce energetic ·action—could it be that this had gone out from her, exhausted in the single hunting down of one criminal and forcing a fatal secret from his lips ?   Could it be, that Joe Gilfert— representative and reminder of bygone days of wrong and suffering, had laid off his garments of dangerous disguise at once and for ever ?

Did the Minor Canon see and mark this indescribable change, which certainly rendered the young girl so much more attractively handsome, and therefore so much more dangerous in a new direction ?   Perhaps so ; or the late conversation may have made him peculiarly susceptible to certain influences, and less than usual under that strict command which he made it so stern a part of his duty to hold over himself.   Certain it is that for the moment he was unarmored — and that the China Shepherdess, could she have seen him at that crisis, would have found all her fears renewed, and considered his case as one beyond the curative capacities of the upper closet.

For as the young girl, recognizing her brother's visitor, whom she had not met for many weeks (accidentally on her part, through prudent care on his), came forward with both hands extended and those words of the very warmest affection and respect which she could never more willingly breathe to any one on earth than to the good Minor Canon—he reddened, paled, trembled, almost stammered his greeting—lost his equanimity so completely, that while Helena only saw her friend and preceptor as a little less at ease in the unexpected breaking in of a lady upon a conversation that might have been important and its interruption embarrassing — her brother must have been blinder than his wont, not to observe the omen, note it, understand it!

"It is a great pleasure to see you in good health and spirits, Miss Landless," at length the clergyman commanded himself enough to say. "Only second—if you will excuse the ungallant nature of the remark—to finding your brother so wonderfully improved in every regard."

"He is improved marvellously, is he not?—thanks to the kindness of many friends, and yourself always first among them, dear Mr. Crisparkle," she responded, little aware how much there might be in so simple an expression of pleasure to that peculiar hearer. "But, by-the-bye, though Neville has lately several times spoken of your calling upon him, I have been so unfortunate as to miss you. Pray do not allow him, when you call, to be so selfish as to appropriate you entirely; for remember that his friendship is of no older date than mine, and that when it comes to a question of precedence, I may even show myself woman enough to be jealous of my twin-brother."

Mr. Crisparkle (hypocrite again, with the same opportunity of demanding lenient judgment) spoke something of his professional duties, (which by no means explained his avoidance of *her*, when he did call !) and closed with a regret (candid, if the former expression was not !) that any occupation or accident should prevent his often enjoying the great pleasure of meeting her.

A few more words, not farther removed than these from the everyday and commonplace—words having in themselves no element of remembrance, except as the lips shaping them have the power to transmute the most trifling utterance to something of untold value; and then, with a good-bye to the clergyman, as heart-warm as had been her greeting, and the kiss of an hour or two of farewell to her brother—Helena Landless passed away from the sight of the two upon whom she had come so suddenly. Passed away, yet leaving them as differently circumstanced toward each other, as if in her brief presence a complete metamorphosis had fallen upon the relative thoughts and feelings of each.

For quite a moment, after the young girl's disappearance there was silence in the room. Both were standing, then—the Minor Canon, as he had risen to make his farewells; and Neville, as he had accompanied his sister to the door, for some little last word. Both were embarrassed beyond question, by the belief entertained by each (no uncommon occurrence, by the way, in other life than that of the stage !), that he knew what the other could not possibly suspect, and that awkardness might grow out of the misunderstanding. But the pause was broken by Neville, whose frank straightforwardness went far to prove that though in his past misery he might have been laboring to deceive himself, he could scarcely have formed the same intention towards others. He came up to Mr. Crisparkle, and grasped his hand warmly, at the same time uttering words that the other was not likely to forget, to his dying day. Words, too, which the clergyman would not have had recalled, after once spoken, at any price within his reach, though he would have been equally incapable of giving occasion for them by any premeditated utterance of his own.

"Forgive me, sir," he said, "and forgive *her*. We have neither of us been aware what we were doing."

Least willing of all men was the Reverend Septimus Crisparkle to use a subterfuge, when it could be avoided; but we have more than once seen him doing so for what he believed a meritorious object; and it was not in human nature, however disciplined by mental and moral headers, to avoid the slight uncandor involved in the question :

"Forgive *you*, and *her?* What can you possibly mean, Neville ? "

" Pray, sir, do not make it more difficult for me to say what I feel it my duty to say, by making me additionally feel that I am intruding where you do not wish to have me come!" returned the young man, with the deepest feeling in his tone, "But again I must say—pray forgive *me*, and *her !* "

The Minor Canon's face has been pale and red by turns, in those unfortunate moments of betrayal; but there was only the one color, now—the deep flush, brother of the one suffusing it, at the time of the accusation by his mother. He might have been seventeen, then, again, instead of at that ripe middle-age, supposed to bring calmness of blood and equability of temperament. He tried to speak, but either could not succeed or judged it best to avoid the hazard; and Neville Landless resumed.

" I may be offending you unpardonably, sir; but I cannot help what I am saying, as you have been so frank with *me*, as well as so kind. Once more—forgive *me* for bringing my sister into the way of your useful and happy life, and forgive *her* for not being other than she is."

" You suspect, Neville, my dear young friend——"

"Pardon my interrupting you, sir; but I suspect nothing. For the last ten minutes I have known, with a pride and shame beyond the power of any words to express, that *you love my sister !* "

The face of the Minor Canon was troubled, then, as perhaps it had never before been in the view of any man; but he did not speak, and the other continued.

" One month ago, sir, I should have quite forgotten my own

unhappiness, I think, in the knowledge that she had awakened such an attachment in the breast of the man of all men whom I should have been proudest to call brother. To-day I am made unhappy, because I know that only unhappiness can be the result. I know that I am offending you quite past forgiveness, but my duty must be done, as I have not always done it : my sister has another attachment, and could never be your wife, if you even knew how dear, good and true she is, and thought her worthy of that honor."

"Honor!" the Minor Canon literally gasped as he uttered the word with something nearly akin to anger at the person, even though a brother, who dared use it in such a connection. "Honor! who could honor *her* by asking her to share his life, even if he offered a crown as an inducement!"

The flood-gates were open, now, as they would probably never be again ; and he poured out the words which succeeded, with the very opposite of his late hesitation and embarrassment.

"No—Neville Landless, there could be no 'honor' done to your noble sister, even in laying down life at her feet! You have discovered my secret—how I cannot guess; and I acknowledge—not my weakness, as some might call it—but my *pride*. She has an attachment, you say? Thank God for that, as it cannot be other than a worthy one! She will fulfil her destiny as a woman, and be happy : Heaven bless and keep her, always, and make her perfect as she deserves to be, here and hereafter!"

"Oh, sir, if I could tell you all!" exclaimed the brother, perhaps with some doubt whether his privilege did or did not extend to disabusing the mind of the clergyman, of his fatally mistaken ideas as to his sister's "happiness;" but he was not allowed to continue. The Minor Canon extended his hand, and said :

"Give me your hand again, my dear young friend, not only as that friend, but as the brother of the noblest woman whom I ever met—the woman whom I should have been proudest to call 'wife,' had such a thing been possible. But it cannot be—it could not from the first. I have betrayed my secret; and I am sorry, because the knowledge may add to your unhappiness. It must not add to *hers*, or detract from any happiness within her reach. Promise me, if you believe that I am and have been a friend,—that not a word of this shall ever pass your lips to your sister! You will make that promise, Neville, I know that you will, for *her* sake!"

"I do make it, most solemnly, sir, and with a sorrow that I cannot express, for the necessity," answered the brother, with the extended hand still warmly grasped in his. "And as I do so, and make this new acknowledgment how good and true and noble you are in all your dealings with my unfortunate race—I must add one word more, to say how silly I now know myself to have been, only half an hour ago, in boasting of my own knowledge of a suffering that you had not experienced! Pray forget that too, sir, with so much more that you may kindly attribute to the arrogance and presumption of youth."

"I will forget, Neville, just what you wish me to forget, and remember just what you wish me to remember!" said the Minor Canon, his voice nearly restored to its usual cheery tone, and his manner again composed, as that of one who either lays down difficult burthens at once, or carries them well, with the strongest of all assistance. "And now, I must leave you in a few moments. Too much of myself, and too little of *you*. How are you progressing with those studies which have done you so much good mentally and are eventually to win you a place in the great world? Nearly ready to attempt that meritorious but difficult task, of proving to My Lords or the intelligent jury that four and one make six, or that Mr. Thompson, writing *this*, plainly intended to say *that*, and nothing else?"

Neville Landless did not reply for a moment—hesitating as the Minor Canon had done just before. And there was something strange—cheerfully solemn, if the phrase may be allowed—on his handsome dark young face, as after a moment, he set upon their edges, so that the backs could be plainly

22

read, the half-dozen books lying on the table. When last in the room, a few days earlier, Mr. Crisparkle had seen lying there, and found him poring over, Chitty, and Blackstone, and Coke-upon-Littleton, and several other of those elemental works by which the foundations of that "perfection of human reason," known as law, are believed to be best laid in the mind of the student. What did he see now? Pious old George Herbert; the Holy Living and Dying, and a volume of the Sermons, of Jeremy Taylor, sometime Bishop of Down, Connor, and Dromore; Paley, Butler, and Hooker! Certainly a very different collection of weapons, and for a widely different purpose!—and the half-stare of wonder on the face of the clergyman, as he saw, may not have been extraordinary. But the Rev. Septimus Crisparkle was not habitually slow of observation; and he was by no means deficient in a certain *esprit du corps* belonging to every pr•fession—not to credit him with any higher feeling. And so the expression of satisfaction blending with the surprise, and eventually supplanting it, may have been quite natural, as he said, in a voice very low and earnest:

"Neville, my dear young friend!—what does this mean?"

"Simply this, sir," was the reply. "These hours of comparative loneliness—yes, of misery—have driven me to more communion with my own heart than I might otherwise ever have found. I have become more and more satisfied, that a Hand, mightier than my own, and so much wiser, has been directing me in the way He would have me go. I have heard words uttered by my dear sister, so long ago that she has no doubt forgotten them, ringing in to me on the sounds of the street, and even coming in my sleeping hours: 'Follow your guide, Neville, and follow him to heaven!' I am going to try it, sir. My life is broken, so that the sacrifice I offer is even poorer than it might have been; but such as I have, I offer it. I will 'follow,' sir, as I have been bidden; and perhaps the day may come, when I may be so favored of Him as to 'lead' some other poor and broken man in the Way, with the Truth, and towards the Life."

For a moment, again, the Minor Canon was silent,—as to the sound reaching any earthly ears, at least. And when he spoke, without either quite knowing how the change of posture had occurred, Neville Landless was on his knee, with the dark bright face upturned, and both the hands of his friend were laid upon the brown young head.

"His name be praised, and His peace and His blessing be upon you, my dear friend and brother indeed!"

There was another tap at the door, even as the young man rose; and when he went to it, hastily dashing from his eyes the tears of an agitation which might have shaken many a stronger man under the same circumstances—Mr. Grewgious it was who entered, rounding his Angular face in the unexpected pleasure of meeting the Minor Canon, and speaking with no Angularity whatever:

"Reverend sir, I am delighted at the chance of meeting you. Mr. Landless, pardon my intrusion, but I have the miserable excuse of business that requires your attention—at some time this morning—no haste whatever. Reverend sir, I hope that you have had a pleasant journey from Cloisterham, and that the excellent lady, your mother, is in good health and spirits."

And so, for the moment, the trio of the disappointed was complete. Something more: the trio of *the brave patient and determined under that disappointment most difficult to bear of all laid upon humanity*. There was a very pretty legend, current years ago, of a chain of circumstances through which three uncrowned kings met and passed the night together, at some humble place of refuge in the German mountains—each for a time ignorant of any other rank than his own: was that scene more picturesque or more instructive than the meeting of these three, with a fourth similarly circumstanced just gone out of their midst, — each so calmly wearing, that at ordinary times its existence was quite unsuspected, and on a brow so different to that of each of the others, the withered chaplet-crown of a Dead Hope?

CHAPTER XXII.

THUNDERS OF DOOM.

THE night has been close and sultry, over Cloisterham and all its neighborhood ; and the morning, without changing the condition of the atmosphere as to temperature, has sent the smoke of the Cloisterham chimneys downward towards street and river, with a suddenness denoting much organic weakness on the part of that dusky volume, or much rarification of the air ordinarily destined to float it to the nostrils of others than the makers. Thick mephitic vapors have been lying on the river, reducing the dun-sailed boats to even a more helpless condition than that of ordinary calm, as the nerves of those who might be rowers are unstrung, and the very thought of the least unavoidable labor is an abhorrence. As the morning progresses, dense clouds rise, drift away on a wind unfelt by the lower world—to be succeeded by others that drift away and disappear as mysteriously, and those by others that succeed with corresponding persistence.

Persons of quasi-marine temperament or vocation, who quarter the barometer as their arms, in compliment to their nearness to the coast, or from some connection with the boating interest—are led to notice, this morning, that the needle has been suddenly taken with an attack of St. Vitus' dance, flying hither and thither with a celerity giving suspicion that it has lost its metallic senses and fails to know what weather to foretell. Presumably, at the same time, grizzled and tarry old fellows, on the coast, where playing at sailors is less ornamental—these, carrying huge sea-glasses under arm and walking wide as if with that doubt about nice steering which requires much sea-room to avoid fouling,—observe the unsteady but dropping glass, cock up oblique eyes at the heavens, hitch up the fugitive trousers, transfer the quid to the other side of the mouth, and remark, sententiously, that if they haven't been man and boy on that coast for two-and-forty years, all for nothing, it'll give 'em more'n a capful o' wind afore they're many hours older—blow great guns, more likely than keep Blue Peter hanging down his head.

His Reverence the Dean, connected with one of those great old families entailing other blessings, sometimes, than property, becomes aware of peculiarities in the atmosphere, through the medium of his right great-toe, at the very moment when he is putting on the comely gaiters to proceed to the Cathedral, for a service of more than ordinary (earthly) importance seeing that the sermon of the morning is to be preached by his clerical brother of eminence, the Hon. and Very Rev. the Dean of Baxetter, temporarily at Cloisterham on his way home from the Continent.

Mr. Tope, traversing the limited distance between his house and the Cathedral, to look after its being duly opened for that important morning service, and to take due order that nothing therein or thereto appertaining shall be out of keeping to the nice sense of His Reverence the Dean or the yet-nicer sense of the Hon. and Very Rev. the Dean's visiting brother—marks the omens of the sky, silently prognosticates rain, if not wind, and scarcely opens the Cathedral to the extent necessary for due ventilation, in the apprehension that rain may burst in at any opened window before the close of the service, and occasion a little of that confusion always regarded with such pained feeling by his Reverence the Dean.

Mr. Crisparkle, whose header of the early morning, taken in the neighborhood of the Weir, seems to have been made into mingled oil and water, so far has the element been from refreshing him to the usual extent, with its flash and motion—Mr. Crisparkle notes the atmospheric influences, as he steps out from the door at Minor Canon Corner and measures the infinitesimal distance to the Cathedral doorway—breathing, the while, less freely and buoyantly than is his wont, and wondering, as he enters the Cathedral, whether it would not have been better, after all, to have brought over his umbrella, even for that trifle of space, sufficient, in a certain contingency, to give him a header with the water and not himself as the moving body.

And Mr. Jasper, coming out from his three days of illness and supposed quiet at the Gate House, following upon his midnight visit to the Crypt—induced to make that exertion by the imploring message of Mr. Crisparkle, who has stated that without *him* the service will certainly disappoint the Very Rev. the Dean of Baxetter, and inflict intense mortification upon his friend and patron *the* Dean—Mr. Jasper, proceeding Cathedralward at that late hour, only allowing of his hurriedly robing in time for the very commencement of his duties — he too looks up at the lowering sky, feels the oppression of the atmosphere, and attributes to it something of that intense weakness which seems to affect limbs and body, and that numb pain pressing down on the top of his head like a leaden weight. But there is a difference in the view upwards, between the Choir-Master and the others. They think, and some of them say: "With this heavy and sultry atmosphere there will be thunder and lightning, and they will clear the air!" *he* thinks, too, of the possibility of the thunder and the lightning, but dreads them, and hopes against them, as if they might bear again in sight and sound the strict commands and fearful warnings of Sinai.

The gathering in Cloisterham Cathedral, this morning, is more than ordinarily numerous for any occasion less important than one of the great church festivals. For the coming of the Dean of Baxetter is known, by some inscrutable means defying type and telegraph, throughout the sleepy old town that has not too many sensations; and his admitted eloquence may have an equal share in attracting hearers to his expected sermon (nay, let us be charitable, and hope that it has more!) with the fact that he is the Honorable as well as the Very Reverend, with a Baron for his father, and an Earl as his uncle. So, although the morning threatens, the seats fill at an early hour, as if the occasion was a holiday one. In like manner, the

choir mus'ers in full force—few pleasant rivalries being more
declared than that which forbids that one of the great Cathe-
· drals of the kingdom should be found deficient in thundering
out melodious sound to the ears of the representative of
another; and the choral strength of Cloisterham coming out
in prompt season and excellent array, to delight and possibly
astonish the Very Reverend of Baxetter.

It has already grown dusky in the Cathedral when the last
notes of the organ, playing the voluntary, roll through the old
vaulted pile, making it no difficult matter to believe that the
conflict of the elements has already begun, and that the faint
reverberation of distant thunder is muttering near. It grows
even darker, seeming to shadow over the pile and the congregation with a great raven wing pausing as it sweeps by—when
the first words of the impressive service are intoned, praying
for fit humility to approach into that Presence, so much more
awful than any omen of the physical world,—and asking that
the One sitting so high above all clouds and storms may not
enter into judgment with those who have neither strength nor
will for the great combat. It darkens still, and the candles are
lighted in a brief compulsory pause,—before the commencement of that sublime Confession to which the breasts of all
men, since the very foundation of the world, have had cause to
echo, with more or less of fear and self-abasement. And
there it hangs—that pall of semi-darkness, while the Prayer
of Our Lord is repeated, and the *Venite exultemus Domino*
rings out from choir and organ, with a significance only known
to those who sit in grief, or guilt, or the deep shadow of some
great peril by land or sea. It seems to lighten, though still
the dusk is deeper than that of twilight, as the clear, soft voice
of Mr. Crisparkle, its bright cheeriness mellowed in that
atmosphere and that employment, reads the First and Second
Lessons of the Day, with the *Te Deum laudamus* intervening,
and carrying up the reverent soul to the very height of trembling adoration of the Divine Being. And then it settles and
darkens again, with something of awful import in this verita-

ble overshadowing, making cheeks whiter than usual, and fa
more than usual in the holiest places, blotting away the trifling
things of the outer world, as worthy to be no more remembered
in the face of the greater.

Then there comes a change, breaking in on the *Benedictus*,
and making every one within the Cathedral start and shiver in
an unacknowledged combination of physical and supernatural
fear. The black wing moves, though still retaining its
shadow; and the winds and the rains of heaven come with an
accompaniment of rolling thunder, making the peal of the
organ a faint and puerile imitation. Above the sound of that
organ and the voices of the singers, the sweeping dash of the
rain can be heard, as it lashes the great windows, and the
fierce wind as it bursts, howls and shrieks around the staunch
old edifice. Many cheeks pale, now, as they have not paled
in many a long day—as if the God of the Storm, as well as the
God of Love and Peace whom they ordinarily worship, was in
their very midst, compelling a new knowledge of his attributes. More than once, Mr. Crisparkle, even his bright and
cheerful spirit impressed by the omens, looks up in awed
wonder not unmixed with a certain solemn artistic pleasure.
More than once the Dean—a man in whom the artistic sensibili-
ties are much less fully developed than the sense of propriety,
and the desire that "all things should be done decently and
in order"—and who knows no reason whatever for thinking
more profoundly of the thunder and the wind, this morning,
than on an hundred other mornings of his life,—regrets that
the visit of his Very Reverend brother of Baxetter should
have been made under such inauspicious circumstances, and at
a time when his sermon, if this state of things continues, will
scarcely be listened to with that attention which it will be certain to deserve.

Possibly the Dean of Baxetter may be impressed with
something of the same feeling, and a wish that, if this is the
current sacerdotal weather at Cloisterham, he had concluded to
pass on from the coast without visiting it. Sure it is that

Mr. Tope, the while, has an attack of Tribulation, in a mild form and a different shape to that which it assumed in his communication to Mr. Crisparkle—nothing less than a fear that his Cathedral may be damaged, to the extent of unknown pounds sterling, by one or the other of these extraordinary actions of the climate; the result being that he profits little by the service, looking upwards and around so anxiously as to excite apprehensions that he believes the roof to be coming down, in the breasts of those worshippers sitting near his favorite gate.

And John Jasper?

He has come out from a sick-room, if not from a sick-bed, at the solicitations of Mr. Crisparkle, and in the knowledge of the occasion being really an important one. He has nerved himself manfully, all things considered, to do his duty in the Cathedral, before the eyes (and eke the ears) of those who have known him so long, and of his Reverence the Dean of Baxetter. The knees may have been weak, the eyes may have been dim and filmy, the head may have been filled with a dull pain rendering him capable of little more than the mere mechanical exercises of his office—but what then? He has duties to do, and they must be done—done to the end! Perhaps there has been, now and again, a quaver not called for by the music, in the rich tenor inclining to the baritone, with which he has so often honored the Church, pleased Cloisterham, and delighted the music-loving Minor Canon; but if so, no one seems to have detected the fact. He has held his choir, so to speak, well in hand; and despite all the omens of the storm, rarely have the musical portions of the service been more correctly and effectively conducted than on this occasion. If the Choir-Master's hair is greyer than its wont, and his face more haggard than any one has ever before seen it—those characteristics are not likely to be observed in the semi-darkness of the Cathedral, as he sits prominent among the other white-robed of the earthly service—far-off types of those who know neither defilement, sin nor sorrow.

The *Jubilate Deo*, following, not supplementing, the *Bene-dictus*—possibly in honor of the Very Reverend visit—has just died upon the ear, when suddenly, as if all the prelimi-nary darkness had been nothing more than a mere premonition, a new pall falls upon the Cathedral and all the worshippers within. There is neither rain nor wind, for the moment—as some, calmer or better circumstanced than the others for obser-vation, take note, and afterwards repeat it to the less-informed. The blackness seems almost palpable. The very candles be-come mere sparks, in the heavy and murky atmosphere, and give scarcely the pitiful illumination of rushlights. The con-gregation feel, individually and collectively, that sinking of the heart and that suppression of the breath inevitable on the face of the Stupendously Awful and Untried. If the candles could give more than their insufficient light, absolute terror would be read on more faces than often express that painful feeling when removed from the presence of the direst physical danger.

It is at this most solemn and impressive of moments that Mr. Crisparkle, still officiating in honor of his guest,—after only a moment of awed pause, in which the closing peal of the organ still rolls its minor thunders through the gray arches,—commences, with the voice of more than half the congregation fervently following, the Apostles' Creed :

" *I believe in God the Father Almighty, Maker of Heaven and Earth——*"

Above his voice and the voices of all the others following, comes again the rushing of the mighty wind that has been for a brief space comparatively still; even above this, and the voices, and all else that can be thought or imagined, comes the crashing of the thunder, breaking and booming over the old pile with such awful nearness that the very pillars shake with the reverberation, and the frightened congregation grip their seats as if the power of the earthquake was unloosed. But still the Minor Canon reads on, and the frightened voices make some feeble attempts to follow, until those crowning words, at once of Hope and Fear, are reached :

"FROM THENCE HE SHALL COME TO JUDGE THE QUICK AND THE DEAD."

For that instant, even to the dullest sense, it may almost seem that with the sublime and awful formula the more sublime and awful reality has been reached. Has not The End come, indeed? When has the like of this been? and how long, beneath such terrible blows and pressure, can the solid earth or any structure built upon it, continue to exist? Another thunder-crash, closer, deeper and more jarring and rending in its character, accompanied by a lightning flash of such intensity of glare that all eyes fall shut before it, in the very fear of blindness, only a few catching even one glimpse of the Cathedral interior, every detail lit up as no noon-day sun has ever had power to illumine it. And even at this instant, another burst of wind, if possible a hundred times more fierce than that just died away—literally shaking the pile of massive stone as if it might be a mere structure of cardboard, and creating the natural fear that in a moment more, roof and arches and columns may all be lying a heap of ruins, upon and in the midst of hundreds of crushed and struggling human beings.

One instant more, and then the feared demolition seems to have begun. There is an awful crash, rather accompanying than following the culminating burst of the wind's fury—a sound that is only afterwards recognized as that of breaking, splintering, and falling glass, half-drowned in the terrified cry of hundreds of voices,—as the great stained-glass window of the Chancel, the preceding instant so illuminated by the lightning that every sainted figure has little else than burned itself on the eye-balls—gives way under the pressure and falls crashing inwards. There is an instant redoubling of the cries of terror; a hurried rising from seats and pressing backwards, in the fear that the whole chancel is falling forward into the choir; then an earnest word from Mr. Crisparkle, to calm the terror and reassure the congregation. And then something else, as little expected as all preceding, and possibly lingering quite as long in the minds of the dwellers in Cloisterham, on that occasion present, as even the terror of the storm, and the serious damages to the Cathedral.

John Jasper, necessarily unobserved, like all others, at the moment of the catastrophe, and of whose action at that special instant, consequently, no account can be given—is missed from his seat, when the first terror has passed, and the attempt is made to resume the interrupted services. And it is only by a comparison of notes among the frightened and therefore not too intelligible choristers, and others in the immediate neighbor-hood—that the fact becomes patent of a white figure flitting away and disappearing, just when the physical winds and thunders broke deadliest over the Cathedral, with their accom-paniment of crashing glass and terrified voices, at the same moment when the far awfuller thunders of the coming judg-ment fell, in those warning words of the Creed, from the mild lips of the Minor Canon.

He is known to have been very ill: he has been suddenly taken with a relapse, and hurried away for medical assistance, with the least possible disturbance to the congregation. This is the explanation naturally occurring to Mr. Tope, whose dignity has been more or less assailed by this infraction of rules in his Cathedral; and to Mr. Crisparkle, who has a certain regret for the persistence with which he has called out a sick man, possibly too ill properly to leave his room; and to the Very Rev. the Dean, who regrets the occurrence mildly, as is his habit—and the more mildly as being unusually absorbed, to-day, from the misbehavior of his right great-toe: and to the other Very Rev. the Dean of Baxetter, who preaches his sermon, in the brightening Cathedral and the clearing weather to less attention than he might have absorbed, in the event of the Chancel window not being broken to the extent of needing costly and difficult repairs—and who listens to a less perfect musical service, during the brief remainder, than he might be privileged to hear if the Choir-Master was not suddenly absent.

Absent! ay, that is the word, conveying so much in so little

space. Absent!—how sent or forced away, through what combination of the ominous and the terrible in past recollections
and future forebodings, driven in upon heart and brain by
those feeble reminders of the Thunders of Doom, bursting
over Cloisterham Cathedral—there may be other imaginings
than those of the good, literal people of the old city, who know
no more of John Jasper, except the little conveyed by his
scarcely remarkable exterior, than they know of some resident
of the Antipodes. But absent, for the last time and forever,
from the seat he has occupied and the station he has filled;
unless restless spirits do indeed walk the earth, as believed in
the fancies of bygone ages, and especially affect and haunt those
places in which they have wrought, loved, enjoyed, sinned and
suffered.

CHAPTER XXIII.

THE THORN OF ANXIETY.

MR. BAZZARD was back at Staple Inn. Mr. Grewgious was
no longer alone, in the sense of having no one with whom to
consult and no one to whom to defer—though the same mystery
necessarily remained after his return, that had existed before
his departure—what Staple wanted with him or he with Staple;
what good was to be derived from his being there, or anywhere,
as what harm could possibly have resulted from his being
absent from that place or any other?

His return was as mysterious as his departure—which is
saying much; the causes of both the departure and the return
being (as already indicated) wrapped in corresponding obscurity. In point of fact, he came in the night, with a carpet-bag
of threatening proportions—much more with the air, general
equipment and indefinable impression of one who was running
away with the surreptitiously acquired contents of the carpet-
bag beforementioned, and prudently choosing the night for

that removal, than of one who had good right to bestow it and and its contents where he would. At which period P. J. T., observer of entrances there since seventeen forty-seven, and, Perpetually Jotting Traits of his visitors, though Perhaps Justifiably Tired of doing so as a Purely Judicial Trouble— looked down on him, as he passed through the Portal Jaundice- Tainted into the Premises Jointly-Tenanted, and remarked to himself in his grim silent way, that Positively Just Then the extraordinary person who had already proved the Poor Jani- tor's Torment, was Proceeding Jerkily Through, after a Pro- longed Journey Tenebrous, with his Personalities Jealously Treasured (not to say, his Plunder Jammed Tightly), his Port Jauntily Tense, and no doubt again his Purposeless Jab- ber Threatening any who Tabernacled Joylessly There.

Whence he came, there was nothing in his appearance by which P. J. T. or any other could have decided positively though any one of several hypotheses might be held as sug- gested. Thus—he looked pale and puffy-faced enough, and seemed to have enough damp flabbiness in his complexion to have possibly spent most of the warm period of his absence with the fish and oysters at the bottom of any imaginable river; his hair was cut so much shorter, though still retaining the tangled quarrelsomeness of each particular hair with all the other members of its family, to indicate that he might possibly have been passing away the hot weeks in the cool shade of a prison; and his lack-lustre and expressionless eyes seemed so peculiarly vacant, as to suggest that for a time he might have been blotted out from the world in a sleep of seve- ral weeks duration, on awakening from which so fishy and glassy expression would be only natural.

He was evidently on good terms with himself, however— being more than before given to periods of chuckling, without palpable cause appearing at such moments for the same, and giving good reason for prefixing to the laughter the epithet vacant. He met Mr. Grewgious, on (in a legal phrase) put- ting in an appearance, with a species of sublime condescension

which might have been very crushing in its effect on a man
less Angular and consequently weaker in construction; and it
became evident, at the first moment, that if there had been
anything of inversion in the two positions of principal and
clerk, that inversion was now to be intensified rather than
changed. On the merest suggestion pointing thitherward, at
their first meeting, the morning after his return—he first went
into an air of Injury suggesting to the observer that there
might be such a thing as Asking Too Much; then gradually
changed into one of Conferring Benefits of such extent, magnificence and self-denial, that the devotion of a life-time on
the part of the favored recipient could only go a short distance
towards repaying them; then blandly continued the employment of the Substitute (substitute for *himself*), by ordering
that temporary official down to the cellar for the bottles of
Mr. Grewgious' choicest wine. On its obediently coming up
for due destruction, he continued the Favor by dealing that
destruction to one bottle and three-fourths, without much
apparent suffering, while the owner was with difficulty imbib-
ing the remaining quarter-bottle. In brief, Staple, if for a
short time bereaved of any one capable of representing proprietorship of all the lands, tenements, messuages and heredit-
aments thereunto belonging and appertaining—could not be
said to labor under any such bereavement for a single hour
after the reappearance on the scene of Mr. Bazzard, who
" mightn't like it else ! "

The first night after his return, saw him a Compelled and
Favoring guest at Mr. Grewgious' table, with a neat little
supper from Furnival's, at disposal, and no company, other
than what each supplied the other, to check the flow of conversation that might have been the most confidential. And
confidential that conversation may really have been, even if
uttered so loudly as to be heard in Holborn; for to the uninstructed ear it must have been little else than Choctaw, in
possible honor of Mr. Bazzard's late wanderings and seques-
terings; and it may even be so to the ear flattering itself with
being, like Mr. Sapsea's, far from uninstructed.

"Bazzard!" said Mr. Grewgious, at a certain turn in the conversation, which had been interrupted by occasional other uses of the lips than articulation. "Bazzard!—on this pleasant occasion, which, if I was a less Angular man, or there were more of us, I should be disposed to call a re-union,— allow me to give over again a toast which I have before taken the liberty of proposing at this table."

"Ah!" replied Mr. Bazzard, at once reflectively and patronizingly. "I follow you, sir, though I have not the slightest idea what you may happen to mean."

"Umps!" replied Mr. Grewgious. "If you don't mind my saying so, Bazzard, you *ought* to know to what I allude. Something very near to the hearts of both of us, from different causes. To yours from proprietorship. To mine, because you might not be satisfied else—likewise on the ground of friendship. I give you——"

"Why, you don't mean, sir,"—commenced Mr. Bazzard, interrupting in a manner which might have been impertinent in any other than a proprietor.

"Umps! Yes, I do! That is precisely what I mean!" said Mr. Grewgious, interrupting in his turn, without due regard to the proprietorship in which he, as well as Staple and P. J. T. all happened to be held. "Yes, I say it again, as an Angular man, who from that fact cannot possibly go round anything and must approach it squarely. Not to mention other names, which you possibly mightn't like, I give you the Thorn of Anxiety; and I say again, with three times three understood—May it Come Out, and the sooner the better!"

"Why, what a blessed old bookworm and antiquity you are, sir," exclaimed Mr. Bazzard, commiseratingly—"not to know that it is already Out!"

"Out? Umps! Bazzard — do you positively mean to make the statement, that it is Out, and that I have never been informed of the fact? Bazzard, if I was not a man of peculiarly hard tendencies, without the power to become affected by ill-usage, I should feel the necessity of considering this glass a Flowing Bowl, and drowning in it a certain amount of Sorrow."

"Don't, if you please, sir!" chuckled Mr. Bazzard, with the fatuous tendency very strongly marked, and hair, eyes, and complexion all playing their part in making him appear so, with great concert and vigor. "There is no occasion. You would not have enjoyed the Coming Out, had you been present; as indeed I was not and only became informed of the circumstances through the medium of a friend."

"Bazzard!" said Mr. Grewgious, staring blankly, "if I did not fear that you might not like it — might object, in point of fact, which would be unpleasant for both,—I should be inclined to remark that this Burgundy is a trifle heady, and that it has a bad habit of confusing the distinction between subjects talked about — say, jambling them up together. Candidly, now, is not that the case? Are you not referring, without being aware of the fact, to something else than the T. of A.?"

"Not at all, sir!" again chuckled Mr. Bazzard, with an access of vacancy, if such a thing could be possible, in eyes, hair, complexion and general manner. "Certainly not, sir! It is of the T. of A. that I am speaking; and I tell you that it is Out."

"Umps! Of course, Bazzard, if you assert that it is Out, I must accept the statement; as no one should know better than yourself. But would it be asking too much, to request a trifle of information How it Came Out?" mildly and deferentially suggested Mr. Grewgious.

"On the contrary, sir, it becomes my duty to explain briefly all the circumstances connected with its Coming Out," patronizingly replied Mr. Bazzard, taking a sip of the wine, and loftily waving his flabby hand ; whereat Mr. Grewgious, more or less encouraged, also took a sip of wine, but did not wave his Angular hand.

"If you will kindly permit me, sir, to tell the story in my

23

own way, and not ask too many irrelevant questions, I think that we shall finish all the sooner, and all the better," remarked Mr. Bazzard, with the strongly injured air of one who had always been broken in upon, put out of the course of his narrations, badgered, trampled down in all immaterial senses, and generally rendered an object of pity, by the arrogant and overbearing tyrant at the other side of the table.

"Quite right, Bazzard, I am sure," echoed the arrogant and overbearing tyrant, in his mildest and least Angular manner. "Be kind enough to tell the story in your own way —you mightn't like it, else, you know."

"Well, then, sir," proceeded the victim, with his injured air rapidly changing back to flabby inconsequence, "I will tell you how the T. of A. Came Out. You will understand, of course, that I am not telling you of anything that I have been doing—only relating, in a very brief way, the adventures of a friend of mine."

"God bless me!—no, Bazzard, of course I understand that you are not speaking of yourself—only of a friend of yours. Umps! what did you say was his name?" Mr. Grewgious, thus responding, and thus inquiring, was at the moment perusing the smoky ceiling with great assiduity, as if he expected to find the name inscribed there in large capitals, but had somehow overlooked it.

"Name of Datchery," proceeded Mr. Bazzard, so impressively as to bring down the eyes to their proper level. "Place of birth, immaterial; age, ditto; family, ditto; profession, legal. You quite understand, sir?"

"Bazzard, I follow you, as you have obliged *me* by doing, once and again," replied Mr. Grewgious. "I follow you, and I fancy that I understand you. From motives of prudence, and in fear that any of the rats in the wainscot may have been retained by the other side, we will assume the professional and merely say *alter ego*."

"My friend Datchery," pursued Mr. Bazzard, "came into the case, or in deference to the dramatic character of the a'fair, we will say came upon the stage, precisely at the time when I took the liberty of arranging a short summer vacation and went down to Norfolk."

"Tick that off—yes, Bazzard, you went down into Norfolk," assented Mr. Grewgious, at the moment making a telescope of the bottom of his glass, as if endeavoring to survey that distant county of the North Folk. "And Scratchery — did I follow you correctly, and understand his name to be Scratchery?"

"No, sir—'Datchery'—'Datchery'—repeatedly Datchery," corrected Mr. Bazzard, severely; adding, in a yet severer tone of voice: "Am I to understand, sir, that these interruptions are to cease, or that they are not?"

"Save the man! I was not aware that I was interrupting. Pray proceed!" apologized Mr. Grewgious, putting something red into his glass, to make the bottom clearer for the next distant survey.

"Crime had been committed, at a place called Cloisterham, in Chalkshire, of which you may have heard, sir."

"Am I to answer, Bazzard?—or would that be interrupting?" humbly inquired Mr. Grewgious.

"Answer? of course, sir! How could you follow me else?" at once explained and inquired Mr. Bazzard.

"Yes, Bazzard, I have heard, then, of Cloisterham—possibly seen it, at some remote period."

"Crime, as I said, or ought to have said, had been more or less committed. Intended victim had, in point of fact, escaped through something little less than a miracle. Intended victim, immediately after escaping, was placed in a difficulty—indeed, in what might have been called a quandary. Attempted murderer, and real murderer, as he believed, was relative of supposed victim. Supposed victim, closer acquaintance of my friend Datchery than most people dreamed, having seen a little London life in his company, in a quiet way——. Do you follow me, sir?"

"I follow you, Bazzard, and I drink to the success of your friend Datchery."

"Supposed victim," Mr. Bazzard continuing, "put himself into communication with Datchery, probably as the most consummate ass that he knew."

"I follow you, Bazzard, and I quite agree with you," assented Mr. Grewgious, with gratuitous willingness and energy. Whereupon Mr. Bazzard frowned with a double ferocity of fatuity; but continued:

"In serious doubt, supposed victim, how he could manage to punish attempting murderer, whom he could not avoid sparing, for blood-sake, and whom he must necessarily regard with horror after such attempt. Consulted my friend Datchery, who like a blessed inspired idiot——"

"Save the man!—what admirable choice of terms!" exclaimed Mr. Grewgious, as an "aside," which of course could not be noticed as in the general conversation.

"Advised continued concealment of supposed victim, temporary absence from the country (rendered easy by previous arrangement for employment abroad), and the putting into his (my friend Datchery's) hands, of certain data and materials for working upon the fears and possibly affecting the conscience of supposed murderer. Do you follow me, sir, here?"

"I follow you, friend Datchery—Bazzard, *there;* and I quite appreciate his inspired idiocy."

"My friend Datchery, to whom had been entrusted the T. of A., having a desire to bring it out through certain experiments on the mentality of the guilty, and taking care not to mention that fact to escaped victim, who might otherwise have objected, on the ground that supposed murderer might better be arrested and dealt with at once——"

"Than tortured, and murdered by inches, in that way," Mr. Grewgious obliged him by concluding the unfinished sentence. "Yes, Bazzard, I follow you, and quite agree with what would have been the sentiments of the escaped victim, had he known the whole case."

"Result," continued Mr. Bazzard, apparently growing tired either of the narration or the interruptions, "may be stated in a few words. Supposed victim went away. My friend Datchery experimented, assisted by an old official donkey, named Sapsea, whom he cajoled and flattered out of his few wits; a nondescript dunderhead named Durdles, with several grains of native sense, whom he hired; and a poor little cripple named Little Crawshe, whom he pitied and paid — liberally, for Datchery.

"Bazzard, I drink to the health of your friend Datchery again, without any reservation on the score of idiocy or otherwise!" exclaimed Mr. Grewgious, suiting the action to the word.

"Thanks, sir, on his behalf!" replied Mr. Bazzard, his flabby face for the moment lightened by something more notable than romantic vacancy. "When I communicate with my friend Datchery, Mr. Grewgious, if I ever do, I shall take pleasure in conveying to him your very kind sentiments. But to proceed, and very briefly. At a certain time, not long since, my friend Datchery was surprised by the coming home of supposed victim, who had imbibed a specially idiotic idea that his relative was punished sufficiently, and must by that time be repentant. Besides, as appeared on cross-examination, there was a young woman in the case, and he was awfully spooney to see her. My friend Datchery tabooed the young woman, peremptorily; enjoined continued concealment of person, and no communication with any one but himself, on penalty of throwing up the case; and then allowed the young numskull to see how 'repentant' his precious relative was!"

"Umps!" said Mr. Grewgious, "I not only follow you, here, but I have heard of the incident. Does my recollection fail me, or was the party named Philpits?"

"Recollection quite correct, sir, but unnecessary to be brought in at this stage of the case, in my opinion!" answered Mr. Bazzard, severely, but still continuing.

"Effects of that exposition of his relative's 'repentance,' quite satisfactory to supposed victim, who thereupon put himself even more completely than before in my—I mean to say

in the hands of my friend Datchery. General results magni‑
ficent, though possibly there might be difference of opinion, in
the mind of any party favorably disposed towards the criminal, who became cognizant of all the circumstances. Only one
other interruption, and that occurring very lately."

Mr. Bazzard paused, with a certain air of expecting to be
interrogated; and Mr. Grewgious, thus permitted, again interrupted.

" As what, Bazzard—may I ask ? "

" The presence, sir, at Cloisterham, of a young person of
the male sex, named Gilfert. For whom, sir, I am pained to
say that I believe I—that is my friend Datchery,—must hold
you largely responsible. Be good enough to answer the question—are you, or are you not retained, say in Gilfert *v.* Jasper ? "

" Umps ! Answering with more than the ordinary professional candor, then, Bazzard—I am."

" So my friend Datchery thought, sir, and he—that is, he
blessed you accordingly. For a more difficult person to put
off a scent, or keep from meddling with things beyond his
capacity, I—that is, my friend Datchery, never had the unhappiness of knowing. He is not even certain how much the
youngster discovered, and would probably be a shade more
comfortable if he knew. So young and so fine-looking, too,
though in a sort of feminine way—so at least my friend Datchery says—it seems really a pity that he should exhibit such
Juvenile Depravity."

." Umps !" said Mr. Grewgious, setting down his glass for
the more convenient rubbing of his hands, and then taking it
up again as if with a new relish of it and its contents.
" Bazzard, if you don't specially object, I will interpolate by
giving you the health of Gilfert—Joseph Gilfert, Esq., of any
place you choose to name. Eh, Bazzard ! save the man !—he
doesn't mean to refuse my toast ? "

" No, sir," said Bazzard, taking up his glass and drinking
with so wry a face, that its doughy surface was temporarily

changed, even if scarcely for the better. " I meet your wishes, sir, and I drink to Gilfert, under protest, and with a wish that he may be—not to mince matters—Smothered ! "

" Smothered, sir ! " continues Mr. Bazzard ; " and to promote this consummation, sir—on my part, at least, devoutly to be wished—I am willing, nay, anxious, to expend one-third of my quarterly income for purchasing the necessary feather-beds for the purpose ; for of all young men—and young men as a rule, are excessively antagonistic to temperament—this particular young man, if you will allow me the expression, is the antagonisticest ; and, I repeat—being willing to go to the stake for my opinion—I think he ought to be suddenly and completely smothered ! "

Mr. Grewgious, oddly enough, chuckled a little at this un-amiable wish ; then asked a question of importance to the general issue.

" You were about giving me the result, Bazzard,—which I suppose that I am also to understand as the Bringing Out of the T. of A. ? Yes ? Well, then—what is the exact result as at present illustrated in the condition of the supposed murderer ? Your friend Datchery as authority—remember ! "

" Supposed murderer, sir," returned Mr. Bazzard, loftily, " is, so far as my friend Datchery has informed me—at the present moment, a remarkable proof of the power of Genius as applied to the Unhinging of a man, or so to speak, Disjoint-ing him. He is hovering undecidedly, I—that is, my friend Datchery thinks, between the Madhouse and the Tomb, with odds in favor of the latter, because there will probably not be time left him to reach the former. He is likewise a notable illustration—so my friend Datchery also gives me as his opin-ion,—that Crime, considered as a Fine Art, seldom pays, with Amateurs, whatever it may do in the hands of Professionals."

" And your friend Datchery, Bazzard ? May I be allowed to inquire what has happened to *him* ? " suggested Mr. Grew-gious, with his Angular eyes screwed up into a queer con-templation through the two sides of his empty glass, which produced the pleasant effect so congenial to the human mind, of distorting everything within view.

"My friend Datchery, sir, having Brought Out the T. of A. upon this broad stage of every-day life and action, instead of confining that great drama to the mere walls of a theatre, may be said to have Had Enough Of It. As I am at present informed, yesterday or the day preceding, with nothing more to do, and in point of fact with affairs outrunning any efforts of his—that inspired idiot rubbed out with a damp towel the Rune-marks, in chalk, on the door of the closet at his lodgings, with which he had in a sort of droll way recorded his progress in discovery as well as displayed his knowledge of the Norse system of writing down historical records—paid his last weekly bill, and—Disappeared."

"Poor Datchery!" exclaimed Mr. Grewgious, solemnly, pouring out into his glass and that of the other, at the moment, the wine remaining in the third bottle. "Poor Datchery! if he is really Gone, if you don't mind, Bazzard, we will both drink to His Memory."

"I follow *you* now, and I join you, sir, if you will permit me a slight addition to the sentiment," said Mr. Bazzard, with corresponding gravity. "I drink, sir, to his Memory and his Bequest!"

"Lord save us!" cried Mr. Grewgious, in affright. "You don't mean to tell me that he has left anything! Anything in the shape of another Duty, or Search, or Quest, or Mission, that would seriously mar the future legal prospects of any one accepting it!"

"No—nothing of the sort, sir, I am happy to say," returned Mr. Bazzard. "The only Bequest, that I am aware of, was made to myself, in the shape of Little Crawshe, the crippled fisherman's-boy, for whom I stand pledged under that Bequest, to try whether the best surgical skill in the city cannot invent an apparatus for holding up his head without the constant and painful use of his hand—thus rendering the poor little faithful fellow less a cripple."

"Bazzard!" said Mr. Grewgious, warmly, reaching across the table to shake hands in accordance with the expression. "Bazzard, allow me to shake hands with you, as substitute for your friend Datchery, who has Disappeared! Permit me to express my appreciation of him, as a *benevolent* idiot, as well as an inspired one. It seems to have been a somewhat hair-brained work that he set himself to do; and the amount of good really achieved, balanced against the harm, may be problematical, if you will excuse a plain Angular man using so long and round a word. But I fancy that he has performed the task very creditably, under all the circumstances; and his Bequest is certainly a thoughtful and a proper one. We will cherish, so far as other matters will allow, his Memory. And to-morrow, Bazzard—if you don't mind—certain hindrances and obstructions being now out of the way, to both of us—to-morrow we will devote to gathering up some of the lost ends of Business."

"I understand you, sir, I follow you, I quite agree with you, and I thank you!" said Mr. Bazzard, draining the last drop in his glass and the last that it will be our privilege to drain, even in imagination, in his company.

CHAPTER XXIV.

GOING ELSEWHERE.

AGAIN John Jasper crosses the threshold of the disreputable house in the East— seeking what a thousand thousand of worse and better men have sought, in one or another of the ages of the world, at the same time that they dreaded the possibility of finding it with a dread unspeakable. He is seeking, again, Temporary. Oblivion : how little he, or any other — the guiltiest quite as little as the most innocent — would carry out the words often rashly and impiously uttered, and seek the naked phrase Oblivion without a qualifying precedent! Perhaps the question may rise in connection, whether it is not always more or less dangerous to seek, in any other mode than that by Heaven appointed, Sleep, that temporarily, which must be shuddered at as coming eternally — whether any Brain or any Lip is safe, when its owner rushes too madly upon Present Ease at the possible price of Future Misery,—let wine, the drug, or some modern anæsthetic refuge of shuddering and pain-dreading humanity supply the temptation.

But this man, if any thought he has in the matter, holds a widely different one. The time has come to him, when of all the blessings of that life which is an aggregated distortion, the richest is to be found in a single draught of the waters of Lethe. To be—small matter how, for even a short period, no longer himself, no longer any one, no longer anything—to have, for that certain period, neither part nor lot in the world of thought, feeling, sensation, hope, fear, dread, love, hate, revenge, deceit, calculation—to be, indeed, for that period, one of the very weeds that lie noisome and rotting on the bank of the River of Forgetfulness—this has come to be the chief good. And here he has found it, once and again, and in different measures, according as the changes in his own system and the developments supplied by the dark wisdom of others, have made succeeding stages possible. How magnificently he found that for which he was looking, almost in despair—last time! How splendidly he sank, almost in a moment, like a stone dropped into the very centre of the dark pool,—only making a few pleasant ripples, as he went down, shaping themselves into rosy clouds and fairy forms, to an accompaniment of the most delicious music; and how he came up again, after a time—with no more effort—weakened a little, certainly, in body, but oh, so refreshed in mind, and so ready to grasp, in a moment, what he needed to grasp for the difficult duties of his waking hours! None of that painful striving to get away from himself, on that occasion; none of that fearful wrestling with shapes seem-

ing like Demons of Sensation fighting those of Unconscious-
ness, which had so often troubled him since the habituating
of body and brain to bear stronger inhalations of the narcotic.
It had been, that once as in his first attempt, when every
nerve was fresh and sensitive: he had regained what he believed to be a lost Power—the power of Totally Quitting Himself—leaving his body a mere tenement-shell, to be re-entered
at will; he had regained a lost Enjoyment, beyond question—
the Enjoyment of Death in Life. And why, thus remembering and thus tempted, should he not try it Once More?
Why not, indeed? Why should any of us, at any time, who
have eaten stolen fruit, or trodden upon forbidden ground, or
broken some canon native to the conscience, and as yet suffered no fatal damage thereby—why should we not try it Once
More? What if there is a hand, unknown as to the body to
which it belongs, but awfully distinct as to its shape and
office, writing on the walls of consciousness, now and again,
three warning words that always read the same and so grow
rather wearisome than impressive — "Once Too Late"?
What if even this should be? Must that which has been,
always exist? Some prophecies have been fulfilled—but have
all? Other hands have written upon other walls and with
other words than those inscribed above the feast in Belshaz-
zar's palace; but have the Medes and Persians always followed
the inscription? Humanity trows not, and can cite any number of instances of non-fulfilment. Again, why not Once
More?

He has much occasion for Oblivion, now—the deepest and
the most enduring. Since the last time, he has seen the
spectre in the crypt and heard the warning thunders break
over the Cathedral. The unknown and formless shapes have
been drawing closer and more numerously around him since
then. He has kept his room since the last misadventure,
allowing the services of the Cathedral to go on without him,
and refusing the visits of condolence in favor of the mere
messages. But he has shut out nothing so; for only last

night he went to the window, attracted by the same infernal power which has more than once lured him to additional pain and terror — and there, as he drew aside the curtain and looked out, believing that he should see it,—there he saw the pursuing shape—dog-like and yet so much more terrible than any dog of flesh and bone—erect, black, grim, immovable, inscrutable as to the three possibilities of its derivation. And this very morning—God of Heaven!—the very recollection is enough for madness!—this morning he saw snakes gliding across the floor of his room, hither and thither, under the chairs, over the keys of his piano, and one of them—acme of all that is shuddering and most horrible!—one of them he distinctly saw crawling into one of his shoes, and attempting to coil itself away there, though he failed to secure it or any of the others, that must have come out from the dank old walls and escaped back into them!

So he has come again, deserting sick-room and almost sick-bed for the Once More. He has been so feeble, most of the day, as only to be able to leave Cloisterham late and reach the city long after dark. He has no appointment this time, and really needs none, having escaped one of the chief terrors of his pursuit, and become confident that under the new and better shape of the drug his lips are sealed beyond any danger of a betraying word. He has had an attack of extraordinary feebleness, too, at his hotel, since his attempt at supper — alarming the servants and for a time himself, besides making his visit even later than intended. So it is past midnight when his foot presses the mouldy and half-rotten step of his true *Lust in Rust*.

But he is strangely nervous as he commences to ascend the dark, creaky stairways that he has ascended so often. Does something of the morning remain? Possibly. For certainly, by no means an imaginative man by nature, he has abundance of the faculty now. He knows, in his inner consciousness, that there is no truth in the imagination, the tumble-down old tenement being chiefly occupied by other ramifications of

vice and crime; but in his outer fancy he cannot divest himself of the idea that in certain closets of the landing along
which he stumbles, there lie grinning and gibbering Lascars,
Chinamen, and sailors debauched by trading in the China seas,
fighting with the fumes of the Accursed Sleep (the world's
thought — not his — *he* knows better!) and gripping ugly
knives to stab and slash any who approach. Once or twice
he almost believes that he hears their stertorous breathing
and catches their muttered words—words that may be, after
all, nothing but the scrambling of the rats up and down their
favorite highway.

He passes on, however, with more of those nervous tremors
than he can ever remember assailing him within the same
space of time and in the same place, since the night of his
first visit. He reaches the well-known door—now, standing
half-open in the full darkness without and the worse than
semi-darkness within, a mere dusky formless space—entering
within which he sees, relieved against the miserable window
by the dim light coming in from the more miserable court,
the two awry posts forming the foot of the bed and cutting
the window itself vertically into uneven stripes. He sees this,
as he has so often seen it before, but for some cause seems
to note it more carefully, in particulars, than on any previous
visit. He sees, too, as he has so often seen before, in a distant
point of the room a single glowing spark, that indefinably
awakes the idea in his mind of a tiger's eye glaring out from
a black jungle; and near it a dark shapeless mass that he
knows to be the bed; and between that and the brazier of
the spark, a black form rocking to and fro and moaning and
babbling out words, half cough and strangle, that may be
unmeaning and may only be worse!

It is after he is fairly within the room and has accustomed
his eyes to the partial darkness, that he becomes aware of one
effect of his failing to arrange for his visit, in the shape of a
limp motionless figure lying against the black heap of the bed
and clasping it like some huge vampire bat. How acute this

man's senses are to-night—for what reason none may know. Many a time and oft he has lain on that bed and presented a figure only less repulsive than the besotted brute now occupying it—perhaps more repulsive, considering all the laws governing ascent and descent in the moral scale; and many a time and oft he has seen others there; and yet in neither case has he been so overcome, for a single moment, by an unconquerable disgust and horror towards the old woman, the place, all who frequent it (including himself), and every detail and surrounding in the remotest degree, connected with it! For one instant, he is almost on the point of doing what he has never done before in any resolution of life directed by his own sole power—turning about and going away, before recognized by the crone, at whose lips he sees the golden worms chasing each other around the fiery bowl of his pipe, proving that she is at once recommending her prescription to others, and medicining her troublesome cough, by being herself a free and liberal customer. But the unaccustomed impulse passes away as it came; what has happened, or what *can* happen, to make it proper for him, John Jasper, to forfeit the relief for which he has come so far and under so many difficulties?

He steps forward; the sound of his foot breaks even through the half-insensibility of the old woman. He can see that she lays down her pipe and forces herself to her feet, managing to find a match even in the midst of one of her paroxysms of coughing, and to set it and the candle alight, with more speed than she might have mustered when less under the influence of the drug. And as she lights she coughs and mumbles:

"Who are ye, deary, comin' on the poor old soul in the dark? Wait a minute, and I'll have the candle, though my cough is so dreffle bad and my hand shakes so that it's like to drop off! Who are ye? Oh!"

The candle is now alight and she sees his face; bringing out in that word so much that the hearer cannot understand, and into the wrinkled, discolored, flabby and usually expressionless old countenance, so much that it might be well for him to read, for his soul's sake. He hears nothing but the simple word of surprised recognition—sees nothing in the face, of that fierce satisfaction only known in the human visage when a great ambition, a great love, or a great revenge is about to be satisfied.

"Yes," he says, "you see who it is, do you not?"

"Yes, deary, I see who it is," she mumbled in reply, setting down the candle, so that it will not shine quite so revealingly on the disgusting figure on the bed, and then dropping back into her chair in an access of coughing which threatens to send her flying over the room in fit pieces for cat's-meat. "But ye come on the poor old soul so sudden, deary! Why didn't ye let her know, so that she could get ready?"

"Never mind that!" he answers, brusquely. "I suppose that you are ready enough at any time when I don't object to having somebody in my way—unless you have had so much business to-night, that you need no more. If so, I can find what I need elsewhere."

"Oh, no, no, deary!" she coughs and strangles. "Oh, no, no, business is dreffle bad, and my poor lungs is tied down with ropes and strings, so that they cut me with the cough. O me, O poor me! Here's all I've had, to-night—this thief of a Chinaman and he's gone off with only half his pipes. Oh my poor head—it's splittin' to bits and splinters."

"Stop," he says, severely. "Not so many words, and more to the purpose. I told you that I might come again in a few days, and I have done so."

"Yes, deary, I understand ye," she interrupts, between two dreadful coughing rattles which sandwich her words into a most pitiable compound. "Ye want more of the new mixter that sent ye off so easy and didn't make ye speak so much as a single word—don't ye, deary?"

"That is what I want, if you have it. Can you mix precisely as you did the other night? Mind—no more of your swindling me with trash, or you have seen me for the last time."

"Don't ye be alarmed, deary!" she replies. "O me, my

lungs is dish-rags. The price of the new mixter, that is so strong and sends ye off easy, has gone up dreffle, deary, and ye must pay accordin'; but the poor old soul has some of it, waitin' for ye, and can get it ready in a minute, if ye won't be so hard with her when her cough is shakin' her to bits."

"Ah, well," he says with gratification. "You may get it ready, then; and give me enough of it to make me sleep longer than the last time—mind that! Stop! this carrion must be moved. Do you think that I will lie on that bed, alongside of *him*?"

"Oh, we are squeamish and perticler, deary, to-night, all along of our being so fortinet in our business, maybe! O me —but it 'pears that my dreffle cough *did* tear out a bit of my poor lungs, then. But never mind, deary—ye shall have it yer own way. Kick him—maybe he'll wake; for he hasn't the new mixter as the poor old soul saves for them as needs it and can pay accordin' for it, and don't even take it herself."

"Wake *him*!" he replies, with a scoff. "You might as well try to wake the bed-post; and if you could, *you* may want his knife between your ribs—*I* don't!"

"O me, my head is splittin'! But he hasn't no knife, deary—the poor old soul takes care o' that before they begins, with the Lascars and the Chinamen and sometimes with the sailors as is very old and hard-lookin'. He hasn't no knife, deary; but——"

"But what?"

"If ye don't like him here, where there's no one as has a better right than you, deary, we can carry him out."

"Where?"

"Out there in the hall-way, deary, where there's many of 'em has slept it off, when there wasn't room here."

Within three minutes thereafter, with more strength than one hour ago he believed himself to possess, but not with more energy and determination than he has always known himself to possess—John Jasper has dragged that miserable and su-pine Chinaman off the bed, through the door, and into the hall-way—no more sign of waking from his opium-sleep, meanwhile, than in the quoted bed-post, that may indeed have imbibed something from the repeated fumefactions of the atmosphere, and thus fallen into its helpless and staggering condition. This special Monarch of the Realm of Sleep is dethroned, with the same suddenness and something of the same violence often shown in the abolition of dynasties in his own Flowery Land; and he, who looked like a bundle of very dark foul clothes, lying on the bed—lies in a corner of the hall-way, without, like the same foul clothes waiting for the untidy washer-woman—possibly supplying to any rat that may pass, *en promenade*, text for a lecture at the next meeting of the Society for Promoting the Avoidance of Poisoned Cheese, on the stupidity as well as the helplessness of that dreaded larger animal, Man.

This diversion of the attention of her customer gives the old woman an opportunity to prepare the "mixter" for him —as she does by staggering to the rickety little table at the window, taking from the bosom of her gown what has been so carefully preserved there, as against accident for *him*, and charging the pipe with an amount of it which would probably drive Dr. Chippercoyne into paroxysms of self-upbraiding, and set Joe Gilfert to looking about for the syringe and a pint of cold water. Her theft was one covering a liberal amount of the drug; she has seen that a small quantity only induced sleep, however profound, for a certain brief period; she is confident that twice the quantity will be necessary, with a head so seasoned as that of her customer, to induce that longer stupor possibly needed for her purposes—that full and explicit opening of the sealed lips, without which she must die miserable; and she "mixes" in accordance with those general and special principles.

It is almost ready when John Jasper returns from his little excursion without the door, and after closing it; it is quite ready, the moment after, and the withered and evil old face brought back to its ordinary expression, from whatever unus-

24

ual aspect may have temporarily dwelt upon it. In spite of
this, when she says, holding out the pipe that nearly falls
down from her trembling hand in another of the coughing and
strangling paroxysms :

"It's all ready for ye, deary—good and strong, and will
send ye off quicker than ye ever went in your life. O me, my
lungs and my poor head ! "

Then, moved by something for which he cannot account, he
pauses and looks fixedly at her, at the moment of throwing
off his coat,—with a shade of suspicion in his face that freezes
her small remaining quantity of blood and nearly sends her
quaking to the floor,—uttering, in a hard, grating voice, quite
as threatening as the words :

" Old woman ! no tricks, to-night ! If this is not what you
pretend—if it is not the same that I had the last time—look
out for yourself, for I shall remember, and I shall settle with
you by something worse than merely paying you no more
money. Take care—I say ! "

" Whatever do you mean, deary ? and me so dreffle bad
with the cough and my head splitting like a billet of wood ! "
she whines, in reply. " If ye want the poor old soul to swear,
deary, she'll do it—that the mixter is just what ye had the
other night, nothing else—s'help me ! "

" Very well, then. Give me the pipe."

If there was any doubt—if there was really anything in
the crone's manner, awakening suspicion—the one has passed
and the other been accounted for. His coat has dropped. He
sits down on the side of the bed, so lately occupied by the
repulsive Chinaman and possibly yet warm with his unclean
pressure. She hands him the pipe, and he places the mouth-
piece between his lips and inhales a few fumes. Ah !—how
the dull eyes brighten momentarily, and the whole manner becomes that of a thirsty man just drinking that for which he
has waited so long !

" It *is* the same : it operates like the other : do not mind
what I said," he utters, in a very different voice, the mental

softening with the physical. " Ah ! they are coming again—
the sweet sounds, the beautiful shapes, the brilliant colors.
Heaven ! how bright and glorious it all is ! See that no one
disturbs me, no matter how long I sleep, or I shall—go elsewhere."

He has sunk down upon the bed now, with the pipe falling
into such a rest that the mouth-piece remains as well between
the lips as it would do if held in the hand. He breathes long
and steadily, inhaling the fumes with every breath, and the
room becoming more full of the aromatic air than could be
known, except by an outsider coming suddenly into it. And
the poor old soul, sitting down close beside him, where she
can watch him most closely until the moment when he seems
sufficiently stupefied for her experiment, inhales more of the
odor than she can possibly suppose.

How pleasant it becomes to her, after a few moments !
How the pain of her racking cough has ceased ! How every
nerve and faculty seems to be at ease and peace ! She, too,
though her eyes are open and looking at the sleeper, waiting
for the moment when she can " make you talk, deary ! "—she,
too, hears pleasant sounds; and the next moment she sees
bright colors, too, for the eyes have closed without her being
aware of the fact or having strength to fight the influence
even if she knew. And then—a moment more—she is as fast
asleep as the slumberer on the bed, though far from so sound
in the nature of the slumber : sitting doubled up and half-
fallen forward in her chair, like a tumbled cushion of large
size and very uncleanly character.

How long this may last, she has no idea. Half an hour—
an hour—may have passed, when she wakes with a start of
recollection where she is and what there is to do—that valuable time is passing, and without care she may miss the great
object after all.

She rises, with an effort and the inevitable strangling and rat-
ling cough of any exertion. She sees John Jasper lying there, as
she left him—the head thrown farther back and the right hand

clenched, but with the pipe-stick still between his teeth. All
is not over, then, even if she *has* slept; for his slumber is
still unbroken, and there is yet time.

No time that must be lost, however. What is to be done,
must be done at once. Her head is a little stupid; but she
tries to remember exactly the action of Joe Gilfert under similar circumstances, and succeeds passably well. He is so sound
in sleep that she does not need to go behind the bed—only to
approach it in front, lean over, and put her palms to the two
points before pressed by the handsome boy. She lays one of
the skinny and shaking hands on the top of the head, then
applies the other to the palm of the left hand, which fortunately lies open. At the instant of doing so, she utters a
scream rendered doubly horrible by the rattling cough blending with it—half starting up from the bed and then throwing
herself literally upon it and its burthen.

What is it that she has discovered ?   What!

She puts her old face and ear close to the mouth of the
sleeper, then screams again and feels with the fingers of one
shaking hand for the pulse at the wrist. Then, with yet
another scream, blending rage and fright, she hobbles to the
little table, takes part of a glass of water standing there, and
dashes it full in the face of the slumbering man. Then, with
one longer and fiercer scream, in its hoarse horror not unlike
that of a horse dying in torture in flames or on the battle-field
—she throws herself back on the bed, grasps at the neck-cloth
of the sleeping man, tears it off, throws open the neck and
bosom of his shirt, and forces one of her hands down the
breast to the region of the heart. No motion, all this time,—
none even when his person is touched and that sanctuary of
the person invaded !

He must be sleeping soundly—must he not ?—even for a
slumber under the skilled preparation of Dr. Chippercoyne !

But the bleared old eyes see something on the shoulder that
has been so far uncovered. With a cry blended of rage and
despair, and still the hoarse cough making a third in the ele-

ments of jarring sound, she pounces down again, so to speak,
on that shoulder, tears down the linen still further, and follows
that motion with a veritable howl accompanied by another
motion most unaccountable and possibly most cruel. With all
the power remaining in her enfeebled body, she raises her
right hand and brings it down heavily on that something on the
shoulder, which may be a broad scar or may be a birth-mark.
No wincing even at this, on the part of the sleeper who sleeps
so soundly; but the flesh is more sensitive. A moment, while
the bleared eyes continue looking with a hungry keenness, and
coughing, moaning and cries are still: and then from the
centre of the something on the shoulder there rise two letters,
livid white on a ground of purple red: "T. F."

She starts up, then, chuckling hoarsely and rubbing her
hands, even in the midst of her evident alarm. The fierce
Evil Joy of revenge seems to predominate even over Fear, as
she points one of her skinny and shaking fingers at the
motionless form on the bed, and apostrophizes it with a broken
coughing and rattling vindictiveness more horrible than any
other of the surroundings.

"The poor old soul *has* done it, deary, after all! Ye didn't
keep ye'r secret from her, even though ye died to do it! Ye
haven't always been John Jasper, deary!—not when ye'r
double tongue named ye Jean Jourmeaux, when ye were sowing what I suppose ye called yer wild oats, away over beyond
the water, there—first singin' away and then stealin' away the
only child I had in the world—even if she *was* nothing but a
ballet-girl! I've knowed ye, deary, all along, though I
couldn't get words to prove it! If I could, the poor old soul
would ha' sent ye back, long ago, to the galleys at Toulon,
where they put ye for killin' the only one as stood up for *her*
—where they give you that pretty mark, deary, and where
ye'd have been to-day, but for knowin' how to make yourself
somebody else, and gettin' away!"

She has dropped into the rickety chair, with thorough exhaustion, coughing and strangling as if that last hour so soon

to come has come indeed; and it is from that chair, too weak to rise, that after a moment she again stretches out her skinny finger and concludes her awful apostrophe.

"Ye've gone to a worse place, deary, to get quit of the poor old soul; and *she* sent ye there—*she* sent ye there! Ye did talk, deary, as I said ye would—with yer skin if not with yer lips. And the old woman—O me, my lungs is rags and my head is splittin'—ye'r fine family 'll never know anything of it, or how it come about; but the old woman is even with ye at last, deary!"

"See that no one disturbs me, no matter how long I sleep, or I shall—go elsewhere." Such were John Jasper's last words, lying down to the Accursed Sleep. Without the outrage being committed, he has fulfilled the threat! Nothing has disturbed him—nothing shall or can disturb him, till the sounding of that Trumpet of Doom of which he half believed, the other day, that he heard the thunders breaking over the old Cloisterham Cathedral; and yet he has Gone Elsewhere!

CHAPTER XXV.

WHY? WHY? OH, WHY?

MRS. BILLICKIN was at once in her Glory and her Misery. The statement may seem a contradiction in terms; and yet such a complication of affairs is entirely possible—as any young lady can bear witness, who on the same day has received an offer of marriage from the most elegible of men, to whom she has long been tenderly attached,—and lost a valuable bracelet, impossible of duplication, or fallen into an attack of the *tic doloreux*. Deliberately is the incongruity repeated; Glory and Misery. On the afternoon of that day, Miss Twinkleton and Rosa were to leave the lodgings in South-

ampton street, Bloomsbury square—the former to return to
her duties at the Nun's House, at Cloisterham ; the latter, for
some cause no longer fearing Mr. Jasper or his neighborhood,
to accompany her, not as a boarder but a visitor, during a certain number of weeks, at the end of which a return to town
might probably take place, with other appendiary events not
necessary to enlarge upon at this juncture.

This constituted the current Glory of the lodging-house
keeper.   To be rid of the calm and equable sharp-tongued
woman, over whom she had certainly now no victory if she
had not suffered repeated defeat—to be no longer in terror of
her well-bred scorn, only able to oppose those coarser and less
trenchent weapons of lower breeding—to be freed from a
tyranny which debarred her from entering some of the most
eligible rooms in the house, thus reducing the respectful awe
due to her from her own servants,—this was pleasure and
pride enough to ensure the marking of that day with a white
stone in memory.

But alas!—the other side—the Misery ! Financially and
in that detail of abundant patronage which allows choice and
makes the peculiar pride of the lodging-house keeper, the late
campaign could not be regarded as a success.   For the apartments, sweet rooms though they were and the best in the 'ouse,
were not as yet re-let. Whether the coming of the grave lady
had laid the whole house under a spell—or whether (as the
proprietress sometimes almost suspected) the dissatisfied
lodger had in some mysterious mode circulated reports
throughout the entire community, indicating the apartments as ineligible and the landlady as objectionable —
certain it is that the bill at the door had only attracted a few
applicants of inferior condition, and that seventeen-and-six-
pence, expended in announcements in the morning journals,
had not been more effectual.   So far as leaving the rooms
empty could be considered, there was every probability of
her enemy going out with banners waving and all the honors
of the conflict; and this, apart from the financial question,

was enough to constitute quite an appreciable amount of
misery to the lady of the fugitive heart and the swooning
tendency.

Mrs. Billickin, however, it must be said, came up to the
closing conflict, at this crisis, with great energy and no small
amount of strategic skill.   Defeated she might be, but discouraged never and wherefore try !   Sportsmen, unsuccessful
in bag or creel, have been understood to call at the poulterer's
or the fishmonger's, on their way home, and purchase the
necessary quantity of game or fish to turn aside the venomed
shaft of ridicule as aimed by the objects of their affection or
others ; able generals, depleted in force and unable to resist
an impending attack, have been known to march in, with loud
music and much display of flags, certain corps sent surreptitiously away for that purpose, thus striking terror into the
enemy with the idea of a heavy reinforcement : bankers,
suffering under that want of confidence in the public mind,
illustrated by a " run on the bank," are at least currently
reported to have procured the bringing in at the front door
and throwing down very pronouncedly on the counter, of
large amounts of bullion, supposed to have been just sent
forward by confiding depositors, but really taken out of the
back door, half an hour previous, for that special exercise of
ingenuity.

So the Billickin, who may have studied in the sportman's,
the military or the financial school, or all of them, and who
had probably extracted a portion of her wisdom from each.

Most of the luggage of the two ladies was packed, ready
for removal ; and half a score of trunks and boxes, compris-
ing a large proportion of it, had been placed outside the doors
of the apartments, ready for the coming of the hour and the
two cabs necessary for removal.   But these did not by any
means supply all that the hallway contained. on that special
morning ; for from immediately after the breakfast-hour, Mrs.
Billickin had herself been in the hall, shawl-wrapped, making
occasional clutches at her heart (as if that, too, was about to

leave its lodgings vacant, with no applicants), and suggesting that swooning, to the number of say half a dozen repetitions, would be the most desirable of diversions. But quite equal to the duties of her position, for all this, and displaying vigor that might have excited the envy of the robust.

She was subjecting the stone hallways, especially those immediately outside the rooms of Miss Twinkleton and Rosa, to an amount of scrubbing, scouring and washing down, involving the use of water enough to have extinguished a conflagration extending not beyond a single house, and indicating that she believed herself to be the officer of the deck of a steamer just freed from the cattle-trade, cleaning up for the commencement of light passenger traffic. This had continued and increased to such an extent, that Mr. Tartar, coming in by arrangement to assist the ladies to their vehicles and possibly to the station, when the hour should arrive (and for other purposes, also not necessary here to specify), found himself unexpectedly in very congenial atmosphere, water, mopping, scouring and scrubbing being quite sufficient, and only the holystone and squegee wanting, to carry him completely back to his abandoned quarters on shipboard. Indeed on arrival he narrowly escaped hailing the boatswain, in a severe voice, with orders to free the scuppers and not have everything afloat 'tween-decks, like a land-lubber as he was!

There was something else, which he did not escape—the dear little imploring voice in which Rosa saluted him, on arrival, with a request that he would get their trunks inside again and prevent everything contained in them being ruined by the splashing water. And it was while he was performing that service, in which he wished that every package of *hers* was ten and ten times as heavy, that he might have the longer fancy of being in the act of altering stowage of sea-chests and all heavy dunnage, to clear for a tidy little brush with the yellow niggers or get her on an even keel for a sharp chase—it was during this performance, with its open doors, that the verbal but still more important tactics of the Billickin became best apparent.

These consisted in a series of candid statements made very loudly to the servants, of the filthy condition in which certain persons as she needn't name though she wouldn't disguise the fact that they probably didn't know any better never 'aving lived in an 'ouse with any pretence to cleanliness or gentility, managed to disfigure and put every thing out of order, and it was a blessing that they was goin' as if they stayed much longer the best rooms wouldn't be fit to show to a shop-girl much less a lady and what else could you expect? As also reminders to the servants aforesaid, in even a louder voice than that conveying the preceding, that Mrs. Welstood and her daughters, who had took the rooms, at prices as was prices and yet not too high for such sweet apartments and no thanks to them as had wanted to undervalue them but couldn't try how they would, — couldn't stay any longer than to-morrow morning in the rooms as they had occupied in Upper Baker Street, Regent's Park and they must have the floor dry and the other rooms in order if the persons as was goin' away and the quicker the better she wouldn't deceive them not for her life, ever managed to get off as they had been warned sufficient and time hup.

Miss Twinkleton, half-angry, half-amused at the extraordinary length to which Mrs. Billickin's wrath had reached, was still wishing that the lunch-hour had passed and that they were well on their way towards a place of residence more congenial. Rosa, altogether amused and entirely unconcerned, now that there was no danger of the drowning out of their personal adornments, was clapping hands at the whole affair, combined with certain suggestions and anecdotes of Mr. Tartar's, which illustrated it so capitally—and asking: " Oh, why, why did they ever make such a cross old thing, to make everybody uncomfortable—only that it is all so droll and absurd ! " And Mr. Tartar, in addition to other suggestions and anecdotes, was compelling a smile even on the face of the elder lady, with one of the former,—expressing a forcible desire which he seemed to entertain, of having Mrs. Billickin at sea with him during one cruise in the tropics, where the water would be warm enough to allow of keel-hauling her once a day, which he believed would have the quadruple effect of curing her swoons, fastening down her heart in the proper place, softening her temper, and shutting her mouth.

It was then, and into such an atmosphere as this, that Helena Landless came, managing to reach the door of the drawing-room dry-shod, though after receiving certain venomous splashes, supposed to be accidental, which might have produced an unpleasant effect upon a temper less equable or a mind less preoccupied.

The face of the young girl was very grave, as she met her three friends, embracing Rosa with that elder-sister tenderness which she seemed never tired of expending upon her " baby-beauty," and greeting Miss Twinkleton and the Ex-Lieut. with the warmth belonging to her confidential position towards both.

Notably grave, the face, as of one who was for the moment too earnest for any of the trifling things of the world—and yet with something in it of high, sustained content, that might even be happiness, though not easily or at once that happiness bubbling in laughter.

All marked the expression of the face ; but it was Rosa who first commented upon it, as their chairs so naturally drew close beside each other.

" Helena, dear !—how grave you are !—*we* have been laughing, oh, so very very heartily, over Mrs. Billickin and her arrangements for annoying us.   But for Mr. Tartar, who adores swimming, and likes to do it even in houses,—do you not, Rob—Mr. Tartar ?—I suppose that our trunks would have all floated away, leaving plenty of room for — what is the name of the imaginary woman, dear Miss Twinkleton, who is to succeed to our comforts ? "

" Mrs. Welstood, Rosa dear, I think, is the name of the imaginary person who is to pick up the comforts which must be lying very plentifully about the house, seeing that *we* have

not found or used many of them!" replied the staid elder
lady, demurely.

"Did she come in a carriage, with footman and a crest, to
look at the rooms, I wonder?" inquired Mr. Tartar, in the
soberest but breeziest way; whereupon Miss Twinkleton
smiling quietly, Rosa, without any good reason being apparent,
laughed so heartily, that Mrs. Billickin must have been
annoyed by the sound, even above the rush and swish of her
water-dashing without. But Helena Landless did not join in
the merriment; and after a moment more of silence that began to tell upon the spirits of the others, she said:

"Rosa, darling—you thought I looked grave. Perhaps I
have cause. Do you read the City reports in the newspapers
here, very often?"

"No—scarcely," replied Rosa; and then, suddenly alarmed
by the suggestion of her friend's gravity and a newspaper
report having some connection, she began to inquire, breathlessly:

"Oh, Helena, dear! what, what has occurred?"

"Nothing to alarm you, darling; but something to cause
surprise and a certain grief to us all. Look here!"

Rosa took the morning journal that she handed with a
mark at a certain spot, and read aloud, breathlessly and terribly frightened, — those twenty or thirty lines in the City
intelligence, reciting the discovery of a body, the day before,
at a disreputable opium-smoking house in a certain dangerous
street not far from the Tower—which body proved, on examination of papers found on it, to be that of a person named
John Jasper, lately resident and in some musical avocation at
Cloisterham, in Chalkshire. All indications, the report went
on to say, pointed to long-developing decay and debility
caused by excessive use of the deleterious drug; and there
was no doubt that he had died in a debauch of that character
—though time had not yet elapsed for investigation at Cloisterham; and nothing could be discovered from the occupants
of the house, the tenant of that special room having disap-

peared after providing for irresponsible notice to the authori-
ties, and none of the others admitting any knowledge of the
unfortunate deceased or his antecedents.

The face of the poor little trembler, suddenly grave as that
of her friend, was nearly white as the painted wall before she
concluded, and the last words of her reading were scarcely
intelligible. There even crept up from the warm little loving
and forgiving heart, a few tears that fell in sorrow over the
dreadful fate of the man whom she had lately known so well,
and the man (let the whole truth be told!) who had *loved her
so deeply*, even if so dangerously! For it is not in us to lay
the same severe rule to conduct inspired by warm affection for
us, that we should be sure to apply to it, when dictated by any
other motive; and the wildest of passions has that security
for recognition even in the least responsive natures.

"Poor Mr. Jasper," she said, as she concluded, "How very,
very sorry I am, to know that he has ended so! He did love
me, did he not?—though it was in his own dreadful way and
though he made me so afraid of him!"

"Yes—poor Mr. Jasper, Rosa, dear," said Miss Twinkleton,
in her own undemonstrative manner. "Let us hope, now that
he is gone, that he may have been a better man than we
feared, and that he may have gone to an easier account than
some of us, blind mortals, could arrange for him."

"From the little acquaintance that *1* have had with your
departed friend, I should scarcely select him as a messmate for
a long cruise," said Mr. Tartar, with that fresh voice and
manner showing him equally incapable of fostering narrow-
ness of view or retaining long animosity; "and yet, why
should he not hold a better place on the roll than any of us
would be likely to give him? I have known a general court-
martial, with any number of epaulets and any quantity of
gray hairs above them, condemn and hang a poor fellow, on
circumstantial evidence, who was afterward found to be only
unfortunate and misled, instead of guilty; and it is a good
thing for all of us, I fancy, that the Presiding Officer of the

courts up aloft can see further and better with the naked eye than we with the best sea-glass ! "

Helena Landless said nothing for a time—as one to whom the intelligence had been already communicated. If she had spoken, and spoken her thought, she would probably have expressed her deep thankfulness that she had been mercifully spared from a great remorse, which might have haunted her during the rest of her life, in the event of this death occurring, under similar circumstances, only a few days before—when a certain handsome boy, Joe Gilfert to wit, was trying an experiment so dangerous and so easily fatal ! Well for the repose of her conscientious nature, that she could never know to the contrary—never dream that any portion of Dr. Chippercoyne's subtle preparation remained behind her to work this death in unskillful hands—that she could attribute it, as did others, to opium, the pangs of guilt and fear, and the wearing away of the very powers of life !

A ring at the door, scarcely noticed by either of the four, in the conversation occurring over the death of John Jasper ; and then, after a considerable interval, during which their notice was attracted by a certain amount of altercation and stumbling over obstructions in the hall-way—a tap, two or three times repeated, at the door of the drawing-room. Rosa, partially expecting Mr. Grewgious, to make his farewells and " see them off," and a little wondering that even he should have received such a reception for their sakes, in the house of his relative—went to the door and opened it.

The next thing of which the four within the room were aware was a scream of terror, followed by a cry of joy ; and then they saw the young girl make a rush forward, counterbalancing the late recoil, throwing her arms around the neck of a young fellow who shared in the enthusiastic demonstration, if he did not supply quite the half of it, and covering his face with kisses, of which he was only able to repay a moiety, while she laughed and sobbed and gurgled out a variety of exclamations and inquiries, of which the most intelligible that could be caught were :

"Oh, Eddy! You are sure, sure, sure that you are your-self, and not a ghost? Where, where have you been all this time? And why, why, why did you come so suddenly and frighten us all to death?"

EDWIN DROOD!

At least, Edwin Drood, if anything could be judged from the singularly life-like appearance, the least in the world like that of a ghost—the eye bright; the figure a shade more manly than it had been eight or nine months before; the cheek much browner and therefore healthier-looking, as if the sun of a warmer climate than that of England had temporari-ly shone upon it. And possibly there was something corrobor-ative of physical existence, in the voice, with much of its for-mer manner, though scarcely so merry as of old — as how could it be, with its last previous utterance, half an hour before, in a certain chamber of Staple Inn: "Poor old Jack! —poor old passionate, guilty Jack! How I loved and trusted him, once!—and how he loved *me*, before he went mad, after *her!*"

"Did I frighten you, Pussy? Why, what a brute I am? Myself? Of course I am myself; and I have altogether too much appetite for a ghost. Where have I been? Every-where in general, and around your bothering old Pyramids, in Egypt, in particular! All about that, and a hundred other things by-and-by. And what a dear little handsome Pussy you are, after all!"

Naturally all this, consuming so much time in the relation, had occupied far less in reality. And the brief interval had not been entirely filled by the two principal actors. There had been other cries and exclamations of surprise, and all present were on their feet, manifesting emotions quite in keep-ing with their several characters. Miss Twinkleton was sim-ply frightened and speechless. Mr. Tartar, for the instant, possibly forgetting the past, and only remembering that a pair of plump little white arms, believed allotted to himself in the distribution of prizes after the fight, were around the neck of another and younger man—looked like seizing a cutlass, heading a gang of boarders, and coming to close quarters of a very violent character—until the native good-sense of the man reasserted itself and the frown passed away in a smile of pleasure at the unexpected return.

And Helena Landless?

That she was less surprised than either of the others, at the return of the dead to life, was very possible—for she gave no start to indicate the totally unexpected. And yet there was evidence that she was more moved than any of the others— far more than the impulsive child who rained kisses and fond words on the new-comer. Her brown cheek was totally color-less; and her eyes were full of a strange expression blending an intense joy and a fright almost driving her to rush from the room—as for that moment or two she stood apparently un-noticed. Few women, perhaps, in all the long catalogue of the loving, the suffering, the temporarily or finally bereaved, the suddenly reassured, have ever been placed in precisely such anomalous circumstances as those at the moment sur-rounding the Ceylonese girl. What she had hoped—what she almost knew—had already proved itself. The man she loved so dearly and had mourned like his faithful widow, was alive? But what was she to him? Everything? Nothing? What should she do?—what say?—how comport herself in that most difficult and trying of all positions, when on one side she might in an instant compromise her maidenly modesty and on the other falsify her woman's heart?

But it often chances that while we are troubling ourselves over the coming of the deferred rain that is to revive the thirsty crops, or the overdue ship that bears our fortunes, the rain falls, without any interposition of ours: the vessel arrives, borne in by other winds than the breath of our wishes. And Nature, as Helena Landless might have known had she been a few years older and more experienced, is a better teacher than any sitting in the schools.

Possibly Edwin Drood had not seen her, at the first moment

of his coming, in the virtual possession taken of him by Rosa. But, scarcely disengaged, his eye caught her face and form; and then, had the young girl been better skilled in reading the eye of love, or dared quite to look upon it, she might have read all that she wished. He stepped toward her, as she stood erect, pale and motionless—holding out his hand with an unmistakable fervor of gladness.

"Miss Landless! Helena! Will *you* not welcome the returned runaway, too?"

Would *she* not welcome him! Ah!

She could only speak one word, then, as she held out the taper fingers nearly brown as her cheek, but so perfectly shaped and handsomer for their very warmth of color.

"Edwin!" not "Mr. Drood," as *he* had begun: only "Edwin!"

Perhaps the tone told something; for the young man did not seem satisfied with the prospect of the one hand—wished for both. Both were given him; and then he raised the two to his lips, with a shameless disregard of all the other personalities present, and covered them with kisses. There is some hope that neither this nor what followed, however, was observed by the others; for at that juncture Miss Twinkleton, wonderfully weaned from the proprieties, found sudden occasion to bring something from an opposite table; and Rosa, her ebullition over, smuggled up alongside of Mr. Tartar, as if she might be a fairy pinnace belonging to that stanch though scarcely grim man-of-war, with an inquiry whether he did not think that it had been too, too absurd—her behavior to Eddy?—but how could she help it? for she was so glad to see him, and didn't he know that they had come very near to being man and wife, once?—and then what, what, what would have become of *him*—jealous fellow! And Mr. Tartar himself, his momentary jealousy blown away, was receiving this model confession of penitence, and at the same moment looking very hard out of the top of the window, to discover from

25

the opposite chimney-pots whether there would be a head
wind or a severe knot breeze abaft, on the way to the station.

What all these, or any of them, would have seen, had they
paid full attention to matters not concerning them—may be
summed up in a few words. They would have seen Edwin
Drood, after a moment of devouring the hands of his mistress
with kisses, drop both, as if moved by an impulse beyond control, and hold out his arms, without a word, but with a compelling earnestness far more effective than any language.
They would have seen Helena Landless pale until the brown
cheek might rival that of any of her blonde sisters; then
redden suddenly, till all the brownness and all the paleness
both faded in the very flush of the morning sky; then force
herself back, with a frightened movement, as if she could not,
dared not, must not submit, then and there; then yield, as
we all must yield, struggle how we may, at the hour of our
Written Fate, and meet the outstretched arms with a cry and
a tired, weary, joyful nestling of the head against the breast
to which it was gathered, needing no words to mark the heart-
full Betrothal!

CHAPTER XXVI.

TYING THE THREADS.

TIMES change—upon the old Cathedral town, as over every
other spot of trodden earth. And as they change, a statelier
procession moves along, in the succession of the rolling years,
than opium-dreamer ever saw in lurid visions of the Accursed
Sleep. For if the cymbals clash, as clash they do at times, it
may be but the hands of single men that, beating them together, send out their brassy sound upon the air—and yet it
may be that a nation's angry might combines to strike melodious terror to the hearts of listening men. If bright swords

flash and dancing-girls strew flowers, there may be something
more, in all, than the mere idle pageant of an Orient show;
for half the blades may be those keenest ones of trenchant
thought; and in the wreathing arms and supple limbs, circling
and turning in the mazy dance, there may be nations mad
with wealth and luxury, preparing in those hours of wanton
ease for fearful judgments in the days to come, when pampered
nerves no longer have the power to hold the steel demanded
for a native land's defense, and when the conqueror's foot un-
checked shall tread above the monuments of Art and Pride,
with steps more blighting still than Attila's.   Nay, more—the
bed of sleep that is no sleep, where hands are clutching madly
as at phantom throats, and murderous knives upraised to stab
and slay whoever comes in reach—this bed may be as broad as
earth, and on it nations clutching, stabbing at each other's
lives, as if we travelled back in history, and were approaching,
not receding, from the day of brother-slaying, most-red-handed
Cain.   But something else, thank God'!—may be, as well, in
all those rolling years.   Inventions, making stronger Labor's
weary hand ; Discoveries, bringing nations nearer each to each ;
Benevolences, softening even the asperities of War, and making more endurable the bitter lot of Poverty; Emancipations,
freeing human minds and bodies ; Illuminations from that
brighter sphere where man is privileged to walk in thought
while yet his body feels the clinging clog of clay—these, and
a thousand more of blessed things, may be more evident in each
of all those rolling years, and proving to the heart so prone to
sink in hopeless pity for its kind that all the course of time
has due direction, point and purpose, in the Guiding Mind, and
that the Onward, all confessed, *is* stronger than the Retrogade.

   And in the greater lies the less—even that infinitesimal less
involving the fates of those some portions of whose history lie
in this brief chronicle.   Limned more as the hand of the Great
Designer scatters hues and shapes on some evening cloud, than
as the painter draws and colors on the material canvas—we
may see, as following the events already recorded, the little

that still claims notice in the destinies of each, and fancy the hours and days in the great total bringing each its time.

When Miss Twinkleton is once more in her place at the Nun's House, with a new bevy of budding girls supplying the place of those gone away to return no more—thinking most of all of dear little Rosebud, at once her delight and her torment, and meeting a fate so blended of the gay and the grave, the sorrowful and the happy; remembering Foolish Mr. Porters occasionally, as she must continue to do until memory fades under the graying hair; but for some cause showing to her pupils less of her school-room aspect, now, and more of that genial best-self which was once reserved for the private hour and Mrs. Fisher, than before she went through a certain experience which will always, when she recalls it, make her hold her breath with wonder and a trifle of agitation.

When Mrs. Billickin, stretched and martyred on her own rack of meanness and malevolence, and no longer able, through receding and constantly-less-and-less respectable patronage, to keep sweet rooms in any 'ouse, is supplying disreputable lodgings to and broiling herrings for half a dozen ambiguous lodgers, at prices in accordance with the accommodation—in a foul street of the Seven Dials, keeping but one servant, herself, and that one not paid that liberal as never to complain; and though candid as ever in her lowered way, dispensing with shawls as incumbrances; seldom clutching at the escaping heart, from a want of care whether it escapes or not; and never swooning, from deficiency of time or attendance necessary for that diversion.

When little Crawshe possesses that wonderful invention of steel, leather and whalebone designed by Datchery, carried out by Bazzard, and made by Chevalier—which holds up the poor drooping head, makes him far less a cripple, and enables him to earn as well as enjoy something of the humble living of his position. When Black Tom-boy is older, more quiet, a little afflicted with wonder at seeing that young master of his the possessor of two hands, but quite as ready and willing as ever, on due provocation, to rescue or throttle.

When Stony Durdles, still gruff, lime-dusty and impracticable as ever, and still tenacious of Old 'Uns, but a shade less
intemperate and so more than a shade additionally industrious
and comfortable—has progressed so far with the statue of his
lost girl, that Mr. Crisparkle compliments him warmly upon
his success, and it may reach, before he is entirely gray, and
altogether helpless, to something near enough to the proportions of humanity, quite to fill the poor old fellow's heart.

When Mr. Honeythunder has a wickedly bright young
fellow, with a crippled left hand and arm and a tendency to
whistle in the hall-ways, sometimes calling on him, by permission, at the Head Haven, presumably from school or light
occupation—with whom he is always alone for some minutes,
whom he always dismisses with a kindness indicating that he
must be a relative or favored *protégé*—and from whose company
he always comes out, on such occasions, with a voice less over-
powering and a manner less combative to others, than generally mark the utterance and demeanor of the Aggressive
Philanthropist.

When Mayor Sapsea has swollen, in his pompous donkeyism,
to such proportions that he is quite beyond recognition by most
of the people of Cloisterham—his Mayoralty looked back upon,
by himself, as rather a degradation of intellect, than any
honor ; the wondrous Epitaph seldom alluded to, by one who
could now excel it so far, if he would ; and a probability existing that the dignity of Knighthood, if ever offered, will be
declined, nothing less than Baron Sapsea, of Pompspfusseigh,
in the county of Chalk, being worthy of his later dignified
consideration.

When the miserable old woman of the East has coughed and
strangled herself finally into bits—being found, one morning,
not long after the *finale* of John Jasper, in the same condition,
with a difference, to which she aided in reducing the Choir
Master—and buried in a manner eliciting no regard as to its
dreffle character or the market-price of the operation, the ex-
penses being (always narrowly) defrayed by the public funds.

When there is a new legal firm at the Staple Inn, that of Messrs. Grewgious & Bazzard, Solicitors and Conveyancers, with a specialty of Collecting Rents—of which the senior partner grows less Angular, more suave, more garrulous, and more drolly afraid of doctors'-bottles and medical preparations, as he grows older, and sometimes falls into fits of long abstraction, in which, from the solemnity of his countenance and an occasional use of the handkerchief afterward, he may be thinking of a strange blending of Her and Her Mother—the probability being rendered stronger by the retention of a certain odd sofa, on which there is a seat "first class," from which, when he can do so, he always excludes all sitters, as if he saw some form sitting there, too sacred to be disturbed. Of the junior, meanwhile, it being notable that he seldom visits the theatre, and only on tragedy-nights; that he has an odd penchant for the abstruse and difficult, not to say the tricky, in the line of professional duty; that he exacts a large amount of deference from his senior, and sways full command of the wine-cellar below, under the probable idea that he " mightn't like it, else ; " that he looks a shade less fatuous, inconsequent and doughy-faced, as he grows older and pays more attention to business—to the stony eyes of P. J. T., date seventeen forty-seven, who Probably Judges Truly, from long experience ; and that he has always an unaccountable tendency to forget his hat, after the manner of his departed friend Datchery.

When Mr. Crisparkle, a trifle older and more mellowed, but still cheery and lovable, has conquered the keenest pangs of that sorrow once so poignant though always so manfully borne —his labors shared and perhaps some of his burdens lightened, by the Reverend Neville Landless, for years in holy orders, and of his own choice attached to the service of Cloisterham Cathedral — a cheerful, conscientious, earnest young man, doing with his might what he finds to do, and evidently expending in his vocation an almost fierce energy that might have been very differently employed but for certain rulings of Providence. The Minor Canon still taking his headers into

the river below Cloisterham Weir, and his constitutionals, with
all due regularity—preserving his physical and mental health,
and leading the China Shepherdess, who seems perennial (by
means of or in spite of the upper closet, to look forward to the
proud possibility that she may live to see her dear Sept a full
Canon and even his Reverence the Dean.

When Helena Landless, the name of Drood added by a
different Act to that of Parliament, has lived much abroad,
accompanying her brave, always boyish, but rising and capable husband, on some of those engineering expeditions in the
East which have materially aided, later, in making Egypt
once more the highway of nations; her portrait painted, without objection on the part of the brother who could once found
an insult on the very idea of her face being limned by that
special hand—painted so often and in so many of the gayer
and graver moods of the husband-artist, that the collection
forms little less than a gallery of beautiful whimsicalities;
brother and husband long ceased to be belligerents in deed or
word, in the absence of John Jasper's drugged wine or a cause
of rivalry; her lot in life as truly rounded and completed as
that of her oddly-chosen love-mate; and the tiger's drop all
gone out of her heart now, with the dangerous gleam from
her handsome tawny eyes, in the affection, duty and happiness of the true and noble woman.

When Rosebud, long since the possessor of the diamond-and-
ruby ring of Her Mother, as well as the invaluable libellous
portrait of schoolgirl Pussy, and sailed on a land-cruise of
much duration and few opportunities for quitting the ship,
under command of Ex-Lieutenant Tartar, of the Royal Navy
—sometimes looks up in childish terror at his chosen ascents,
descents and promenades over the roof and balconies of their
pretty little abode on the Dorset Coast, opposite the Isle of
Wight, and says, without the least belief that he will fall, or
injure himself more than a cat if he does: " Oh, Robert, why,
why will you frighten me so?" and "Do come down and be
like other people, that's a dear!" while she would not have

him like other people for all the wealth within her limited reach; as also giving vent to a more serious fear, in the inquiry: " Oh, Robert! how did baby manage to get such a little tiny button of a nose, just like mine? and will it ever, ever, ever grow like yours, so much larger and handsomer, do you think? Isn't it too absurd?"

When the memory of John Jasper's Crime and John Jasper's Secret, Provoking Jove's Thunders over his guilty head, and eventually producing Judgment Terrible—never fading away entirely from sleepy old Cloisterham, has still become shadowed and softened there by time and the presence of the world's hurrying events, until pityingly spoken of as Poor Jasper's Troubles; and when Mr. Tope, still taking his queues of visitors round the Cathedral, though more slowly and carefully than of old, would probably find his recollection misty enough to deny that there had ever been a double wall to the grand old structure, if he did not even attempt to invalidate the truth of the whole relation as connected with it!